praise for carolan's farewell

"Lyrical, ambitious.... A richly imagined landscape.... The melodies of this novel resonate long past its final pages."

—*The Globe and Mail*

"Vivid dialogue and prose.... The brilliance of this fine novel arises from the basic delights of narrative."

—*The Gazette* (Montreal)

"*Carolan's Farewell* is an important addition to Irish literature.... Like a lament, [it] is haunting but vibrant."

—*Kitchener–Waterloo Record*

"This is a beautiful, beautiful book."

—*Telegraph Journal* (Saint John)

"Using the powers of a storyteller, Foran plunges his readers into a totally realistic 18th-century Ireland. The result is a captivating tale of music and brotherhood that is a treasure just waiting to be read."

—*The Sun Times* (Owen Sound)

"Both scholarly and powerfully human, *Carolan's Farewell* is as much about Ireland itself as it is about its two central characters, and that country's God-sodden excesses have rarely been so vividly portrayed."

—*The Georgia Straight*

"Foran is a lively writer who knows how to tell a story and set up tension in his dialogue."

—*National Post*

Charles Foran

CAROLAN'S
FAREWELL

A Novel

For Peter —
Delighted to meet you
here in Quebec City.
Best wishes,
Charles Foran

April 2013

HARPER
PERENNIAL

FOR MARY, AGAIN

Carolan's Farewell
© 2005 by Charles Foran.
P.S. section © 2006 by Charles Foran.
All rights reserved.

Published by Harper Perennial, an imprint of
HarperCollins Publishers Ltd

Permission to quote from "Mabel Kelly" and "Peggy
Browne" by Austin Clarke has been given by R. Dardis
Clarke, 17 Oscar Square, Dublin 8.

First published in hardcover by
HarperCollins Publishers Ltd: 2005
This trade paperback edition: 2006

HarperCollins books may be purchased for educational,
business, or sales promotional use through our Special
Markets Department.

HarperCollins Publishers Ltd
2 Bloor Street East, 20th Floor
Toronto, Ontario, Canada
M4W 1A8

www.harpercollins.ca

Library and Archives Canada Cataloguing in Publication

Foran, Charles, 1960–
Carolan's farewell / Charles Foran–1st trade pbk. ed.

ISBN-13: 978-0-00-639249-1
ISBN-10: 0-00-639249-0

I. Title.

PS8561.063504C37 2006   C813'.54   C2006-902436-7

RRD 9 8 7 6 5 4 3 2 1

Printed and bound in the United States
Set in Dante

The night is bright as the day, for darkness is as light with thee.

—*Psalm 139*

I am his Highness' dog at Kew;
Pray tell me, sir, whose dog are you?

—*Alexander Pope*

Part I

✺

DALL
(Blind)

chapteR oNe

Clip-clop. A snort, not of human making. He feels the sway, the sensation of saddle. He smells horse.

The animal snorts again. Though groggy, he leans forward to shoo flies from its nostrils. "Geminiani," he says.

"Easy, Gull," another voice says to another horse.

Carolan clutches the reins. He takes up the slack occasionally to remind Gem that she carries a forceful rider. He does so while awake and he does so, he has been told, while dozing. Tug, muse a few minutes, tug, snooze a moment or two.

"Did I fall asleep?" he asks.

"Both fell and slept," Owen Connor answers.

"Upon disembarking from the ferry at Lough Derg?"

"Right."

"A swoon?"

"A flop," Owen confirms.

"I was destroyed. Wrecked and ruined. I couldn't take one step to save myself from further disaster."

"That's where I come in."

Carolan has a notion. "A pilgrim whispered something to me the other day. He said your typical Oriental believes his life to be akin to a fellow who falls asleep and dreams he is a butterfly. Upon awakening, he wonders, Am I a man dreaming of being a butterfly or a butterfly dreaming of being a man?"

Owen Connor is quiet. His brown bay, Gulliver, no admirer of heathen philosophy, snorts as well.

3

"Owen?"

"I've never met an Oriental, typical or otherwise."

"Hardly the issue."

"Years ago we were introduced to a man at Lord Mayo's who claimed to be a wild Persian. He carried a sabre the length of a halberd. But someone else said he was actually from Cork."

Carolan waits.

"Perhaps there is a Persian quarter in Cork, little known outside the city boundaries."

He waits longer.

"Nor have I ever been to Constantinople," Owen adds.

"It's what is known as a parable, son."

"What is?"

"Fine."

He registers the amusement in his guide's voice. Shame on Owen. Carolan is destroyed from his pilgrimage on Station Island. Saint Patrick's Purgatory, as it is better known, with its penitent beds and unsparing regime, its cave entered into by pilgrims for the final vigil only after a requiem mass has been said on behalf of their souls, which might soon go free. Our Lord spent the night in prayer before his arrest. Saint Patrick suffered a fasting vigil for the good of his subjects until God appeared to him with a staff and a book of the Gospels. He took Patrick to a deserted island and a covered pit, declaring that whoever entered the cave for the duration of one night and day would be purged of his life's sins.

"I am wrecked, you know," Carolan says.

"And shame on me for making light of it."

"Ruined."

"The island is to blame?"

"Along with my own foolishness."

He is trying not to think about what happened out there. Nor about her. His heart will burst from his chest like a butterfly, or a soul, if he fails.

Or like a bird? Birds, birds. His spirits should be lifting to their music right now. The air should be sprinkled with their song. Finches and blackbirds and meadow pipits. The wheatear, a scratchy whistler.

"Where are we?" Carolan decides to ask.

"Up above the lake and on the road to Pettigoe. A rutted track, muddy from the rains."

He knows that already. The squelch of hoof-falls tells him of the muck. The bumpy ride informs him of the road. His befuddlement, aligned with his ruination, runs deeper.

Owen Connor guesses as much. "Mid-afternoon on August twenty-fifth in the eleventh year of the reign of George Second. The year 1737, for those without a head for numbers. The southeast corner of County Donegal in west Ulster, one of four provinces in the formerly recalcitrant, now sleepy, kingdom of Ireland. Where Persians and Orientals roam wild," he says.

"Pup."

"And where are we bound, you also wonder?"

"A fair question."

"To the glum village of Pettigoe, four miles south, and the lodgings I have procured for this evening and the next. A chamber where you are to recover from your ordeal, complete with a meal and bath."

"Plus drink."

"After that, it is home to County Leitrim," his guide says, "an easy two days' journey, and the ministrations of those who love you wholly and uncritically, for reasons some of us can't fathom."

"But first we have a visit?"

"A visit?"

"To the estate of an esteemed patron somewhere in these parts," Carolan replies, unable to recall any details at present. "Where I will be feted with quality wines and a bountiful table, and only then be asked to sing for my supper."

Owen clicks his tongue at his horse.

"Have I a tune ready?"

"You, a tune?"

"Composed in honour of the squire. Or his lovely wife, or fetching daughter, or the cousin with the laugh capable of shattering the glass in a man's hand. I must have a new tune," he says. "It's what I do."

It's me, he reassures himself. Carolan. And Terence Carolan is the legendary composer and harper, a familiar sight along the paths of that sleepy kingdom and a cosy presence within its finest homes. "There goes the master," people whisper as he ambles past their fields and villages. "There goes the bard." The bard without a chieftain to praise through poetry and song. The master of all he does not survey. A blind old man, matter of fact, attired like a gentleman in tatters or a peasant costumed in mockery of his born betters. Cuffs filthy and collars frayed, cloak worn and splattered. A codger in a saddle, portly of gut and flabby of jowls, cheeks ruddy and hair lice-ridden. Pity the poor horse bearing this sack. Pity any creature within range of his belches and farts. Specifically, pity poor Owen Connor, Carolan's guide for the past twenty years. A mountain man, by most accounts: freckles and side whiskers and unruly carrot curls. Blue eyes, the hue of stones in a stream, and a gaze that many find unsettling. Alert and clear seeing, too much so at times.

No stinks off Owen, at least. He has enjoyed the dignity of soap and water.

"I reek like a peeled onion, you know," Carolan says. "Feet and crotch, pits and breath. Small wonder Gem doesn't shake me off in disgust. There's a girl," he adds, patting the horse's neck.

"Fortunate for her we ride into a breeze," Owen agrees.

"My last bowel movement was days ago. My guts are in knots and my mid-section is bloated. I emit squeaks of odourless gas, pitiable as a kitten's."

"Charming."

Thinking of the meal ahead spittles his lips. "Three courses will suffice for this evening," he says. "Start with a vegetable soup and partridge pie. Then a roast loin of veal and plate of rare mutton, a fricassee of eggs and mushrooms in cream. Sides of sweetbreads and pickled salads, a terrine of fresh peas. For dessert, a warm apple tart or peaches in brandy, with a dollop of cream."

Carolan pauses at the sound of panting. The gasps aren't coming from Owen Connor or the animals.

He blames the mention of brandy.

"A meal best taken with a few pots of ale or a beaker of claret," he resumes once his breathing is steady. "A sup of rum followed by a drop of whiskey. Only a decanter, a few drops. Not wishing to overindulge."

"Indeed."

"Ten days I have gone without proper food and ten nights with hardly any sleep. Two hundred and forty-one hours since my last libation."

"Terence?"

"Hmm?"

"Your lips are spittled."

He licks them. "It need not be both veal and mutton," he says as a concession. "One or the other meat will do. Likewise with the rum. The chances that an inn in such a remote location will keep decent rum are slight."

His guide clicks his tongue again.

"Two hundred and forty-one hours, Owen. Two hundred and forty-one."

"I heard you."

"An oaten farl at sunrise and another at sunset. As many glasses of boiled lake water as I could swallow without dry heaving."

"Modest fare, to be sure."

"My knees are bloody from kneeling in prayer. My back aches from sleeping on a rock. It rained most nights on the island, and the days were breezy and sunless."

"At least it was dry inside the cave?"

"The cave?"

"The penitent cave, where you spent your final night and day. Don't tell me you've forgotten about the vigil," Owen says.

Forgotten it, Carolan has not. The incident occurred in the cave. In the dirt and the cold. Her hand and voice. Bone stems, a bird cupped in the palm.

Astonishing. But he can't think of her now. If he does, he'll burst.

"Kind of you to take time from your various pursuits to collect me at the shore this morning," he says.

"My pleasure."

"You slept well in the lodging house?"

"I did, thanks."

"No regrets at having refused to accompany your master on his pilgrimage, as many another guide would have done?"

"None at all."

"Nor at passing up the opportunity to atone for your own sins and be absolved of them by the Lord?"

"And catch a fatal chill in the process?"

"Answer my question."

"As I am not yet prepared to declare myself more sinner than sinned against," Owen says, "I doubt I am ready for Station Island."

The reply unnerves Carolan. His guide has obviously been pondering theology. Given that Owen thinks best aloud, he must have had a partner in his scepticism and apostasy.

"'The meals provided—they were acceptable?" he asks, probing.

"The beef in gravy was especially savoury. The woman of the house serves it with shives of warm bread, for soaking up the sauce. She also makes a fine bonny-clabber and black pudding."

"Any amusements?"

"I had a new shoe cast on Gull's near front foot and groomed both the animals," Owen says. "Cleaned your saddle and polished your extra boots, washed and dried our clothes in a stream. Also I read. Naturally."

"By a roaring fire?"

"Evenings I spent in one of the village public houses, taking a glass of ale by myself or in company."

In company? He'd better inquire. "Ale?" he says instead.

"Devlin's inn serves the finest of a dismal lot. Still flavoured faintly of urine, if you want my opinion."

"Sounds delightful." Carolan struggles once more with his breathing. "A noggin of urine-flavoured ale would not go amiss right now," he says.

"So I am gathering."

"Or claret reeking of vinegar, or whiskey tasting of turf."

Owen hiccups his disapproving laugh.

"This Devlin's inn you mentioned. It keeps afternoon hours?"

"It does."

"Will we be passing it along the route to the lodging house?"

"We will."

"Well, then," Carolan says.

They ride in silence. *Clip-clop, clop-click:* Gull and Gem in lockstep. He could compose to the beat, *clackety-clack* on his cloak buttons, tapping it out, jaunty and spry. Compose a tune for his next patron, whoever that will be. Especially if he could do so to birdsong, his favourite accompaniment.

"Where have the birds of Donegal got to?" he asks.

"Sligo or Leitrim, if they know what is best."

"I was expecting mallards and coots on Station Island, finches and blackbirds by the shore. Dabbling ducks and squawking gulls, ravens croaking overhead. Yet a solitary crow was all I heard the entire sojourn. A crow—*craw, craw*—along with wind whistle, a shrill void. Most discouraging," he adds.

"Some bird glides now across the black bog that surrounds us," Owen says. "At a distance."

"A curlew. I detected it."

"Even though it makes no sound?"

"The beat of its wings," Carolan explains.

They are both stalling, without good reason. He will indulge himself in the end. Owen Connor will leave him to the job.

"I have my instructions," his guide begins.

"Must we go through this?"

"She said you would say that. She said you would do anything to have your own way, as usual."

"My own way, Owen?"

"Don't."

"When did I, sightless since age eighteen, at the mercy of friends and strangers alike for the simplest of functions, the most basic of dignities . . . when did I truly ever have my own way?"

"She said you'd say that as well."

His tone stiffens Carolan's spine.

"Her recommendations?"

"Instructions, Terence."

"As you wish."

"Have a local physician waiting for us at the lodging house. Ensure that a meal of thin soup and bread is prepared and a bath drawn, a bed with a goose-feather mattress and pillow. No disturbances that first night and selected admirers the next day. Cheese and milk the second evening, if you seem able for it. Meat only once your digestive system has shown evidence of resuming its normal functions. And no drink," Owen says, half-swallowing the one sentence of import, "for forty-eight hours after you depart the island."

Carolan draws in the reins in shock. Gem snorts a query but keeps her walk. Another forty-eight hours? Might as well be forty-eight days.

"The hag," he says of his lifelong patroness, Mary Macdermott Roe. "She knows you."

"And her quack—he played a part in this conspiracy?"

"The good doctor isn't the only one to have observed the effects of spirits and ale on your mood. Where others are left sleepy by a night's revelry, you are positively revived by it. Worse, your head gets filled with notions you insist on acting upon, at strange hours and in states of disrepair."

"Nonsense."

"Quack's orders, I'm afraid."

He cannot stop himself. "Your predecessor never had difficulties managing Mary Macdermott Roe," he says.

Owen fumes.

"'Yes, Mrs Mac,' John Glavin would answer. 'Whatever you wish.' He'd promise to obey her every command and would report back what she wanted to hear. But out here in the wilds he'd do as his real master asked. An outstanding guide, John Glavin. A decent drinker and a fine singer in the old style."

He waits for the groan of disgust and, more important, defeat. Hearing nothing, Carolan wavers. The allusion to Glavin's drinking prowess was fair, but the mention of his singing, excellent by comparison with Owen's warble, was cruel. The shame is on him now.

"You're still happy to see me, aren't you?"

No reply.

"I am delighted to have your companionship again, Owen," he

says. "I missed our chats and disputes. Many times each day I shared a thought or complaint with you in my head, sometimes actually hearing your tart, smart replies, as though the miles separating Station Island and Pettigoe couldn't prevent us from chattering in our customary manner. I was lonely for my guide and friend every moment I languished on that wretched isle."

"Is that so?"

"You smiled just there, didn't you? You take air into your nose when you do, as if drawing on a pipe."

"A flicker of a smile," Owen says.

"It is still more than I can manage. Me, with my cadaver's grin, a fright to children and cats alike." He makes a face, holding it until his cheeks ache. A dead expression, he has been informed, for lack of another face wearing a corresponding expression to confirm the emotion and effect. Smiles are like that, it seems—alive only in relation to other ones.

"My dear boy," Carolan says with feeling, "we mustn't quarrel. We are too close, you and I. A single being, really. Shake my hand on it. Better yet, embrace me."

"Terence?"

"A hug will do neither of us lasting harm, my reek notwithstanding."

"We should dismount first."

"Dismount?"

He has forgotten where he perches. His torso is twisted and his arms are outstretched, his backside sliding from the saddle with the ease of a nightgown off a shoulder.

"Oh dear," he says.

Carolan is falling. The earth will receive him with a squelch. He'll probably pass out again and be revived by the taste of his own blood.

He hears Owen tug on Gull's reins to narrow the gap. Suddenly, he is being buttressed by an arm, his leg pinned between horse flanks. Then he is once more upright and secure.

"Honestly," Owen says.

He apologizes. Still, while content to have avoided a tumble, he is sorry they did not embrace. The contact with fabric and skin and bony shoulder would have pleased him. Also, Carolan could have read his guide's body the way the sighted read one another, and so known how best to interpret his mood.

"Grip the knob with both hands."

He does as told.

"Shall I mention who else Mrs Mac instructed me to have ready and waiting at the lodging house?" Owen asks.

"Please."

"A priest, to deliver last rites."

"Were you able to locate one?"

"I wasn't, on account of the sub-sheriffs sniffing around Pettigoe hoping to catch pilgrims before the season is done. But I did inquire after one priest, now a farmer near Belleek. Care to know why?"

Carolan nods.

"Because I spent those ten days and nights anticipating a knock on the door from the friars who oversee Station Island, informing me that my charge had expired atop a penitent bed or in the cave. Not in his room in Alderford, as befitting his stature, nor in his cottage at Mohill, as any family man would wish. Out here in this wasteland, rather," Owen says, "engaged in a ritual of atonement both prohibited by law—the only sensible aspect of the Penals, it is commonly agreed—and rejected by modern Christians as an embarrassment."

"Modern?"

"From *modernus*—of the present, the now. You don't recognize the word?"

Carolan recognizes the word. His query concerns its use in the context of his stalwart church. But that discussion is for later.

The Penal Statutes. Abominable laws, he thinks to himself, turning friends into enemies and suppressing natural religion, including an admittedly extreme expression of that faith—the pilgrimage at Lough Derg. Sheriffs hanging about Pettigoe, hoping to arrest the weary and meek? Silliness. He has no doubt that pilgrims have occasionally expired out on the island. Younger, less decrepit fellows than he, too.

"To die unshriven is a woeful fate," he grants. He recalls the incantation. *Dirige, Domine, Deus meus, in conspectu tuo viam meam.* Direct, O Lord, my God, my way to Thy sight.

A pipit cheeps in the distance, the note held by the glen they are travelling through. The mist has tapered, and the air is once more fragrant with hazel and bog. Carolan pulls off his hood, assuming the village to be near.

"Is it turf I smell?" he says.

"Pettigoe is upon us."

"And it's straight to our rooms?"

"Mrs Mac's instructions."

"Recommendations, you mean."

His guide says nothing.

"We'll be passing Devlin's inn shortly?"

Silence.

"Famed for its piss ale and vinegar claret?"

"Don't bother."

"Be at ease, Owen. What harm could come from a single glass?"

"Quite a bit, in my experience."

"A single glass."

"Stop it."

"I'll take it standing at the counter, if they have one. Or the keeper could bring the noggins out to us. I needn't even dismount."

"Stop."

He really shouldn't. "John Glavin could keep a secret from the old hag without suffering moral distress. He knew who his proper master was and how best to serve him. And did I mention his singing voice?"

Owen Connor mumbles.

"What's that?"

"Dismal," he says again.

"It's the truth," Carolan says. "But don't I know it and aren't I rueful?"

The questions aren't mere rhetoric. All men must take the solitary journey through their lives. The more confident know the roads by heart or navigate using the heavens. The more daring blaze new trails and venture along paths as yet uncleared. Horses are commanded to canter or even gallop, and obey. Families are kept secure back at hearth sides. Titans like these confront danger and stare down peril and lock gazes with the devil himself until the coward slinks off. They do not hesitate or await assistance. Nor do they tremble at the occasional loss of God's light upon their features. Prowess of this sort is rightly lauded. Wives, when visited, are grateful. Children, when held, are awed. "My bold lad," wives say, resting cheekbones against chests. "Dear Father," children sigh with hugs and kisses. Women can't disguise the admiration in their eyes and the heave of their bosoms. Irises widen like blossoms. Pomanders of rosehips waft up from secret gardens.

Such men, braced atop their frothing steeds, spurs cutting and crops striking, are bold lads indeed. Carolan, sadly, is otherwise. His horse ignores his commands, as though the bard is a sack of grain flung across the saddle. He can't stare down a hound, never mind a demon. The pockmarks scarring his cheeks and egg-yellows bulging from his sockets ensure that women blanch and look away in his presence, breasts heaveless and perfumes damped. He has had no say in his fate, and to this day others choose almost all his paths on his behalf. His meat needs to be cut and his glass refilled. He must be instructed where to piss.

"How about we take these animals out for a proper run?" he suddenly says.

"Beg pardon?"

"Fly, Gem." Irritated, he stiffens his legs, lifting his buttocks from the leather. Geminiani tosses her head without altering her pace.

"Fly!"

The horse slows, fearing, no doubt, her rider is about to tumble off. He has done so before.

"Is it unreasonable of me to expect that I should control my own steed?" Carolan asks.

"It is."

The mirth in Owen's voice is as grating as an audience member chattering while he plays the harp.

"Might I inquire . . .?"

"Take this instance," his guide says. "We are, as it happens, on the outskirts of Pettigoe. Gem knows this. You, apparently, have forgotten. Who then should be making the decisions about pace and direction?"

"I'll ask Mrs Mac for a set of spurs or a crop. A good crack across the flank should convince the beast to do my bidding."

Now it is Gem who snorts again, the pulse fluttery.

"You've upset her."

"Sorry, dear," Carolan says to his horse. Then: "I should like to be wild and windswept one time before I die. That seems a fair request. To choose my own destination and ride towards it, confident as any other man."

"What you are not, Terence," Owen says, "is any other man."

"Is that right?"

"I'm afraid so."

As though on cue a woman calls to them from a doorway. "Is it himself?" she says.

Unsure he is being addressed, he hesitates.

"Direct from the pilgrimage? It's what everyone is saying."

"Madam?"

"The bard praying and fasting on Station Island. People are talking."

"Are they?"

"Hush," Owen says.

"And you survived the penitent cave?" she asks. "If barely, judging by appearances."

"With the Lord's guidance I did."

"Hush," Owen repeats. "The fewer who know of your presence in the village, the better."

"Your courage and fortitude," the woman says, "they're an inspiration to us all."

"Too kind," he replies. He is merely being polite. She is in her middle years and, by the gargle in her speech, consumptive. The exchange will stay with her the remainder of her days and be a comfort.

"It's Master Carolan," she shouts back into her cottage. "Look, look!"

Owen groans.

"Well, aren't you?" the woman says.

"Aren't I . . .?"

"Himself."

"And no one else," Carolan answers.

CHAPTER TWO

"She had the most graceful hands of any girl I've known," he says. "Fine and soft and constructed with the bones more of a songbird, a dove or a thrush, than a human. Her metacarpi, especially."

"Her what?"

"Bone stems, Friar—the bones running from the base of her fingers to her wrists. Right along here," Carolan explains. Raising his right hand to the men seated across the table, he outlines his stems with his left forefinger.

"Bone stems," Friar Seamus says.

"Like those of a songbird," Owen Connor echoes.

"When she squeezed or made a fist, the stems would rise and collect into a bundle. Once I gathered up a robin that had been intent on extracting a grub beneath my feet. I bade her imprison the bird in her cupped palms and allow its wings to caress her skin. Only then, I declared, could she appreciate how I felt each time I took her hand. A living thing in my clumsy grasp. A sensual wonderment, to a boy."

He sighs and sups. A fine observation, if he does say so, and one he never tires of making. Can he help it if Owen tires more easily? And Devlin's barrel is flavoured of raw barley, not urine, being underbrewed. The malt failed to sprout properly.

Carolan must speak of her now. He must confess what happened. A drop more courage and he should be ready.

"You refer to Bridget Cruise?" the friar asks. "The landowner's daughter you courted as a lad?"

Friar Seamus is the boatman who rowed him out to Station Island eleven mornings ago and back to shore earlier today. He is also, by the by, the Franciscan who helped rescue Carolan from the penitent cave the previous afternoon—a connection Owen may not realize. At present, the friar-boatman with the booming laugh and hearth-smoke smell is their table guest, having appeared at the inn, as if by arrangement, an hour before. An amiable guest, too, if somewhat brash.

"The very one."

"Back in County Meath?"

"Outside the village of Nobber. Where I was born and raised in a farmer's cottage and she on the ten-thousand-acre estate known as Cruisetown."

"I imagine that courtship ended happily," Friar Seamus says.

"You don't know the story?"

"Of Carolan's muse? The girl he wooed and lost while sighted and then kept alive in his heart as inspiration, despite the darkness that enveloped him? Everyone knows it. I can even hum the tune you wrote for her."

"Four tunes," he corrects.

"Four?" the friar says. "Why so many?"

"No reason."

"Only one of them has the soul of a great melody," Owen offers.

"As only one pot of this ale so far has not tasted of grain," Carolan says. He knocks his noggin on the table. "Our vessels are empty, innkeeper," he calls. "Our purses are not."

James Devlin shuffles over.

"Will I give the table a wipe as well, sir?" the keeper says in the church-solemn manner of the devout or the obsequious.

"No bother."

Another whiff of the rag and Carolan's bowels may spontaneously void, like a bucket with a false bottom. The cloth stinks of stale ale and clotted blood. There is a breezeway for nature's calls, he was told, with a chamber pot kept in a corner, should the need prove dire. Owen described the inn when they first arrived. A low door, obliging even a short man to duck under the lintel, and no windows. Two tables before a cold hearth, surfaces stained and gouged, benches showing the polish of countless breeches. A solitary candle, its flame emitting trails of smut and flickers of light. Mice scurrying inside the walls.

Dinner has yet to settle in his guts. He was sensible to order it—without food, a single glass would have toppled him—but unlucky in the offerings. The mutton was marbled in gristle, and the cheese had to be carved free of mould. Crows would have found the bread tough pecking. A meal, even his guide agreed, to be taken only with drink. To Carolan's surprise the rum has been potable. Not the whiskey, though.

The friar's arrival coincided with a switch back to ale.

He feels queerer than he has all day.

"I was a lad like any other, Friar Seamus," he begins. "Swaggering and loose-limbed and as shoeless as on the morning of my birth fourteen springs before. She was my junior by a year, with blue-green eyes and a dimpled smile, flaxen hair nearly to her waist. We courted in secret for a spell, mostly around the chapel on the edge of her family estate, talking and giggling and lying on our backs watching the sky. The month of June it was, the air warm and flavourful, and all nature in bloom. Once and once only she whisked me through a wood and across an apple orchard to a spot where a priory stood by a stream. A moss-covered ruin, its floor littered with grave markers and its bell tower a choir of starlings. There, we kissed upon a grave, light pouring through a gap in the wall, my hands stiff by my side, too shy to take her by the shoulders or, heaven forbid, the waist."

He drinks, spilling some.

"I'd not been kissed before," he says, "and not really been kissed in the same way since. Bridget said I had bluebells for eyes. She said I was her bold laddie boy."

Owen scratches his scalp with canine vigour.

"I thought her a barrow fairy or a sprite and I the fortunate mortal granted its attentions. The softness of her lips, as though mine pressed against a flower petal, the fineness of her hair . . . Yes, Owen?"

"Why are we telling this tale?"

"We're not—I am."

"But why now?"

"Bone stems," Carolan says.

"So?"

"A bird cupped in the palm."

"What, have you fresh news concerning the owner of those stems? Fifty-four years have passed without further contact with the woman, Terence. She might as well be dead—and may, in fact, be so."

Nonsense. Bridget Cruise lives, as do her immortal hands. Not that he would expect Owen or the friar to accept this on faith. But he has evidence and is ready to share it. Almost. "I'm telling my story," he says, dribbling more ale. His drinking hand isn't steady.

"He's telling his story," James Devlin says from across the room, "and in my very own establishment! A pity there's no one else present."

"Well?" Owen asks.

"If you'd allow me to finish," Carolan says.

"*Duh-dah-du-dah, dah-dah-la-la,*" the innkeeper hums, "*duh-la-lah-la-lah-lah.*"

The first of the Bridget Cruise compositions. In the wrong key and with dropped notes.

"Very nice, Mr Devlin."

"I noticed the harp tied to the back of one of your animals outside, Master," the man says with abrupt nerve. "Any chance of a tune?"

Carolan pauses.

"I'd be honoured," James Devlin adds.

"And you'd also be whispering to the wife to rush out and inform the entire village of who's performing," Owen says. "Wouldn't you?"

"Sir?"

"You'd get a crowd, I promise, and would earn a pocket full of pennies off the extra trade. Equally, you'd have a yarn to embellish for years about the evening the bard played here. But let me ask you this, James Devlin," Owen says, his voice climbing the register as it does when he is angry, "what of the reputation of your inn if it is known instead as the site where Terence Carolan was arrested? What of that?"

"Easy, Owen," Friar Seamus says.

"Arrested?"

"I counted four sub-sheriffs sniffing about the village during my days here. Why, one such gentleman sat on this very bench a few evenings ago, boasting that the fine for making pilgrimage yet stands. Ten shillings, or twenty lashes for those too poor to pay. Do you not recall that fellow?"

"I do, now that you mention it."

"Would you wish to see Carolan arrested and obliged to ride in chains to the Enniskillen gaol?"

"Arrest the master? They wouldn't dare."

"One or more Ulster sub-sheriffs? They surely would dare, if only out of ignorance of who, or what, he is master of."

James Devlin whimpers.

"No more talk about music," Owen says. "And we've been unwise to stay so long in this hovel."

Friar Seamus calms him. "Three travelling gentlemen sharing ale and cheer of a late summer evening," he says. "There is no crime in it. Unless, that is, you brain poor Mr Devlin here with your noggin. Then it's to the Enniskillen gaol for sure—only not for the guilty pilgrim."

Owen respects the Franciscan, Carolan can already tell, and may be in his thrall. Is Friar Seamus the "company" Owen kept, mulling over various apostasies, while Carolan staggered about Station Island? He suspects so. Meaning, in effect, both bard and guide have had separate encounters with the man, about which the other knows nothing. When Friar Seamus led the efforts to open the cave door and release the distressed pilgrim, Carolan showed his gratitude by engaging his liberator in conversation. But the friar had little to say for himself, beyond revealing the county of his birth, Galway. No family title or ancestral village. Scant personal details, although he did mention a period of near starvation up in Dublin and admit to only middling qualifications to serve as a Franciscan, including—truth be told—middling faith. The order had accepted him more for his brawn, he confessed, as a boatman during pilgrimage season and a farmer the rest of the year, than for his devotion or his grasp of theology.

Such is the age, Carolan supposes, that men are obliged to hide their true natures and capacities. Is Owen Connor a "natural" guide? Probably not. Or Terence Carolan a "natural" harper and bard? Hardly.

Not that he is so confident of his own era or, most days, concerned about it. But times past do seem better outlined than times present, as well as more honourable. A half-century has gone by since the Siege of Derry and the Battle of the Boyne. Another forty years must be subtracted to summon Cromwell's army and the slaughters of 1641, Catholic on Protestant, which supposedly justified the invasion. Kings no longer fight European wars on Irish soil;

lord protectors with flaming swords have ceased burning towns to the ground. Still, terrible ages do produce leaders of the requisite stature. Gone are the likes of Patrick Sarsfield and Oliver Plunkett, the duke of Ormond and Ironguts Oliver Cromwell, Hugh O'Neill and Red Hugh O'Donnell. Gone are the acts of enormity and gestures of fearsome will.

Once, men measured themselves by the boldness of their actions. A life was the sum of activity, a record by which a character, and legacy, could then be assessed. Of late, however, such markers have been stripped away. In lieu of wars there are famines and foul weather. Instead of crusades there are quarrels over property and horses. The honour of facing an enemy on a battlefield has been supplanted by the dishonour, and frustration, of skirmishing with opponents who hide behind petty laws and sheriffs-for-hire. In the absence of action there is only constant reaction, insults heaped and tyrannies enforced, hard on the body and spirit alike.

Hard on the young, especially, who must speak and act, or wither and die.

Or else emigrate, an "action" often reluctant and nearly always fateful: all joy vanquished, and even the sweetest memories blighted, by the separation of seas that rise and fall.

It comes down to the Boyne, Carolan suspects. The battle ended far more than the hopes of James Stuart to regain the crown he had lost two years before to William of Orange. On a July afternoon in 1690 the former monarch defended the River Boyne using a slim line of Jacobites and French soldiers against a disciplined crew of Dutch, Danes, English, Huguenots and Ulstermen. After a few hours of desultory fighting James retreated to Dublin and shortly after that to France, leaving his followers to their fates. The brave souls who soldiered on, less for the return of a Catholic monarch to the throne in London than for the rights of the majority in Ireland to retain their lands and control their parliament, were marked men. The disasters that followed—the Pass of Aughrim and Siege of Limerick, principally—finished the job off. The best were now dead or banished to the continent. The rest had to suffer the endless punishments and indignities married to defeat.

The Boyne. Every able-bodied man and boy should have rushed to County Meath that warm summer day to take up arms alongside James. No excuse for avoiding the fight ought to have been entertained, let alone accepted. Even the crippled and diseased could have lent a hand loading muskets or bandaging wounds. And what of the newly blind? Might they have helped out somehow?

"Were you at the Boyne, by any chance, Friar?" he asks.

"The Boyne?"

"Fighting for faith and tribe?"

"I'm afraid that was well before my time."

Of course it was. By his voice Carolan guesses Friar Seamus to be just short of forty. "Most of the recruits were raw, you know," he says regardless. "They stood no chance against a trained army."

"I dare say."

The friar's lack of interest is a surprise.

"Owen would have fought for James, wouldn't you have, Owen?"

His guide is slow to answer, also surprising.

"You've said as much before," Carolan reminds him.

"I've expressed a longing for a worthy cause," Owen replies, addressing someone else. "Any cause. I don't believe I've ever claimed otherwise."

"The restoration of a foreign monarch, be he a Calvinist Dutchman or a half-French Englishman of Scottish descent, is poor reason to risk an Irish life even as miserable as my own," Friar Seamus declares. He isn't speaking to Carolan, either.

Such a remark is too radical for his old ears. Aware that he has steered the conversation as recklessly as Owen maintains he would steer a horse, Carolan makes a point of ordering another jug of ale.

"But the present one is yet half full," James Devlin says.

"Or half empty, Mr Devlin, depending on your view."

The keeper goes off.

"A fool," Owen says. "And a shrivelled wee fellow at that."

The comment suggests that Seamus must also be strapping. Owen is a giant, and when annoyed he is prone to measuring a person by his physical stature. Yet Carolan's height, some fourteen inches shorter than Owen's own, is immaterial. In the eyes of the guide, it seems, Terence Carolan simply isn't like other men.

Another sour thought escapes him. "How indeed could a sub-sheriff ever arrest me?" he asks after a swallow of ale and a burp. "It would be like arresting a lark for a melody or a butterfly for dreaming he is a man. And did I mention, Friar, that I, too, never defended the Boyne?"

The two of them exchange glances. He hears it.

"I'd have signed on to fight, I'm sure, being from just up the road in Nobber, and likely been dispatched without delay by a rapier or cannonball, due to an innate clumsiness. I was saved, if you will, by a blinding bout with the pox. How's that for queer chance?" he adds.

No one speaks.

"You were telling us about Bridget Cruise," Friar Seamus finally says.

"I was?"

"Her metacarpi?"

Grateful for the change of subject, Carolan blurts the truth before he can decide whether he has imbibed enough courage. "I saw her," he says.

"Master?"

"I can't put it less directly."

"As a lad of fourteen?"

"I saw her," he says again. His hands now quiver and his brow, he can sense, normally as smooth as a pebble, is furrowed. As well, a fish-hook tugs on his guts, plea for a chamber pot or bush. "Saw her and never forgot. Her face alone has stayed by me through the darkness, as you earlier described it. And it is plenty dark in here, I can assure you. Darker than any purgatory or crypt. Dank as any dungeon."

He is raising his noggin to his lips when the vessel is snatched away from him.

"Not another sup," Owen says.

"Give it back."

"You've indulged already, and I will pay for my poor judgement."

"Pup."

"It's bed for you this instant."

"Insolent pup."

"Call me names if you must."

Carolan has a better idea. "Lend me your hand," he says, extending his own outwards, elbow on the table.

"I think not."

"Friar?"

"Don't encourage him, Seamus."

"I'm afraid I must oblige, Owen," the friar says.

"But why?"

"He doesn't know how it ended," Carolan says to the Franciscan.

"Ah."

"I don't know how what ended?" Owen says.

"The hand, please. I promise not to slobber over it."

A coarse, walnut-knuckled hand slides into his own. The appendage of a farmer, Carolan thinks, though that isn't quite correct. The friar's palm is too dry—a farmer would be nervous sharing a table with one so illustrious—and his grip is too relaxed. Here is a man confident of his stature and influence.

"We were a dozen pilgrims in the cave," Carolan says. "Anonymous, sworn-to-silence companions from the previous nine days.

Several had assisted me about the island, penitent bed to penitent bed, or else had helped find spots where I could lay my head at night. The friars had seen to my tortured bodily needs." The hook tugs harder, and he shifts on the bench. "But in the cave there was no escaping our rank smells and barking coughs, our moans and groans and scratchings. Better than half the pilgrims were women, and as is my wont, I'd exchanged whispers with them. One lady, however, had kept to herself, displaying rare devotion in her prayers and fasting, even for Station Island. With her I'd had no contact at all. But there came a moment, perhaps two hours into the vigil, when this woman needed to slip past me in order to find, as she relayed it, a deeper, more pure darkness within the chamber."

"It is closer in shape to a tunnel," Friar Seamus says. "Pilgrims are obliged to line up in there, as if awaiting an audience with Lucifer himself."

"For her to pass we both had to make room. I assumed she was now more blind than I was and suggested she take my hand. She did so," Carolan says, adjusting his grip of the friar's appendage to more resemble the hold, "and thus—"

His guts snarl like a cornered animal.

"Terence?"

"'By the blood of my forefathers,' I announced, 'this is the hand . . .'"

He stands, knocking into the table. Plates and noggins rattle.

"Do you require—?" Owen says.

"'. . . the hand of . . .'"

"Your grip is clenching," Friar Seamus says.

"'. . . Bridget Cruise.'"

There. He has confessed. He releases the friar.

"Beg pardon?" his guide asks.

"The chamber pot, Owen," he says next. "Without delay."

A moment later he is in the breezeway and resting atop the

pauper's throne. The chill of the rim, in conspiracy with the night air, contracts his bowels, opposite to the desired effect. The pot also sits too low.

Owen and Friar Seamus retreat to the other side of the door.

"The recognition was immediate," Carolan calls to them. "The slightest graze. The words came unbidden—'By the blood of my forefathers, this is the hand of Bridget Cruise.'"

"What are you saying?"

"She was in there. She was that other female pilgrim."

"Impossible."

"Why?"

"All those decades later, and you recognize her by her hand?"

"I've explained it already."

"Bone stems," Friar Seamus says.

Carolan pushes. Only piss so far—a gorged stream, splashing around the bowl and misting his buttocks.

"You were delirious," Owen says.

"Probably."

"Demented."

"That came afterwards."

"Many pilgrims do suffer traumas in the cave," the Franciscan says. "They enter it in a weakened state and then struggle to keep awake, and pray, for twenty-four hours without food or water. Some yet claim the chamber is an authentic purgatory, where pilgrims descend into the underworld to have their faith tested by demons."

"Ridiculous," Owen says.

"I couldn't agree more. But I have witnessed, or at least heard, extraordinary monologues being spoken behind that door. Pilgrims believe they converse with not only the devil and the Lord but Saint Patrick and Saint Paul. Likewise, they are visited by apparitions of lost relations and loved ones."

"I encountered my first true love," Carolan says.

"Then you saw Moira as well?"

"I do not speak of Moira."

"I am well aware you do not speak of Moira, who apparently never kissed you in all the years you were man and wife."

"Easy there, son," the friar says quietly to Owen. "He is off his head, poor fellow."

Owen is silent.

"He was in a grievous condition when we pulled him out."

"Right, Seamus."

Friar Seamus is unaware of the acuity of Carolan's hearing, even in a breezeway echoing the splatter of rain onto the flagstones beyond it. Owen Connor, naturally, is well aware.

"And I saw Bridget," Carolan says. "May God have mercy on me."

His guide mutters something.

"Did I not beg to be freed shortly thereafter?"

"He did," the friar says.

"You did?"

"The reunion overwhelmed me, Owen."

"What reunion?"

"Once she left my side, I experienced the dark as I never had before. *Never,*" Carolan says with an involuntary shudder. Unless he is mistaken, he is swaying. Either the floor is on a tilt or the pot is.

"You mentioned this impression when we liberated you from the cave," Friar Seamus says. "Most interesting."

"Most distressing, Friar. The Lord has always lifted me up into His light. That He would hold me in His brilliant gaze has long been the most fervent of my prayers, in fact, aside from those for my own precious ones. Yet in the wake of my encounter with Bridget I became convinced He no longer did so. I was alone now, with only my affliction and failings as company. The resulting desolation was acute."

"A ghastly place," the Franciscan says. "I am ashamed at having any part in its operation."

"Actual conditions of light and dark mean little to me, remember. I speak, rather, of my soul."

"'May the Lord lift up the light of His countenance and give you peace.'"

"The Aaronic Blessing," Carolan says of the citation. "You know your Old Testament well."

"You are surprised?" the friar asks.

"Not at all," he answers, a small lie.

A meow carries down the breezeway.

"Is it a cat," Owen says, "or another apparition of your first true love?"

The animal calls as it approaches, its cries like a rusty door hinge. Carolan steadies himself. He adores cats, aside from their habit of leaping onto him without warning.

"Puss, Puss," he says.

The creature knocks against his knee. Leaning forward carefully, he scoops it up and spreads it across his naked thighs.

"A woeful thing," he comments.

"Wormy, I am sure," his guide says.

A few strokes confirms the diagnosis. Only a starving cat would let itself go this badly. The animal is skull, spine and ribs. Its ears are ribboned and its tail severed, its coat filthy and knotted with burrs. Purring so loudly that Carolan must raise his voice over the thrum, it kneads his thigh with its claws.

"Have we room for him?"

"Room?"

"In a saddlebag or sack?"

"Mrs Mac placed an embargo on strays years ago, Terence. You were cluttering her estate with them."

"He has no mother to wash him, I fear," Carolan says. "Nor any home where his purring is appreciated as melodious throat song."

Holding two fingers to the cat's throat, he marvels at the pulse. There it is, he thinks with his usual humility—God whispering to us. In measured rhythm and hushed rhyme.

"Agh," he suddenly says. Though worried he will burst his innards, he redoubles his efforts.

The creature digs.

Carolan moans a second time.

"Are you managing?" Owen asks.

"Nice pussy," he tries.

Waste is expelled, more ooze than solid. That will be all, he guesses, and his distress won't be eased.

The pussy leaps. He lunges after it.

"Dear me," he says, the pot suctioned to his arse.

They steady him, each taking an arm, not a moment too soon.

"What a great man you are," Friar Seamus says with a roar.

"My breeches . . ."

Liquid trickles down one leg.

"You bleed," his guide says.

Carolan's left thigh, gouged.

The men haul him back inside, his feet dragging.

"Inquire of Mr Devlin if he has scraps for our new friend," he says.

"You mean the skeleton that lingers in my breezeway most nights?" the innkeeper replies.

"Has it a name?"

"No name."

"A colour?"

"The beast is filthy and diseased and not long for this life," James Devlin says. "I wouldn't bother naming or feeding it."

"I notice the wee fellow padding about the village most days,"

Seamus comments. "A coat of cinnamon, which it will lick until it shines, once it has dined on even the most meagre fare."

"Cinnamon?"

"Orange-brown," Owen says.

"A feed of mutton for Cinnamon the cat, Mr Devlin. Leave it in a bowl outside. We'll pay."

The man departs.

"I'd best settle our bill," Owen says.

"I'd best accompany you," Seamus says.

"Devlin won't be getting a farthing more than fourpence from us. Even then, he'll need accept a note of promise."

"He'll be wanting five, in coin."

"Could I be deposited back at the table?" Carolan asks. "My legs are about to give out."

They return him to the bench.

"Do you truly not know the colour cinnamon?" the friar says.

"Nor orange nor brown any longer."

"You can't remember?"

"I remember everything, Friar. I've simply lost the visual images to accompany those recollections."

The Franciscan is silent.

"Images have dissolved," Carolan says. "Even of those people and locations I hold most dear. My mother and sister, both of whom died during the same epidemic that took my eyes. My poor father, who soldiered on for a lengthy, if sorrowful, period. The cottage we called home and the village nearby it. Details of the Meath country-side, cows in the fields and sheep along the slopes, the River Boyne burbling past. All receded over time, and all now gone."

"How strange."

Carolan shrugs, a rare physical reaction. "I'll give you an example," he says. "The 'Bridget Cruise' that James Devlin hummed earlier was composed almost four decades ago, when my imagination was yet full of the sighted world. I still recall how I would perform the melody to the picture of a swan paddling in a stream. Its head would be bowed and its wake so faint, it barely disturbed the surface. Some years after that the swan began to dim. A while later again it faded to black. Likewise for the waters and the sky."

"They vanished?"

"Or perhaps were simply replaced. What I 'see' now of a swan is its nasal honk and bell-beating wings. Of the stream I 'see' wind skitter over the surface and sedge grasses sway by the shore."

"And this course your blindness has taken," Friar Seamus asks, his tone respectful, "it cannot be reversed?"

"A tunnel, Friar, not unlike your description of the penitent cave. Too narrow to turn around in and too steep to climb back out of. Down and down the tunnel I slide, no longer attempting to dig in my heels or seek a hold. Not of my choosing, this path."

"Yet you acquired a gift in return?"

"Apparently."

"A rare genius for melody?"

"According to some."

He refuses to declare the exchange a fair one. He is by nature a contented person—his recent meditation on the Battle of the Boyne notwithstanding—and so has been at peace with his fate. But the issue, once again, is choice. An exchange is a negotiation. An exchange involves agreeing to terms and then shaking on them.

"What a great man," Friar Seamus repeats.

Can Carolan say the same of the friar? He isn't sure. Seamus is, however, at least as impressive as Owen Connor is impressionable. Cause enough for Carolan to wonder whether they should keep his company any longer.

The conspirators are away for ages and can be heard whispering in the breezeway. Carolan, though, is now satisfied. Among the detritus still littering the tabletop are two half-full jugs. A waste, he decides, especially at five pence. Also a necessity, in the aftermath of the reunion in the cave. To pour himself a glass, he similarly reasons, would be to risk spillage or a noisy accident. Better to drink directly from the vessels, using both hands.

Speaking of waste, he can't fathom why he bothered to confess what occurred to a table of men. Bone stems, a bird cupped in the palm. He'd have been better off confiding in a wolfhound. Women alone possess the requisite sensitivity. Women alone have emotional lives the match of their physical existences. And speaking of women—he inverts the first jug, liquid trickling down his chin—he should be composing a tune in praise of Bridget Cruise. A fifth melody, why not, even though Owen and the friar give his story no credit.

He loved his wife. He hadn't meant to imply otherwise when he spoke of being kissed.

Such a waste, talking to men instead of women. Such an indignity, not being allowed to command his own horse. Carolan should be footloose and wind-tossed and up the lane. He should be legging it, the lad.

chapter three

"We're legging it," he says above the rain.

"We are?"

"Footloose and wind-tossed."

"Who?"

"Up the lane, bold Geminiani!"

Owen Connor sucks air into his mouth, a watery burble.
"Dr Lynch had you pegged, loath as I am to admit it."

"That quack?"

"He warned me you might try such a stunt. They both did."

"Quack, quack."

"Queer notions at strange hours in states of disrepair," his guide
says. "Can you deny any of it?"

Carolan runs through the list. He is certainly merry and in a muddle. The hour is also gone ten o'clock, with the lodging house
where they were meant to board twenty minutes behind them. As
for the road to Enniskillen, upon which the horses tread—*shlip-
shlop, shlop-shlip,* Gull a muddy step slower than Gem—it is desolate,
the next prospect of accommodation two hours ahead at
Irvinestown. According to James Devlin, the road is notorious for
the highwaymen who haunt it, keen to lighten purses. According to
Friar Seamus, it is favoured as well by marauding ex-rapparees.
Those vigilantes, once committed to righting wrongs done to
Catholics, trade on the romance of their half-forgotten cause to
take random revenge on travellers, along with cash and jewels. And
the notions that drove Carolan from the security of Pettigoe and the

warmth of a goose-feather bed? Something to do with talking to women and not being a sack of grain. Also, about shaking hands with a natural leader in need of fresh recruits for his campaign.

"The charges are groundless," he concludes.

"What are we doing out here, Terence?"

"We've a visit to pay."

"In the dead of night?"

"An esteemed Ulster patron," he says. "I should be composing a tune for him this instant. If I don't, we may be refused at the door."

Clackety-clack on his four cloak buttons. A spry planxty, perhaps, or a bright song in the Italian mode. He wishes his fingers were more nimble. He wishes he had the seeds of even the most banal musical idea growing in his brain.

"Who would dare turn us away?"

"Whoever it is we are calling upon, of course," Carolan answers. He still can't recall the name of the patron in question.

"Your visits to gentry are favours, not charity," Owen says with the usual vehemence. "And you are off your head tonight, as Seamus suggested. Exhausted beyond measure."

"I feel quite alert."

"Potted, too."

"A mild buzz only, sorry to report."

"We found you sprawled across the table, the last of the ale spilled down your shirt and into your crotch."

"The position was . . . comfortable," he replies. Even with his head bowed, water is tracing the rim of his hood and changing course at his neck, icy fingers over his breasts and belly. The cold latches his hands to the saddle knob.

"Madness," Owen says.

"We'll quit soon enough."

"Where, in a ditch?"

"The bold lads, eh, Owen? You and me, galloping through the

night atop our frothing steeds. Whips cracking and spurs jangling, the earth trembling beneath. Women find that quite splendid, I am told," he adds.

Owen Connor ignores the comment, calming the horses with clucks of his tongue. Normally, Carolan can smell Gem's fear. This evening he senses it in the strain of her neck as she pulls her head back to probe the dark with her superior eyes. When the path narrows, probably before a gully marking the lean side of a turf wall, the animals snort in unison.

Fair enough. Horses and men alike are leery of moonless travel. Accustomed to striding through a landscape, the route already blazed, they cannot abide genuine darkness. It is both thief and bully, robbing them of their resources and humiliating them as humans or as steeds. Carolan is sympathetic. Only a fool does not avail himself of the smallest advantage when on the move. Such arduous journeying is required of us all. A whirlwind of arrivals and departures, mounts and dismounts: room to room and house to house, estate to estate and county to county. The pace is frantic, and the wayfarer halts his travelling only for illness or worse. Given such terms, it is wise to choose a judicious plan and the best of circumstances. Wise to mark the distinction between day and night.

Unless, that is, the traveller is blind. If asked, he explains with an analogy. Were Carolan the sort to thatch his own roof, he suspects he could manage it. Once up the ladder he could sew the scraws to the purlins using a needle and fir-ropes, then secure the layers of thatching with rods. He could swing the mallet and wield the trimming knife; he could staple and patch. He could do these tasks much like any other man. But the difference would be that Terence Carolan could work as easily at midnight as at noon, head bowed and hands engaged, no more afraid of a slip in the perilous dark than in the safe light.

"Did you notice Gem's snort?" he says now. "Long and with a flutter. Through the nose, the mouth shut tight."

He imitates the sound.

"It's what you'd expect from a horse in such circumstances," he continues. "'There may be danger,' she is saying, 'though I can't yet discern it.' Gull's squeal a minute ago, on the other hand, was a surprise. A squeal suggests urgent concern. He is warning some enemy that he is prepared to fight."

"Maybe Gull knows what lies ahead."

"Compare those sounds to the whinny or the neigh. They are melancholy communications, implying the horse is lonely. Or the nicker. When low-pitched, it serves as a straight hello or thank you. A mare's nicker to her foal is an exchange the newborn forever associates with her mother. Imitate it properly, and the foal will follow you instead."

The rain pummels his hood. Carolan could go missing inside the storm and be relieved of his anxieties. He travels most comfortably by giving over to flow. Rain is flow for him, like wind or rushing water, and once within the current he gets carried along unawares, almost unmindful. There is the *thwap* of it into the earth and the *thump* on the horses' coats. There is the drumming upon the saddlebags and the *rattle-tat-tat* across his own head. There is pattern and pitch and supernal God-driven syncopation. Or else there is rain drone, an even deeper release, nearly a dissolving, akin only to dreamless sleep. While he could probably venture to this place as well, it is one from which return can be difficult.

Anyway, Owen Connor won't permit him such an escape. Why should he? They are lost in the wilds of a Donegal night, thanks to his caprice. They are all at risk of bodily assault or injury, especially the horses, with their delicate legs.

"I saw her, Owen," he says.

"You are going to press the matter?"

"I held her hand."

"I won't hear it."

"'By the blood of my forefathers,' I said, 'this is the hand of Bridget Cruise.'"

Owen starts to whistle.

"Why won't you believe me?"

No reply is forthcoming.

Carolan repeats the question.

"Why won't I?" his guide finally answers. He pauses, perhaps to suggest an abundance of reasons. "Because you are a child of nature, impulsive and indulgent, and a stranger to discipline. Because your imagination, ever on the wing of some fancy, is eccentric in its flights. It is also unsteady and untrustworthy."

"Even at the harp?"

"Only there do you show composure, as though some finer instinct rules when you pluck the strings. Curious," he says almost to himself.

Owen Connor has always shown more interest in Carolan's creativity than anyone else, including the harper himself.

"I managed the pilgrimage," Carolan feels obliged to mention. "Fortitude was displayed there, was it not?"

"I am duly astonished."

"As am I," he admits. "The ten days were well beyond my native capacities. Only my yearning kept me afloat, so to speak. Good that it did. Otherwise, I'd have missed the reunion."

Owen is quiet.

"Bone stems," Carolan says with, he grants, the obstinacy of a child.

"You were mistaken."

"The way the stems rise and collect into a bundle."

"So do my own. You've remarked before on my spindly hands. Could it have been me in the cave yesterday afternoon?"

"Not unless you have shaved the back of your right hand of hairs and washed your palm clean of calluses."

His guide smiles through a skein of water, another, more faint, watery noise. His hood must be off.

"And not unless you asked me to please refer to you as Mrs Arthur Barnewall, rather than Bridget Cruise," Carolan says. "In deference to your husband. Do you recall making such a request?"

"You are impossible."

"I saw what I saw—or felt what I felt, rather."

Owen has heard enough.

"Years and years of nonsense about some mossy priory and flaxen-haired muse," he says. "Starlings reeling in a tower. Light angling down into a nave. Will it never be over, this adoration of a gentry girl of neither flesh nor—excuse me for saying it—bone? Will you remain forever incapable of honouring those who were your own blood? Or of showing the same ardour for the woman who willingly entered the real cave of your existence and stayed by you all her days?"

"If you knew what she said to me in there . . ."

His guide's next statement causes his horse to toss his head, like a dog at high notes on the violin.

"Can you even name them?" Owen says.

"Owen?"

"Your children. Can you?"

"Don't be miserable."

"In order of birth, please."

Carolan sighs. He is shivering now.

"Siobhan, in March 1712," he says.

"April 19. Next."

"My only son, Tadhg, born the following year."

"In 1714, in fact. The final day of October."

"You intend to quibble?"

"Next."

"Martha Carolan. 1715 . . . No, 1716. Am I right?"

"Go on."

"Eileen, born the summer of 1718. Then Maev, the following June."

"Anne Carolan, July 22, 1719."

"Did I say Maev?"

Owen does not oblige him.

"I am in no condition to be doing this," Carolan pleads.

"Next."

"Anne, I mean, Maev, in what, 1620?"

"Back in the reign of James First? There was a noble age."

Ignoring the quip, Carolan pries the fingers of his right hand loose to take a count. The arthritis will be awful once he is indoors. One . . . two . . . three . . .

"Mary!" he says, a hand spread and the other with two fingers raised. "How could I forget that sweet child? She came to us last but hardly least. In 1722, I am nearly certain."

Seven children bearing his name. Seven offspring that he sired, courtesy of a Leitrim cottage and a butterscotch wife whose hips were wide. It is what a man does in his prime, even a man like him, as easily as sucking on a sweet.

"Not too bad," Owen says.

"I can't believe I almost forgot Mary," Carolan says with more wariness than relief. The children, he fears, were a mere warning shot.

"And the mother of this fine brood?" his guide asks accordingly. "Who birthed you six girls and a boy in the span of a decade without complaint or much assistance? Does a name come to mind?"

"Owen . . ."

"Does one?"

A name, along with a few lines of his own poetry. *Happiest the husband / Who puts his hand under her head / They kiss without scandal / Happiest two near feather bed.*

"Careful," Carolan says.

But Owen is in no mood for caution. "Moira Carolan, née Keane," he says. "Born 1692 in Cavan town. Died in November, or was it December?"

"November 15, 1733."

"Good for you."

"You insult me in this manner?"

"You insult her memory in every manner possible. Why, she never even kissed you properly, did she?"

Though his accuser can't witness it in the dark, Carolan grimaces at the reminder of that comment. Regret settles over him even as a sound distracts his attempts at a reply. The sound is closer to a vibration, like thunder so far out to sea it reaches land as an echo inside the earth. In this instance the vibration reaches Carolan via Geminiani, passed up from one body to another. Owen Connor probably can't feel it yet.

"I am the most desolate of creatures," he says.

"Are you really?"

"I never laid eyes on my wife or children, Owen. Never laid eyes on anyone I attempted to love, once those I had cherished were sent to heaven. Neither could I be of much practical assistance as a husband or father. Could I take in a harvest or thatch a roof? Play cup-and-ball with my son or tie a daughter's braids? The buttons on my wife's dress I managed, and her nightgown I certainly did raise. But help her birth those children or rear them healthy and safe? Keep her from succumbing to illness at a terrible young age?" Carolan pauses to chart the rumble climbing up through his horse. "Such helplessness hollows a man," he resumes, "making him doubt he is present at all. Call it a tunnel or cave, this room where I reside, or an exile across a vast, churning ocean. The truth is, I have dwelt here so long, and grown so accustomed to the solitude, that I am no longer fit to be friend or companion, let alone parent. Who is the great

Terence Carolan?" he asks, astounded by his own words. They are new and, in their manner, fresh. "He is the bard and master. He is no one, dressed up as himself."

Owen's sputter confirms the newness of Carolan's thoughts. "But you are revered," he says. "If I merited even a fraction of the same esteem, I would count myself lucky. If I—"

"Hush."

The sound is now distinct—the clumping of hooves ahead on the path. Both the horses squeal.

"Can you not feel it? Or hear it, rather?"

Owen goes quiet.

"A single rider," he finally says.

"He could pass for a regiment."

"At a canter. He must carry a functioning lantern."

"Can't you see anything?" Carolan asks.

"The hand before me is obscure. But wait."

"A light?"

"A glow."

"Should we flee?"

"We should halt and wait," his guide answers. "And you should let me do the talking."

❋   ❋   ❋

"Fools or highwaymen?"

"Travellers," Owen says.

"Travellers?" the rider asks. His horse, a colt with a fluting to its breaths, snorts. Gull replies with a friendly nicker.

Lantern light washes over Carolan's face.

"Sheriff," Owen says for his benefit.

"I ask again—fools or highwaymen? Or rapparees maybe, out to avenge the phantom injustices of the age?"

The accent belongs to Fermanagh, the tone to the sort of Ulsterman often recruited into the service. Hard-headed and gruff, like a dog that won't surrender the shoe in its mouth.

"It's we who are relieved not to be encountering some scoundrel out to steal our coins or crack our skulls," Carolan says. "Not that our purses aren't already empty after a sojourn in a humble inn and our skulls—mine, at least—permanently cracked, Sheriff."

"Travellers," Owen says again.

"At this hour? On this night?"

"A soft evening it is."

"Soft?"

Grrr, Carolan hears, the hound wiggling its head and tightening its clench on the shoe.

"A few drops of water never harmed a man," Owen says.

The lantern shifts to him.

"Are you making smart with me, lad?"

"He wouldn't presume," Carolan says.

"I'll be the judge of that. Where was this humble inn?"

Owen names Pettigoe.

"James Devlin's house?"

"I didn't learn the keeper's name."

"That explains it, then. Your kind are the only respectable folk on this road after dark and in all weather. Too poor to hire the most pitiful room in the village. A ditch shared with curs can't be much worse than the accommodations offered on Station Island. Did you really squander ten days on your knees praying and fasting, as they say?"

"We are bound for Tempo, Fermanagh," Owen says. "The Maguire estate."

Tempo. The estate name that Carolan could not draw up from the well of his memory. Three thousand acres and a manor house owned by his friend and patron, Brian Maguire. Sir Brian married the least splendid of the Nugent girls. They had four sons. Carolan wrote a tune for Brian Maguire once and another for the eldest boy. A planxty for the wife—named Elizabeth, with a cackle-laugh and vanilla scent—might be prudent. Especially if he and Owen show up soaked and stinking.

"I think that improbable," the sheriff replies.

He hears Owen stiffen. Gull twists his muzzle side to side. When Gem follows suit, Carolan leans forward to rub the glaze across her forehead, as he does when standing before her. The motion reminds him that he is yet mellow and at greater risk than ever of sliding off the saddle.

Sensing a temper he can flare, the Ulsterman presses the insults. "The likes of you won't get much beyond the front gate of Tempo," he says, "unless they are receiving beggars in the servants' hall, offering them feeds of cold gruel."

"Is that so?"

Carolan makes a decision. Better that he speak out of turn than Owen say too much more. A hacking fit, the coughs rasping, delays him. The men have the courtesy to wait.

"My friend Brian Maguire is the middle son of Constantine Maguire, hero of the Pass of Aughrim," he begins. "The story is famous in these parts. Having destroyed the second regiment of British horse, Con's men were cut to pieces by grapeshot. Maguire fell and was left on the battlefield. A lad by the name of James Durnien happened upon the corpse. Recognizing his commander, Durnien drew his sword and severed the head. He rode hard for Enniskillen, where he hired a boat to take him out to the Isle of Devenish, burial ground for the Maguire sept. Thus the great Constantine was reunited with his ancestors in the family ground."

"Or his head was, at least."

"You are of Enniskillen, are you not, Sheriff?"

"What of it?"

"Then you must be familiar with the tale of Con Maguire."

Carolan speaks the words with careful congeniality. Unlike his guide, he has no argument with authority. Ever.

"Ancient history," the Ulsterman answers.

"Easy for you to say," Owen snaps.

"Is that right?"

"Ancient history, indeed," Carolan says. "As it happens, though, I can still recall the boom of the Aughrim cannonades drifting across the plains of Roscommon that summer of 1691."

The sheriff's impatience seems to rise with the pounding rain. "What I know of the present-day Maguires of Tempo is that their estate nearly went under the gavel not long ago, though whether from debt or the statutes I can't be sure. Is there even a papist Maguire left in that wreck of a manor?"

Carolan is startled. "Brian Maguire remains true to his—"

"Have you business with us?" Owen asks, a judicious interruption.

"I might or I might not."

"Could you be quick in deciding?"

"Let me have a look inside these saddlebags," the man says. "They are of peculiar bulk to contain the lawful possessions of pilgrims. Could be gunpowder in there, or the setup for a Catholic ritual. Unstrap the saddlebag closest to my lantern, if you would."

When his colt is inched closer, all three animals express their wariness. Carolan, still clinging to Geminiani's neck, seeks an ear. "Easy there, girl," he whispers to her. And please heed me this once, he adds wordlessly.

A dash may soon be their only option. He probes the bag hanging behind his right buttock, confirming his fears. It bulges, likely with stolen goods.

He wishes for those spurs or that crop.

Whip or gouge a horse? Not on his life, or on the lives of his children, whom he could likewise never have harmed.

"Books," he announces. The play, though weak, is the best he can manage. His heart hammers in his chest.

"Books?"

"Our bags burst, Sheriff, from the effects of a poor scholar's fidelity to his tools-in-trade."

Carolan listens as the straps on one of Gull's bags are undone. Those saddlebags are set between a large, oddly shaped object—the harp, in its leather case. Were he a constable, that case would be arousing his suspicions most.

"There's a library in here," the sheriff says.

"Don't hold it up in the rain," Owen scolds him.

"I realize I carry more volumes than I could possibly read on my travels," Carolan says. "The truth is, I cannot bear to be apart from them. Where others suffer for their attachment to claret or whiskey, my own addiction lies with the calfskin binding and gold tooling, the endpapers yet uncut."

Owen must be biting his tongue.

The lantern shifts again.

"You, a reader?" the sheriff asks.

The mere mention of whiskey has set his lips quivering. He raises his face to the spigot sky and drinks. "In a manner of speaking," he replies. "My manservant does the reading and I the listening. Virgil and Bunyan and the sonnets. Plus Bedell's Bible, a few verses every evening."

"The pox, was it?"

Carolan confirms the cause.

"It's the scars on your cheeks that tell the story," the Ulsterman says. "An unlikely face for a brigand or pilgrim. You should be indoors, old fellow."

"These aching joints agree."

"As for your honoured friend Brian Maguire, my understanding is that he currently lodges in the stable, not the house. A nephew holds the estate, Colonel Hugh Maguire, and he is no Jacobite traitor."

Again, Carolan is surprised. But the report makes little sense. For Hugh Maguire to hold Tempo, his uncle Brian would have to be either dead or in debtors' prison. Carolan would have heard.

The sheriff is now a dog with a ripped and gummy shoe on the floor before its front paws, a pleasurable chew ended. "You'll get nowhere near Tempo this evening," he says to them.

"We intend to put up soon."

"There's a village fifteen minutes ahead. Sties, for beasts and Catholics alike. You may find shelter there, however wretched."

"Most kind," Carolan says.

"We can find our own way," Owen says.

There is a pause. Though the rain affects his hearing, he still detects it—the men, exchanging the glances that men do. Regardless of the dark.

"A fine horse your master rides," the sheriff says. "Worth more than five pounds, I'd venture."

"Seven, and not a penny less," Owen answers. "Are you making an offer of purchase? In coin only, naturally."

"Do I require in excess of five pounds to confiscate it?"

"I can't imagine how else you'd come to possess such an animal."

"Four pounds at most, sir," Carolan says. "Gem's a wreck, God bless her. Like myself."

"You value her too little. Typical," the man adds.

"Of what, may I inquire?" Owen says.

Carolan sneezes. Twice, the second sneeze like an unfriendly slap on the back. His intervention is well timed.

"You'd best get this one indoors."

"It has long been my ambition."

"I'll leave you ₁o it, then," the sheriff says. Without so much as a good-night he orders his steed to walk on.

❋   ❋   ❋

They resume their journey in silence.

The sheriff's report about Tempo must be wild rumour, Carolan thinks. Even the Penal laws can't just run a Catholic off his lands. It is true the statutes forbid marriage between the religions and banish all bishops, deans, monks and friars. True as well they deny Catholics the right to practise as lawyers or hold public office, obtain degrees from Trinity College in Dublin. Property grabs, however, more than punishments for the Boyne, lie behind the laws, and while a Papist can't purchase new land or bequeath holdings by primogeniture, unless the oldest son converts—a ploy to carve up the few surviving large Catholic estates—he likewise can't simply be evicted.

Some families try circumventing the Penals with secret arrangements to transfer ownership in name only. Here is a tricky business, rife with betrayals. But the statutes have done more harm to the honour of men than to their possessions, turning them into knaves and schemers and muddying relations between neighbours and friends. Then there are the partitions within clans. One sibling refuses to convert and so is disinherited. Another changes coat and is rewarded with the acreage. One flees to the continent to fight alongside the king's enemies, now his allies. The other has a traitor for a brother or child.

Worse still, the majority can't see this evil occurring. They fail to recognize that they are being divided for the purposes of having their dignity, rather than their property, conquered. Carolan can see it, of course, but he is a mere spectator—a queer, faintly ridiculous one, at that.

Why, a Catholic is forbidden from possessing a horse valued at greater than five pounds. Any animal can be procured on the spot for that fee in cash, regardless of its actual value. Few Protestants have dared deprive a Papist of a steed in so offensive a manner. Still, remark how the sheriff used the threat. From Owen Connor, he earned a rise that nearly sparked a confrontation. From Carolan, he won a grovel, a humiliation that leaves a taste of bile, summoned from those yet unrelieved bowels, in his mouth.

"I did not require your gallantry back there," Owen finally says.

"One of us had to be the rightful owners of those books."

"And it should be you?"

Carolan refrains from answering.

"Could I not claim to have purchased the volumes with my own funds? Or even had them on loan from the squires whose names can be found on certain of the front plates?"

Again, he is silent.

"Then I am such an obvious poor scholar?" his guide continues. "The word *Gael* branded across my forehead?"

"It's the order of things, son," he answers mildly.

"The order?"

"You understand."

"I do not."

"I am your elder."

"That is hardly what you mean."

"The sheriff would assume you are in my employ. Thus he would grant that I might possess a library and be eccentric enough to lug the books around on my journeys. He wouldn't be so accepting of another story."

He is right, and Owen knows it. But Owen, in turn, is right that Carolan meant something else by "the order of things." This discussion, about status and virtue and society's judgements, is for another day.

"Seamus claims we accept too much and contest too little," Owen says. "Not so much from fear as a lack of purpose in our lives."

Carolan's voice tightens. "Does he."

"He excludes you, naturally."

"Because I am a great man?"

"Or because you are a great age."

To stop his mouth, he drinks more rain. The water pricks his sockets and runs up his nose. Carolan cares not at all for the friar's conjectures about the defects of the native temperament. Serving God and one's fellow man should be purpose enough for any life, Irish or otherwise. Seamus attacks first the monarchy and now the church. Who will be next? Himself, he reasons—Terence Carolan, feeble Christian and dogsbody to the landowning class.

"The Franciscan is tall?" he says with manufactured calm.

"Not like I am. But he is broad across the chest and arms."

"I sensed it both times he assisted me."

"Both times?"

"Out of the cave and then from the chamber pot."

"Right."

He deliberates before speaking further. "His eyes display similar force and appeal, I assume?"

Owen does not reply at once. Instead, he clucks his tongue at Gull.

"It has been a long while since you asked me to describe some-one's physical appearance," he eventually answers.

"The information ceased being of any benefit," Carolan says. "Not with my visual memory of expressions and their meanings almost lost. I now operate purely from the black, as I explained to Friar Seamus."

"Then why inquire about him?"

His reason—because of what the description may tell him about his guide—can't be shared. "His voice intrigued me," he says.

"But not his words?"

"Those as well."

"I am most intrigued by his words," Owen says.

Now it is Carolan who clucks his tongue, despite Geminiani's rule of ignoring his commands. He needs to reach the village the sheriff mentioned. His every limb quivers from fatigue.

"It doesn't have to be that way for you," Owen suddenly says. "What you said before about feeling isolated by your infirmity."

"Also by my gift," he replies. To his own surprise he is willing to revisit this subject.

"Your gift?"

"It marks me out. It separates me from my fellows as surely as the sky separates heaven from earth."

"But you are a man, like any other."

"Am I?"

"I do recall my earlier remark," Owen says to defend the contradiction. "I refer now to something else. If family is taken as the measure, then you are more normal than I am. Who had the wife and seven children?"

"I could not see my wife."

"You chose not to see Moira."

The effrontery of the comment, more than its rawness, causes Carolan to draw a breath.

"You chose a path away from her. To mount a horse and ride off for weeks and months on end."

"Me, choose a path? When was I ever allowed?"

"I watched you ride away," Owen says, "and even assisted you, being a dutiful manservant. The same holds for your flights from Siobhan, Tadhg, Martha and Eileen, Anne, Maev and Mary."

Carolan drops his chin.

"The girl is to blame, in no small part. She overshadowed the others."

"Bridget Cruise?"

"Must we speak her name aloud again?"

"I still haven't told you what she said to me in the cave," Carolan answers. "You must be curious, after hearing about her for two decades."

"There was no conversation for you to report, aside from the one that occurred in your delirious brain."

"But she said—"

"Stop it."

The force of the command nearly propels him from his horse. He embraces Geminiani for support.

"Though I was too young to understand back then," Owen says, "I believe I do now. Because I am not your manservant, am I? I am your guide."

Carolan is quiet.

"Paid to steer you with boldness and vision."

"The pilgrimage has wasted my faculties, true," he admits.

"The pilgrimage, and this infernal night ride. Perhaps both were necessary, however. And perhaps the journey can be different from here onwards."

"You think so?"

"Even for your music, it needn't be too late."

His music requires guidance as well?

"Now is not the occasion," Owen adds, anticipating the obvious question.

In truth Carolan has no strength left to hear his craft likewise assaulted. "Tell me we are upon that village," he says. "Gem can't support such a load for much longer."

Geminiani thrusts her head, a forward movement usually suggesting impatience. Tonight the action implies discomfort, probably at the dark and cold.

"A gathering of hovels," Owen confirms after a moment, "the first one immediately at hand."

"Will they take us in?"

"There's scarcely a house in the land that would refuse you. The offerings, though, may be humble."

"I should be honoured to be received by regular folk," Carolan says. "Our Saviour was a carpenter, after all."

He feels Owen's grip on his thigh and hip, assisting his dismount. His hood falls back, a swift drenching.

"So, will you allow me to guide you, Terence? You might begin to feel less isolated. You might even be with her at last."

"Her?"

"Moira."

Why should Carolan's life be helpless and his fate a legend already told? He will allow it.

"The house has a door?" he asks.

"I can barely make it out."

"Knock, so."

His guide—also his servant and friend, and now his determined redeemer—knocks.

chapter four

"Peace on this house."

If there is a reply, the rain swallows it.

Owen repeats the greeting.

"Sir?" a woman answers.

"Two travellers, madam, in need of a dry corner to toss down our cloaks as beds."

"So late?"

"I apologize for the inconvenience."

"We've sickness here," a man says. "Otherwise, you'd be welcome at this or any other hour."

"A child," she adds. "It may be grave."

It is grave, Carolan can already tell. With just those few words the woman betrays the severity of both the illness and her worry. He distinguishes three separate strains: disbelief that such a thing could have happened, dismay that it has, and a refusal to acknowledge the likely outcome.

"Carry on up the lane," the man says. "The next house belongs to a brother, Geroid, and his wife, Mary. They have five children but are charitable. Do you possess a lantern?"

"I can't keep it lit."

"Geroid will take you in."

Owen thanks him.

"I may be able to offer assistance with the child," Carolan says. The unexpected words slide from his lips with the ease of a rosary.

"You are a physician?" she asks.

"I've long experience with illness."

"The sickness, we're told, may impart a contagion. Other children along this shore of Lough Erne have been spirited away."

He hesitates for only a second. "I've no fear of catching my death," he replies.

"But you are not trained?" the man says.

"I may be able to assist."

The door opens.

"What are you doing?" Owen says into his ear.

"Following my guide," he answers.

Carolan crouches under the lintel, as per instructions. His olfactory powers, gone missing in the storm, return with near sensory violence. He inhales dung and bulrushes, vomit and sweat. He does not pick up the after-scents of a fire. The pressed air tells him the ceiling hangs low, and heat from bodies suggests the same cramped conditions as in the penitent cave. The mud walls smell dry.

A candle is lit.

"May I shake your hand, sir?" he asks.

The hand finds his, the grip proud.

"Patrick Connelly, of Kesh," the man says. "My wife, Grainne."

She stands, Carolan estimates, to her husband's left. His hand goes there, six inches lower.

"Terence," he says, receiving a soft shake from her, "of Mohill, County Leitrim. My companion Owen Connor, of Sligo town. Owen?"

"He is tending the horses," she says.

They still do not know about him. The sooner the better, Carolan has always found. People need a few moments to adjust. So many assumptions about hosting a visitor must be reconsidered. So many instincts about judging character have to be given over. No one wishes to make strange with the affirmed. Rather, they wish to show kindness and to help.

"Raise the flame to my face," he says.

"Sir?"

"As explanation, Mr Connelly."

The heat scorches his skin. He tries to hold his expression.

"But . . .?" she says with a gasp.

Next the husband will issue a remark he will regret.

"Tell me," Carolan says, hoping to spare them the embarrassment, "how old is the child?"

"Three years and a month."

"Her name?"

"Deirdre. How did you know she was a girl?"

From her breathing, he does not reply. "She lies against that far wall?" he asks. "Flat on her back, arms sprawled? Raven hair over her eyes?"

"Her hair has much red in it," Grainne Connelly says.

"Red or orange?"

"The colour of ripe apples."

"Lovely."

"You possess the skills of a physician?"

"Patrick," the wife admonishes.

"The fever runs high?" Carolan says to her.

The man's fury gives off a warning scent, but the wife's distress, especially in its hint of supplication, is a perfume, and he the swooning suitor.

"Some believe it the plague loose again," she answers.

"Not the plague, I assure you."

"Her forehead boils while her cheeks are like ice. Her stool is liquid, and she is in too great discomfort to eat."

"Fatigue?"

"Some days she hardly stirs."

"A sore throat?"

"She can't sup water."

Diphtheria. An assassin who rarely misses his mark. Were Carolan a doctor, accustomed to dashing hopes, he would carry on in the same tone. But he is not. He is a father, like any other. "Any swelling," he says, swallowing his own distress, "about the neck?"

She sobs.

"Hush, Grainne," her husband says.

"No cause for tears," Carolan offers out of mercy.

"We pray to the Lord for her deliverance. Night and day, sir, we pray. She is our only blessing, little Deirdre. Without her . . ."

He longs to touch her hand.

"It may be a simple ague," he says.

"It's what I've been telling her."

"Other bairns have been spirited away," she says.

Owen Connor appears, his choppy breaths suggesting a yoke of saddlebags over his shoulders. He pauses, presumably to take in the sight of a woman quaking in her man's arms, with Carolan standing idly by.

"Are the horses secure behind the house?" he asks.

"There is hay in the poultry shed," Patrick Connelly says. "You're welcome to feed them on it."

Unless Carolan is mistaken, the husband has already found an excuse to end the embrace and his own discomfort with such a display.

"We've oats to spare," Owen says.

"Oats? Lucky animals."

Grainne Connelly, taking a cue from her spouse, composes herself enough to inquire of the sack that Owen has leaned against the wall.

"Explanations in the morning," Carolan says. "We don't wish to keep you up any longer."

"But the child?"

"My curative is eccentric, Mrs Connelly. I wish I could claim otherwise. All I ask, and can offer, is to sleep next to her this night."

"That is your medicine?" the husband says.

"My wife and I raised a brood, sir. Six girls and a boy, without a loss. Over the years every variety of epidemic swept through the countryside outside our cottage. Spotted fever and the bloody flux, typhus and my own mortal enemy, smallpox. The insight behind our good fortune?" he asks rhetorically. "Keep the children close by at such times. In our bed, inhaling secretions from our healthy bodies and imbibing our strong faith. Embraced by such love, no harm could come to them."

Owen hiccups in disbelief.

"And your wife?" she says.

"Beg pardon?"

"Your wife—she shares your faith?"

Carolan requests a chair.

"We've had a long and difficult night, madam," Owen says from behind him. "Sunrise will show us all in a more sensible light."

"Then he has nothing to contribute to my Deirdre's recovery?" Patrick Connelly says.

She admonishes him once more by name.

"Some believe the blind to be possessed of special powers," Carolan says. "Fortune's children, we are called."

No one responds.

"I can contribute only fervent prayer, Mr Connelly, and the healing properties of this sorry old corpse. Little else."

"Fervent prayer is exactly what our daughter requires," Grainne Connelly says. She brushes the back of his wrist with her fingertips. "Its power as medicine is beyond dispute."

The man sets about further spreading their mattress of bulrushes to accommodate the extra sleepers. The family owns just a single blanket. Owen, though, assures Patrick Connelly they will be fine with their cloaks.

Amazingly, she touches him again. "Were you born with the condition, Terence?" she asks, her manner intimate.

"I was eighteen," he replies. "The pox, as I mentioned."

She blesses herself.

"Others?"

"My mother and sister."

"I am sorry for your losses."

He reaches out with his right hand to take hers and squeeze. Either she does not notice or she finds the gesture rude.

"I always thought that 'Fortune's children' referred more to a musical gift possessed by your kind," she says.

"My head is gone, Mrs Connelly."

"You are a good Christian, I can tell."

"A pilgrim, direct from Station Island," he says.

"I guessed as much. Ten days and nights out on that rock. It demonstrates your great faith."

"Or folly."

Her laughter is guilty but gay. It certainly isn't girlish. A quality to her voice has been weighing upon him, a quaver he can't put down to fatigue or trauma. She must be thirty, even thirty-five. A late marriage, he reckons, or else difficulties in delivering a child. Either way, Deirdre has to be more precious than her own salvation.

"Terence?" she says.

"Hmm?"

"You mustn't think of sleeping in those clothes."

In fact, he is desperate to be out of them. "It would be improper to disrobe," he answers. "Not to mention unpleasant smelling."

"Our family slept in *stradogue* every night. The little ones, by their ages, then the parents and any guests. We were all naked and warm under the rushes."

"We were the same."

"Once this candle is snuffed, it will hardly matter to me what you do or do not wear to bed. Only the opinion of your wife matters then."

He should reply in kind to her wit. Instead, hunger for her quavery voice and cold-fingered touch gets the better of him.

"My wife died at age forty-one," he whispers. "May her soul rest in peace."

After making another sign of the cross, Grainne Connelly rests her hand on his arm, as if they are being introduced at a ball.

"A womanly ailment in the chest," he adds. "She suffered terribly towards the end."

Her breasts actually turned swollen and hard. Awful, awful. Dr Lynch could do nothing. Carolan, even more ineffectual than usual, fled for the last week to an estate in Roscommon. Moira understood, and forgave him, as did the children. Owen Connor did not.

"The loss of so many women . . ." she says.

"Aye."

"You poor man."

"I could be of so little use in the final account," he says, "with my infirmity. As well, my occupation necessitates much travel."

"Now, now," she says.

He hears it plainly: the uplift, the purpose. Consoling—touching—is doing her spirit good. He is happy to accommodate.

"Do I interrupt?" Owen asks.

Pup.

"Mrs Connelly was just explaining to me about the bedding," he answers. A shiver of a different sort passes through him with the force of an ocean gale across a field.

She must notice. "We would light a fire, but . . ." she says.

"A fire for the cooking of breakfast," Carolan assures her. "No sooner." He thanks her again for the hospitality.

*　*　*

Owen Connor removes his boots for him and peels off his socks. His breeches come next, after some tugging, followed by his vest and chemise, all fit only to be burned. Carolan begs his guide to bury him in bulrushes, to spare their hosts the reek, and then absorbs the weight of the cloak, heavy as a yard-cut of turf. Owen positions a saddlebag as shared pillow.

Exhaustion swarms his head and body equally. He could fall away in a beat and sleep until the lark sings. But now he must be vigilant.

"Are you ready?" Grainne Connelly asks.

"Let me roll onto my side."

He shifts with a groan, the rushes prickly, not much padding between his flesh and the dirt floor. Though he extends an arm to serve as buttress, his hip still complains.

She nestles her daughter against his chest. The girl mutters and kicks without awakening. His paunch—shaped, he has been told, like the haystacks of County Mayo—makes the fit a challenge. Deirdre, however, soon curves her body around the dome, resting her arm atop it, as children do with a beloved dog. Carolan adjusts the cloak to cover her as well. They lie face to face, her braided hair, which he strokes, smelling of sickness rather than fruit. Her breath is still more dismaying. He marked the fall of his own children from innocence by the changes in their night-time breaths. One month their scents would be sweet all the sleep-time long. Then a souring would begin, faint at first, like spring moss, and finally as acrid as a bog at the end of a wet autumn. The girl he holds has the breath not only of a grown-up but of someone whose body is rotting. The rot of age is one betrayal. The rot of illness in a small child is another.

Carolan runs his nails over her arm. His seven bairns purred when he drew them into him and scratched their arms and bellies, up and down their legs. Moira liked a good scratch no less. She smelled of uncooked dough and tasted of butterscotch. Every evening she washed first the children and then herself, face and neck and under the arms, the water a tinkling in the basin and an occasional shower when she squeezed the cloth. Then she washed him, especially his scarred cheeks.

Kissing without scandal.

What kindness did Bridget Cruise show towards those same pockmarks? A remarkable gesture, one that still causes him to tremble. He couldn't have conjured the reunion with her. Even Terence Carolan lacks such fancy.

Shh. Owen Connor can eavesdrop on his very thoughts.

Owen joins him on the ground. As soon as he lies down, he blocks the chill pricking Carolan's backside from the crack beneath the door.

"Well?"

"I haven't checked," Carolan says.

"Any point in waiting?"

He probes the girl's neck. Her skin is hot, as though she slumbers near an unquenchable flame—the dreadful truth, he supposes—and her throat is swollen to twice its natural width. She wheezes in her sleep, the sound marking the struggle of air to escape her closing passage. Once the throat is sealed, she will suffocate.

He sighs.

"I suspected as much," Owen says.

His guide is perched on one elbow behind him, his words passing directly into his ear. Carolan, in contrast, must shield his mouth to funnel his replies. His voice carries towards the child and her parents.

"It's a bond," he finally says.

"A fraught one."

"Is it fair to pick and choose?"

"People do so all the time."

"We knocked on a door," Carolan says. "This is what we found."

"A vulnerable female?"

"A family, Owen. I am tending the girl, not the mother."

"Curing her?"

He says nothing.

"And if she succumbs?"

"Beg pardon?"

"You heard me."

"Is Deirdre settled?" Grainne Connelly calls.

He recognizes the concern buried in her query. "It is very dark in here?" he says to his guide.

"Pitch black."

"Poor woman. Though her child lies just a pace away, she can't see her. She feels helpless and is only half convinced the girl isn't a happy dream, from which she will soon awaken, once more barren and alone."

He raises his voice. "She sleeps comfortably, Mrs Connelly. Her forehead is cooling and the swelling has subsided."

"Truly?"

Now Carolan detects Grainne Connelly's other fear, the one she may not be conscious of nurturing. *If my own daughter can't see me, she is wondering, am I any more real?*

Or perhaps he is thinking of himself.

"Fire a candle, and you'll be able to smile your love across at Deirdre," he says. "Is that what you'd wish?"

"I . . . I wouldn't mind," she answers with a sniffle.

"Of course, I'll have to shake the girl awake."

"No, don't do that."

"Hush, woman," her husband commands. He is desperate for sleep and close to it.

"She is safe and contented, and you are her world," Carolan tells her. "All this will come clear in the morning."

It isn't that people must see to believe. It is more that they must *be* seen, within the iris of an eye or the flash of a smile, to maintain faith in themselves. The blind cannot provide this service, and as a result the sighted lose track of them, forgetting they are present. The sightless, in turn, collude in their own disappearance. As they have no eyes to serve as mirrors, they stop seeking contact with other gazes. Lacking the smiles to light fellow smiles, they sink into an abstracted countenance, genial but vacant.

And at sunrise Deirdre, tickled awake by light she can both see and feel, will probably squirm for release from the beast mauling her. Carolan won't express hurt. Even his own children never quite grasped their father's condition.

"When I close my eyes," his daughter Siobhan once said, "you can't see me."

"I'm afraid not," he replied.

"Then when I open them, you can?"

"Not exactly, darling."

"I see you, Daddy, so you must see me!"

Or his boy, Tadhg: "See the bird?" Tadhg asked one time.

"My eyes are no good," Carolan answered.

"But I can see your eyes."

"I know you can, Tadhg." He then blinded his son with his palms. "Can you see the bird now?"

"No," the child said.

"Then you are like me." He removed the hands.

"And you're like me, too," Tadhg said. "See the bird? Look, it's flown away!"

Moira regularly instructed the children to place themselves near Carolan. "Show your father," she would say, meaning come closer.

Various bairns would announce, "Look, Daddy," when laying a drawing or a leaf in his lap. But almost inevitably they would add: "Isn't it pretty?"

"You certainly are," he would reply, consoling himself with the touch and smell of them.

Only on a single occasion did he fail to find words to smooth over the awkwardness. Mary, the youngest, adored the tale of Rapunzel, the maiden who let down her hair. "If I cried, Father," she said, "and the tears fell in your eyes, you'd be able to see again, wouldn't you? Just like in the story?"

Mary would be fifteen now. She lives with her sister Maev and the woman hired to mind them in the cottage near Mohill. The girl is already tall, although born a runt, and possesses a sweet singing voice. It is the same house where she was raised, sleeping most nights in her parents' goose-feather bed. It is the same bed her mother died in, nearly four autumns ago. He visits the cottage infrequently and has not slept atop those feathers since.

He can hardly breathe sometimes for missing her.

Silence descends over the Connelly home. Branches stir and the door rattles, the thatch smothering the rain. Carolan could slide into these sounds, their cadence and flow. He could be gone until sunrise.

"Help me, Owen."

"With what?"

"Fighting sleep."

"Fervent prayer won't keep you awake?"

"Probably not," he admits.

"You take on too much here."

"We knocked on that door . . ." Carolan says again.

"You cannot help her," his guide objects, blowing air from his cheeks. "I mean, you simply are no physician."

"No quack?"

"Do you seriously think you can save this child?"

"I have my rosary," he says, raising a hand twined by beads, the silver crucifix likely a glint in the dark. "I can pray the Hail Marys as well as any old woman in this land."

"That you can," Owen says.

"And I have other resources as well."

"What, your gift for composition?"

"I am a father, like any other," he answers, ignoring the dig.

Owen says nothing.

"Answer me this," Carolan asks. "Am I not the most sociable of men?"

"I suppose."

"The table has yet to be laid that I would decline to grace," he says, still caressing Deirdre's hair. "The glass has not been filled that I would refuse to empty. Company all the day and night, why not? Better a brood of kicking children or a nagging guide than an empty bed. Better a hound with meaty breath."

"A hound?" Owen says through a yawn.

"Nor do I covet solitude for the creation of my music. Quite the opposite. I play the harp for how it gains me companionship. I play to be admired and loved as well as fed and watered. As well as to gratify the Lord, naturally."

"Naturally . . . ."

His guide is fading. But Carolan feels alert, if sore in the shoulder and hip. He will require two-hands' help to rise in the morning and will be hobbled, the pain as sharp as thorn pricks. Climbing back on Geminiani without the boost of whiskey or port will be a task.

"Why then am I so alone, do you suppose? . . . Owen?"

He nudges his guide with his elbow.

"Ouch."

"Apologies."

"I like my teeth in my mouth, not scattered over the ground."

"Sirs!" Patrick Connelly calls.

"Sorry, Mr Connelly," Owen says.

"Well, Owen?"

His guide yawns again. "You should inquire of the parents," he says, dismissing Carolan's loneliness. "You know you should."

He pretends not to understand the question.

"The child—has she been given last rites?"

"Quiet."

"To die unshriven is a woeful fate. You've said it yourself."

"I'll ask no such thing."

"Do you not need. . ."

He does need to piss, badly.

"I'll manage," he replies, pinching himself there.

"I intended to suggest a trip outdoors before you accepted the girl into your care. Can you hold it until morning?"

"I'll have to."

"Then I am done," Owen says.

He is asleep before his head touches the saddlebag.

Across the room Patrick Connelly slumbers noisily while his wife, who has succumbed at last to her fatigue, takes in air with deep, fluttery breaths.

Even Deirdre is settled.

Only Carolan is awake. Only he is so alone.

Outside, rain pummels the roof, water streaming off the thatch. Without any wind the storm will exhaust itself before dawn. The day will be fresh and fine, should it ever come.

"*Dirige, Domine, Deus meus, in conspectu tuo viam meam,*" he intones. Direct, O Lord, my way to Thy sight.

My way to Thy sight.

Not the girl. Not her.

Take him instead.

Eternal shame for babbling on about his supposed skills at protecting his own from disease. Twice shame again for seeking pity over the death of his wife.

He could not hold her gaze with his own, could he? He could not assure her she was cherished and would be remembered. Nor was he able to console the children with facial gestures of fatherly authority. Impossible, being dead-eyed and vacant-smiled. Impossible, being scarcely present. So he scurried off to the O'Briens of Boyle, where he performed splendidly as the bard and so stayed merry, merry, all the nights and most of the days. Until it was finally over, and then he got to be the grieving husband. There, too, was a part Carolan played with gusto. Another solo recital.

Still, he can make up for it now. He can find a bond.

And it's true, Owen, he declares inside his head.

What is? he imagines his guide answering.

I can hardly breathe sometimes for missing her.

Don't speak to me of that woman again.

Not Bridget. *Her.*

Who, the wife you neglected? The one whose deathbed you fled?

I can hardly breathe.

CHAPTER five

A girl dances around his chair.

Carolan is lilting for her benefit. A slip-jig, in D major and nine-eight time. Or thereabouts.

"*Ladly-fol-da-dee-di-diddle-dum,*" he says. "*Ladly-fol-da-dee.*"

"Tee-hee," she chimes.

"*Ladly-fol-da-dee-di-diddle-dum.*"

"*Ladly-fol . . .*"

"Tee-hee-hee-hee."

So ending, he drops his elbows to his knees.

"More," she says.

"A moment's rest and I'll lilt you another."

"More."

"You'll wear our guest out, Deirdre," her mother says.

Her voice, though, is too bright to scold. Grainne Connelly has already joined her daughter for a turn of the room, quitting with a laugh that was thanks enough for him.

"How old are you?" Deirdre asks.

"Ancient."

"Do your eyes hurt?"

"Not at all."

"Can I touch them?"

"If you want."

"Did you watch me dance?" the girl says, changing her mind.

"Yes."

"But you were staring at the ceiling."

"Was I?"

He hears her hair brush the collar of her dress. A garment, he noted during the night, cut from a sack previously filled with oats. She wears no shoes and probably doesn't own a pair.

"I saw you nod your head there, Deirdre."

"But you're still not looking?"

"Magic."

"Your fingernails are long."

"On both hands," he says, raising them.

"And they're dirty."

"I'll have to clean them."

"You smell."

"Deirdre," her mother offers with more conviction.

"From the mouths of babes, Mrs Connelly," Carolan says.

"Call me Grainne, please. After all, I've seen you in your *caitech* now," she says, referring to a shirt of beaten rushes.

"And you're still in shock from the sighting, I can tell."

She laughs again. In its inflection he discerns her surprise that she would yet be capable of this simple pleasure. He has heard the same in the voices of other women in similar situations—mothers of sick children and wives of dying husbands—and always finds it worrisome.

"Gin-her-bread," Deirdre says.

"Don't eat it all at once."

He extends his arms for her. Now that he has held a child after so long, he wants to hold one forever. But the girl is awake, and he is a smelly stranger with egg-yolk eyes and dirty nails.

"Run, run as fast as you can . . ." she says, evading him.

"I'll not catch you . . ."

"I'm the gin-her-bread man!"

She bolts through the open door, chased by her mother's caution.

Wren song, horse snorts and bee buzz nose back in. The air is after-rain fresh and the light is warming.

"Sweets for Deirdre," Grainne Connelly says, "flour and sugar for the house. You are too generous."

"I only wish I hadn't promised you that ball of yarn before Owen checked our saddlebags. I could have sworn we had one left."

"It's no bother."

"Your shawl couldn't use mending?"

"It could."

"There you go," Carolan says. He is treasuring every minute of their time together. Dare he try once more?

"Your hand, Grainne. May I hold it a moment?"

"Terence?"

"Never mind," he says.

Two failed attempts in the space of a few hours. He seems determined to examine another female hand. He imagines Grainne's fingertips to be calloused and the pads of her palms coarse from working the flail and butter churn. Still, her bone stems must be as refined as her voice and demeanour. An excellent country wife, Carolan is already convinced.

She rushes as well to put the awkwardness behind them. "The look on the child's face just now," she says. "Her gaze and smile. She could not suppress her wonder at feeling so improved. If you could have witnessed it."

"Aye."

"Oh," she says, covering her mouth.

"I appreciate your words, Grainne."

"It's a miracle."

He is concerned she may find God's work in the recovery. How, then, will she fare once that same God takes her girl away? "Her fever broke," he answers carefully. "I merely hastened it along."

"A miracle of faith, as you said last evening. Faith, expressed through prayer."

"The Lord sees our sufferings."

"'God is light,'" she quotes, "'and in Him there is no darkness at all.'"

The Gospel of John, first chapter, verses four and five. He feels such warmth for this woman, and such empathy. His touch would convey it, too, were he allowed.

"My own wife liked to quote that passage," he says. "She had small hands and thick, somewhat inelegant fingers. Powerful for the washing of children, mind," he adds, fearing she may misunderstand him, "and the massaging of her old husband's back, sore from a long journey."

"Patrick often requests a shoulder rub after a day in the fields. But I lack the strength to bring him much relief."

"She was a real country woman," Carolan says. He drinks from the noggin his hostess has provided, forgetting it contains buttermilk. "Wore the same shawl every day and didn't let the hearth go cold in twenty years. A man for cutting the turf, she believed, and a woman for minding the fire."

He is describing his mother more than Moira, he realizes at once. He has never confused them before.

"Was she also of Leitrim?" Grainne asks. She pours the batter she has been stirring onto the griddle.

"Cavan town."

"Then how did you meet?"

"By arrangement," he replies, his stomach growling at the suggestion of food. "My patroness—er, my friend Mary Macdermott Roe—was acquainted with her people. Both parties thought we might make a match. Mrs Mac organized the introduction, and Moira and I were married not long afterwards."

"And by then you were already . . .?"

"Blind? For more than two decades when I met her. A contented bachelor, set equally in my drinking and thinking. Except for desiring a child or two, that is."

"And she gave you seven?"

"Healthy babies, each and every one."

"I should have wished . . ." she begins.

"The oatcakes, Grainne," Carolan says, smelling burn. "They could probably be turned."

"Foolish me."

"Do you mind if I work these hands over the griddle?" he asks. Several of the joints throb, as anticipated.

"I apologize for not lighting a fire last night when you arrived," she says, flipping the cakes. "The summer has been so wet, and my husband is worried the new turf won't dry for winter."

"I understand."

"We're uneasy about the corn as well. Much more rain and the harvest could be ruined."

"I'm sure that won't happen."

Grainne Connelly must deliberate before speaking. "I still have nightmares about the winter of twenty-six," she says after a pause. "Patrick says I am silly to let the past haunt me so."

"He's right," Carolan says as brightly as he can. But he knows she is not silly at all to shudder at the memory of 1726, when a disastrous harvest left Northerners gnawing on nettles and boiled grass. Owen and he rode into a Galway village one afternoon that terrible winter just as a packhorse collapsed in the street. The animal was swarmed by locals and torn into pieces for meat. On the same outing his guide witnessed a scene he at first declined to relay to his master. Carolan insisted, and Owen described the sight of an infant suckling the breast of its mother's corpse in a doorway. Owen claims the image is seared upon his retinas even now, like freckles on skin.

Still, this morning in August 1737 is too hopeful for such talk.

Especially with Deirdre dancing, and her mother cheered, and breakfast cooking—or burning, rather—on the griddle.

"They smell done to me," he finally says.

The burn stinks of scalded milk.

"The cakes!"

"I like mine cooked through," Carolan assures her.

"I hope you do," she says with still further mirth.

The scents, and the heat of the fire, summon much older memories. He is thinking about how his mother refused to let the hearth go cold, irrespective of the season. Her smooring skills at the end of the day were impressive; come dawn, all she needed to do was stir the bedded embers and flames would leap from the mound, desperate to feed on air. Soon the hearth would be glowing, cosy as the night before. No one wanted for fuel back then. Not in County Meath, anyway.

"Meath was a garden of plenty," he announces.

"The county?"

"My native hearth. I spent a charmed childhood there more than a half-century ago."

"When did you move westward?"

"At age fourteen."

"On account of a plantation?" Grainne Connelly asks.

The question implies much, and Carolan appreciates her confidence.

"My father was a tenant farmer. In the year 1684 he received an offer of employment in Carrick, County Leitrim. He accepted it, and we moved voluntarily. Odd as that decision might sound," he always feels obliged to add.

"What sort of offer?"

He hesitates for only a moment in advance of expressing a truth known to just a handful of friends. "A powerful local family objected to my courtship of their daughter," he says. "Rather than warn me off with a sub-sheriff or even a notice of eviction, the family sent word among their relations, asking if one could provide employment for a lowly Meath farmer. The St Georges of Carrick responded with the position of foreman in a foundry they then operated in the Iron Mountain, a hundred miles from Cruisetown. My father could hardly refuse."

"Cruisetown?"

"The girl's family belonged to the Cruise clan."

His hostess is quiet.

"And your kin?" he says quickly.

She relates the forced flight of her ancestors from Down to Tyrone during the great Ulster plantings under James First, who expelled Catholics from the best lands in that corner of the country, replacing them with Presbyterian Scots. Her husband's people were likewise dispossessed two generations later, courtesy of Cromwell's decision to reward those Roundhead soldiers who helped him subdue the island with Irish smallholdings in lieu of English pay.

But Grainne Connelly won't be put off. "There is a famous tune named after a woman called Cruise," she says. "Composed by a no-less-famous harper who also went by Terence."

He can almost hear her eyes drift over to the sack by the wall.

"I am familiar with the melody," he answers. "Who isn't?"

"And for all our talk of clans this morning, I don't believe you've mentioned the name of your own."

Someone enters. A man, by his step.

"I had to run to the brother's for a drop of milk," Patrick Connelly says.

"Our guest here was telling me—"

"Your roof held up admirably during last night's storm, Mr Connelly. Is it an uncommon thatching you use?"

These obfuscations serve no purpose. Carolan will reveal his identity soon enough. To refuse would be to deny the family the satisfaction, and mild fame, of having once hosted him. Besides, he has the first name, and the harp, and the fingernails. He has the affliction. Who else could he be?

But he is tired of the fuss that will ensue and the abrupt loss of ease the revelation will induce. He can no longer abide such distance between him and other people—the solitude of being, in effect, himself. Better a butterfly than such a man. Better a melody, for certain.

"A standard scollop," Patrick Connelly replies. "Sop and mud coping. It's the best design for this part of Ulster. Nearer to the sea they need rope thatches on account of the winds. Here we require sturdy cover to support all the snow."

Carolan offers to share a pipe with his host.

"I wouldn't feel right smoking by myself," he says. "And I've an extra pipe in one of the saddlebags, should your own not be handy."

Owen Connor has been standing in the doorway. He fetches the spare clay pipe without being asked. Following Carolan's instructions, Owen fills the bowls not with the regular mundungus but pure Virginia tobacco, a gift from Lord Mayo, who has mercantile concerns on the far side of the ocean. In the open air the quality of tobacco matters little. In a closed space, however, the cloud formed by slow-cured leaves, the scent rich and deep and flavoured with heather honey, can alter the weather of a room. He means to honour Patrick Connelly by the choice.

His guide strikes a match.

"Now," Carolan says, sucking in air until the tobacco hisses.

"A lovely aroma," Grainne Connelly says.

"Not as lovely as the scent of those oatcakes."

Her laughter is dutiful. His secrecy is irking her or perhaps reviving her earlier suspicions. It is time.

"The first cake has cooled enough, Terence," she says.

"I'll eat only once Deirdre has had her fill."

"She is yet up the lane," her father says. He is drawing on his pipe with the frenzy of a starving cat eating mutton. "She complained to my brother of her thirst, but then could not swallow a drop of water."

The news stops the conversation.

"I'd be delighted to sample the first oatcake, Grainne," Carolan says. He balances the pipe on his knee.

"Patrick?"

"Right here," he answers, passing her something.

A glass plate, Carolan suspects, also borrowed from the brother. He accepts the plate and then, folding the tepid cake, takes several noisy, appreciative bites. Too much salt was used in the batter, out of habit, and too little sugar, for the same reason. There is a taste of burn.

"Salty?" she asks.

"Perfect."

"I am not used to having sugar in my larder."

"Perfect," he repeats, finishing it.

"Don't fuss so, Grainne," her husband says.

Sharing the Virginia tobacco was a mistake. *Thrawn,* or excess pride: the Ulsterman's failing. But Carolan is being unkind. He slips into Patrick Connelly's one pair of boots. Strangers at his hearth, eating his food and cheering his wife to the point of gay, girlish laughter, while his only child, who ought by rights to be the gay, girlish creature in the house, dribbles water down her chin, her throat as bloated as . . .

As a child in the choke-hold of diphtheria. Carolan can summon no simile.

It is definitely time.

He stands. "You asked last evening about the case Owen lugged in. What say he opens it and I play us a real tune?"

Grainne Connelly covers her mouth with her hand again.

"Terence?" Owen says from behind.

"A tune or two, and then we'll be off."

"You're still determined to carry on to Tempo?"

"I believe I am."

His guide sits him back down, begging the Connellys' indulgence. The couple are soon whispering as well.

"It must be him, Patrick," Carolan hears her say.

"Who?"

"*Him,*" she replies, and then his name.

Owen drops to one knee. Though his body and clothes emit no strong scent, his breath is sour.

"Not all the sheriff said last night about Tempo was bigotry, I'm afraid," he says into his ear. "While waiting for you in Pettigoe, I heard rumours. Brian Maguire has apparently signed over the estate to his nephew, a retired army man, to avoid creditors and allow for a partial sale of the lands. The colonel, in turn, has brought an English wife along with him, a woman he wed more for her money than her charms. The wife, though, has hidden the funds, and this Colonel Maguire has imprisoned her within the manor until she gives them up. Brian and Elizabeth Maguire suffer accordingly."

"Isn't Brian master at Tempo?"

"The estate may be under a different name now."

He is silent.

"The rumours could be false," Owen concedes. "Still, we should be braced for a house transformed since our last stay there. And Tempo need not be our destination this morning."

"No?"

"We could turn east at Enniskillen and ride south to Councillor Brady's. Another day in the saddle, and it is home to Alderford and the rest you need. It's my advice to you," he says. "As your guide."

Carolan is tempted, and not for his own sake. Tempo has a small library, a room Owen Connor has frequented during previous visits. Owen's fondness for books is well known, and most of their patrons indulge it. But of late a visit by Carolan's guide to a library has coincided with the disappearance of volumes from these collections. There is talk. There are also the bulging saddlebags.

"Haven't we alerted the Maguires to our intentions?" he asks.

"We heard no word back."

"We've always been welcome at Tempo."

"I'm not saying we wouldn't be now . . . We'll be right with you, Mr and Mrs Connelly," Owen says in his public voice.

How odd they must appear. A gangly, freckled man on one knee, lips mutely moving; a squat, unkempt elder on a stool, muttering in reply. Others have told him the pose suggests a priest hearing a confession or a monarch heeding secret counsel.

"Perhaps I can be of assistance to Brian," Carolan says.

"By performing?"

"That, and through friendship. Who knows, my presence in the manor could help mitigate circumstances."

"Mitigate?"

"Why not?"

"Have you a new composition ready?"

"Not quite."

"Is a tune forming in your head?"

"Sadly, no."

"Well?"

"Well, we should stop talking and I should start playing," Carolan says for all to hear. "Or singing, rather, in gratitude for the hospitality these weary travellers have received in this house."

✳ ✳ ✳

He runs his fingers along the upper strings. Two Cs, a B and a D have gone flat. Drawing the wrench from his vest pocket, Carolan counts off the pins and adjusts the tunings. A descent of the lower octave with his right hand reveals fewer problems. Next, he strikes the strings in a glissando, for flourish. The clashing harmonies of notes, like a wobbly staircase up to heaven, are no more remarkable to him than his own heartbeat. But he hears Grainne Connelly's fluttering sigh and the held-breaths of her husband, who has stopped smoking the pipe. In their places, he would be astounded as well.

Owen has stood behind him during the tuning, a bundle of wire and a cutter ready should a string snap. He withdraws.

Carolan talks for a few minutes about the harp, on the assumption that the Connellys have never seen one before, except emblazoned on King George's coinage. He travels with a lap harp, forty inches in height, played off a stool or block or from an actual lap, as he is doing this morning. It has a soundbox cut from a piece of sally and a fore-pillar of ash, a low-head curved for harmonics and a bellied arch. Thirty-two strings in all, of brass, unlike the gut strings favoured by harpers these days. Being of the old school, he can't support composing on strings that don't tinkle in the upper registers and growl in the lower. He can't support playing an instrument that does not allow for dampings.

"Hence these alarming nails," he says, raising his hands for inspection. He demonstrates.

"Catch the string between flesh and nail." Carolan plucks an A. "If it's staccato you're after, immediately damp it with another finger to halt the vibration." He plays a passage from the slip-jig he lilted to Deirdre. "But if you leave brass strings to warble on," he says, "you wind up with this sound instead." He repeats the passage without damping, the tones the muddy clang of pots on a kitchen wall.

"If your ambition is to play legato, however," he continues, sounding a phrase from a popular air, "then you wish certain strings to vibrate as long as they can. The ringing creates harmonies all its own."

He proceeds through the divisions in style, a sequence lasting two minutes. The routine has been perfected over the decades and performed to crowds ranging from a half-dozen to a hundred. Curiously, playing before a farming couple in a cottage smaller than a gardening shed gives Carolan a rare attack of the jitters. He can't recall feeling this nervous, even in advance of an encounter in a Dublin room packed with Italians, including Corelli's own pupil, Francesco Geminiani, after whom he named his current horse. Of course, he also can't recall a performance given while so sober.

To conclude, he delivers the usual disclaimer. "I am no master musician, friends, despite the honorific. My talent, such as it is, lies in composition. Apologies in advance for any stumbles."

A notion occurs to him. Could he compose a tune for Deirdre? Making it up, more or less, as he goes? He has never resorted to spontaneous composition before. But he does write quickly, often producing a melody in a morning on horseback or an afternoon by a fire, and is convinced a good one ought to sound effortless, or perhaps inevitable, like birdcall at sunrise. In his experience tunes are either present or they are not. One has the knack for them, in which case the melody summons the composer as much as the composer conjures the tune, or else one forms part of the grateful audience. He thinks of it in terms of pleasure. The moment his pleasure in the act of creation begins to diminish is the moment he knows the resulting piece will be wan and woeful. A heavy head produces slow hands. Tired fingers result in tiresome notes.

There it is: *dee-dle idle-dee*. Not bad. There it is again: *lad-la-da-dee-dah*. Not bad at all. Arrange the left hand only—he can sort out the bass notes later. There it is, a full part: *dee-dle idle-dee, lad-la-da-dee-dah*. A solid opening, in Dorian mode, better known now as A minor, and standard time. And tempo? Allegro or risoluto, as the Italians would put it. Next, clack out a second part, building in some harmonies and maybe a raised accidental, a B flat or C sharp, an effect requiring a hasty de-tuning of a string using the wrench. Finally, slap together a middle section—*idle-dee da-dee-da-dee*—and weave it into the A-B mix. How about A-B-A-B-C-B-C-A-B-A? Sounds grand. Sounds like Carolan. For his songs he claims neither proper form nor virtuosity. Rather, they have an innate melodicism and powerful clarity, intelligible to everyone.

A tune for the child? He'd love to compose one on the spot, less to please her than to soothe her parents, especially her mother. Call it "Deirdre the Dancer" or "Deirdre of the Apples." But the truth is, he has no music in his head this morning and hasn't been blessed with a part or even a phrase in a long while. How long? He can't say, or maybe prefers not to think on it.

"I'll play something from the old days, will I?" he says.

His hosts find their voices at last. "We are not prepared, Terence, er, Master . . ." Grainne Connelly says.

"Neither am I, Grainne, if these trembling hands are any indication."

"We're honoured, sir."

"You could honour me most, Mr Connelly, or at least improve your chances of hearing a decent tune, with a noggin. For medicinal purposes only."

"Will I run up the lane and see if anyone keeps ale?"

"He jests," Owen says.

"I do, I suppose," Carolan admits.

Grainne Connelly confesses that she is mortified beyond words.

"Something from the old days, then."

He launches into "The Lament of the Three Marys," a piece he associates with mendicant friars from the sixteenth century. To the best of his recollection he has heard it exactly once before, performed by Thomas Connellan at Belanagare in January 1697. At the time he found the melody graceless, its emotions lost to antiquity, and declined the older harper's offer to teach him it. Now, before he quite realizes that he committed the tune to memory anyway—an involuntary process, for which he is nonetheless renowned—Carolan is playing the opening part, his fingers sounding each note as if striking a church bell. He hesitates for so long between pluckings, as per his recollection of the tempo, that he must keep his hands from falling by his side. The music impresses him today as no more strange than wind whistle across a bog. Its emotions are likewise intelligible. "The Lament of the Three Marys" rocks his body in waves of recognition, as if he is inside the bell each instance it is struck. Only its melodic charms continue to elude him. People must have had different ears then.

Next, he bridges with just a half-beat pause into "Molly MacAlpin," a tune by William Connellan, younger brother to Thomas. The Connellys will appreciate a turn towards the familiar. When introducing "Molly MacAlpin" to audiences, Carolan often remarks that he believes it superior to any piece he has composed. He can praise the tune unreservedly for the simple reason that he is incapable of writing anything so pure. Unlike the Connellan brothers, he did not really know the country before the final collapse of the old society. Unlike his predecessors, and despite the title that others give him, he is no bard. His own music is as influenced by Arcangelo Corelli and Antonio Vivaldi as by Carrol O'Daly and Myles O'Reilly, to name two great harpers of the last century. His compositions lack integrity of construction and impulse, if not of expression. Worse still, for all his love of genealogy, of affixing individuals to their proper families and septs and ancestral lands, as a composer of music Terence Carolan belongs to a clan of exactly one.

Then there is the issue of skill. His is middling at best, and most nights he is thankful he was born long enough after O'Daly and O'Reilly that few listeners appreciate how poorly he plays. Practising from time to time might help, he grants, as would a degree of moderation in his personal habits. But in his own defence, Carolan pleads consistency. He rarely fails to make the same mistake twice. He almost never rises above his limitations. For instance, as he glides through a thousandth rendering of "Molly MacAlpin," he braces to muck up the *di-di-dum* passage towards the end of the second round. Even slowing the tempo probably won't prevent the error. Sure enough, he plucks *di—dum-dum-di* and then, anxious to skip over the rough patch, loses the beat, finishing too fast.

"You get the general idea," he says to the silence.

He understands not to be offended. His fame binds the hands of many a crowd, especially ordinary folk. By the volume of murmurs he estimates that twenty to thirty villagers have assembled outside the door. Every man, woman and child in Kesh in attendance.

"We're honoured, sir," Patrick Connelly says again.

"The state of our dwelling," his wife adds. "I am mortified."

He wishes she weren't. He wishes she could be the same woman who humoured a dishevelled codger an hour before.

"Is Deirdre nearby?" he asks.

She is, he can already tell, her wheezing like the rasp of a saw on wood.

The girl comes to him, rests a hand on his knee. She is having difficulty swallowing.

"I promised you another tune, didn't I?"

She must be nodding.

"Answer the master," her mother says.

"*Ladly-fol-da-dee?*" she says.

"Something better," he replies after clearing his throat.

"Fetch our guest a sup of water, Grainne. He's gone parched, for the attention we're showing him."

Carolan resolves to give these people what they want. He is an itinerant, after all, like any other, hired to entertain. "There's a tale to this next tune, Deirdre," he says in a voice pitched to carry into the laneway. "Will I tell it?"

She curtsies, her sack-dress crinkling.

"'Sheebeg and Sheemore,'" he announces to gasps of recognition. "My very first composition."

He tells the tale. When Carolan was twenty-one and newly trained on the harp, his patroness, Mary Macdermott Roe, of Alderford, County Leitrim, arranged a debut call. The house, on nearby Lough Scur, belonged to a family friend by the name of Squire Reynolds. The squire was a great man and a sturdy drinker. He obliged the novice with a listen of his music, his ears probably pinned to the sides of his skull, and then wondered if the young harper's real talents didn't lie in composition and verse. Carolan replied that he lacked fit subject for a poem or song, but the squire persisted. He related the legend of the hills near his estate, Sheebeg to the east and Sheemore to the west. In ancient times Fionn MacCool and his army fought a battle on the plain situated between the rises. Thousands of warriors were slain, their mortal remains buried in the barrows and cairns that dot the slopes to this day. For generations thereafter rival fairy queens tricked humans into warring on their behalf. The carnage continued until the humans, awakening to the mischief of gods, arranged a truce among themselves.

Fine material for an aspiring bard, Squire Reynolds reasoned. Fairy queens and good people and such. Will you give it a go, lad?

"So I did," Carolan says, raising his hands back to position, "melody and poesy both. And here is the tune, as played for the squire. The words I've long since forgotten."

Forgetting the melody as well might have been prudent, he muses, striking the first notes. While pleasant, "Sheebeg and Sheemore" would have deserved its fame only if, as his friend Toby Peyton once quipped, Carolan had composed it using the toes on his feet. As for the lyrics, if he had written them using an even rarer appendage, they would still have been banal. He has no knack for clever phrases or rhyming words, as his own poems amply attest, except when he versifies about women. "Mabel Kelly," for instance, with the lucky husband and the feather bed: "He sees her tumble of brown hair / Unplait, the breasts, pointed and bare." Or "Peggy Browne," a verse recited only in certain company: "Her voice is music, every little echo / My pleasure and oh her shapely breasts, I know / Are white as her own milk, when taffeta gown / Is let out, inch by inch, for Peggy Browne."

These women, by the by, Carolan has had no carnal knowledge of, the first being the youngest daughter of the Kellys of Ballyforan, Roscommon, and the other a wench who served him in a Longford inn. Whose voice and gown and tumble of brown hair, unplaited, has he been summoning? Whose breasts, white as milk?

He inverts two phrases in "Sheebeg and Sheemore." Everyone notices but no one minds, him included. For his sin he repeats the round.

In truth, that first composition wound up a foundling. Carolan wore the bardic mantle poorly for a while and then cast it off for good. His melodies became original and his poems less awful the instant he disavowed any grand purposes for them. He composes now, when he composes at all, in honour of friends and patrons and women and alcohol. Should a lament be required, he keens it exclusively for the departed. Even his much maligned church compositions—Owen Connor thinks the songs dismal, and says so—have no public design. He expresses his desire for his Lord in his own manner and hardly cares who else might be listening.

Why, then, is he presently endeavouring to infuse this wee tune with more emotion than it can sustain? Thinking of Deirdre, perhaps, and Grainne. As well, of Bridget in the cave, and his mother and sister so long in the grave. And of the woman whose absence still causes his breath to catch sometimes and his heart to flutter, a bird in cupped hands.

In her taffeta gown.

The crowd comes unbound.

"Too kind," he says to the applause.

Owen reappears behind him, a signal.

"Packed and ready," he says.

Outside, showered in shy greetings and praise, Carolan decides he can't depart without bonding once more with Grainne Connelly. His path back to her involves a family ritual. Calling to mother and daughter, he explains the plan. Before Grainne can object, he emphasizes that his own dear Moira, trusting his judgement, always approved it. There is no danger, he assures her. There is only the certainty of a memorable experience for the child.

She agrees.

"Want to touch the sky, Deirdre?" he asks.

She says she does.

He raises her up to his chest and then, arching his back, hoists her. Never do his fingers separate from her dress. Never is she free from his grasp. Still, Deirdre squeals and Grainne gasps and Carolan's mouth goes dry at the shock of almost letting go.

"Again," she shouts, back in his clutch.

"You'll have to close your eyes this time."

"And be like you?"

"Exactly."

"Mind yourself," Owen says in private. He presses up against Carolan.

"Are they shut?" he asks the girl.

He hoists her with all his might. At once he knows she will climb the air. He knows also that his right arm, naturally the stronger, has applied extra thrust, and that her body might shift while above his fingertips, complicating the descent. He remembers this concern with Siobhan and Tadhg, Martha, Eileen and Anne. He recalls it less with Maev and Mary, born to a decrepit old excuse for a father. But in every instance he returned the child safe, his or her trills of delight the purest expression of joy he has ever heard, outside the bedroom.

Deirdre trills as well.

He feels a twinge in his left leg, along with a throbbing up his side, even before her weight buckles him. When the throb reaches his arm, raw as a toothache, he understands that he might not be able to hold her. She will fall through. He will fall first, he hopes, and provide her a cushion.

Owen Connor rescues them both. In the instant it takes Carolan to tremble, his guide seizes his arms and extends them outwards. Then, as Deirdre crashes into his chest at the predicted angle, Owen leans Carolan back into his braced body while closing the puppet limbs around the girl. Her hair brushes Carolan's cheek and her knees dig into his belly. His girth slows her down. So does the clutch of his—Owen's, really—hands on her garment.

She lands on her feet.

"Again!"

Though he tries to speak, his words are slushy. The left side of his body has gone numb.

Owen saves him once more. He lifts Carolan up onto Gem with a powerful motion, wrapping his fingers around the saddle knob and pushing his boots into the stirrups.

"Think you can hold on?"

He nods.

"Wave, if you're able."

"God bless you all," Carolan tries to say.

chapter six

They reach Tempo in the late afternoon. Robins and wrens, thrushes and blackbirds herald their climb up from the village. Once through the gate, however, this music is lost to the monotone of quarrelling jackdaws. The Maguire estate, planted with sycamore and beech, alongside native elm and ash, normally attracts choirs of songsters. The grounds also buzz and drone, the air narcotic with fern tang and waft of mushroom, the abrupt stink of a nearby fox. But today Carolan hears only *cra-cra-crah* and smells only decay, especially when they ride past the pond, whose surface, according to Owen, is the colour of stagnant urine. Gem swishes her tail at flies.

Good Geminiani. Intuiting his disability, the horse kept a steady pace the entire journey from Kesh. Feeling returned to Carolan's arm and leg over the course of the morning, and by noon he was his old self once more, aside from a slight speech impediment, as if he has a chestnut lodged in one cheek. His guide can't properly explicate what happened. Something about eating an oatcake and playing the harp, Owen claims; about tossing a child in the air and almost dropping her. For his part Carolan struggles to recall much beyond a nocturnal drenching that put them at risk of injury or assault or both. The *shlip-shlop* of hooves and the timpani of rain on his hood. The musk of frightened horses. But after the storm, nothing. No recollection of what was said or where he slept or whom he might have met. Only the certainty that he drank too much at an inn the night before and too little at breakfast today, and that his bowels remain noisy and unrelieved.

As for launching a child into the sky, it is preposterous. He hasn't tried a stunt like that in ages. Someone would get hurt.

The man who answers the manor door isn't Thady Bourke, the butler at Tempo these past forty years.

"Sirs?"

Owen announces him

"Sirs?" the man says again in the hardscrabble accent of East Ulster. He has not withdrawn to allow them entry.

Owen repeats the information.

"The colonel isn't home to visitors this afternoon."

"It's Brian Maguire we are here to see," Carolan says.

This other servant bids them wipe their boots on a rug. "Don't be climbing the stairs to the upper floors," he says, "nor passing through that doorway to my left. If you find yourselves in the larger dining hall, with the panelled walls and swaying chandelier, you've strayed. Perilously," he adds after a thespian's pause. "I knew a lad once who insisted on that route, against my instructions. He hasn't been heard from since. Brian Maguire's quarters lie beyond the doorway opposite. An antechamber, a sitting room, and a small dining hall at the rear. Follow the trail of rubbish and you can't miss him."

"Thank you," Carolan says.

Owen grips his arm.

"One further instruction."

The grip tightens.

"Servants around back, please."

"Beg pardon?"

"The colonel insists that menservants enter the house through the staff hall and confine themselves to the quarters below. For order's sake, and to keep floors from getting scuffed."

Carolan nearly cries out at Owen's grip. His boot, meanwhile, makes contact with an object. He guesses hair and skin and possibly flesh. A dead animal?

"A wig," Owen corrects.

"I suppose I could make an exception in your situation," the butler says, pronouncing the word as *situ-eh-shun*. "Given how easily this old one could cause himself harm."

When Owen Connor hiccups a laugh as challenge, Carolan takes flight. More than a few steps on his own and he'll knock into a table or tumble over a hound. He already smells wood and dog.

He passes through the doorway into the antechamber without a collision. Owen catches up.

"In a hurry?" he asks.

"I sense no reason to linger."

"There's a pane missing from a window in here," Owen says over his shoulder. "You've need of a glazier."

"Brian Maguire's side of the house," the Ulsterman replies from back in the reception hall. "Speak to him."

"The gap must leave the manor vulnerable to invasion by all sorts of unsavoury creatures."

"Think so?"

Carolan picks up his pace.

Tempo manor, rebuilt after a fire at the beginning of the century, is said to cross-breed a Norman castle with a Palladian mansion. The exterior boasts a castellated façade with assorted turrets and battlements, leaded windows so transparent that birds fly into them, providing easy meals for cats. Wooden ceilings and thick plasterwork, some thirty fireplaces, many of them hand-carved, lend the interior the cosiness, if not the intimacy, of a hunting lodge. A dozen bedrooms ensure the house can accommodate an actual hunting party, without recourse to the straw-chamber downstairs. If paintings adorn the walls or sculptures pose on pedestals, no one has described them to Carolan. If any of the furnishings are noteworthy, this aspect, too, has gone unremarked. But he isn't put off. Brian and Elizabeth Maguire are country gentry. Household staff are treated like family. Dogs are invited to table. The couple have no pretences and exactly one ambition: to offer sincere welcome to their guests.

He will be enjoying that welcome momentarily. Carolan envisions ale, bread and cheese to sustain him until dinner, followed by a table of Fermanagh edibles, heavy on the roasted meats and puddings, along with clarets so hearty they pour more like gravy. There may be games in the early evening, basset for the women and backgammon for the men. He vows to fling regular quatres tonight, instead of the deuce-ace five times running, as he did his last visit to Tempo, twelve—or was it eighteen?—months before. The family owns a harpsichord, and a lady or two will no doubt be persuaded to sing. Should the Maguire children be present, a dance might also be on offer. A fading or a trenchmore; the popular Trotting the Hay, its steps borrowed from the French. Only then, with lesser amusements ended and revellers mellow, will Sir Brian rise and entreat their guest of honour to grace them with a tune.

Honoured, sir, Carolan will reply.

Next, his foot kicks a bottle, setting it spinning over the wood. He notes the modulation, as if the aural distance widens when the neck of the bottle points away. Owen warns him of a further impediment.

"Another wig?"

"This one has a head attached to it."

"There's a picture," Carolan says to be cheerful. He brushes against a second door frame.

"Here is an entire mural for you, Terence. A battlefield strewn with the fallen, though perhaps not the brave. Beakers in lieu of rapiers. Beef bones instead of muskets."

"Any familiar faces?"

"Allow me to make introductions. Sir Cady Riordan, I believe. Better raise your foot up over his paunch. It rises like Sheebeg itself. Or Sheemore," his guide says.

"Sheebeg and Sheemore"—his debut as a composer. A plain tune he rarely plays any longer.

"Cady, old friend," he says to the owner of the adjoining estate.

"He is unconscious at present."

Following instructions, he steps over the hillock. For dramatic effect, he has to believe. Owen could have steered him around the body.

"Carolucky!" a voice calls.

"Sir?"

"Arthur Magennis," Owen reports, "lying sprawled atop the dining table, a bottle clutched to his chest."

"Arthur."

"May I present my son, Morgan."

Morgan Magennis declines to present himself. But there is an odour.

"Where is the boy?"

"He bathes, Lord Arthur," Owen says, "in his own vomit. On the floor beneath you."

Carolan requires no explanation for what occurs next. He hears Arthur Magennis, lord of four thousand acres at nearby Brookeborough, shift to table's edge to inspect his son, hears his bottle plummet to the ground with a thump and him follow.

"Is Mrs Magennis at Tempo as well?" he asks nonetheless.

He wrote a tune for the wife once, to commemorate a dinner invitation to Brookeborough that deteriorated into a debauch lasting a fortnight and costing Carolan his watch, lost in a wager as to who could ride the family wolfhound the longest, without a saddle. "Kitty Magennis," an indifferent piece. If memory serves, she is a genial lady with a preference for sherry over port and a burp that reminds him of gull call. Her husband, sadly, is an ass.

The scent of hound, come to think of it, is cutting through competing smells like a crow's cry in a nest of sparrows. The hairs on his forearms spike.

"Dead, the wench," Arthur Magennis answers from his new location.

"In Dublin, Father," Morgan Magennis says, "spending those funds obtained by mortgaging our estate. On more hats."

"Hats," the father repeats.

"Has anyone a spare handkerchief?" the son asks.

"Don't offer yours," Owen advises Carolan.

They step over a final guest. He is Captain John Noble, squire of a small estate north towards Archedall and a veteran of the Siege of Derry. Here is a lesser catastrophe from the near-recent past. On reaching Derry in March 1689, the would-be-king-again found he lacked the artillery to storm the walled city, whose population had lately swelled with Protestants flocking in from the countryside for protection. James laid siege instead, determined to starve the citizens out. A fifteen-week-long civic defence ended when an English ship broke the boom across the River Foyle, scattering the Jacobites. According to Captain Noble, the siege is almost a half-century removed only for those who didn't live through it. Carolan maintains he suffered alongside the brave Derry residents, courtesy of the captain's well-stocked arsenal of anecdotes, ranging from Catholic cannonballs blasting into chapels to papist rats the size of puppies nibbling on corpses. He composed an air for John Noble's daughter some while ago. Suddenly worried that it, too, might be mediocre, he seeks the melody on his cloak buttons. *La-da-ladly-low,* he clacks. *Low-lah-lah-la.* The tune, mercifully, is charming.

Next to appear is Thady Bourke himself, tucked in a chair and wrapped in a curtain no longer shading a window.

"Thady will look after us now," Carolan says.

"Once a bucket of water is thrown over him."

"He is worse for the drink as well?"

"I'm afraid so."

"Madness," he says with a thin laugh.

Privately, Carolan is dismayed. Thady Bourke has been senior butler at Tempo the length of his four-decade acquaintance with the family. Thady has also sounded the sole note of sobriety throughout that period. The Maguires do not practise good land-lordship. Carolan has personally attended countless negotiations between improvident squire and prudent retainer. Take the nag of bills. Grocer and milliner, butcher and baker, farrier and tailor and linen-draper: all in arrears, and all threatening non-delivery.

"Bah," Brian Maguire would say. "A dozen more hogsheads of ale instead."

"Now, Sir Brian," his manservant might reply. "We must keep body and soul together."

Or the ledger for the estate. There have been crown taxes ten years past due and sheets of unpaid attorney bills. There have been bonds for money borrowed for those purposes only to be squandered elsewhere.

"A pox on the crown," Brian might roar, "and a dose of clap for the king."

"Well put, sir," Thady would respond. "But what say we provide a complement to the receiver and hush-money to the sub-sheriffs to avoid a quit-rent?"

Carolan was even present the day news reached Tempo of an Enniskillen clothier who, owed a substantial sum for an extended period, confiscated the corpse of Sir Murtagh Maguire, brother of Constantine, in default of payment. The clothier threatened to ransom the deceased, maintaining the body in brine, until the family forwarded him his money.

"Let them pickle Sir Murtagh," Brian Maguire thundered. "The old gasbags will soon have his smelly revenge."

"Indeed he will," Thady answered. "But think of how lonely your father must be, waiting to be reunited with his sibling out on the Isle of Devenish."

Except for Thady Bourke, the house of Tempo might have already collapsed. Except for him, rack and ruin.

"If Thady and his kind won't set an example for the nobility," Owen says, reading his mind, "who will?"

He will not be drawn into a dispute. And his guide is equally shocked by the butler's condition, he can tell.

"There is a powerful stench in the air," he offers instead. A tall, wide-mouthed hearth is close by, the fire smoking and hissing. He protects his nose with his sleeve.

"Three dogs, sprawled on the hearth stones," Owen says.

Finally, the voice sounds. A bass grumble, like a barrel bumping over slats. It, at least, is unchanged.

"The aroma of damp dog," Sir Brian Maguire announces. "Is there anything like it, gentlemen? I ask you."

He asks, and he answers as well.

"Nothing like it in this world," he says. "Begin with your classic setter. Quite the larder of odours off these squireens. Gamey hams and sweaty coats, breaths that would drop a Connemara pony in its tracks. Earwax of peculiar fragrance, nearer to ragweed, and not too terrible a taste, though don't inquire as to how I possess such knowledge. But setters, such as dear Jenny and Lucy here . . ."

Maguire pokes the toe of his boot or tip of his cane into the flanks of two resting dogs, eliciting good-natured growls.

"Setters have some wits about them. They'll withdraw from a fire if they sense themselves becoming the broiling meat in question. Not so the wolfhound," he continues. "Not so that lad. There's an Ulsterman's natural companion. Stinks of every variety rising off him, bog and briar and wetland, with a special affinity for the bouquet of his distant cousin, the moulting sheep. Compound these smells with a perpetually bubbling nose and a proclivity for slobber, flung about like holy water. Ever catch a whiff of hound drool? Eh?"

Again, Brian Maguire prods the subject of his discourse. Carolan remembers this dog only too well. The beast is indeed ridable, with or without stirrups. It drags the carcasses of hares and partridges into the manor for gory suppers and pays visits to guests who fail to seal their doors at night. Conbec, the favourite of Fionn MacCool.

Fionn, who once fought on the plain between Sheebeg and Sheemore. A legend Carolan declaimed before a small crowd not so long ago. He can't think why or where.

"Gaze upon Conbec sprawled there by the hearth," Brian Maguire says. "As though felled by grapeshot and waiting to be interred. Why, I've known sub-sheriffs with greater mental capacities than this creature. He won't budge until the heat has singed the fur right off him. His coat as hot as a coal and his nose flayed, his eyes rolling up into their sockets. Then there is the smell. Roast brisket of hound. Grilled cur on the spit. And is the beast even aware he is the evening's bill-of-fare? Apparently not. On how many occasions have Thady and I been obliged to grab a hock each and lug his lordship away from the blaze? After a point Conbec won't save himself from a searing. He can't be bothered, it would seem."

"Sir Brian," Owen says at last.

"Ask Thady Bourke if I exaggerate. Thady is expert at sensing when the hound is past caring. It's the drool sizzling on the hearth-stones that gives it away, isn't it, Thady?"

Thady Bourke revives with a start, tossing off the curtain. "Another chair for the fire, Sir Brian?"

"We've additional guests," his employer replies. "Better spare a few."

The remark explains the hiss and spit of the fire, and the stench of dissolving paint.

"Additional guests?" the old servant says. "Who could . . .? If it isn't Master Carolan! I didn't notice you there, sir."

"Hello, Thady."

"Not Terence Carolan?"

"Aye, Brian. But I'm the one meant to be blind."

And accustomed to being received with courtesy, he adds to

himself. He does not expect a stranger to know to say "I sit by the fire with my dogs" or "Thady rests below the window." He does not expect a recent acquaintance to be aware enough to offer, "It's good to see you, Terence, though you are looking like a corpse before the wake," or "Let me come to you for a proper greeting." But he does expect such sensitivity from someone he has called friend for many years.

"My spectacles," Brian Maguire answers, finally climbing to his feet. "They've gone missing."

Owen, guessing he is miffed, guides him over. Carolan holds out his hand. Maguire brushes it aside and embraces him. A strapping man with the robustness of one of his tenant farmers but neither the stooped shoulders nor curved spine, Sir Brian clings for several heartbeats, burying Carolan's nose in his chest and patting him on the back, as might a father with a prodigal son. His garments are less than fresh and he smells of whiskey, hay and dog.

"Has Thady searched the house for the spectacles?" Carolan says. He has already forgiven his friend.

"Top to bottom," Thady Bourke replies. "They disappeared some time ago now. A number of Sir Brian's personal belongings have vanished."

"I see plenty," Brian Maguire says. "Too much at times."

"What about the window in the antechamber?" Owen asks.

"The glazier awaits settlement of a bill," Thady says.

"And the water stains on these walls?"

"Shingles in need of replacement. But the slater is likewise demanding satisfaction."

Though aware that Owen is posing the questions for his benefit, Carolan still interrupts. "What does a guest have to do to procure a draught of ale in this castle?"

Brian Maguire orders Thady Bourke to locate a glass and pitcher and bring them over.

"Plus a chair," Carolan says. "With its legs intact."

He is soon seated and draining a beaker.

"You are a wild one for the dogs, Brian Maguire," he says.

"Why shouldn't I be? The creatures are companionable and trustworthy and certain to stand up to trouble. Dogs and dogs alone will do so, I am discovering to my chagrin."

"Mrs Maguire, she is well?"

"Well indeed, for living in Westmeath these past six months with her sister Grace."

"Grace Nugent," one of Carolan's loveliest tunes. The woman herself is no less lovely.

"And the boys?" he continues, baffled by Maguire's responses.

"Grown men now, Terence."

"Of course," he says. In reality, he is taken aback.

"With their own ways and my means, or what is left of my means, to support those ways. Two are in London and two more up in Dublin town."

Carolan holds out his vessel until the butler obliges him by refilling it.

"To what do I owe the pleasure?" Brian Maguire asks.

"Beg pardon?"

"Your visit. It is unexpected."

Carolan requires a few seconds to digest the remark. Sir Cady and Captain Noble, the Magennises, father and son—are they not assembled to bid him welcome? He sent word to Tempo two weeks ago, fixing this day or the next for his arrival from Lough Derg.

"Station Island?" Brian Maguire says on being informed of Carolan's itinerary. "Whatever compelled you to submit to such an inspection? Isn't everyday life trial enough?"

Carolan drains off another glass. "I hope we'll have a proper conversation about the pilgrimage, Brian. It was revelatory on many counts," he says, emphasizing the mystery.

"I'm sure," his host answers flatly.

"Your constancy in such times, Master Carolan—it gives us all courage," Thady says.

"Thady, look after Terence's room, will you?"

"Gladly," the butler says. He halts partway across the floor. "You mean, Sir Brian, his usual chamber up the stairs?"

"And down the long hall. Where else would he lodge?"

The observation gives them both pause.

"A bath would make me more fit to join this illustrious party," Carolan interjects with, he hopes, the gentlest of rebukes.

"Who, the dogs?"

"Indeed," Owen Connor says.

"If it isn't Owen Connor," Brian Maguire says, as though just noticing him. "I am surprised to find you yet in the service of the master these two years later. Long crossed the ocean is what I expected to hear, sending back reports of fortunes being won on a West Indies plantation or in the great city of Philadelphia. Still not ready for what the New World can offer, Owen?"

"Aye, Sir Brian," Owen replies in a neutral tone.

A full two years since his last visit to Tempo? He has never muddled dates this badly before. "Without Owen, I would be helpless," Carolan says.

"I suspect you are anyway. Like the rest of us."

"Would asking one of the staff to draw me a bath cause undue hardship so close to the dinner hour?" he asks.

"I can't think why it should."

But then Brian Maguire and Thady Bourke communicate again. Though the exchange is wordless, Carolan catches the gist. Silence, he long ago discovered, rarely contains no information.

"It might be simpler if the bath is drawn in the staff hall," Brian Maguire says. "Nearer to the kitchen. That way, a scullery maid won't be obliged to haul water up all those flights of stairs."

As a scullery maid has hauled water up for him many times before? "Whatever is most convenient," Carolan says. He is here for his friend, not himself. To provide entertainment and support. To mitigate, even.

"Go on then, Thady."

"Sir Brian?"

"Go inform that man . . ."

"Gordon Smith?" Thady says with a quaver.

"Inform him that I would like a word with my nephew."

"Colonel Maguire?"

"Have I another nephew at Tempo?"

"I am to speak only with Smith, correct? Not with the colonel himself?"

"I will raise the question directly with Hugh."

"Right so."

Finally, Thady Bourke plucks the courage to confront his presumed equal—the butler who greeted Carolan and Owen.

"One further instruction," Brian Maguire says. "You'd better ask Mrs Moore to lock up the library. We've a keen reader in the house now."

"If I am not welcome . . ." Owen says.

"I'm only making sport, Owen. I couldn't care less about those books, as you well know."

The creak of Thady Bourke over the hardwood stirs a guest.

"A popish incendiary in her ladyship's bed!" Captain Noble cries out from his slumber.

"Easy there, Captain," Brian Maguire says.

* * *

Ten minutes later Carolan sits by the fire while Brian Maguire and his nephew converse in the reception hall. Their exchange is no less heated than the malingering dogs. The voices carry so well, Owen is relaying, in part because they are raised in dispute, and in part because the intervening chambers lack the usual impediments to the passage of sound. These include doors, drapes, carpets or furnishings. His guide even describes the object burning in the hearth: a brown panelled armchair made of ash, the original coat of red bleeding through like a wound from a bandage.

"I am perplexed," Carolan admits.

"Sir Brian will settle matters," Owen says without the slightest conviction.

Regrettably, Brian Maguire's efforts at settling matters reach their ears. "In the straw-chamber? Are you jesting? . . . Who is he? Who is he! . . . He *will* lodge in the room upstairs, Hugh, and he *will* dine tonight in the proper— So help me, God . . . What, one and six per plate? Charging me, in my own— Push any further, sir, and I swear I will—"

"Tempo has been partitioned," Owen says, projecting his remarks below the distant conversation and nearby snores, "with Brian Maguire retaining control of these small rooms only. Later, I will obtain details from Thady. But it seems obvious Sir Brian did have to sign the estate over, and that the colonel has, in turn, made himself master of a goodly portion of it."

"He and his wife, you mean."

"Not if what I heard in Pettigoe is true. I explained some of this to you this morning, though perhaps you don't recall. Are you still unaware of what happened during the night and earlier on today?"

"In the cave?"

"The cave?" Owen echoes sharply.

"I was under the impression you didn't wish to hear another word about the place or about her," Carolan says. He is off the mark, he realizes, but can't do better. Contrary to his earlier diagnosis, his left side still tingles and his hand still aches, not from arthritis. He is also finding it hard to keep the final two fingers from cramping up.

"Did I fall off Geminiani again?" he thinks to ask.

"Not lately."

"I almost need to be strapped onto her now."

"You honestly can't remember?"

"About Colonel Maguire and his wife?" Carolan replies, rubbing his palm. "Nothing, I am afraid."

His guide's perturbation increases his own.

"About Maguire," Owen says, "and the Connellys of Kesh. But also a conversation between us, one long overdue and of lasting import. I'd hate to think it has vanished as well."

"Little truly vanishes," Carolan says to console him. "It's more that certain occurrences lodge in our memory without our awareness. Thoughts and actions may then come under obscure but powerful influence."

"But you don't remember the words we exchanged?"

"Was the subject so rare?"

"Rare and valuable."

"Remind me then," Carolan says.

Owen hiccups. "Where to begin?" he says. "The rain was torrential."

"I remember the rain."

"The horses were in distress."

"Dear Gull and Gem," he says.

"We had an unpleasant encounter with an Ulster sheriff."

Carolan bites his lip.

"Don't tell me even the sheriff has gone missing?"

"Was this before we put up at the inn?"

"The inn, Terence?"

"Where we must have lodged?"

Owen hiccups again.

"Push me no further, sir!" Brian Maguire threatens from out in the reception hall.

"Brian sounds much agitated," Carolan comments.

"With reason."

Now he succumbs to a sigh. "Have I also been told, and forgotten, the context for this harsh exchange?"

"Only some of it," his guide answers. "We were speaking before of Colonel Maguire's wife. Her name is Lady Cuthbert, and she is said to be a prisoner within this manor."

"Prisoner?"

"For her money."

"Doesn't the colonel already possess it, by marriage?"

Brian Maguire is now shouting. "I'll do damage, Hugh, I swear I will!"

Then a new voice, steely and composed: "Sir, your threats lack both authority and proper footwear."

"Sir Brian wears only a single shoe," Owen tells Carolan.

The negotiation settles back down.

"Her thousand pounds per annum are not enough, by all accounts," his guide resumes. "Colonel Maguire wishes her jewels as well, valued at ten times that figure, in order to pay off his gaming debts and the debts of the estate. She refuses to divulge their where-abouts. He keeps her under lock and key in the tower situated over the manor's east wing."

"Curious."

"There is more. The colonel is also . . ."

Owen goes quiet at the return of their host.

Brian Maguire's voice is more sad than chastened. "It's settled, then," he says. "There is confusion below, Terence, new people in the employ and so on, meaning a bath can't be arranged at present. Apologies about that. What say we stick close to the hounds, you and me equally, to blanket our stinks, and that we bathe in aqua vitae instead this evening."

"Grand, Brian."

Carolan struggles to mask his despondency. He does not relish his own decrepitude or think of himself as base. Aqua vitae, it will be. A tub of it.

Owen asks if he should unload their gear.

"Certainly. But listen," Sir Brian says in an attempt, largely through gestures, to cloak from Carolan his request that Owen use the servants' entrance . "Would you mind terribly?"

"I don't mind," Owen says.

"The colonel is particular about such matters."

"Fine."

"Thady will relate the entire tawdry tale to you, I am sure."

Carolan notes the gentleness in his guide's handling of this awkward apology. He begins his own apology to Sir Brian for his failure to have a composition ready for the night. It occurs to him suddenly that the circumstance at Tempo is at once fraught and unfamiliar. Would the tune even have been appropriate? The notion that Terence Carolan could ever compose music other than perfectly fitting causes his stomach to flip and then to churn.

His remark is cut off. Someone has entered the room and is waiting for him to finish. But Brian Maguire can't wait.

"Yes, Mr Smith?" he says.

"Excuse the intrusion, Sir Brian," the butler with the mouth-full-of-biscuit accent says. "Colonel Hugh Maguire requests the company of you and your friends for dinner this evening. In the main dining room, at eight o'clock."

To Carolan's further chagrin, his friend responds to the invitation like a man who has just had his missing shoe returned to him. "Thank the colonel for his offer," he says. "I accept, on behalf of my guests."

"That would seem prudent," Gordon Smith says.

Owen issues a grunt of amusement.

"Minus the hounds," the butler adds.

"Understood."

"And reasonably upright."

"Curb yourself, sir."

"Oh yes," the man says, his tone now scornful, "the colonel also wishes me to mention that he has sent to Enniskillen for a harpsichord player. In honour of your special guest, who is also an itinerant of some variety?"

"He has done what?"

"Music, starting at ten."

Gordon Smith must be wearing riding boots. He clacks, crisp as musket shot, back out of the room.

"Outrageous," Owen says.

"Terence . . ." Brian Maguire starts to apologize.

"If the harpsichord player is Italian, I'll likely know him," Carolan replies. Truth be told, he is relieved.

"I had no idea . . ."

"Will we take a good long drink tonight, Brian?"

Sir Brian sniffles, not from a cold. His dear comrade, once reckless and outsized, now a heap of regrets and ill manners.

"Return some of the old madness to our souls?" Carolan says.

"The old madness," Brian Maguire repeats back to him.

"I'm ready for it," he says, despite being something close to the opposite. "Ready to roar."

✳   ✳   ✳

"It's said that Lady Cuthbert is permitted down from the tower once a week to attend chapel with the colonel," Sir Cady offers sotto voce. "She takes air in the grounds after the service, but always with Gordon Smith nipping at her heels. The lady has demanded the butler wear the same cologne as Maguire. Being a stinking ex-army man, his proximity is otherwise intolerable."

Several gentlemen at the table snigger, though not Captain John Noble, survivor of the siege, whose horse laugh normally leaps out like an alto among baritones.

"Shh," Arthur Magennis says.

"She can be heard wailing from as far away as the village, if the wind is favourable," his son says.

"You've heard her, Morgan?"

"Not personally, Sir Brian. But people say."

"The sobs of a woman couldn't possibly carry such a distance. Not unless Lady Cuthbert's wails are the match of Dido's for her lad, what's his name . . . Eh, Terence? Terence?"

"Brian?"

"The fellow from that book you find so pleasing. By the Italian?"

Carolan, adrift in memories of Tempo dinners gone by, is slow to digest the question.

"Still mad for all things Eye-talian, Master?" Sir Cady asks.

"*The Aeneid,*" Carolan finally answers. "By Virgil, the court poet of ancient Rome."

"There you go. Dido and her lad . . ."

"Aeneas. An aloof and distracted man, undeserving of her. *Burning with love, infected to her very marrow,*" he recites in translation.

Book IV, his treasure. Owen has been reading aloud from *The Aeneid* since he was first retained as Carolan's guide. Although his predecessor, John Glavin, did his best with the poem, John's Latin was halting. And for all his dramatic efforts Owen can still never recite Virgil with the intensity the poetry deserves. Moira Keane would have done the passion of Dido justice, had she been better learned in words. Carolan rarely thinks of his wife now and can't bear to summon her burning love for him. Dead at forty-one, her breasts swollen and hard.

As he was saying to someone recently. To whom? The demise of a spouse is an intimate sorrow.

"You must hear Lady Cuthbert regularly, Sir Brian," Captain Noble says. "Given that you share the same house."

Brian Maguire, seated on his right, drains his glass. Carolan silently implores his host to inform the other guests that there is no honour in discussing a lady this way. Especially, he might add, a lady who ought to be dining with them at present, alongside her husband—who has also yet to appear.

"I've not heard her weep, to be honest," Brian Maguire replies. "But I have discerned certain equally private sounds."

There are more sniggers and a horse laugh. Candle flames jump at the commotion, *pssht, pssht.*

Troubled by his summoning of Moira and by the beads of sweat trickling down his spine into his crack, Carolan attempts to envision the dining room. Three candlesticks flicker along the tabletop and the chandelier tinkles overhead. The fire burns behind him. Five musty revellers, cheeks ruddy and lips wine-stained, wigs askew and shoulders powdered, boom to his left and right and directly across. A hound pants at his feet, redolent of bog.

But he soon gives up, and not only because lips spittled by wine or shoulders flecked with wig powder conjure almost nothing in his imagination. He withdraws from more and more public situations these days, finding it difficult to separate out voices and assign individuals their locations, to chase conversations zigzagged by acoustics and inebriation. He lacks the concentration and, often enough, interest. Even when not coming off a pilgrimage and a night in a storm, he is too fatigued.

Carolan is equally out of sorts with the tone of the discussion. Pride should preclude men from debasing themselves before the era. Honour should prevent them from engaging in petty sniping and futile revenge. He believes the character of the country's citizenry can close up the divides that history and bad lawmaking have opened across the land. Unless, of course, that character has been likewise breached and the partition internalized. Then the old—old ways and old songs, old harpers and their courtesies—may indeed be of scant value to the new.

Brian Maguire, sadly, is lashing out like one of the divided. "Her imprisonment in this house does not keep the lady from berating servants and smashing crockery, Captain. Nor did it prevent her from addressing my wife so improperly that Lady Maguire fled to Westmeath for her dignity's sake. Neither," he adds, his voice dropping a half-register in conspiracy, "does Lady Cuthbert's confinement in the tower prevent regular conjugal visits, if you catch my meaning."

Someone says, "Shh."

The gunfire snap of Gordon Smith's boots in the hallway from the back stairs lends the request credibility.

"The colonel apologizes once again for his tardiness," his butler announces. "He intends to join the party shortly and is convinced the conversation will take a turn for the respectful before he does."

"Right you are," Arthur Magennis says.

"Inform my nephew that any further delay on his part may result in his going respectfully hungry this evening," Brian Maguire says. "Not that the table he set was very bountiful to start."

They dined on salty mutton and still-bloody quails, sweetbreads and bitter greens. The ale, at least, has been bountiful, along with a claret purchased by the barrel from smugglers who ply the Donegal coast. Carolan has been hard on the wine for an hour now, in the absence of savoury fare or sincere cheer.

"Colonel Maguire has already taken his evening meal," Gordon Smith says.

"He has?"

"Gentlemen."

Carolan has a request. "My guide," he says. "I should like a word with him, please."

The demand that Owen Connor wait in the staff hall below yet stings. Owen is almost never removed from Carolan's side. His duties include settling him in a seat and listing the dishes on offer, filling his plate and preparing his meat. In most homes Owen is provided a chair in a corner, where he can survey the proceedings, including the watermark of his master's glass, without disrupting the meal service. Entire evenings he sits there, silent and watchful. Hosts often insist he take a noggin of ale and even seek his opinion, as a servant and commoner. Owen is known to have views and to be forceful in expressing them. He is known to be a bright, if vexing, man.

Still, Carolan obliged. Convention left him no choice, especially when Brian Maguire failed to speak up on his behalf. All estates have their rules. If a guest cannot suffer them, he should leave.

"The fox-haired lad covered in rashes?" the butler answers. "The one who thinks a broken pane of glass is letting unsavoury sorts into the manor?"

"Smith . . ." Brian Maguire says.

"Owen Connor is his name," Carolan replies.

"I know his name."

His host pushes his chair back with such force it topples. The dog in attendance—Jenny or Lucy, by the scent—adds her own *grrr*.

"Let me see if I can locate this Owen Connor," Gordon Smith says in response, presumably, to both growl and glare.

More smuggled claret is in order. Carolan's glass has been empty for ages. Certain that a decanter is within reach, he runs his hand over the table surface, a cautious search. Though he finds the vessel and uses a finger to draw its mouth towards the rim of his glass, he still spills wine. The trembling doesn't help. Nor does the tingle.

"Blast," he says.

"Your hand, Terence?"

"The claret, Brian."

Another servant in the family employ since the days of Constantine Maguire, Martha O'Hara, is summoned.

"How is Mrs O'Hara?" Carolan asks her.

"Your honour."

"Apologies for the mess."

"This mess?" she says. By the tremor to her words, he surmises she is wiping the spill with the apron tied around her waist. "It's nothing, I can assure you, compared to the disasters elsewhere at Tempo."

"That will do, Martha."

"Aye, Sir Brian."

"Don't go," Carolan pleads.

"Master Carolan?"

"I mean, we haven't had a chance to chat."

She says nothing.

"Later, I hope," he adds, his cheeks suddenly warm. He abandons the idea of requesting her hand, to make a study of her bone stems.

"Pray tell us you aren't injured," the neighbouring squire Cady Riordan says to him.

"I am fine."

"Your mishap only further proves the wisdom of my own caution around bottles and such," Sir Cady continues. "Are you aware, sir, that I wear white gloves at the table this evening?"

Brian Maguire groans.

"Gloves?" Carolan asks.

"Gloves, Master. And I recommend you do the same. My own reasons are private. But you, our one true bard, the great Carolan, his fingers snapped like tender twigs . . . I shudder at the thought."

"As do I, Cady."

In truth, he doesn't. Cornelius Lyons soaked his fingers in warm water before performances. Young Denis Hempson is meant to avoid shaking hands before he plays, for fear of breaking a nail. Other harpers wear gloves in damp weather or refuse to perform if a chamber is unheated. Yet Terence Carolan, most famous of them all, isn't so fussy. His hands certainly beg no special treatment. They are pudgy and knob-knuckled, the palms as pink, he has been assured, as a sow's belly. More to the point, they are to composing tunes what a mussel rake is to harvesting mud flats. As a broken rake might halt a gathering, so a sprained finger could postpone a night of playing. But the sea is still there, dark and abundant.

"And what would be your reasons for wearing gloves at the table, Sir Cady?" he eventually says. "If I am not prying."

"A solemn oath made to my late loving wife, Lady Riordan, shortly before we were parted."

"Ah."

"The most solemn of oaths. But to speak further . . ."

"I understand."

"If you insist," Cady Riordan says. "A promise to my beloved on her deathbed that I would never again touch alcohol."

"Most gallant," the captain says.

"Never a drop touched, gentlemen. Never a drop."

"Was it not true, Sir Cady, that Lady Riordan's final words to you were of a more practical nature?"

"Sir Brian?"

"The incident, recalled with the clarity of one who was present, saw her ladyship lying on the forest floor, having been thrown from her horse. And yourself, recovered from your own tumble—which, by the by, had induced her fall, as one domino topples another—kneeling over her, a hand wisely pressed to the ground for support. Her last words to her husband?" Brian Maguire asks without mirth. "'Were you to remove your knee from my chest, Cady, I'd be grateful.'"

"Calumny," Cady Riordan says pleasantly.

"The lady," Carolan inquires, although he has heard the tale before, "she succumbed to her injuries?"

"In time."

"Without speaking to you again?"

"Except through her solicitor."

"A stirring show of matrimonial devotion," Arthur Magennis of Brookeborough says. "Mrs Magennis would be moved, Sir Cady, and would express her emotion at exasperating length and volume, were she not also dead."

"Hats, Father," his son corrects.

"Gentlemen," Cady Riordan says, rising from his chair. "To the memory of Lady Riordan, gone spitefully to the crypt these years, and to Kitty Magennis, shopping away the family fortunes in Temple Bar."

Carolan raises a glass with his fellow diners but does not drain it. Claret, he has learned from hard experience, is chugged at the risk of a raging morning after, the heaves first wet and then dry, as though one's throat were being extracted. He is also thinking of the harpsichord player from Enniskillen. If the fellow is Italian, he will arrive at Tempo chilled and homesick and anxious to drown his melancholy in wine. The company of a lonely Latin pleases Carolan to no end, regardless of how garbled the signore's English may get, especially from the bottom of that decanter.

"But you were saying, Sir Brian?" Arthur Magennis asks, his tone once more pitched for scandal.

"I was?"

"About Colonel Maguire and Lady Cuthbert and noisy conjugal visits?"

"Shh," Morgan Magennis says.

"I really shouldn't speak," Brian Maguire replies.

"Hear, hear," Carolan says.

"The colonel may be joining us at any moment."

"Or he may have no intention whatsoever of gracing the table he badly set," Cady Riordan says. "Besides, it's your own damn manor, Brian Maguire. Or it was, in a former age."

There is a silence, full of communication.

"He rides her hard most nights," Brian Maguire begins. "No

mistaking it. Their animal frenzy dislodges vases from tables and paintings from walls. Those sounds alone, sirs, were enough to launch Lady Maguire in the direction of Westmeath with the haste of an arrow from a bow. The suspicion among the servants—"

"Brian," Carolan says as softly as he dare, "indiscretions of this sort can bring no honour."

"The suspicion is that he takes her with such violence and variety the better to survey her hair, which is a dazzling stack of ringlets and curls. It is believed that Lady Cuthbert hides her jewels up there."

"In her hair?"

"The lady's jewels, I would propose, are kept elsewhere," Sir Cady says.

"Finally, the jewels," Captain Noble says. "Now we talk the pounds and pence of this dark union."

"She had three husbands before Hugh," Brian Maguire resumes. "All with fortunes, and all early to the grave. She must have ridden those poor lads directly to the gates. Whether or not Saint Peter was especially—"

"Shh!" the Magennises say.

But Sir Brian Maguire has abandoned his pride outright. "She purchased his commission for him, you know. Two hundred pounds is what it costs to call yourself an officer in King George's army."

"Shh!"

This time, the footsteps in the hallway slow at the warning.

The candles jump again.

"Do I interrupt?" Owen Connor asks.

"For God's sake, Owen," Brian Maguire answers. "You scared us all half to death."

Carolan's guide squats next to his chair. "Terence?" he says, one hand on his shoulder and the other on his arm.

"Nothing per se. I was just missing you."

"In a room of dear friends?"

He is quiet.

"There is much to report," Owen says, drawing even closer to him. "Tempo is in an uproar."

"Then you have already visited the library?"

"Beg pardon?"

Carolan winces at his own remark. He is definitely under the influence of the wine and the company. Also, the absence of women rarely improves the behaviour of their men.

"These are serious matters," Owen says through a quaver of hurt.

"Master Carolan," Captain Noble interrupts, "has Sir Brian shared his latest scheme for beautifying the privies?"

"He has not, Captain," Carolan replies with a weariness he can no longer disguise.

"Go on, Brian," the captain urges.

"A modest effort," Brian Maguire says. If he is aware of Carolan's agitation, he elects to ignore it. "To do with the chamber pots themselves. Martha O'Hara's son, Thomas, is stableboy here, and he has a gift for drawings and caricatures. I asked Thomas if he thought he could sketch the image of the colonel—check the hallway, will you, Morgan? All clear, is it?—on the bottom of my own pot. The boy said he could. And it is indeed a fine likeness of Hugh Maguire that awaits me each morning as I lower my breeches."

In an instant the sniggers and snorts dissolve into throat clearings and coughs. Even Carolan hasn't heard the footfall.

"Honoured guests," the same voice from the reception hall says, "forgive my tardiness. Crude of me, I realize."

Colonel Maguire, speaking from the far end of the room. How long has he been lingering in the adjacent chamber?

"Hugh . . ." Brian Maguire sputters.

"Lady Cuthbert sends her regrets," the colonel says. "She is preoccupied with feminine matters this evening—fixing her hair and smashing crockery and such."

Long enough to have overheard his uncle's original insults of his wife, it would seem.

Sir Cady Riordan mutters his regrets over the regrets of Lady Cuthbert.

"She has no regrets, sir. She merely sends them."

"Ah," Cady says.

Colonel Hugh Maguire crosses to the table. Owen Connor had caught a glimpse of the new lord of Tempo earlier in the day and described him to Carolan as "exactly what you would expect." As Carolan hadn't any expectations for the man, visual or otherwise, he requested details, assuming his guide would paint a lurid portrait. Owen did not disappoint. The colonel is severely handsome, he began, in the clichéd manner of the salon roué or stage cad. He is tall and lanky and attired to emphasize less the cut of his jib than the size of his bulge. Of his features—including black eyes and a downturned mouth, a sharp jaw and goitrous Adam's apple—none inspire confidence. He also wears spurs indoors, a low conceit.

"You must be Mr Carolan?"

He tries to rise. "And you are Colonel Maguire," he says, allowing Owen to assist him to his feet.

"No need to stand."

Carolan extends a hand. Instead of a punishing grip he receives a firm squeeze, along with a bow, which he returns. The colonel wears a pulvil of musk, sandalwood and cloves, popular among the younger set in Dublin. His own raw cologne further shames him.

"My uncle informs me you are a musician," the colonel says. Though brusque, his tone is cordial, wrong for a cad or roué. His accent, meant to denote an Englishman of standing, betrays a lowlands Scot.

"He is—" Brian Maguire begins.

"I play, sir. A little."

"Lady Cuthbert and I attended a concert this past May at the new music hall in Fishamble Street."

"I know the venue."

"Do you?"

"It was built by John Neale, an acquaintance of long standing."

"You are friends with the Neale brothers?"

Carolan reaches for Owen, who now waits beside him. Unless dissuaded, his guide will almost certainly launch into a summary of the relationship between Terence Carolan and John and William Neale. He will begin with the 1721 volume *27 Pieces of Musick, Airs, Minuets and Dances, Contributed by Mr Dermt. O'Connar, of Limerick, Compositions of harper T. Carolan, of Leitrim,* issued by the Neale brothers of Christ Church Yard, Dublin, at twopence, eight and a half per. He will mention other booklets that have included Carolan's work as well, including a 1726 volume of minuets by the Neales. Number Twenty-Nine in that collection, "Squire Wood's Lamentation on the Refusal of his Halfpence," might especially interest the colonel. It features music by T. Carolan and words by Jonathan Swift, a collaboration borne of a dinner at Quilca, the estate of one Thomas Sheridan. Yes, *the* Thomas Sheridan and *the* Dean Swift. Merely two of his illustrious friends.

All this Owen will say in a manner he believes commanding of a respect that transcends social rank. Colonel Maguire, of course, may not agree.

To his relief, his guide says nothing.

"The playbill may be of interest to you, then," the colonel continues. "Purcell's *Te Deum* and *Jubilate,* an anthem by Dr Blow, plus three concertos by Corelli—the first, third and sixth, I believe."

Carolan suspects it was the eighth concerto, not the sixth, and that the concert took place at St Patrick's Cathedral rather than in the Fishamble Street hall, which lacks a quality organ. His friend

Charles O'Conor described attending just such an event in the capital in a recent letter. Three pieces by Corelli, in St Patrick's, of a May evening. Bliss itself. Curious that the colonel would get the setting wrong.

"A fine night of music, Colonel," he says.

"You are familiar with these composers?"

"I am. The first Purcell you mentioned benefits from the availability of a proper church organ."

"The piece cannot be performed otherwise," Colonel Maguire answers with a trace of self-doubt.

A few bars of the *Te Deum* come to Carolan. *"He-hum, la-he-dah-dum, he-he-da-dum,"* he hums.

"You, sir, can play Henry Purcell?"

"He can play anything, Hugh, after only a single listen," Brian Maguire says. "Can't you, Terence?"

Carolan keeps to himself. It does no good to boast, especially of such a trivial talent.

But his friend disagrees. "His genius in this regard is known far and wide," he says. "There's a story of the time a twitter of Italians demanded he have a listen to a piece one of them had just composed. Some pompous thing, skittish and silly. No chance Terence had heard it before, let alone devoted hours to figuring the tune out. Still, he not only duplicated the music note for note, he actually improved one or two passages as he went along."

Brian Maguire roars at his own anecdote.

"This is so?" the colonel asks.

Though Carolan understands the question is directed at him, he waits, a test of courtesy.

"Mr Carolan?"

"The room lacked a fire," he replies, "and the violinist complained of numbness in the fingers. It was obvious he had sounded certain notes in error, not design." Satisfied, he returns the courtesy. "May I sit back down, Colonel?"

"By all means."

Owen steers him into the chair. His guide's hold betrays an anger he only half-wishes to contain and probably isn't hiding.

"A query for your guest of honour," Colonel Maguire says. He now paces the length of the table, spurs jangling. "I am still new to this island, sir, and yet unfamiliar with its customs. Inquiring of men of discernment and learning is one sure road to wisdom. Could you oblige me for a moment?"

"You've never posed a single question of us, Colonel," Arthur Magennis says. "And we're at Tempo most days."

"Indeed, Mr MacMurphy."

"Magennis."

"Macdonald, did you say?"

"I'm afraid any answer I provide will disappoint you," Carolan replies. "I've no head for serious matters. You'd do better asking Owen."

"Who?"

"Owen Connor here."

The colonel refrains from comment. One, two, three seconds pass, and no one, including Owen, tells Carolan what is transpiring. But the mocking twitter that greeted his suggestion did not come from Colonel Maguire. Cady Riordan, he guesses, who is also apparently an ass.

"If you could name one gentleman whose words and deeds do greatest justice to your people, Mr Carolan, who might he be?"

"My people, Colonel?"

"The Gael."

"Living or dead?"

"As you see fit. But please," the colonel says, resuming his stroll, "do not try my patience with the name of Jonathan Swift, who I am informed is a friend of yours. One need not trade in the latest gossip out of Dublin to realize the man is mad. A survey of his writings is evidence enough."

"The Dean would not be my choice," Carolan answers. "Much as I am honoured to call him a friend, of sorts."

"Mad as a hat, Swift is," Sir Cady says.

"And will you remove those ridiculous gloves?" Colonel Maguire snaps.

"Colonel?"

At last Brian Maguire speaks up. "You need give my nephew no satisfaction, Terence. His manner is most rude."

"Sir Brian," the same nephew says, "I forgot to mention that Smith has found your other shoe. Compel him, and he will guide you to it."

The lurches from civility to childishness are difficult to predict and impossible to condone. How many people are present in the room? Carolan has lost track of the butler Gordon Smith. For all he knows Morgan Magennis, who took too much ale at lunch, may have done the same with claret at dinner and be once more under the table. His ambition now is to find an excuse to expel Owen Connor before his guide utters something disastrous. Then he wishes to retire.

He empties his glass, suspecting that being half seas over won't be half enough to sail through this exchange.

"James Butler would be my selection," Carolan finally replies. "Son of Thomas Butler and grandson of Earl Walter. Chancellor of Dublin University and lord lieutenant of Ireland. The first genuine duke."

"Ormond," Owen says under his breath.

"The duke of Ormond?" Colonel Maguire says. "A surprising selection."

"I was reared on tales of the duke," Carolan explains. "He yet lived then and loomed large in our house. My father, who revered the Butlers above all the old families, never tired of relating the duke's exploits in Strafford's parliament and in exile in France, and his return to the viceroyalty with Charles Second."

"Your father's choice, then?"

"Butler was a man of constancy. A dutiful husband and parent and a faithful servant to country and crown. A gentleman, obviously, possessed of a native splendour, but also someone with an appetite for adventure. Willing to bow to the inevitable. Able, time and again, to make a virtue of necessity."

"I am still surprised," Colonel Maguire says. "Ormond, after all, was privileged by birth and marriage and inclined to his own kind. Charles even advanced him a dukedom in the English peerage during his final visit to the court. Unless I am much mistaken, James Butler would not have been caught sitting by a hearth with your father, hearing his praises sung firsthand. You are of common stock, are you not?"

"He is the bard," Sir Cady says.

"John Carolan was a tenant farmer, Colonel Maguire, and I am that farmer's son. Also a Catholic," he answers.

Whole and undivided, he acknowledges to himself. If still a codger.

"So I was given to understand. And was Ormond not also a lifelong adherent of the Protestant faith?" the colonel asks. "One who served the very kings that have subjected your people and confiscated your lands? It seems incomprehensible that such a man could be hero to the sullen majority of this island."

Carolan waits while Maguire takes up a position behind him, in front of the fire. Owen must be nearby, arms crossed and expression mutinous.

"I recall how the news of Ormond's death was received on the estate in Leitrim where I was then living," Carolan says, turning to face the colonel. "The year 1688 was momentous in many regards. Villagers were sad but not forlorn. They mourned his passing in the spirit, so to speak, of his own moderation. If there is a way to measure the truly great, it may be this—the extent to which, upon their deaths, their better attributes widen out to become values held by all."

He waits for reinforcement or rebuttal. But attentions have suddenly shifted. He feels the tension.

"No greatness without goodness," he adds. "Am I right, friends?"

"Those attributes Ormond supposedly bequeathed to his fellow Irish, what might they be?" Colonel Maguire says. Though he is addressing Carolan, he is challenging someone else. "Dreaminess and sloth? An affinity for actions at once intransigent and compromising? Weakness, dressed up as caution?"

"We are a nation of—" Captain Noble starts to say.

"And what was it James Stuart said to Lady Tyreconnell on his arrival in Dublin after fleeing the carnage at the Boyne?"

The speaker is Owen Connor. He has no right to enter the conversation freely. In doing so, he is showing disrespect, probably by design.

"You address me, sir?"

"What did James supposedly say?" Owen continues. "'Your countrymen, Madam, run well.' To which Lady Tyreconnell is meant to have replied, 'But I see that Your Majesty has won the race.'"

Carolan struggles to his feet, for no other reason than to draw gazes. He wonders whether the colonel is armed. In the view of many a gentleman, a rapier and a readiness to wield it are prerequisites of the class.

"Owen Connor has been in Terence's service for twenty years," Brian Maguire says, hastening to the fireplace. "It's the same with Thady Bourke. After a point, even the most loyal retainers betray a certain insolence."

"And what, sir, did William say to the boatman who rowed him across the River Boyne after that same battle?" Colonel Maguire offers in retort. "'Who won, Sire?' the boatman asked. 'Why should you care?' the king answered. 'Regardless, you'll still be a boatman.'"

"Hugh, please," Brian Maguire says.

"Tell me, Colonel," Carolan says, "the harpsichord player you have arranged for this evening—is he by any chance Italian?"

"I beg your pardon?"

"The musician you hired for tonight's entertainment?"

"I made no such hire."

"I understood otherwise."

"Excellent news," Brian Maguire says. "Then there is hope yet we might hear from the master."

"What master?" the colonel says.

"It's to bed for me shortly, Brian," Carolan announces. "I am destroyed in the head and in most other parts as well."

"Better a bleating piper or squeaky fiddler, eh, gentlemen?" Colonel Maguire says, now cutting for sheer sport. "We could order up some kitchen wenches to dance for us. Heaving bosoms and flouncing tails—superior entertainment for an assembly of country squires like yourselves. What do you say, Sir Cady Riordan? And you, Captain John Noble? Up for a squeeze and tickle and possibly a closet ride? Better that, surely, than some harper tinkling away for hours for the reward of a bath and bed and the howling approval of the family hounds."

The scuffle of feet suggests to Carolan that the colonel and Owen are menacing one another from close proximity. Given the climbing tenor of growls, Brian Maguire must be wedging himself between them as referee.

"Easy there, Jenny," the master of Tempo tells the animal.

"I take it you mean business, boatman?" the colonel asks.

"I do, Your Majesty," Owen Connor replies.

"'Hang all the harpers,'" Carolan declares with what authority and determination are left in his voice.

Man and beast alike fall silent.

He repeats the proclamation.

"The orders of Elizabeth herself, since we are citing monarchs this evening," he begins. "Spoken to her viceroy, Lord Barrymore, in or about the year 1590. 'Hang all the harpers, wherever found, and destroy their instruments.'"

"I hardly see . . ." Colonel Maguire says.

"Her father, Henry Eight, was the first English king to desire absolute dominion over this island. Were you aware of that, Colonel? The surest manner to subjugate a Gael, Henry understood, was to silence his artists. Not inside the Pale, either, where the old ways had long been diminished, but out here in the wilds." He gestures with one arm, latching the other onto the back of the chair to halt the swaying. "Where chieftains still ruled and their *fili* and bards still produced verse and song in praise of that rule. Ban musicians and poets from sitting at high tables with nobles, like yourself, Sir Brian, or yourselves, Sir Cady and Lord Arthur. Imprison them if they show defiance. Execute one or two, even, to shrink hearts with fear."

"Sir . . ." Hugh Maguire says.

"It's what Henry did and what Elizabeth did as well. And yet the queen was still keeping a harper in her court in London and requesting private performances of Irish dance. Why, Barrymore's own household had a harper on its rolls as late as 1603, a full two years after Kinsale, the battle that launched the flight of the ancient order from this island, never to return. Isn't that curious? Even the ambitious Tudors had a soft spot for the bards."

A glass is abruptly in his hand, and he drinks from it. Owen has now secured him, meaning his guide is no longer at risk of exchanging blows with his born better. For this, Carolan is grateful.

The claret fortifies him. "But then along came Ironguts," he resumes. "The right man to finish the job. In three short years, between 1649 and 1652, Oliver Cromwell confiscated and burned five hundred harps in Dublin and another two thousand throughout the countryside. Burned them! Calculate the loss of those instruments, if you're able, many of great antiquity. Fancying himself a flaming sword, Ironguts went further than any monarch would dare, hunting down harpers and crowding the prisons with them. Previously, the musicians had sought refuge in the courts of their patrons. But now, with so many houses in disrepair—with the subjugation complete and the old society destroyed—they found no shelter. And what, I wonder, caused these musicians greater sorrow—the loss of their benefactors or their audience? More than one ruined poet ridiculed the surviving clans for parroting English manners and customs, right down to the waistcoats and riding crops. Cowardly nobles, the poets chided. Not worth a barleycake, for all the good they were doing their own people."

He devoured an oatcake for breakfast that morning, he realizes with a start. Too much salt and not enough sugar. Cooked by a woman named Grainne.

But Carolan dares not pause to sort through these memories. "Harpers were in a quandary," he says. "The old music was finding little favour with either the remaining gentry or Cromwell's soldier-planters. What could a fellow do? Adapt or perish. Quit playing tunes few could hum, let alone dance to, and start playing music that would please parlours of ladies and gents."

Deirdre the dancer. He feels her in his grasp, and then no longer. Did she fly? Or crash to the ground? He took a tumble himself, he now suspects, struck down by God in punishment for discussing his late wife with a stranger.

Discussing Moira with Grainne Connelly, to be exact, whose touch was a thrill but whose frailty had him as worried about her as her sick daughter.

"It's what we have been doing ever since, Colonel Maguire,"

Carolan still manages to say. Owen holds him by one arm and Brian Maguire, he presumes, the other. "Playing to the crowd and singing for our suppers. Wandering from estate to estate begging alms of lords and squires. The name *bard* may still be applied to us, but it is inaccurate, a disservice to the memory of the tradition I have described. Quite right, and quite fair, to compare me unfavourably to pipers or fiddlers. They, at least, provide music that sets ordinary folk dancing. Entire villages at the crossroads, rosy-cheeked and merry, on a Sunday afternoon . . . A glass, gentlemen, if you would."

"Terence?"

"One final refill, Owen. One final toast. Sir Brian and Sir Cady. Captain Noble and Colonel Maguire. Magennises, father and son. Oblige an old fool, will you? Humour him."

Curiously, Carolan is now certain it is Hugh Maguire, and not his uncle, who has hold of his right arm. The caution of the grip alerts him.

"Farewell to Hugh the Great, earl of Tyrone," he says, employing the formal meter used by his own father during toasts. "Farewell to James Butler, duke of Ormond. Farewell to Patrick Sarsfield, hero of the Siege of Limerick, and to Constantine Maguire, of the Pass of Aughrim. Farewell to John Carolan as well, dead from slow grief at just fifty-six. And farewell, last and very much least, to the only son of John Carolan, middling harper and composer of tunes belonging not quite to the crossroads and not quite to the court."

Carolan, dead?

On his feet, anyway.

He chugs the wine without pleasure or accuracy.

CHAPTER SEVEN

He was in the cave with her.

It's me, Bridget. It truly is.

The boy with bluebells for eyes?

Son of the Carolan who farmed the land over near Nobber.

He was sweet, that boy.

You were loveliness itself.

We kissed once.

So we did.

My first kiss.

Likewise.

But then he went away. Went away and died.

In a manner of speaking.

Who are you? she said. Why do you rub the back of my hand?

Do you mind?

This is a holy site. It is improper.

Can you see me?

Hardly.

I see you, Bridget Cruise. Your blue-green eyes and dimpled smile, the flaxen hair to your waist.

The boy died of the pox, she said again. May his soul rest in peace. And my name is Barnewall. Mrs Arthur Barnewall.

Of course.

Married to the second son of Mathias Barnewall, captain of Galmony's Horse. Mathias fled to the continent rather than convert. His son converted, and so obtained the fifteen thousand acres.

Trimlestown, near Kells. I abandoned my faith alongside my husband. For the sake of the children.

I understand.

A Catholic could not go up to Trinity or be called to the bar. Nor could he obtain a commission in the army or a seat in parliament. Arthur said I had to think of our children first. He said it would be selfish to cling.

You gave birth to four?

Then lost them all.

I am sorry.

Almighty penance, she said.

Hush.

For my weakness, and my turning.

Hush.

And now I've come here to Station Island to beg the Lord's forgiveness and plead for readmittance. I wish to die among my own. To be with God at the end of my days.

He welcomes you back.

Cease your rubbing, she said, withdrawing from him. What is so interesting about an old woman's hand?

Bone stems.

Beg pardon?

Nothing.

I demand you allow me to pass. I must find the darkest, coldest corner of this cavern, encounter Lucifer and his demons, and then enter the purgatory for the test. There is no other way to prove I am worthy.

The night is bright as the day, he replied, for darkness is as light with thee.

How did you find out about the children? she asked.

A cousin in your employ kept me informed.

The bard wrote four tunes bearing my name.

That's right.

I ordered an itinerant to play the melodies once. He knew only two by heart. Household staff were forever humming one of them.

The first, most likely. It alone has the soul of a great air, I am told.

Four tunes for four babies. I made the connection.

Did you?

But the melodies were so gay. How could they be lamentations?

Others have remarked on this as well.

And who was I to the great Carolan or Carolan to me?

He is . . . he said, wavering. I am . . .

I must be dreaming.

Perhaps.

Aren't you dead? she said savagely.

My mother and sister and father are. Also my wife. I contracted smallpox but survived.

Your cheeks bear the scars.

Then you can see me?

I've watched you pray for the last nine days. Watched you sleep and wake and sleep once more. We all have. Others gossip about your identity. They say you are him. Can I touch them now?

Bridget?

The pox scars.

You wish it?

I lost my babies and betrayed my faith.

He grasped both her hands and raised them to his face. He guided her fingertips to where the skin was pockmarked from papules that had swollen and burst or swollen and then hardened. Like the etchings of bird feet in snow, his wife once said. Like a thousand tiny cuts, his guide had told him.

She touched the scars. Her fingertips upon his skin, playing him. The contact summoned a thunderbolt from heaven. His knees folded and his head jerked back, scraping the cave wall. He would crumble if he did not flee this terrible place. The dark, he understood, was too dark, and there was no light, no light at all.

✳   ✳   ✳

Emerging from a fitful sleep, Carolan realizes he is not alone. Someone has entered the bedchamber. The intruder has cursed the creaky door and the maid who bothered to draw the curtains. Now he has shifted a chair to bedside and begun his watch, a palace guard fearful his king will be visited by midnight assassins. Though Carolan is glad once again to be out of the cave, he isn't happy to be back inside this house. He is also still potted, the claret a paste over his tongue. The buzzing in his ears bodes ill for the morning.

"Owen?"

"I didn't mean to wake you."

"I am grateful you did."

"You are?"

"I saw her again . . . She touched my scars."

His guide issues a warning hiccup.

"Moira," Carolan explains with haste. "What did she compare them to—the patterns left in the snow by birds?"

"You saw Moira?"

"Or sensed her, at least."

"It's good she visits your dreams."

Not wishing to compound the lie—for it is a lie, surely, to substitute Moira for Bridget, although the switch does not feel duplicitous—Carolan keeps quiet.

"Perhaps she came to calm you after this evening's debacle," his guide says.

"Such behaviour," he answers. "No estate can survive for long in the wake of the flight of its women. Left to themselves, men soon bring the roof down upon their own heads."

"Then you must count me among the badly behaved?"

"None of us are above censure any longer."

"I wanted to brain Maguire, truth be told," Owen says.

"Be careful around the colonel."

"I refer to Sir Brian."

"My friend is . . . diminished," Carolan says. He hopes the admission will put an end to this talk.

"Thady tells me the new butler, Gordon Smith, formerly served as Hugh Maguire's footman. Smith lobs stones at the windows in Sir Brian's quarters after dark. He also hides his spectacles and shoes. The colonel intends to drive his uncle from Tempo and seize control of the estate."

He wonders if this is the case. There are the debts, and the four Maguire sons.

"Brian will never leave Tempo," he says. "The manor defines him no less than do his children or dogs."

A voice sounds within the house. The call is remote and pared of words, like a plea from the bottom of a well.

"I examined the chamber pot in the privy earlier this evening," Owen says. "In the company of Thomas O'Hara, the boy who painted the caricature. I had to lower a candle into the bowl to study his sketch work. Sure enough, the likeness of Hugh Maguire, painted onto the clay."

"And did you . . .?"

"A steaming piss. I couldn't resist it."

Amid their sniggers the ceiling creaks.

"She's up there," Owen says in a hush, "pacing the floorboards and addressing an empty cell."

"Lady Cuthbert?"

"Thady claims she sleeps by day and prowls by night. She also sings lewd songs from her career as a courtesan and dresses in scarves and hats, for dancing with her shadow."

"Then it is illness, and not a dispute over jewels, that keeps her confined to the tower?"

"Dementia, apparently. Martha O'Hara witnessed a fit. Lady Cuthbert rolled about the floor, her mouth foaming."

"Poor woman," Carolan says, drawing a blanket to his chest. He is naked from the waist up, he now notices, with no recollection of who undressed him. "Poor Tempo."

"The situation is indeed dire," Owen says almost cheerfully. "The duke of Ormond himself could not have resolved it."

"A new tune wouldn't have achieved much, that is certain. It occurred to me in the afternoon that any melody I might have produced would have been off-key. The notion was distressing."

"Not wishing to heighten your distress . . ."

"Yes?"

"I've been hinting at this for ages," his guide says.

"Then say it."

"Moira passed away in November 1733?"

Carolan waits.

"And it is now August 1737?"

He waits longer.

"Four years, less three months, since her death," his guide says. "In all that time, Terence, you have not composed a single new tune."

"Not one?"

"Fragments only. You might manage part of a melody, possibly a full part, but then stall or lose interest. You patch the half-creation onto a composition you wrote ten or twenty years ago and declare it done."

At once Carolan is drumming his fingers on his chest and humming those melodies he associates with the recent past. "Lady Athenry," for instance, *duh-dah-la-la-lah*, composed for Mary Nugent at her castle near Tuam before her untimely death in 1725, he seems to recall. *Dum-dum-de-dum-dah*, the lively drinking song "Kean

O'Hara," its namesake, formerly sheriff of Sligo, dead for a decade or longer, come to think of it. Or his friend Toby Peyton, who yet loves the smell of a glass, but whose eponymous melody in praise of that amour—*ladly-lol-la-di*—dates back to a three-day session at Alderford attended, Carolan is almost certain, by Sir Henry Macdermott Roe. Sir Henry, of course, died in 1727. Still, the instant he clacks out the wistful *la-lah-du-la-lah* opening to "Blind Mary," his lament for his colleague, the harper simply known as Maire Dhall, he is convinced he has found a new melody that is entirely whole and worthy.

"The year 1731," Owen interrupts.

"Hmm?"

"Maire Dhall passed away, and you wrote that fine tune for her, nearly two years before Moira took ill."

"You're sure?"

"We were at Belanagare with Denis O'Conor when word was received that their old teacher had died. You composed the melody that same afternoon, in order to perform it for the O'Conor children before we carried on to Galway."

"Your memory is acute."

"Notoriously. But then," his guide adds, "I have never loved the smell of a glass with nearly the same passion as you and your friends, have I?"

As ever, Carolan is undone by Owen's ability to read his thoughts and, in this instance, his fingertips and murmurs. Flustered, he quits seeking evidence.

"Owen," he says with an anticipatory wince, "don't make me supply the actual words. Show pity."

"How do the half-creations of recent years sound to the ear?" Owen says, using, indeed, the exact words he would have chosen. "Not terrible. Not distinctive or memorable, either. Ordinary, I suppose."

Carolan can't help himself. "Ordinary?" he says. "Me?"

"Mrs Mac doesn't bother to have them transcribed. Haven't you wondered why she no longer calls someone in to note the melodies down?"

"Mrs Mac is aware . . .?"

"Of course."

"Anyone else?" he asks in a chastened voice.

"Charles MacCabe and Toby Peyton. Plus Charles O'Conor."

"Have they opinions as to why I am in the doldrums?"

"Grief," he answers.

"And you?"

"Guilt."

He waits.

"Why haven't you composed for your wife? Or any of your children?"

"Or for you?"

That stops him momentarily. Carolan can almost hear his friend turn over the remark, as one might turn a coin found in a stream, examining it for value. Soon he will dismiss it, rightly, as worthless, a weak attempt to put him off.

He does not wait for Owen's reply. "I compose for patrons and friends mostly," he says, "and always have. My tunes work best when they are clear and simple and pitched to please. Anything more complex is certain to flounder. Why, I wrote not one or two but four tunes for Bridget Cruise."

"Upon the death of each of her newborns?"

"You knew?"

"Everyone knew."

Carolan must swallow this latest shock. Which other of his secrets are, in fact, common knowledge? "And even *those* compositions were bright and, I suppose, filled with a certain kind of light. She, too, noticed it," he says.

"Who did?"

He chews his lip, grateful for the darkness that is presumably masking the consternation on his face.

"Your excuses are lame," Owen says.

"They are not excuses. They are explanations as to the nature of my narrow gift."

"Why are you so sure your gift is narrow?"

"You've heard my church music?"

His guide draws air into his nose again, this time without censure.

"Or my laments?"

"'Blind Mary' is decent enough."

"Decent only."

"But your gift is your own."

"My own?" Carolan answers. "It belongs to the Lord. When I compose, I am doing His bidding."

He isn't dissembling. The silly wee man Terence Carolan couldn't possibly come up with tunes of such inspiration and, he dares to say, immortality. He hasn't that kind of stuff in him. God, and God alone, could be directing his fingertips when they locate pleasing sequences of notes on the strings and then bundle perfect arrangements of those sequences into a tune. The Lord is indeed his musical shepherd, and with His guidance he shall not want.

Except, it would seem, for the past three years and nine months.

Surely he did not make pilgrimage on Station Island for this secret reason? To entreat God to resume guiding his fingers to those harp strings? If so, he kept the secret even from himself, most likely because it was unworthy.

Owen, naturally, has been overhearing these deliberations as well. "Must the Lord be your sole creative taskmaster?" he asks. "What of your own private longings and sorrows? Why not transpose those into a composition?"

His reply is as lame as his other remarks. "The result might not be pleasing," he says.

"Or it might achieve a power and originality the likes of which haven't been heard on this island before," Owen says with a force suggesting a much rehearsed and too long unspoken comment.

"Owen!"

"You don't think I am serious?"

"I think you mistake me for an artist of a calibre I would never presume or even wish to be. A Jonathan Swift, perhaps, or that Alexander Pope, whom you so admire. Or yourself," Carolan adds.

"Myself?"

"Your intellect, rather. The quality of your mind. It is a fine thing, if too sharp by half, as I explained to Colonel Maguire before. It's you who ought to have been answering those questions he asked."

"The colonel was certainly keen to hear the views of a manservant," Owen answers. But he can't hide his pleasure at the compliment.

"He might have been persuaded."

"There was much persuasion in your speech earlier this evening."

"Ah yes, the speech. I was wondering when you'd ask."

"It was prepared?"

"A few days," Carolan admits.

"Days?"

"Months."

"On the assumption you'd have occasion to deliver it soon?"

"Some time or another."

"As farewell?"

Yes. No. He isn't sure.

"What makes you say that?" he asks.

"Was it not a eulogy?"

"More a threnody, I suspect. I did not relish the clack of my own voice. It reminded me of too many dinner guests at too many tables I have adorned. Chatter, clatter, without measure or cadence."

"Regardless," his guide says, "the remarks were out of character in the same manner a tune that addressed the depth of your feelings for those you have loved and lost would be out of character. The beginnings of something new."

The room is frigid, Carolan suddenly notices, like a crypt unsealed in winter. Hearing Owen rub his arms, he bundles up the top blanket. The dark isn't half as deep as it feels against his own skin, he hopes.

"Take this."

"I'm fine," Owen replies. But he wastes no time in wrapping himself in the blanket.

"The hour must be late?"

"Between three and four. The sun will be up in two hours."

"That soon?" he says with a yawn.

"I should leave you be."

"The colonel's demand that you sleep in the straw-chamber was most silly," Carolan says. "Like so much else about this evening."

"The man presumes himself a cut above."

"He is a complicated fellow," he says with deliberate mildness. He hasn't forgotten Colonel Maguire's taunts at dinner. Nor, however, can he forget the colonel's clumsy efforts at courtesy and transparent desire to understand the place, and the people, that were now his surroundings.

"He is a mercenary, Terence, a brigand in an army uniform."

"Did he look at me when we spoke?"

"You couldn't tell?"

"Not for certain. The room was too crowded and he paced it during much of our conversation."

It matters to Carolan whether a person bothers to address him directly, as he or she would the sighted. It tells him something.

"Colonel Maguire was careful to hold your gaze, so to speak," Owen answers.

"And the others—Cady Riordan and Arthur Magennis?"

"Hazard a guess."

"And Sir Brian?" he says, unsure he desires further evidence of his friend's diminishment.

"He studied your face like a child seeking the approval of his parent. Or rather, he did so once he located his spectacles."

The ceiling creaks again. The soliloquist has gone quiet, leading Carolan to wonder whether Lady Cuthbert has detected *their* voices within the house and is constructing a tale of woe for her fellow inmates. Fair enough, he reckons: prisons take as many forms as do prisoners.

"Why not stay here the rest of the night," he says. "Share my bed, if you can stand the reek."

"I'll leave you be."

"I don't want you to leave me be."

"Get some sleep."

"Is there a candle in the room?" Carolan asks. "You can't wander those corridors in the dark."

Especially the corridor across the landing on this same floor, the one leading to the library.

"I'll be careful."

Neither of them speak.

"No headaches of late, I take it?" Carolan finally says. Owen Connor has suffered sore heads since he was a boy.

"One or two in Pettigoe, while waiting for you. Seamus diagnosed them as the manifestations of an unquiet spirit."

Friar Seamus, once more. His influence is most definitely a concern. "The friar is also a physician?" he asks with, perhaps, bared teeth.

"He believes—"

"We haven't discussed your future in a while, have we, Owen? It's going to be brilliant."

"My future?"

"There may come a time . . ." Carolan says. He is hoping the sentence will expand outwards in a vague but positive direction.

"You need rest," Owen says. "That's all. Whatever happened this morning need never happen again. I have been faulty in my judgements these past days. Had I shown greater resolve, much of what transpired could have been avoided."

"I was delighted to meet that family. The Connellys, was it?"

"You remember them?"

He does, a little. "The memories resurfaced over the course of the evening. Did I lift the child?" Carolan says, rubbing the fingers on his left hand. That side of his body yet aches, leg, hip and shoulder, with even his cheek still inflamed, as though from a lingering slap. He sustained an injury, he now suspects. A rough sleep on an uneven floor? Another tumble off Gem? His mind apparently went blank in consequence of the violence.

"Toss her into the air, as you once did your own children?" Owen replies.

"And catch her?"

"Of course you caught her."

"Thank the Lord."

"She is deathly ill, Terence."

"Aye."

"Speaking of untrained physicians, the mother believed you cured her girl of diphtheria."

"Grainne," he says, summoning her quavering voice and sensual touch. "She was lovely . . . wasn't she?"

His guide's volubility vanishes when the subject turns to women. Owen colours, too, Carolan knows, reddening a complexion already freckled to the point of disfigurement. The boy is still a virgin, he is convinced.

"An attractive woman," Owen answers.

"That's all?"

"Her eyes, maybe. They were dark and brimming. A man could be mistaken for thinking them a pool into which he could dive."

"There you go."

"But I wouldn't know about such things."

"Annie has such eyes, I am told," he ventures, referring to Annie MacManus, the scullery maid at Alderford, the Leitrim estate of their mutual benefactor, Mary Macdermott Roe. Here is a subject worth exploring.

"Annie?"

Carolan waits, doing his best to stifle another yawn.

"She is not quite twenty-one," Owen replies.

"And a fine lump of a girl, everyone says."

"Everyone says that about Annie?"

"You know they do."

"I'll be on my way then."

He mustn't be allowed to leave. Not with the house quiet and the library corridor black. Thady Bourke, equally concerned, informed Carolan earlier that the key to the library door had gone missing, allowing bibliophiles to enter and exit at will.

"I can recall everything now," he announces.

Though Owen keeps silent, the tightness of his breathing betrays his interest.

"You advised against coming to Tempo. Back in Kesh, in advance of my performing for the villagers. I should have listened."

"You hoped to mitigate."

A sigh escapes Carolan, followed by equally deflated words. "I place too high value on my own influence, I suspect, prone as I am to confusing the dignity expressible through music with the indignities enforced by life. I dwell too little in the real world. Most men, in contrast, dwell too much in it."

He waits for Owen to correct this harsh self-judgement. But the creak of the chair suggests his audience may be pronouncing on him in the harshest manner possible—with his feet.

"The conversation about Moira," he says, reaching for Owen's arm, "and my cowardly flights from her. We spoke of it on the road out of Pettigoe, did we not, and then again in the wake of our encounter with the sheriff? You wish to lead me back to her. You think it your duty as my friend and guide."

"Back to her and the children," Owen says in a tone that suggests he no longer quite believes the scheme himself.

In this regard, Owen is half correct to have doubts, Carolan thinks. The children probably aren't possible. Far easier to make amends with the past than the present. Especially if you are also, in effect, of the past. Farewell to the only son of John Carolan? Indeed.

"She was a fine country woman," he offers of his wife. A weak compliment, by intent.

"She was the best," his guide answers with precisely the ardour that leaves Carolan uncomfortable.

"Your hand, son," he says, reaching for him again. "Allow me to hold it for a moment."

"Your fingers are frozen," Owen says.

"I am wrecked and ruined and won't be able to do this much longer."

"You just need rest."

"And I think the world of you, Owen Connor. Your loyalty and honour and deep feelings for others. It has been my pleasure to travel with you these past two decades."

"We are a single being almost?"

The comment, he acknowledges, is his own. "You've a great future ahead," Carolan repeats. This time, the blandness is instinctive.

"Old man . . ." Owen says. He chokes back a sob.

"And why not stay right here? Help warm these frozen bones. Forget some smelly straw mattress."

But then a bird sings. A lark, first to rise in country gardens.

"Did you hear it?" Carolan asks.

"I am thirty-nine years old," Owen replies.

"*See-you, see-your,* it sings. I'll not be able to slumber now, with the lark calling to me."

"Yes, you will. Like a baby."

"I love the scent of babies," he says. Sure enough, he is suddenly as drowsy as a kitten satiated on its mother's milk.

Thinking of lark song.

And of God's gift to him, lately gone unused.

And of Moira, not in the cave on Station Island. In the four-poster bed at Mohill, rather, with her hair unplaited and his arm as her pillow.

chapter eight

Carolan does sleep like an infant, especially once Owen reconsiders and joins him. He can't say for certain when his guide slipped into the bed. But he can comment on how Owen, normally a docile companion, prods him with his elbow, indifferent to the condition of his bladder. He is bothered not so much by the peculiar cologne the younger man wears—can Owen Connor really be almost forty?—as the tiny hairs that end up in his mouth. Fire-singed, to the taste.

The feuding jackdaws revive him.

"Your arm, son," he says, "it pins me as securely as any Lilliputian ropes. Could you not shift over?"

Nothing.

"And the stench . . ."

His bedmate emits a gummy expulsion.

"Master Carolan?" a voice calls from across the room.

He hasn't heard the door open.

"Thady?"

"Conbec?"

"Conbec? I assumed it was Owen."

The hound whimpers.

Carolan moans.

"The smell in here . . ." Thady Bourke remarks.

He issues an additional moan at the jab of a paw into his abdomen. Conbec consoles him with another whimper. The dog's breath invokes raw partridge and lathered testicles.

"Can you move at all?" the butler asks.

"A chamber pot, Thady. Make haste."

"Conbec, away with ye!"

Conbec does not away.

"This must look odd," Carolan says.

"It isn't for me to comment."

"An elderly couple, still keen to sleep entwined."

"That beast is no lady, sir."

"As I am probably no gentleman."

He tries twice to extricate himself from under the wolfhound. Both instances he flops back, the sag of the mattress rendering the task Sisyphean. The second failure awakens his morning-after ache. His sockets itch and his throat feels rasped by a dull razor. His sinuses are blocked.

The claret. More fool he.

Only when Thady Bourke whacks Conbec across a flank does the animal leap to the floor, rocking the posts. One old man helps another to his feet.

"My buttons," Carolan says.

"Master?"

"On my breeches. My hands aren't steady enough. Could you?"

Thady unbuttons his crotch. "Should I? As well?" he asks.

"That I can manage."

Just barely, as it happens. He fumbles for his tool as though for an eel in a barrel. At last he has the creature in his grasp. "The pot is before me?" he says, probing for it with his toes.

"It is."

"A foot farther back, please. Then withdraw."

The butler follows instructions.

He hums while he pees, to muffle the splashes, but still sprinkles the floor around the chamber pot, along with his own feet. No further ignominies, Carolan resolves silently. Comfort henceforth, at any cost.

"Better," he says.

"I'll fetch the basin of water."

"I could certainly do with a wash. Twelve days have gone by since I last bathed, as you've perhaps remarked."

"Station Island is no easier on the body than the soul," Thady Bourke says.

"You've made the pilgrimage?"

"In my youth. Before the Penals, if you can imagine such an era."

"I can, with pleasure."

"The church and residence had already been razed by soldiers," Thady says. "There were a few simple buildings, as I recall, plus the covered pit that served as cave. Still, better conditions than you had to endure."

"I found the accommodations adequate, at best," Carolan admits. Muscles in his back quiver at the memory of sleeping on rock.

"But did you make the descent, sir?"

"The descent?"

"Down into purgatory."

"You mean Saint Patrick's?"

For centuries pilgrims believed that confinement in the cave on Station Island could open a portal into the underworld, where faith would be tested, and sins atoned, through a series of ordeals overseen by demons with horns and hooves and curled tails. It was accepted that for every pilgrim who survived the trials, and so found reward in a garden paradise of choirs of angels in white robes, a dozen more failed. They went missing, their corporeal selves burned in pits of fire. Even for Carolan, an avowed non-believer in the modern, as Owen Connor recently pointed out, such legends are wild and remote.

"Saint Patrick's Purgatory, naturally," the old servant says. "I experienced its torments, I did."

"Is that so?"

"The likes of which I never thought I'd encounter again. But I was wrong about that," he adds.

Carolan can't decide whether he really wants to be apprised of Thady Bourke's recent torments. "A wash would be pleasing," he says a second time.

Thady fetches a basin and pitcher from the far corner of the room. He wrings out a cloth and presses it into Carolan's hand.

"These are Owen Connor's duties, by rights," Carolan says in apology.

"No bother."

"What hour is it, anyway?"

"Noon."

"So late?"

The butler confirms the fact.

"I can't recall such a helpless sleep."

"It must have been, for you to have slumbered through the uproar. The entire house out of bed at daybreak."

"Roving dogs?"

"Aspiring pugilists," Thady answers. His tone betrays the name of at least one combatant.

Carolan accepts assistance back to the bed. "Any wounds?" he asks.

"None mortal."

"He drew his rapier?"

"He owns one?"

"I imagine Colonel Maguire must possess a collection of sabres. Most army men do."

"Not the colonel," Thady Bourke says. "Thank the heavens. It was with Gordon Smith that Owen Connor exchanged first taunts and then blows. On the staff hall floor, shortly after sunrise."

"Did Brian pull them apart?" he says, remembering Brian Maguire's timely intervention between Owen and Hugh Maguire.

"Sir Brian wasn't in the house."

"No?"

"Colonel Maguire separated the men. He cuffed them across the backs of their heads and declared neither worthy to remain under his roof."

"Oh dear," Carolan says. He is careful to hide his relief that his guide fought a fellow manservant instead of an officer.

"The fisticuffs were Owen's doing, I'm afraid. He appears to have—"

"Thady, old friend," he interrupts, "could I hear the story first from Owen Connor? He has been loyal to me these many years."

"Gladly, your honour."

"The news is distressing enough. Has the sheriff been called for?"

"Not that I am aware."

"Good."

"Sit, please, while I put your boots on."

"It's for Owen to dress me."

"No bother," the butler says again.

"And you've already stripped the same fetid clothes off this corpse once before."

"Master?"

Carolan explains that he assumes it was Thady who undressed and put him to bed the previous evening.

"Sir Brian had me escort Owen Connor from the dining hall in the wake of his exchange with the colonel. I did not bring you to this chamber," Thady says. He has dropped to one knee and is lacing a boot, his breaths laboured.

"Then who did?"

"I can't say."

"Brian himself?"

"He followed me down the stairs to the staff hall. You were still in your seat at the table at that point, finishing a glass."

"A glass that nearly finished me," Carolan says, rubbing his brow. Pain skitters across his forehead like ants over a skull. Or do the ants race through the various holes in that skull: the sockets, nostrils and mouth? What a grim image.

"It was a strange night in this manor," the servant says. "And loath as I am to even make such a suggestion . . ."

"Thady?"

"Loath as I am, I fear you may wish to end your visit here prematurely. This day, perhaps. Within the hour, if you can gather yourself."

"It is so bad?"

"It's been bad for a long while now, Mr Carolan. The brawl earlier only renders it that much worse."

"I am sorry."

"The times that are in it," Thady Bourke says.

Carolan imagines how the butler must look. The same as he does, he reasons. Squat and portly, hairy-beaked and craggy-faced. Eyes whose coloration has worn away, like stones smoothed by water, and teeth gone grey and mossy from mundungus. Thady Bourke has more hair on his head than Carolan ever did, and his side whiskers are said to be the white of fresh snow.

He hesitates before sharing a thought nagging at him since their arrival, anxious that Thady hear it as concern, not criticism. "I must confess to some surprise at finding you in such disrepair yesterday afternoon," Carolan says. "You are usually the most sober of men."

"I surprise myself of late."

"Has life at Tempo been that fraught?"

"It has. But it's not the reason."

The butler is still on one knee. Carolan implores him to rise and, detecting a struggle for balance, returns the favour and hoists him by the arm. The effort sets off the ringing in his ears.

"Are you my age now? Sixty-seven?"

"Sir Brian reckons I must be seventy. My father held the same position with Constantine Maguire as I do with his son. Old Con kept records of births and deaths on the estate, and my name is meant to be listed under 1667."

"Then Tempo is your family seat as well."

"You might say so."

Anxious that they converse as equals, Carolan encourages the butler to sit next to him on the bed.

"No hiding it," Thady finally says, "I've been dealt a blow."

Of course. Carolan rebukes himself for not hearing the grief note sooner. His sensitivities have always favoured women. Unfairly, he realizes—men simply lack the confidence to be at once vulnerable and strong.

He racks his memory. Thady Bourke's wife, Eileen, passed away some years ago. Their only daughter is employed by the Magennises at Brookeborough. Then there are the sons. Michael and . . . Shane, is it? Or Seamus?

"Your boys, Thady?"

"Aye."

"Seamus?"

"Shane. He booked passage to New France back in the spring of thirty-five. Courted a Strabane girl all the way to a town called Qwee-bec."

"I've heard of the place."

"A savage land, apparently. Full of red Indians and black bears and snows that blow from October to June. Pretty lasses, mind, and farms for the asking."

"Any word from Shane since he left?"

"None."

"I'm sure the lad is prospering over there," he says. He is now equally sure the other brother is not.

"Michael signed on with the Earl of Donegal's Regiment in

Belfast," Thady Bourke says. "For want of better opportunities, including here at Tempo, once Colonel Maguire began bringing in his own people. Those failed harvests a decade past started many of us talking about emigration. Michael was told Donegal's Foot regularly served in Gibraltar and the West Indies and other far-flung spots. But he managed no further than a billet in England, where he fell last month in a skirmish with brigands. I only learned the news through another local who enlisted along with him—one of the Garveys from down in the village."

Carolan murmurs in commiseration.

"A full-grown man was my boy," the servant says. He has accepted the offer of a seat, his clothes acrid with hay and tobacco. "Forty or forty-one. Still, you grieve the loss as though that of a bouncing baby."

"This is the case."

"Rue the day you ever brought them into this vale of tears."

"The Lord attends our suffering, Thady. He hears our prayers."

Thady Bourke makes no comment.

"And your Michael was a rascal. He couldn't wait to dig into my waistcoat pockets. 'What have you for us, Master Carolan?' he would say. 'A fig or a gingerbread?' Do you remember that about him?"

"I might."

"I do, as if it were yesterday. 'I've nothing for a pup like you, Michael Bourke,' I'd reply. 'Unless you can tell me who Cuchulain fought in his defence of Ulster and what his hurley stick was fashioned from.' He got every answer correct and so ate more than his fair share of the sweets I packed for such purposes."

In the quiet he hears laughter in the garden below the window. Maids, hanging out the wash.

"A bold lad," he adds. He retains no memories of Thady's children, in point of fact, aside from their names, a reality he suspects their father knows. "I'm sure he did his parents proud."

The old butler's silence suggests he wishes to say more. Carolan lays a hand on his thigh in encouragement.

"What was the very final thing you saw, sir?"

"Saw?"

"Before . . . before your sight was taken?"

"Ah."

Carolan pauses at a wren's bubbly warble.

"Is my question impertinent?"

"Not at all. I am simply recollecting, not easy without a glass of the hair of the dog that shared my bed."

His humour goes unappreciated.

"The pox left me delirious for two days, during which time I flitted in and out of awareness. I saw my mother, nursing her son despite being deathly ill, her eyes huge with terror. I saw my father . . ." He waits while the wren sings another verse. "Perhaps this is the final image, now that I reflect on it. Having been instructed to check that I yet breathed, a look of consternation soon distorted his features. My face could only have inspired such horror."

He touches the scars with the washcloth, as she did. Not Mrs Arthur Barnewall in the cave, once, but Moira Carolan, née Keane, every day. With a cloth and, sometimes, her lips.

His Dido: Burning with love, infected to her very marrow.

Her Aeneas: An aloof and distracted man, undeserving of her.

"And you remember his face even now?" Thady asks. "Along with your mother's?"

"Hmm?"

Thady Bourke waits.

"Remember their faces? Afraid not."

"But didn't you just describe them to me?"

Carolan doubts Thady is much interested in the tunnel of his blindness. "It is difficult to put into words."

"What about dreams? Do loved ones appear before you then?"

"I see nothing."

"Master?"

"My dreams have all gone dark."

"Can this be?"

"Such is the path my affliction has followed. But I hear, smell and taste with exceptional force, and even a kind of creativity." Again, he doubts the servant would be interested. "Your son, Thady—he occupies your dreams?"

"How did you know?"

Now it is Carolan who must wait.

"I am afraid to shut my eyes, for fear my heart will break overnight at the reoccurring sight of Michael."

"And your final glimpse of him in waking life?"

"Ambling down the lane with his mate, Sean Garvey, a swagger in his walk but a thin smile on his lips. He turned and waved to his da, and I saw it as plainly as I see you here—he feared he'd never see his hearth and home again."

"His eyes told you?"

"The sadness in them, sir. The resignation."

"You are haunted?" Carolan says.

"So much so, I sometimes wish my own dreams would go dark as well." Thady Bourke stands in a manner suggesting he is convinced he has given insult. "Meaning no offence," he adds with a bow.

"For heaven's sake, man. I am not your lord or squire. We are two old friends having a chat."

"I should get you dressed," the butler says. "But could I ask one further question?"

Owen Connor should be getting him dressed, Carolan abruptly worries. Owen should be assisting his morning toilette. Where is his guide?

Thady poses his question.

"How did my *father* react?"

"Forgive the impertinence. It must have been an awful blow for him. A wife and daughter taken and a son much . . . altered."

Carolan stands as well. "We'd best be locating Owen before he finds someone else to fight."

"Right so."

He regrets his tone. He does not talk often about John Carolan. Even now he hardly knows what to say.

"He was never the same," he offers anyway, extending an arm to be encased in sleeve. "Lost to his desolation. Lost to me, certainly, as though one or the other of us had, in effect, perished with the women. He ought to have quit Alderford, I sometimes think, and made a fresh start elsewhere. Instead, he accepted the kind offer of Mary Macdermott Roe and took up residence in a cottage behind the manor. Lived there as a near recluse for eighteen years until the Lord finally called him to His side."

The plain truth. His father should have quit Alderford after the tragedy. He should have started over in Dublin or London or across the sea in Qwee-bec. Had he understood then what he understands now, Carolan would have pushed John Carolan off the estate, away from him.

"And when your wife passed on?" Thady says.

"Was I, too, lost to desolation?"

"I suppose . . ."

"Lamplight dimmed beside her," he replies, quoting one of his own lyrics, "and sunlight stayed around her through the day. Her voice held water and her touch lit flames. Mouth and eyes and breast and thighs, all that we desire."

"Sir?"

"Indeed I was lost. And still am, I've recently learned."

But Thady Bourke is no longer listening. "That's what becomes of the likes of us, isn't it, Master Carolan? Forced to go among strangers in strange countries. Severed from land and clan. We can expect no better in this vale of tears."

❊   ❊   ❊

He waits on the front steps while Thady walks over to the stables. Rain falls once more, slanting and cold. He hears a crow *caw-caw* from the roof. He smells and tastes chimney smoke.

Clip-clop. Gull and Gem, being led by their reins.

"Terence."

He embraces his guide. He also pats his back, as Brian Maguire patted his own.

"Thank God, Owen."

"It's not as if I'm returned from the bloody fields of France."

"What about your mouth?"

"A swollen lip. And you should see Smith."

Before Carolan can ask why a swollen lip would be causing Owen to whistle his *s* sounds rather than slur them, Thady Bourke speaks.

"Martha O'Hara found your tooth behind a meal bin, Owen. She's wrapped it in tissue paper."

Owen accepts the tooth without remark.

"I'm missing a few myself," the butler says to be kind.

"Thady helped me with my ablutions," Carolan says. "As well as saving me from being ravaged by a wolfhound."

His guide expresses gratitude to Thady for his efforts. He doesn't inquire about the dog.

As he goes to mount Geminiani, Carolan deliberately brushes against the saddlebag nearest him. The bag feels no bulkier than the day before. "Where on earth is Sir Brian?" he asks.

"He'll meet us up at the gatehouse."

A window is shut as they pass beneath the east wing. Lady Cuthbert, he assumes, in her eyrie cell.

"She spends long hours gazing out," Thady Bourke comments.

"A prisoner in her own house," Carolan says.

"Mostly in her head, sir."

This statement, too, rattles in his memory. It has indeed been a queer visit to Tempo. Too queer for him.

"Would that Lady Cuthbert's difficulties could be resolved by the mere mining of her hair for jewels," Owen says.

The pond gives off no stink today. The jackdaws have suspended their disputes, probably to rest before finding fresh excuse for disagreement.

Brian Maguire awaits them at the gate.

"I am most distressed, Terence," he says.

"Excuse me if I don't dismount, Brian. I might never get back up on Gem."

"Better the company of animals than men, eh?"

"Houyhnhnms to Yahoos," Owen says, the first word, whistled through the gap in his teeth, closer to an exhalation than language.

Gull gives a blow, as if to acknowledge the reference to his literary brethren and the book that produced such odd names, including his own.

"You, sir," Brian Maguire says. "You and your kind."

"My kind, Sir Brian?"

"Now, now," Carolan says to Owen. His stomach flips at the prospect of further dispute, another indication that his tolerance, exhausted overnight, may never be restored.

"On the subject of hounds, Brian," he says, "I must relate to you the most singular dream. But stop. Why do I find you lurking out here at the gatehouse?"

"It's where I've lived these past months. Myself and Thady, on beds of straw, with only the dogs for companionship and warmth. And now even Conbec has deserted us."

Sir Brian Maguire, son of Constantine Maguire, hero of the Pass of Aughrim, laments the absence of a beloved, not his wife.

"I've forsaken it, haven't I, Terence?" he says from close beside the saddle.

"Brian?"

"You know full well."

"Dignity is a quality that can be regained, Brian Maguire."

"Yes, but grace cannot."

Carolan offers him no consolation. Instead, in the conventional manner he bids God bless to his host. "And you, Thady," he says, reaching down to have his hand shaken. "I'll offer a prayer for both our souls."

"Long life to you, Master," Thady Bourke answers.

* * *

They ride through the rain. Once more there is pattern and pitch and quiet syncopation, if Carolan can only give over to the music. There is also rain drone, a deeper, less cautious release, suggestive of sleeps that never end and nights that fail to brighten back into day. But the anxieties won't dissolve easily this afternoon. Not with his conversation with Thady Bourke yet active in his mind, especially his own thoughts on John Carolan and parental duties. Nor with a sore head and raw throat, guts so gnarled they must resemble the roots of a tree.

Or with the further clamour of hooves on the path. A rider, approaching from behind.

"The colonel," Owen reports. "In haste."

"Does he bear arms?"

"You mean a weapon?"

"We'd best make a dash."

"But he rides a stallion."

"Fly, Gem!"

As usual, his horse stops.

"Sirs."

Another bristling steed draws up.

"I'll distract Maguire and block his path," Carolan whispers in the direction of his guide. "Run for it, lad."

"Good day, Colonel Maguire."

"A miserable day so far, Mr Connor, thanks to you."

Both men dismount.

"You know my name, at least," Owen says.

"As does my footman, Gordon Smith. As will the Enniskillen sheriff, if I don't receive satisfaction from this exchange."

Again, Carolan is secretly relieved. The colonel still has no plans to challenge his guide to a duel.

"Mr Carolan," Hugh Maguire says, "a word in private, if you would."

He accepts assistance down off Gem. The hand on his waist is gloved in fine leather. The cologne has been reapplied.

"I'll be just a few steps away," Owen says.

Colonel Maguire waits for Owen Connor to attain that distance. "You left in such haste this morning," he begins.

"Apologies for our manners."

"No need."

Removing the gloves, the colonel slaps them into his palm, like a rider with a crop. The rhythm is designed, Carolan suspects, more to regulate himself than intimidate others.

"I wish to amend two remarks made during our conversation last evening," Colonel Maguire says. "One is minor, the other grave. The concert Lady Cuthbert and I attended this spring, with the program of too much Corelli—it was held in St Patrick's Cathedral, not the Neales' new concert hall. I suspected I had the wrong venue but could not order the details correctly."

He is silent.

"Equally, I fear I overstated my criticism of the duke of Ormond. I am mostly in accord with your assessment of his character. Are you familiar with his efforts at disguise while agitating for Charles in London?"

Though Carolan knows the tale, he holds back.

"The duke," Hugh Maguire says with the eagerness of a man so desperate to talk he will ignore all awkwardness, as well as a pounding rain, "both mussed and dyed his hair, hoping to pass for a native of Cheapside. The dye, intended to turn his head from black to red, instead produced a shock of colours. Ormond's response was audacity itself. Figuring the hair would disguise him as a ninny, he strolled the streets of London in broad daylight. Who would accuse such a buffoon of being a popish spy?"

"A great man, James Butler," Carolan finally says. Astonished by the colonel's words, he struggles to read his temper.

"My wife, sir, is not well."

"I am sorry."

"Tempo is mired in debts that neither I, nor my children, should I have any, nor Sir Brian's children, should they ever take a serious interest in the family estate, will be relieved of."

"The practical affairs of Tempo have often escaped Brian's attention."

Owen Connor coughs censoriously.

"Your manservant has the ears of a village gossip."

"He is my guide, Colonel Maguire, and my friend."

Owen's criticism is unfair. Carolan isn't appeasing the officer; he is making civil with him, a skill unfamiliar to some.

"And if his powers of listening are overly acute," he adds, "it is my doing. Too much time in my company has caused him to evolve alternative methods of gaining information. Isn't that right, Owen?"

"You address me, Terence?" Owen says.

The colonel pats his horse. Carolan wonders if the animal bears mottled scars across the flanks from the spurs its rider wears.

"Then what they said last night is the truth?" Colonel Maguire asks. "You are able to duplicate a piece of music after a single listen?"

"A low party trick."

"I hardly think so."

Carolan offers his usual analogy. "A gentleman is giving a costume ball. He has drawn up the list of invitees and greets each masked guest as he or she arrives. Later he is able to name every individual who attended, despite not glimpsing their faces. Is this genius? Far from it. Because he already knows who is likely behind the mask, he can make the assumption of identity with success."

"And?"

"The same holds true for me and music. I do not need to know each tune personally to be familiar with its natural structure. Thus I can produce it after a listen and generally get the notes right."

"Feel free to ignore the explanation," Owen says. "It is ridiculous."

"I shall ignore it, Mr Connor," Hugh Maguire replies, once again strapping his palm. "Just as I shall feel free to ignore further interruptions by you of a private conversation."

"I am not blind to music," Carolan says in haste. "I see it, in effect. Directly in front of me, without impediments or distractions. When I had sight, I saw nothing. Now the notes appear behind my eyes in their inviolable order. It is not my own doing, I swear. It was certainly not my choice."

"None of us chooses our lives," Owen says.

"True."

"And yet a person makes many clear-eyed choices," the colonel says, definitely not to Carolan. "Choices that can, in turn, become his life, for better or for worse. He can choose whether to steal from those who have sheltered him under their roof, for instance. He can choose whether to stand like a gentleman or flee like a thief."

"'I am his Highness' dog at Kew,'" Owen recites. "'Pray tell me, sir, whose dog are you?'"

The Pope epigram. Carolan has long worried that his guide's admiration of those lines would bring him grief.

"That is your reply? The levelling of further insult?"

"My reply to what, Colonel?"

"Friends . . ." Carolan says.

"Do you take me for a bounder as well, Mr Carolan? The rest of them do. My uncle's pious wife and loafing companions. The staff at Tempo, most of whom have sunk to the level of their betters. Do you, like your reckless servant, also think me worse still than a planter—a Williamite mercenary using the Penals to secure his fortune?"

Carolan feels for Colonel Maguire. The feelings are different from those he holds for Grainne Connelly or Thady Bourke, but still real. No one can enjoy being haunted by ambition. No one can wish his intelligence capped or his empathies compromised by the age. A man should possess instincts about whom to serve and what to believe, and those impulses should never cost him a night's rest. A war waged on others can produce a conflagration. A war on the self can end only in immolation, a few charred bones left smouldering.

But he hasn't time for the colonel. Owen Connor must claim all his attention at present. Does Carolan know what his guide needs most? He certainly has a list of his own requirements. He needs a wash and a groom, a feed and a hogshead of ale. He needs a warm bed and purring cat, the fire smoored and the window left open for birdsong. He needs Mrs Mac's adoration and Betty O'Neill's barleycakes, the press of Annie MacManus's bosom while she arranges his sheets. As for company, he requires the fellowship of those who appreciate tales of Con Maguire and the Siege of Derry, and admire saucy lyrics praising milk-white breasts. Men with a touch of the old madness yet in them. Who hold sobriety in frank disregard.

He needs his nostrils cleared and ears deforested.

His nails clipped.

And Owen Connor gone from his side.

Better, Owen must be banished from his master and the estate where he has spent most of his life.

No!

Not into the clutches of Friar Seamus either, whose radicalism is too bitter and whose persuasions may be too strong.

It is what Carolan can still do for Owen. His farewell to the boy, who he has loved more actively, he suspects, than his own son.

"My question does not merit the honour of a reply? . . . Mr Carolan?"

"Apologies, Colonel Maguire," he answers. "My mind drifted. You were asking?"

"The matter is of no consequence," the colonel says in apparent dejection.

Carolan recalls Maguire's jeremiad. "I believe County Fermanagh is where you now live?" he asks.

"It is."

"And I believe more and more Irishmen reside in France and Spain and across the seas in the various colonies?"

Hugh Maguire agrees to this contention as well.

"With so many Irish now gone abroad, and so many English and Scots come here," Carolan says, "it is clear even to the likes of me that a man belongs where he dwells, not where he was born."

The colonel, hearing some form of endorsement in this muddled remark, issues profuse thanks.

Carolan asks Owen to assist him back onto Geminiani.

"As for you, Mr Connor—our business is not done."

For my sake, Colonel, Carolan almost says. But Owen would never forgive him such a plea.

"Gordon Smith informs me that two books went missing from the library at Tempo last night, and you are responsible. The volume of

Newton you may keep, as I can make no sense of his discussion of optics. But your lifting of the philosophical work from the table next to the reading chair is unacceptable. The volume is signed, sir, and though the inscription isn't to me, it is to someone I hold dear. As well, I happened to be reading Francis Hutcheson just yesterday afternoon."

"Francis Hutcheson?"

The name seems to shock Owen more than the accusation.

"Author of the second volume you thieved," Colonel Maguire says. "The one published anonymously."

"I trust the volume you mention will prove an edifying read, Colonel," his guide says. "It and the Newton."

"Then you don't possess these books?"

"Correct. And kindly remove your hands from that saddlebag."

Carolan's chin sinks at the lie.

"Have you no sense at all?" Colonel Maguire asks.

"Why would I, being a mere boatman?"

"Master Carolan, oblige your friend to see the reason here. I ask only for the return of what is rightfully mine."

Owen mutters under his breath. The comment, concerning the rightful ownership of a wife's jewels, is the sort of provocation that could get any man, squire or servant, run through with a blade.

"Much as I might wish to," Carolan answers, "I fear I lack the influence. Today, at least, I do. But if in the future I am able to impose my—*wooh!*"

His guide hoists him into the saddle without the usual warning count. The thrust nearly hurtles Carolan up and over Gem.

"I shall wait a fortnight before pursuing further action, out of respect for you," Colonel Maguire says to him.

He manages a head bow.

"Beyond that period and you shall be hearing from me, Mr Connor."

"I look forward to the communication," Owen says.

Now miserable, Carolan nearly forgets to show his own respect. "Thank you for helping me to my chamber last night, Colonel," he says. "It was most kind."

"Common courtesy," Hugh Maguire replies.

He rides off.

❈ ❈ ❈

"It's home for us," Carolan says once the hoof-fall has receded.

"Mohill?"

"Alderford."

"You've two daughters in that Mohill cottage who would be delighted to be given the chance to nurse their father back to health."

"You'll bring them around to Alderford when it is time. Today we are bound for the estate of my matron, also your very own hearth. The both of us have affairs needing to be settled there."

"We do?"

Carolan clicks his tongue at Gem. To his surprise the horse heeds his command.

"I'd appreciate a quiet ride down to Councillor Brady's," he says. "To clear my head a bit."

"And dissolve into the rain?"

"If I'm able."

"I am sorry about all this, Terence."

"I know you are."

"Can I be allowed to defend myself?"

"Perhaps later."

"I never intended to—"

"It's some deep thinking I need to do," he says. "You know how rarely I give that summit a climb."

"I'll leave you to it, then," Owen answers after a silent struggle.

He has much of the plan already formed. Before the day is over

Carolan will declare himself needing a respite from travel. He will plead sore fingers and fatigue. He will express a desire to redress those lost years as a composer. Now that Owen has informed him of the lapse, he wishes to take prompt action. He is too old to be composing on horseback or in someone's parlour, especially if he hopes to craft the sort of tune of which his guide believes him capable. A melody featuring more of himself. A melody like no other. To compose it will require robust health and extended quiet. Alderford is the place for the task.

In the meanwhile Owen will want to keep busy. He can journey over to Dublin for a spell or even across the waters to London. Carolan and Mary Macdermott Roe will supply letters of introduction. Patrick Delany, for instance, will recall Owen from their visits to his chambers in Trinity or the house in Stafford Street. Thomas Sheridan may remember the tall fellow who accompanied the harper to Quilca, on the occasion they dined with Swift. Or even the Dean himself, if he is in his right head on the afternoon Owen calls into the deanery behind St Patrick's. Scattered across the country are lords and ladies, squires and bishops, of long personal acquaintance. To a person they hold Terence Carolan in the highest esteem. They also have interests in mercantile and shipping enterprises both here and abroad. These patrons will be only too happy to grant his request for a position for his guide, a youngish man of singular character and potential.

Sixty days is all the task should require. If postal facilities or bad weather extend the period, so be it. He has the leisure. Once Owen is resettled, with Friar Seamus out of favour and Annie MacManus his intended, Carolan will consider his own prospects. But then perhaps he will never again worry over time or the future. So many things are in ruins now. So many things are gone. Among them the bluebells boy and the itinerant harper, whom some insisted on calling a bard. It isn't only that he is sixty-seven and a wreck. It may be that Himself has passed on as well. He is No One, in effect, now and forever. Or else He is the strange notion that all of us, from all times gone by, are Everyone, united beneath a dome of sky identical in curvature and light to the eye of a newborn. Is this vague thought a heresy? Carolan can't think how it could be. Better, he can't think how a man as conventionally devout, and meekly supplicant, as he is would be capable of holding a thought at variance with God. Everyone is rain drone and bird call and the meows of a starving kitten. Everyone is *hush, woman,* and *there, there* and *ladly-dol-da-dee.* Tap it out, one-two-three. Not so jaunty or spry. More slow and ruminative. A threnody of sorts.

He can't breathe sometimes for missing her.

And wishes to be with her again.

Reunited with his family and his Lord.

"There's a lad," he says again after an hour of riding.

"I am sorry for the trouble I've caused you," Owen Connor resumes at once. "You don't know how sorry I am."

His friend is suffering. But Carolan can't share these autumnal deliberations with him. Yet in the late spring of life, more or less, Owen is rightly anticipating the summer ahead, the long days and short nights, the blossom and bloom and fruits ripening on the vines. Wishing to offer reassurance, he reaches across the gap between the horses. Owen squeezes his hand, his palm moist. *The Lord is my shepherd,* Carolan wants to tell him. *I shall lack nothing. He guides me in righteousness for His name's sake.*

"My dear boy . . ." he begins instead.

Part II

~

BALLACH

(Freckled)

CHAPTER ONE

October 1, 1737

When he opens his eyes, it is light. And she is there.

Not his birth mother, obviously. Nor Teresa Devaney, the woman at the charity school in Sligo. Even Mary Macdermott Roe, the only "mother" Owen has known, isn't the face he sees when he awakens that morning. It is Annie MacManus, scullery maid and nag. The most annoying girl in Leitrim. Also the most radiant creature in Connacht, especially framed by autumn light across a floor.

Small wonder he often fails to hold her actual gaze or that her smile causes him a hiccup of nervous excitement. Annie looks the way she does; regrettably, so does Owen. As usual, the eyes tell most of the tale. His are watery and dull, a fish after the life has gone out of it. She claims his irises are easy to misread. Where others discern severity, she notes shyness. Where others glean pride, she recognizes both a hunger for affection and a shame at the craving.

Being homely does not serve his confidence. For Owen, standing before a mirror is akin to stepping on the same rake over and over. He can live with the fox hair, despite how it curls and frays like the fleece of a sheep left unshorn for a winter. He can stomach the pinched forehead and bony skull, a telltale sign that forceps were employed at birth, with fatal consequences for the mother if not the child. He can even abide the liver lips and missing upper right tooth, which is doing him scant good stored in an old snuffbox.

What he can't accept are the freckles. He is smeared in them. Better, he is lathered: ears and nose and cheeks and chin, chest and arms and belly. Achilles emerged from his drenching with a heel tragically unprotected. Owen Connor was dropped into the vat and left for drowned, a comedic touch.

Owen Ballach.

With the freckled member and spotted sack.

Annie MacManus might quit saying she likes her lads the pink of undercooked pig if she learns of that blemish.

Now, hours after her face helped him greet the day, he checks the looking glass a final time, damping the curls with spit. Lunch lies a copse and a horse pasture to the west. He has missed the actual meal and worries that the cook, Betty O'Neill, may have closed the kitchen, reducing him to another feed of bread and cheese. Removed from household noises and idle chatter, he often loses track of the hour. As exiles go, the cottage in the woods up behind the manor isn't perfect. But if a person has serious reading to do, he can't ask for better. In the thirty-one nights Owen has passed here since their return from Tempo, he hasn't once failed to silently thank Mary Macdermott Roe for evicting him from the main house.

Newton's *Optics* owns his attention this afternoon. So much so, he opens the ill-framed door without so much as a parting glance at himself. He wears boots and breeches, a collarless shirt and wool vest. The same outfit as yesterday, he grants, and the days preceding it.

Light, Sir Isaac Newton discovered, is composed of coloured rays that fall upon surfaces in a predetermined order. Newton used prisms to separate out the spectrum. There are seven constituent colours: red and orange, yellow and green, blue, indigo and violet-purple. But then why does light—the brightening light, say, of the pasture up ahead—appear to the naked eye as white? On account of how those rays are united. And for what reason do colours arise within nature in the first instance? Related to the disposition of bodies to reflect certain rays while absorbing others.

Simple enough. If Hugh Maguire can truly make no sense of Newton, as he confessed on the path below Tempo, then the colonel must have found a lively intelligence harder to purchase than an army commission. Admittedly, the section in the *Optics* out lining the "corpuscular theory of light" is more challenging. Those coloured rays within a band are actually arrangements of hard objects like billiard balls called "movable particles." Light beams consist of particles. So do trees and rocks. People as well, if Owen understands the theory correctly. He tried sketching it the other evening, using his own corporeal self as model:

According to Isaac Newton, the particles are in perpetual motion, splitting apart and then coming back together. All changes in nature result from various associations between them. He identified two types: "fragment particles" and "entire particles." Earth and water are entire ones. Lesser entities are fragments, inclined to knock about until they can be formed or reformed. The problem is, both kinds are too small for the human eye to discern without prisms. All this thrilling activity—the very mechanics of the universe, Newton claimed—and no one can see it, except by refracting light through cut-glass pendants onto a bare wall.

Owen certainly can't. He has reread the pages detailing the "corpuscular theory of light" a dozen times without quite grasping their essence. The difficulty, he suspects, lies in the language needed to describe the science. He keeps hearing a metaphor where none is probably intended. Take the "fragment" versus "entire" particle notion. Terence Carolan must be a full particle, akin to the ocean or the sky. Owen Connor, in contrast, is a fragment. He is in bits, his various impulses and inclinations churning within his head the way dust motes churn in a shaft of light. Annie is probably an entire fragment, along with Betty O'Neill. Mary Macdermott Roe is definitely fragmented. With Flinn, he can't really tell.

And his friend Friar Seamus? As big a mess as the man is, he starts from a larger, more compelling particle, Owen decides.

The horses feed at the north end of the pasture. Even on a fine day the field holds a low mist within its fencing, like a bowl of boiled water that confines the steam inside its rim. "Afternoon, Gulliver," Owen calls. "Greetings to you, too, Geminiani."

How many movable particles does each of those animals contain? A staggering quantity, he guesses. Jonathan Swift would likely declare the creatures divine and indivisible, and brook no dispute from any inferior Yahoo mind.

❊   ❊   ❊

He kicks his boots clean of mud and removes his hat. The door is open, the kitchen floor four steps down.

"Peace on this house."

The servant hall is empty, except for her.

"If it isn't Owen Ballach."

"Where's Betty?"

"Having a rest, as she does at this hour every afternoon."

"Right."

"Come in, Owen. Don't be afraid."

Annie MacManus stands at the sink plucking a chicken. Her tugs are brisk, cording her forearms, and the pits of her dress are stained. Her upper lip also perspires, strands of her hair come loose.

"How's Annie?"

"Grand."

"Yes?"

"Why wouldn't I be?"

She stops to examine him.

"You're doing better than that bird, at least," he says, returning her look. An instant later he is studying the floor again.

The scullery maid has staring eyes. If she needs to blink, she makes certain to first turn away. Though her lashes may be as luxuriant as cat whiskers, he doubts they can protect her lenses. Penny round and protuberant, Annie's eyes remind Owen of a harvest moon in a cold sky. The whites are of pearl and the irises of azure. The pupils, diamond in configuration, are permanently wide, as if on the verge of still more astonishment. A man could easily find himself within those pupils, he suspects, and grow addicted to the sightings.

As for the rest of her face—her cheeks, nose and lips, the smile that pulls across her mouth, dimpling the corners, and the chin she keeps high, as if to grant admirers a better profile—the rest of her face merely causes his breathing to turn choppy. Her nut-brown hair, combed tight and tied with a headscarf, has the same effect, along with her swan neck. Even the base of her throat, a shallow pool where perspiration often gathers, can alter his respiration.

Now Annie stands beneath a rectangular window that angles light down into the kitchen between noon and four o'clock most days. Yellow-white light, to the pre-Newton eye.

"Do you know what an anchoress is, Annie?"

"A what?"

"My friend Seamus was telling me about them. Devout women from olden times who asked to be sealed into the walls of cathedrals and shrines so they could give over their lives to God. They spent the remainder of their days imprisoned in the buildings, with only a tiny window for receiving food and passing chamber pots. People went to them for blessings."

"Where was this?"

"France and Spain and maybe England. Long ago," Owen says, noting how her form blends with the light. She raises her chin for his benefit, like a model at the request of the artist painting her.

"I've never been to Carrick, Owen."

"I realize."

"What made you think of these . . . what did you call them?"

"Anchoresses. No reason," he answers.

He is being less than truthful. The sunlight hardly incarcerates Annie MacManus. But in other respects she is trapped within her body. A full-grown adult, Annie rises to just above Owen's mid-section. The deformity, the result of her having drunk infected milk as a child, curved her spine, stunting her torso and legs. Because her head is of normal size, it appears gargantuan, the kind found on certain marionettes. Her breasts as well, belonging to a buxom female, resemble a yoke rather than a natural endowment. Born in the hamlet outside the gate, the scullery maid has never travelled more than six miles in any direction from it, including beyond the church at Keadew, where she attends mass along with Mrs Mac and the rest of the household staff. She tires easily and perspires readily and requires unscheduled days off, which she spends "resting" in the room next to the kitchen that she shares with the chambermaid Bridget O'Donnell.

"And for all that, I've still been kissed before, Owen Connor," she suddenly says. "Have you?"

Not exactly, would be the honest reply. His innocence is still another source of embarrassment. Blame the shyness that Annie routinely notes or the ugliness he confirmed in that self-portrait. Also, the motherless childhood that has left him in muddled awe of women. Blame Carolan even, or rather his loins, for the lesson— taken perhaps too much to heart by Owen—that the mere brush of a wife's cheek with your lips could induce a swollen belly.

At first he was astounded by how Annie could intuit his thoughts. Her gift rivalled his own with his master. She eventually confessed the secret of her skill. "It's not your mind that I read," she said. "It's your face. You've no knack for disguising what you are thinking."

The consequence of years keeping company with a blind man, Owen concluded. He was no longer fit for the intricacies of sighted discourse.

"I should be on my way," he answers now. He will find some food later.

Annie flashes a pout, presumably at his refusal to joust. "A bit early to be calling on Master Carolan, isn't it?"

"I thought I'd visit Flinn first."

"Flinn?" she says. "He'll be delighted, especially if it's your backside you show him, walking up the drive to the gate."

"How do you mean?"

"He believes you are bringing disrepute upon this house and the name Macdermott Roe. He thinks Mr Carolan's reputation is also suffering. But Flinn is a dour old man," she adds with false insouciance.

"He shared his opinion with you?"

"Not me. Betty."

"When did this happen?"

"There was post this morning," the maid says.

"Right."

"Flinn studied one envelope closely and seemed to find it grave. Mrs Mac met him out on the landing."

"I'd best go see about that letter."

"Owen?"

"Yes?"

"You're at it again."

"At what?"

She is silent.

He has cupped his right elbow in his palm and raised the hand to his face, the inset of his thumb resting on his cheekbone. He is massaging his forehead with his fingertips. *Tap, tap, tap,* the sound faint and internal, like a mouse gnawing on wood somewhere inside a house.

"I've suffered a sore head since I was a boy," he says.

"But don't you get aches only at certain times?"

He is still tapping. The motion spreads the pain out, thinning it. "When sedentary," he admits.

"And you haven't stepped foot off this estate in a month?"

"Carolan is still recovering."

She bites her lip, flushing the lower one pink.

"And yes, I had the dream last night," he adds, guessing her thought.

"You did?"

An incorrect guess, apparently.

"It doesn't matter," he says.

"The dream about a winter storm?"

"Never mind."

"Blowing snow and howling wind?" Annie MacManus asks. "Unmarked graves and abandoned cottages with their doors ajar?"

"You remember the details better than I do."

"It sent a chill up my spine," she says, rubbing her arms.

Absurdly, the remark causes his groin to tingle.

"I'd best be going," Owen repeats. His hands are now back in his pockets.

"The master was telling me his dream earlier today," she says.

"Which one?"

"About meeting Bridget Cruise in the cave on Station Island."

"That's what it is, Annie," Owen says. "A dream."

"He believes it happened."

"He is mistaken."

"There's no cause for that tone."

"The reunion occurred only in his imagination," he says.

"Fine."

"I'm just telling you."

"He begged the loan of my hand," she says, her smile so bright he almost shields his eyes. "He must have held it for ten minutes, turning it over and rubbing it like a sacred stone, mumbling about my bone steps."

"Bone stems," he corrects without pleasure.

"What are they again?"

"He begs the hand of every woman who enters his lair," Owen says. "Along with the paws of hounds."

"Aren't we sour this afternoon."

"And aren't we sweet."

"Flinn is out in the manor," she says, returning to her yellow-white light and half-plucked bird. "Go on with you."

As always, he is grateful for her tolerance.

* * *

He finds the butler behind the table in the dining hall. Flinn is on both knees, shifting cuts of turf from a wicker basket into the creel beside the hearth. His motions, as slow and deliberate as those of a priest consecrating a host, mesmerize Owen. J. Flinn, whose first name is almost certainly Joseph—he will neither confirm nor deny it—has been in the employ of the Macdermott Roes since well before the Battle of the Boyne. As a young butler he knew the Meath-transplants John and Mary Carolan, plus their children, Terence and Katherine. He recalls Terence as a genial boy, bright-eyed and obedient, if far from the sharpest spade in the soot house. His younger sister Kate had shown the real glint, poor girl. Flinn was sixty when the foundling Owen Connor was first brought to Alderford. He sided against the new arrival from the start and has declined ever since to moderate his view.

"Any post today, Flinn?"

"Eh? Someone there?"

"It's Owen."

The butler turns in the direction of the doorway. His face has long ago sunk onto the bones of his skull, his eyes hooded by scrub-brush brows. "I didn't notice you, Owen Connor."

Carolan once compared Flinn's voice to the scrape of a knife over toasted bread. Burnt toast, he specified.

Knowing the old man's game, Owen waits.

"You were asking after the post from Carrick? There were letters, aye—a fair few of them."

He waits longer.

"None of the envelopes, as I recall, had the good fortune to possess your name on it."

"I wasn't expecting any would."

"Then you must be satisfied."

He will beg no further.

"One or two to Mrs Mac, it's true," Flinn says. "But mostly addressed to Master Carolan himself."

"He has received more post in the past four weeks than in the entire preceding year," Owen says.

"Stands to reason, given the quantity of letters he is writing," the butler replies. He climbs to his feet, his frame shuddering. "I can manage the turf myself, thanks," he adds.

"Carolan, writing letters?"

"Daily."

"Not by my hand. Though it ought to be, given that such a task is one of my official duties."

"Official duties?"

"As his personal guide."

"Ah," Flinn says. "It's Mary Mac herself who takes the dictation. Then seals the envelopes, and addresses them, and passes them on to me for forwarding to the courier."

Owen is careful to swallow the news without, he hopes, any betrayal of emotion. "Planning future travels, I would imagine," he says. "He is anxious to be out again as an itinerant."

"Is he?"

"We discussed a swing through Galway and then a ramble over to Longford and Meath. Home before Christmas, with any luck."

"You discussed this when?"

"Shortly before he made pilgrimage."

Flinn keeps nodding. Again Owen thinks of a priest, raising the host in response to the bells.

"I'm for a pipe in the staff hall," the butler says.

"Flinn," he says in exasperation.

"I serve what I am ordered to serve, Owen. Burgundy and port, whiskey and March ale. In noggins or beakers. In buckets better used for catching rainwater, even, if such a vessel is requested. It isn't for the likes of me to decide who has reached his capacity. Especially with a gathering of gentlemen."

A fair remark, Owen acknowledges. But he wasn't planning to berate his fellow manservant about the drinking parties in Carolan's chamber.

"You never married?" he asks instead.

The brows flare, revealing irises the grey of an autumn storm cloud. Flinn's eyeballs jiggle in their sockets. "Beg pardon?"

"All these years by yourself?"

"I share a room with John Stamford."

And have never been kissed before, either? he thinks to himself.

"Married to the service, I suppose," Flinn says.

"And children?"

"What about them?"

"No regrets at not becoming a father?" Owen says.

"Some."

"There was never a girl?"

"Not for me," the old man answers. He fixes his best effort at a direct gaze upon Owen. "A letter arrived today from Tempo, now that I think on it. From the pen of Brian Maguire."

Owen thanks him with a weak smile.

"Ask her ladyship," Flinn says. "She unsealed it on the stairs up to his room."

* * *

It isn't for the likes of J. Flinn to question a gentleman's capacity. Neither is it for the likes of Owen Connor to beg the senior butler for scraps of information about the daily mail, regardless if the contents pertain to his own fate. Owen has been entertaining such distinctions, and abiding by them, his entire life. Even so, the rules confuse and frustrate him, inducing outbursts of verbal disobedience and sporadic, ill-reasoned acts of rebellion—such as, he supposes, thieving books from libraries. His conversation with Flinn recalls his encounter with the stableboy at Tempo, Thomas O'Hara, in the wake of the incident with Colonel Maguire in the dining room. The disaster of that night had yet to fully flower. Exhilarated by his verbal sparring with the colonel, whose insults of Carolan had been outrage enough to risk a rapier thrust, Owen eventually persuaded Thady Bourke that he was both cooled off and calmed down and could be trusted to sit alone in the Tempo staff hall. Thady, it was true, refused him permission to go put his master to bed, making Owen promise to keep to the servants' quarters until morning.

He chanced upon Thomas O'Hara smoking a pipe outside the scullery door. A lanky, mop-haired boy with his own freckle smudges across the cheeks, Thomas pronounced himself now almost fifteen and near ready to begin shaving. To celebrate this doubtful fact, Owen filled two beakers of ale from the barrel, dismissing Thomas's worry that they were breaking manor rules. They hid behind the stables.

"It's a mad thing you've gone and done, Mr Connor," the boy

said, shyly clinking noggins with him. "The colonel has a terrible temper."

"As do I, Thomas," Owen replied. "As do I."

"He lands blows across the back of your skull that kick the feet out from under you."

When Owen asked if Colonel Maguire had ever hit him, the youth said he'd deserved it, both times. "Did he discover your caricature of him inside Brian Maguire's chamber pot?" he asked.

Thomas O'Hara shook his head so emphatically that he spilled the ale he seemed too nervous to enjoy. "You didn't tell him of it, did you, sir?" he answered with frank alarm.

Owen assured him, falsely, that the drawing was a secret Brian Maguire shared with only his most trustworthy friends.

Thomas nearly wept in relief. "I was loath to fulfil that commission," he said, "especially once my mother warned that I could be dismissed from Tempo, should the colonel find out. But Sir Brian pressed me into it, claiming no harm could come from such a lark." Then, after a pause in which what little spirit the lad possessed drained from his eyes with the inevitability of liquid from a tipped noggin: "He's right, Mr Connor, isn't he? That drawing won't cost my position in the stable? I don't know what would become of me if I lost my service here."

The exchange deflated Owen more than a single glass of ale could account for. He had planned to while away the evening reminiscing with Thomas O'Hara about his own early days at Alderford. He, too, had started off as a stableboy, sleeping in the loft and enjoying evenings in the staff hall listening to John Glavin's tales of his adventures as guide to the blind harper Terence Carolan, dear friend of Mary and Henry Macdermott Roe and a frequent resident at Alderford, a genial but distracted man whose reputation as both a drinker and composer of tunes preceded his every tour across the land. Owen had planned to mention to Thomas the daily lessons he took in the Alderford library, at the insistence of Sir Henry, who had resolved to educate a lowly orphan alongside his own sons, as if to groom him for some greater task than stableboy or manservant. He might even have described the afternoon in 1717 when her ladyship, Mary Mac, invited him into the large sitting room and inquired whether Owen, though only eighteen, might be ready to assume the duties managed by John Glavin, whose chronic sore back now prevented him from riding a horse for any period, and become the new guide of that same Terence Carolan. A commission of the highest importance, Mary Macdermott Roe had stressed. A rare opportunity for a youth such as himself.

Owen had planned to respect Thady Bourke's wishes that he lie low until sunrise, while also doing lanky, freckled Thomas O'Hara a good turn by sharing these details of his own life, outlining one path to social betterment. But the boy's timidity soured Owen, and after swearing on his honour not to tell anyone else about the caricature, he snuck upstairs first for a peek at the infamous chamber pot—he still isn't sure why he informed Carolan he urinated in the bowl, and in the company of the fledging artist—and then for a chat with his master. Finally, he resolved to pay a visit to the small library situated down the hall from Carolan's room. The library boasted a decent collection of books, knowledge free to any man learned in words, along with a door that could no longer be locked.

* * *

He runs into his mistress at the bottom of the landing to the second floor. Owen, at least, is on the first step, ready to climb. Mary Macdermott Roe waits at the top, staring down at him, hands on her hips.

He heeds the warning.

"It's still early," she says.

"Good day, Mrs Mac."

"Your afternoon appointment isn't for another ninety minutes."

"I am aware," he answers, his fingers once more plying his forehead. If remaining still for too long won't induce the aches, the disapprobation of Mary Macdermott Roe will. No one expresses disapproval with the same sting as his employer, or leaves Owen feeling so cowed.

"Five to six o'clock," she says. "A generous allotment."

Now Mary Mac expects him to be grateful for his full hour with Carolan each afternoon, in addition to a fifteen-minute morning slot. On this matter, he cannot oblige her.

"A schedule was necessary," she says to his silence.

"I'm sure."

"He was entertaining visitors at all hours of the day and night and getting no rest. Someone had to establish order."

"You are just the person for it."

She squints down at him, her brow furrowing. "Did I banish you from the room next to your master's?" she asks.

"Not exactly."

"Not at all."

He shrugs.

"What did I ask of you, Owen?"

As the question is rhetorical, he does not reply to it.

"Only that you return the books to Colonel Maguire, and so avoid prosecution as a thief and dishonour as a man. That, or else remove yourself to the cottage. You chose of your own free will."

"Yes, I did."

"You chose to exile yourself."

"Not such a distant exile," Owen says. "Not like Aeneas."

"This is amusing?"

"Definitely not."

"I am not amused."

"I gather."

"Terence is not amused."

"If you say."

"Nor are your fellow household servants. You bring disgrace not only upon yourself, but upon all of us."

"I'll come back in ninety minutes."

"And why aren't you wearing any of the clothes that are your natural fit?" she demands next, her forehead unclenching.

"Mrs Mac?"

"The trunk. You can't have forgotten it?"

He hasn't forgotten. His ladyship sent him two gifts within twenty-fours of his departure from her house. The first was a hefty candlestick with a circular base and a sconce covered in silver wall plates. Though ostentatious, the candlestick has proven useful, especially for night reading. The second gift consisted of a wooden trunk with leather straps and the Macdermott Roe crest across its top. Inside the trunk are shoes and boots, kneesocks and pantaloons, frilly shirts and scarves. There are two waistcoats with twenty buttons each and a cloak blended of cotton and wool. There is a wig. The wardrobe belongs to a country squire with a fashion flare but a suspect eye for colours. It belonged, more exactly, to Henry Macdermott Roe, Owen's saviour and mentor. Sir Henry had been of equal height. He had also been cursed with the same maypole frame, including hip bones that protruded like helmet nosepieces and a stomach more concave than flat. None of his own five sons inherited his physique. Only the stableboy Owen Connor grew to be a match.

Even so, the gift makes no sense. Henry Macdermott Roe died in a riding accident in 1727. Owen was just as tall and shabbily attired eleven autumns ago. Why offer the clothes now? And for what occasion is he dressing? A masquerade, by his own guess.

"Do you disapprove of Sir Henry's garments?" she asks.

"Hardly."

"Then why not wear them?"

Owen can't think of an excuse. "I'd look an impostor in such finery, wouldn't I?" he answers.

"My husband did not look an impostor."

"But he was Sir Henry Macdermott Roe."

"And you are Owen Connor."

Her reply is meant to be kind. But he can't quite believe her sentiment and doubts she believes it, either.

"Was Annie MacManus in the kitchen?" Mary Mac says.

"She was."

"And you saw her?"

"I did."

"May I ask on what subject you spoke?"

"The wonder of women incarcerating themselves inside the walls of cathedrals, the better to serve the Lord."

"Owen?"

"The plucking of fowl," he corrects.

He wishes she would descend the twenty steps to address him on his level. Unless she starts down the staircase, he can't start up it. There is an emblem in their respective postures, Owen recognizes. She is at the top, elevated by her standing, and he is at the bottom, his assigned rung.

"Terence still rests?" he asks.

"He bathes."

"Again?"

"He enjoys a long soak twice daily now," Mary Macdermott Roe says. Try as she might, she can't conceal her own disbelief at the routine.

"Any chance he could be composing?"

Though the second floor is in gloom, Owen's eyesight—the vision of a horse, Carolan once complimented—allows him to note how she cocks her head at the query, a curious bird.

"A new tune," he expounds. "A new sort of tune, even. He said he hoped to try something different."

"Different? Terence Carolan?"

"Why not him?"

"When did he supposedly make this remark?"

Owen has trouble affixing a date to the conversation. "On the road to Tempo," he answers, "after our night in Kesh. No, that can't be right. He was in no condition to discuss music that morning."

"In the wake of the accident with the child?"

He had told the other servants the tale of Carolan's attempt to hoist Deirdre Connelly into the sky. For his trouble he was hauled in twice by Mrs Mac to repeat the story, the second instance in the presence of the family physician, Brian Lynch. The doctor assailed him with questions.

"There was no accident," he says once more. "He tossed and then caught a wee girl. She was sickly and has since died, I assume."

"Terence did not suffer some kind of paralysis?"

"Possibly," he says. "Though the term is Dr Lynch's."

"He did not lose his powers of speech for an entire morning?" Mary Mac says, endeavouring to hide her dismay behind a tongue-lashing. "Along with all sensation down one side of his body?"

Owen is quiet.

"An injury that might have been prevented had you made more effort to intervene?"

"We've discussed this already, Mrs Mac."

"You were his guide."

"I guided him away from Tempo, didn't I?"

"Are you implying there was actual danger at the Maguire estate?"

"Not necessarily. But there was disorder and dissoluteness. Terence is affected by such an atmosphere. His spirits, and maybe his health, would have further deteriorated had we not departed."

"Preposterous," Mary Mac says. Her expression, though, suggests she knows already what he reports. The decline of Tempo has been the subject of much discussion among the gentry of neighbouring Leitrim and Roscommon.

"The roads of Ulster are less and less safe these days," he says, "and the rutted paths of Connacht scarcely any better. As I am still his guide, I will continue to see him safely along those roads, regardless of his own navigation impulses."

"You needn't worry about that any longer," she says under her breath.

"Beg pardon?"

Mary Macdermott Roe refuses to repeat the assertion. Instead she looks towards Carolan's chamber, which stands out of Owen's frame of vision. From behind the door comes the sound of water sloshing in a tub.

Owen suddenly understands why she isn't descending the stairs. She is barring him from climbing them. He must swallow three times to digest his bitterness.

"His fingernails . . ." he says.

She cocks her head again.

"He plays only brass strings. Yet someone—Flinn, I assume—trimmed his nails to the pink. They'll take weeks to grow back."

"Terence requested the manicure."

"But how will he compose?"

"You are too much in a hurry," she says, shifting again into kindness. "Let him recover first. Give him time."

"He's lost so much of it already."

"How so?"

"He hasn't got forever, Mrs Mac."

"Neither have you, Owen."

Aware that he has squandered her limited goodwill, he humbly inquires about the contents of the morning post.

CHAPTER TWO

November 6, 1737

She enters without knocking and drags the chair to his bed. Though Owen has been anticipating her return for hours, her staring eyes and pressed lips, how she rehooks strands of hair behind her ears, he feigns indifference.

"It's you," he finally says.

"Your lashes are crusted together," Annie MacManus observes. "Should I give them a wipe?"

Pulling himself up on his elbows, he clears the grit before she can.

Annie, whose own brow is dappled, gives Owen a slow, unblinking once-over. She must notice his bristly cheeks and oily skin, the orange mop in need of a wash. She must remark on the cap and shirt he has worn for a day and night and day again of immobility.

"I tried crossing to the hearth yesterday," Owen says, wetting his fingers with his tongue and pressing the hair down, "to peek in the mirror. I am a fright, I'm sure."

She makes no reply.

"Halfway across the floor my head began to throb again. I had to counsel myself to take my skull in my hands and walk it back to the bed, laying it atop the pillow as though it were a porcelain vase."

"I've brought the physician," Annie says.

"I asked you not to."

"He can help."

"It is well established that the doctor can do no such thing."

"Good morning, Owen Connor."

"Dr Lynch," Owen says to the figure in the doorway.

"Annie tells me you've a worse ache than usual?"

"Longer in duration, at any rate," he answers.

Brian Lynch, a portly man with lopsided shoulders that lend him a weary posture and eyes expanded to twice their natural size by spectacles, groans as he sits on the mattress. He has already passed judgement on the chamber, using first a frown and then a jiggle of the jowls.

"We've never gotten to the bottom of these periodic aches, have we?" he says, pinching Owen's wrist.

"I can't recall a time when they didn't bedevil me."

"As far back as the orphanage?"

"A charity school, it was called," Owen says. "Run by pious laywomen at the behest of the remaining Dominicans in the abbey."

"Was there any charity shown to the foundlings who boarded there?"

"We were fed," he replies. "Twice daily."

"Birchings?"

"It's just an ache, Doctor."

"Always the same spot at the centre of your temple?"

"Like a bull's-eye," he says, aiming for a laugh.

Annie winces instead.

"Most queer," Dr Lynch says. He is now probing the spot with his fingers, as if expecting to find an arrowhead lodged beneath the skin. The pain has its own pulse.

"I'm not bothered by it too much," Owen says. "Except for these past days."

"What do you say, Annie?" the physician asks. "Is Owen better accommodated in this hovel than inside the manor?"

She presses her lips together.

"He is more his own man in this habitat," Owen says.

"His own fool, I dare say."

He shrugs.

"You'll be wanting to render the cottage habitable for the winter months," Brian Lynch offers. "The door does not seal properly and the thatch in that corner won't keep out the January snows. And you've had no luck with that fire, I can tell. James Egan, the boys' final tutor, complained in his day of how the hearth spluttered and gave off insufficient heat, even for so small a space. Then, as now, a proper chimney is required."

"James Egan was my instructor as well," Owen says. "Reading and writing and history and maths. Plus Latin."

He wishes Annie to know this about him.

"A little learning is a dangerous thing, in the wrong hands," the doctor says.

"As is a scalpel."

Dr Lynch concedes a smile. His eyeballs bob behind the lenses as he examines Owen's neck for swelling.

"Regardless, I won't be living here long enough to need fix the hatch or put up a chimney," Owen says.

"No?"

"A month longer at most."

"Then they've found you a new position?"

"A position?"

"An arrangement has been made with one of Terence's patrons?"

His face must register confusion.

"I may have mistaken your meaning," the doctor apologizes.

Owen fights the urge to join the search for that arrowhead. "I assume I'll be off travelling again with Carolan," he says, braiding his fingers in his lap. "He can't still be ill after two months of convalescence, can he?"

Brian Lynch stands back up. "I am not at liberty to discuss his condition," he says, as if reading from a card.

"You can't confine him to bed forever, Doctor. It isn't good for his health, or mine. He hasn't been housebound for such a period in all my days at Alderford."

"Except upon the death of his missus," Annie says.

The men look at her.

"He didn't travel for a full season after Mrs Carolan passed away. Kept to the same room he stays in now, with Mary Mac by his side most daylight hours and long into the evenings."

Her expression betrays no awareness of her own remark. The doctor trades glances with Owen but says nothing. He takes his leave with a bow and a parting frown at the woeful state of the patient or the dwelling—or both.

"I feel better already," Owen says once he is gone.

"His examinations of the master are scarcely more thorough," Annie MacManus says. "I do wonder what yet ails Mr Carolan."

"An excess of whiskey and rum and roast pig and plum pudding, to start. Too many men to drink with and call him the master," he says. "Too many women to indulge his every whim."

She rubs her arms. "Fix the fire, whatever your plans," she says. "There's a deathly chill in here." She does a quick tour of the room. "Flinn told me that John Carolan lived in this cottage for years."

"That's right."

"Was he as kindly as his son?"

"I never met him. But I heard he wasn't."

She nods.

"I mean to do some repairs. The door and the thatch. Maybe a chimney as well, if I'm here much past December. And I did build that shelf, Annie, for my books. Are you impressed?"

Owen wedged two clevies into the wall using brackets and then ran a board across the gap. All twenty-two volumes fit, their spines facing out. Still, the shelf isn't hung evenly, mud-and-wattles affording the brackets a precarious hold.

"Not very, to be honest."

"I've no talent for handiwork," he admits.

When Annie smiles, her eyes glimmer like a cat's in the dark. He watches them until she notices.

"I'd best rest a while longer," Owen says. "Wouldn't want to miss another appointment."

He has not seen Carolan in five days, four of them on account of his trip to Sligo, where he escorted—at his employer's request— Mary Carolan from Mohill to the house of her eldest sister, Siobhan, wife of Captain Allan Smedley. Any further delay will cast him into despair.

"He was asking after you," she says.

"Was he?"

"He inquired every day you were away."

Owen waits several heartbeats before speaking, to dull the yearning. "He must be desperate for a decent conversation. Charles MacCabe and Toby Peyton may provide amusement, but they extend no challenge to his intellect or spur to his creativity. He needs more serious company."

"They were certainly amusing themselves last night."

"Who?"

"The master and Mr MacCabe, along with Councillor Brady and an Italian whose name I can't pronounce. Laughter rang out from his chamber well into the morning hours . . ."

Noting his reaction, she trails off.

"There was music played?" he asks.

"A little," Annie replies, drawing her shawl around her shoulders.

"On the harp?"

"The harp?"

"Did he—Carolan, I mean—perform a few tunes for his loafing, mulvadered friends?"

"The instrument has sat untouched in a corner for nine weeks now, as you well know. Charles MacCabe invited the fiddler Sean Doherty from over in Drumkeeran. The foreign gentleman played the pianoforte."

"In his chamber?"

"Mrs Mac ordered Thomas and James to bring the piano up from the large sitting room. Just for the occasion," she adds with downcast eyes.

"They lugged the pianoforte up all those stairs?"

"I almost forgot," Annie MacManus says from the doorway. "She wants you to have tea with her this afternoon. At four, if you're able."

"Tea? Me?"

"It's what she said."

"Fine."

Light from outside burnishes strands of her hair the gold of poured honey. She presses her lips together again.

"I'm glad you're recovered," she says. "I was worried."

"Thanks, Annie."

"You don't take proper care of yourself."

"It's those books I read."

"I'm serious."

"Thanks," he repeats.

✻ ✻ ✻

Tea with Mrs Mac. Won't that be an occasion. Owen was initiated into tea drinking by none other than Moira Carolan, in the same cottage outside Mohill where he recently collected her youngest daughter for transport to Sligo. Moira introduced him to the beverage better than two decades ago. She loved a steaming cup, and though she never lacked for leaves to brew, thanks to gifts of the fashionable drink extended to her husband by admirers, she often lacked someone to share a pot with, given Carolan's indifference to any liquid that had not been fermented. Owen liked tea just fine. Better, he liked the company of Moira enough to suffer cup after cup of the oriental concoction. He sat with her by the fire while she cooked or sewed. He drew a chair next to their oversized four-poster bed in the sleeping chamber while she nursed a baby, careful to avert his gaze from her chest or from the rumpled sheets and blankets that surrounded her, evidence of nocturnal activities he preferred not to ponder. Her face boasted little of Annie MacManus's high drama, being wide and flat, the mouth plain and the teeth crooked, the eyes so globular and serene they put to mind—or to his mind, anyway—a newborn calf. Owen, though, appreciated that plainness. He appreciated Moira's gentle glint, the placid smile she wore with the same regularity, and for the same reason, as she did her shawl.

Because it fit so naturally and so well.

Not that he ever imposed himself upon her. It was his business to ride down from Alderford to collect his charge, in advance of an arranged visit. He could hardly be blamed for Carolan's inability to prepare himself or even remember the itinerary. A delay of several hours was routine. A wait of a full day and night was far from exceptional. That left time for carving a hurley stick with Tadhg and offering piggyback rides to Siobhan and Martha, playing patty cakes with Anne and Eileen. Time as well for drinking tea with their mother, who was, after all, only seven years his senior and appreciated, he sensed, the company of an adult with whom she could share a grin. If Owen could discern Moira's occasional frustration not so much with her husband's affliction as with the effect of that condition on her—the damping, so to speak, of her own exuberance—it was simply because he experienced the same. Who else could claim fair rivalry to Carolan's attention, if not him? Who else might privately declare himself the harper's principal companion, based on time spent and practical needs fulfilled? Natural, the bond between Carolan's guide and Carolan's wife. They shared the same master.

Owen certainly never meant to spy on Moira feeding or catch a glimpse of her exposed nipple, as he did the morning she abruptly separated a biting infant—Maev, it must have been—from her now mottled flesh. But neither did he intend to chance upon a boy of two or three suckling the breast of his dead mother in a doorway, one of several dismaying scenes witnessed during the winter of 1726. While he eventually described the sight to Carolan, he stopped short of sharing the blasphemous vision that settled unprompted in his brain: here was the Virgin Mary with the Christ child, in eternal repose.

Some things a man just sees, with his eyes or his imagination, and can't forget.

* * *

He has put aside *Optics* in recent days to concentrate on Francis Hutcheson's *An Inquiry into the Original of Our Ideas of Beauty and Virtue*. Here is an argument Owen can follow, even with a sore head. Virtuous actions, the philosopher maintains, arise out of virtuous character. "Good dispositions of mind" cannot be produced solely by instruction. They must be "originally planted in our nature by its great Author, and afterwards straightened and confirmed by our cultivation." But a person of deficient natural quality may be redeemed through reading and writing and beneficial social interactions. By such means, Hutcheson believes, a low man can summon the virtue within his nature and convey it to others.

Finally, a book that addresses his own conditions, and one he feels competent to engage. Owen isn't deluded in thinking a bond exists between him and the author. Francis Hutcheson is no Sir Isaac Newton, his cognitions as beyond mortal grasp as the stars are beyond the earth. Rather, he is a native of Drumalig in County Down. *An Inquiry* was issued in 1725 by a publisher in Dublin, where the philosopher once resided. Owen accompanied Carolan on several tours to the capital that decade. During one visit their host, Patrick Delany, organized a soiree in honour of the harper. Having found Carolan a seat and a glass of claret, Owen withdrew to a corner of the room, where he could both study the crowd and keep an eye on his charge, whose signal that he required assistance often consisted of little more than a raised vessel or a tug on the ear. But then a man, not a fellow servant, approached him. He was a plump fellow of thirty with a soft Ulster accent and no wig. Named Francis—he offered only his Christian title—the man had bright round eyes, their lashes long and feminine. For only the second time ever Owen decided he was admiring the eyes that Terence Carolan would have shown the world, had smallpox not intruded.

As was his custom, he assured Francis that he was present at the soiree to be of service to a guest. He was not important enough to have been invited; he was, in fact, not important at all. The invitation to break off the exchange before it got started rarely met with refusal, he often remarked, especially in Dublin, where a gentleman did not take tea without a strategy. Francis, though, merely grinned at the disclaimer and started asking questions. They wound up chatting about all manner of things, including the Penal Statutes, a subject Owen would never have dared raise, and which dropped his voice to the whisper he normally reserved for dialogues with Carolan. The conversation staggered him. Francis from Ulster treated Owen from Connacht as an equal, paying the compliment of not only listening to his remarks but critiquing them, in the hope of cultivating his thinking. Owen thrilled to the challenge the way a duck thrilled to water. So much so, when his new friend mentioned that he lectured in philosophy at the Academy of Dublin, he blurted out that he would like to be his student one day. Many a member of society would have soured then, as if at a fart. But Francis expressed his sincere hope this event would happen.

They might have talked even longer had not Dr Delany himself, professor of oratory and history at Trinity, requested a word with his colleague. Owen reverted to silence before the clergyman, to avoid seeming presumptuous.

This meeting occurred in the summer of 1727. Owen was twenty-eight, a rare country bumpkin in the capital without a cap or a beggar's bowl in hand. When allowed, he would slip out the back gate of the house in Stafford Street and wander, his pockets empty but his heart bursting. He could count the different Dublins. There were the fashionable new streets and squares southward to Stephen's Green, homes of limestone and granite soaring as high as five storeys above the earth. There were the grounds of Trinity College, where teaching was done in Latin, and of Chichester House across from it on College Green, meeting place of the parliament. Further west lay the castle, residence of the lord-lieutenant, and its barracks, from which power, if not order, emanated. Along the quays below the barracks rival gangs, the Liberty Boys and Ormonde Boys, the Weavers and Butchers, fought bloody battles, often rendering bridges across the Liffey impassable for days on end. Even a tall man ambling in plain sight had reason to worry if he strayed into the Coombe or Oxmontown. Expect an emptied purse and a bump on the head. Don't be surprised if a blade is flashed.

To the west again stood the duke of Ormond's great project, Phoenix Park, a royal deer park larger than the city itself. Servants at the Delany house warned Owen away from the park, as well as from the streets surrounding Kilmainham Hospital and those immediately north of the Customs House on Essex Quay.

But it was the castle district that drew him in, especially the cobbled lanes between the cathedrals. With Christ Church looming behind and St Patrick's rising ahead, the castle in the lee and the river farther below it, Owen could feel at once trapped within the city's maw and secure. His sense of comfort was linked, irrationally, to Jonathan Swift. The author was born in Hoey's Court, a square reached by climbing the slippery slope of Cole's Alley, off Castle Street, and now lived in the residence attached to the cathedral. In those ancient streets, where the brick houses, narrow and gabled, leaned into one another as though from mutual fatigue, the country bumpkin could walk among the pickpockets and apple-women, bishops and attorneys, the old soldiers knocking bowls against their wooden legs and harlots flashing bosoms at passers-by He half-expected to run into Swift himself, whom he had been in the presence of at a dinner the previous year at Quilca, home of Thomas Sheridan. Owen lingered outside the Dean's private garden, where the great man was said to stroll daily in the company of one of his women friends. He made a point of circling back past the church door, on the off chance he might discover a verse pinned to it in praise or censure of the mysterious Drapier, a rabble-rouser whose identity he felt privileged to know, thanks to the night at Quilca. Why should a man who is free in England, asked Swift-as-the-Drapier in the notorious Third Letter, suddenly become a slave when he crossed the Irish Sea? Why, indeed. Owen noted the badges that Jonathan Swift, determined to tend only the destitute who resided within the actual St Patrick's liberty, obliged applicants to wear if they wished to receive charity from the church where he acted as dean.

Owen even laid down an outlandish full penny for a cup of coffee in Eade's Coffee House, also in Hoey's Court. Surely Swift would favour an establishment adjacent to his birthplace. If not the Dean/Drapier, then Owen might at least glimpse some of the city's other grandees, the poets and pamphleteers, printers and adventuresses, whose exploits provided the gossip course at many a dinner table. Aside from a gaggle of law clerks, however, Eade's remained deserted for the hour he sat there pretending to read the weekly *Gazetteer*. Liquid coal could not have tasted more putrid than coffee, with or without sugar.

Still. A man like Owen Connor guarding the Drapier's secret and chatting with philosophers! Could he have made a go of it in Dublin back then? He considered trying it, although the prospect of leaving Carolan's service and losing contact with Moira Carolan and the children had caused him a fierce anticipatory anguish. But Owen did cling to the hope that he might somehow end up a pupil of the scholar named Francis and prove himself as natural in a Latin classroom as that duck in a pond. *Aptata ut anas aequori?* The wrong participle, he suspected.

Instead, he had to steal *An Inquiry into the Original of Our Ideas of Beauty and Virtue* ten years later to learn that Francis had even written a book. Worse, the volume was published anonymously, and Owen snatched it from the library at Tempo because of the word *virtue* in the title. When Colonel Maguire mentioned the author's name to him, the news nearly knocked the wind out of his deceit. Later, he checked the inscription. *To Lady Cuthbert,* it read in well-bred script. *"Long is the way / And hard, that leads out of hell and up to light." Francis Hutcheson, Glasgow, 1736.*

He would have paid six months' wages to be the rightful owner of the text. Had their visits to the city not been curtailed in recent years, he might have plucked the courage to seek out the professor at the Academy of Dublin, and so have learned that Hutcheson had relocated to the university in Glasgow. Over time Carolan grew impatient with the condescension of the capital, where even the bard often came under the same suspicion as any other peasant driven into the Pale, and began finding excuses to avoid it. Owen, in turn, lost his chance to pursue an admittedly half-formed dream.

"Men like us will blunder about more than most," Friar Seamus said one evening back in Pettigoe, "doomed as we are to both an awareness of our circumstances and a determination to challenge them."

Owen misses his conversations with Seamus. Those nights in Devlin's inn feel three years, not three months, removed. The friar takes himself more seriously than any other low-born man he knows. Seamus is also impatient and decisive, a pleasing contrast to Owen's fellow servants at Alderford, for whom forbearance and self-denial seem as innate as faith. He longs for such bracing company, especially now, with another winter looming.

"I do wish to play a greater role in my own fate," he remembers answering the friar. "Were it not for my present responsibilities . . ."

Seamus replied with typical bravado. "The age doesn't allow for us, Owen—neither our passions nor our innovations, and certainly not the ambitions we rightfully hold." To Owen's questions about what they could do about those circumstances, the Franciscan said: "Begin with our names. There's nothing to yours and nothing to mine, either. No sept or clan, ancestral manor or family holdings. The trick lies in believing this anonymity our greatest freedom. I am convinced of it. Are you?"

* * *

Mary Macdermott Roe awaits him in the large sitting room. Afternoon tea is laid out: a bone-china pot with matching cups and saucers, a creamer and sugar bowl, a plate of Betty O'Neill's ginger biscuits. The hound called Grace, survivor from the days of father–son hunts along the western slope of Arigna, flops on her side before the fire, front paws crossed. She flicks a rheumy eye at Owen.

"Tea?" Mrs Mac asks, already pouring.

He perches on the settee across from her. Next to the biscuits is a letter, carefully refolded.

"The room feels different today," Owen says, his gaze settling on where the pianoforte would normally be.

"I've a mind to ask John Stamford to apply a coat of paint to these walls. It has been more than a decade since I devoted myself to this house. In the spring, perhaps, we shall undertake certain improvements."

Her observation is just. The sitting room, for instance, besides wanting that fresh paint, has couches frayed from too many backsides and rugs trodden upon by excess humans and dogs alike. The coverlet itching Owen's back, embroidered by tenant women in lieu of rent during one of the famine years, is equally threadbare, while the wall decorations—a row of engraved plates, collages made from rhododendrons and hollyhocks, along with a crooked portrait of the late squire of Alderford—are notable for their blanched colours and faded patinas. And Sir Henry's portrait suffers from worse ills than the poorly constructed frame that tilts it to the southeast. Viewers all agree the likeness is odd. Even Henry Mac had more beef on his bones than the artist rendered. His face, too, while gaunt, chin pointed and ears winged, also featured a playful mouth and squinting but kindly eyes. In this painting the lamented husband of Mary Mac is mostly a needle-for-a-torso and a muzzle-for-a-face, black hair upright in eternal shock. Owen finds the image curious for a different reason: the weighty tome clutched in the fingers of Sir Henry's right hand. He can't recall his patron ever carrying a book, never mind reading one. His wife has always been the bibliophile.

Owen nods at her remark, aware that she isn't soliciting his participation in any repair schemes.

"Where is the head presently at, Owen?"

"Not buried in a book, at least, Mrs Mac."

"Has it ever occurred to you," she says, playing her voice in the usual manner, which Carolan once described as similar to the notes sounded by a church organ, with each word given its full measure, "that the aches may relate to the dream you suffer? The one concerning foul weather and abandoned children, the village in disrepair? Suppose there is a forgotten incident from your childhood that matches the scene? The soreness along your brow could mark the scene's occurrence in your sleep world."

Though he vows to have a word with Annie MacManus about her gossipy habits, Owen holds his tongue.

"Take old Grace," Mrs Mac continues. The dog raises a cheek off the hearth tiles at the mention of her name. "As a puppy she became entangled in the legs of a draught horse, catching a shoe in the snout. The blow sent her flying across the yard. John and I laid her in hay, assuming she would soon expire. But a short while later Grace wobbled back to her feet."

"I remember the accident," Owen says. Well he should remember—it was he, not John Stamford, who rescued the animal. His mistress is more and more forgetful of late, a disrepair no coat of paint will remedy.

"The hound has been plagued by nightmares ever since. Have you not noticed the twitches and clacking when she slumbers?"

"And you are convinced . . ."

"The kick to the head triggered them," Mrs Mac says.

"Therefore I must have received a similar blow?"

"Is it not possible? That horrid institution where you were reared," she says with a mock shiver.

He recalls Brian Lynch's comments in the cottage. Owen's latest bout of headaches has obviously been dominating chatter in the servants' hall, exchanges then forwarded to Mrs Mac by the shameless Betty O'Neill. "Grace has confirmed this link between a shoe to the snout and teeth-clacking dreams?" he asks.

"Don't make smart."

As he did earlier in the day with Dr Lynch, he clasps his hands in his lap to keep them from straying up to his temple. "I wouldn't know how," he answers.

Whose dog are you, Owen Connor? he thinks.

"Maybe it is the same for Carolan in the cave," he says regardless. "Two hundred and forty hours without claret or whiskey could have caused every variety of delirium. It's a wonder he did not encounter his mother as well."

"Then you are convinced no reunion with Bridget Cruise took place?"

"Aren't you?"

"He spoke of her with such clarity for so long," she says.

"Has he stopped talking of Station Island?"

"In the last few days. But then this letter arrived."

"Letter, Mrs Mac?"

"Nothing," she replies. At once her focus is on the mantel and the portrait of her husband.

Owen shifts his own attention to Sir Henry, to see what she is seeing. Even the hound opens a rheumy eye.

"It is peculiar," he offers.

"Beg pardon?"

"His face simply wasn't that narrow. Nor were his shoulders. And as for the artist's rendering of his chin . . ."

"Whatever are you talking about, Owen Connor?"

Her expression, he notices, is vacant. Owen drops his critique of the portrait. "The letter you refer to," he tries instead. "If it relates to our travels, I think I have the right to be kept informed."

"Travels?" Mary Mac says.

"Perhaps it is an invitation to visit an estate? There is time for one trip before Christmas."

Mary Macdermott Roe cocks her head at him. As ever, she puts Owen to mind of a clipped bird, content to have traded its freedom for seeds and nectar. His mistress is a compact woman with white hair worn in a bun, the better to accentuate her sharp features, especially her cheekbones and nose. Her eyes are hazel, cool and dry, and her habit of pursing her lips has settled into a tick, nature's revenge for a lifetime of disapproval. Owen must remind himself that fifty years ago this same woman, newly wed into the Macdermott Roe clan, rescued a blinded teenaged ironworker from certain destitution by hiring a harper to teach him the craft. That act of mercy showed character. Of course, Mary Mac, née Mary Fitzgerald of Castlebar, was herself just twenty-one then and passionate for the old culture. For the price of an instrument and tutor she purchased a bard to call her own.

A bard she has kept a half-century now, her passion undiminished.

Nothing, including a husband and family, has come between her and Carolan.

"Your trip to Sligo was a success?" she finally asks.

"I dropped Mary at her sister's and then stayed on for a day to satisfy my curiosity about something. A shame her father could not see her before she left," Owen adds after deliberation. "She won't be back until spring."

"He was indisposed the morning you passed by."

"You informed him Mary was downstairs?"

"Of course."

"And he could not manage even a few moments for his youngest child?"

"He said they would sit together in the garden come April or May, when the flowers are once again in bloom," Mrs Mac says. "Is that not what I reported to you both?"

"It is," he agrees.

"Well, then . . ."

Owen knows better than to press the complaint. After all, he was grateful for a commission he could accept, especially one that involved travelling to Sligo. His decision to decline all other work requests, including during harvest week, when everyone on the estate pitched in, has made him unpopular. But he has no choice. He must assert his own worth, however much he doubts it in private. Owen Connor isn't a reaper or thrasher or even, any longer, a groom. He is the personal guide of Terence Carolan. The position is one he would be foolish to surrender without a fight.

The explorations were indeed a success. Once he bade farewell to the Carolan daughters, Owen closed his eyes, more or less, and traced a route to Temple Street, a lane in the back of the great Dominican abbey that he last set foot in more than twenty-five years before. The abbey, many times sacked and set ablaze, most recently during the uprising of 1641, remained as majestic as it had seemed to him as a boy. Ten paces into the street he was already reeling from the remembered clang of the smith's hammer, and the reek of soapcake used by washerwomen. Even before Owen found the doorway, his memory breached the pinched building. He saw the ground-floor room where Teresa Devaney lived, keeper of the only fire. He saw the stairwell to the chamber above, the stairs all with different creaks and the walls caked in dried mud. He saw the hay strewn over the floor as bedding and the chamber pots stacked in a corner, the box each boy was allotted for his belongings, including the shoes few of them possessed. He saw the window, set high in the wall, that angled light down, purposeful as a church beam but as warm as the shadows that enclosed it, and the crucifix over the doorway, also in shade. And he felt once more the loneliness—loneliness more than fear—that had dampened his spirit every day he lived there, aching for the parents he had never seen and, according to those pious women, never deserved in the first instance. The darkness of the place. The cruelty.

Once he is sure Mrs Mac won't ask him about the "something" in Sligo that aroused his curiosity, Owen forces the matter. "Do you recall very clearly the circumstances in which Sir Henry found me?" he asks.

"Not this business again," she answers with a grimace.

"Why not?"

"It is tiresome."

"It is my life."

"A life we gave you," Mary Mac says. "A roof over your head, an education alongside our own sons and then meaningful employment."

"For which I am grateful."

"Then show it."

Owen knows to allow her a scolding. Upon its completion, he can proceed. "How should I do that, Mrs Mac?"

"You could begin by attending mass with the rest of us on Sundays," she replies. "You could also cooperate more with your fellow servants. Heeding the advice of your betters, who want only what is best for you, would be equally advisable. Then there are your relations with Annie."

"She's a fine girl."

"She'd make an even finer wife."

"And here I was thinking you wanted me banished from my position as guide and from Alderford. Instead, you wish me to marry a girl who's never been more than a few miles from this house."

"Take her with you," Mary Macdermott Roe says simply.

His mouth falls open.

"Take her where?"

"We'll come to that."

He has tolerated her bullying long enough. "The charity school where I lived until the age of twelve still exists in Temple Street," Owen says, "and is still operated by the abbey Dominicans, albeit in greater secrecy than during my time. A registry survives, and my mother's name can be found in it. 'Jeny Connor,' or 'O'Connor' as it is spelt elsewhere." He makes sure to confine his gaze to the arabesque pattern in the rug. Mary Mac knows the story already. But she may well have forgotten the particulars, which have not come up in a long while. Regardless, tying the narrative threads together will provide the stitch to his confidence that Owen needs. "She died the same day I was born, July tenth, 1698, and someone remarked in the margin that as the name was presumed false, there was little chance of finding her people. An elderly woman I spoke with—Martha O'Donnell, whose face and voice I recalled at once— felt certain Jeny Connor hailed from the Ox Mountains in Mayo. The priest denied her last rites and she was buried in a pauper's grave. She dwells in purgatory even now, I suppose," he adds.

Hearing nothing, he keeps talking.

"Martha O'Donnell, who neither recognized me nor remembered my residency there, wasn't surprised by my height, for the girl had been brought to them by a man of similar stature. He left a purse for the physician's fees and the upkeep of the mother, should she survive. According to Martha, he was by all appearances a gentleman."

Flinn is in the doorway.

"He is asking after you, Madam," the butler says. "There is a letter he wishes to dictate, before Owen Connor's visit."

Mary Macdermott Roe clears her throat.

"Owen," Flinn says, turning to him. "I didn't notice you. How is the aching skull today?"

"Is there anyone in Roscommon that Annie hasn't told of my difficulties?"

"She cares about you a great deal," Mrs Mac says, once the butler has left with the message that she would be upstairs shortly, "and is of the opinion that you are worthy."

"She is too kind."

"I suspect so as well."

He swallows the gibe, along with a bite of ginger biscuit.

At last she unfolds the letter. Owen has suspected its contents since he first entered the room. Still, he braces himself.

"I must have a word with Terence about this," Mary Mac says, shifting in her chair as if to rise.

Grace whimpers.

He waits.

"From the sheriff in Enniskillen."

"A summons?"

"Your presence is requested at the Enniskillen gaol. On charges of stealing articles from the library at Tempo this past August."

"He really needs to hear about it?" Owen asks before he can stop himself. "The matter can't stay between us?"

"The sheriff threatens to journey here before the new year if you do not surrender to him first. And Terence knows already, Owen. He knew what you had done the morning you left the Maguire estate. You should be ashamed," she says.

"I am."

"Then give the books back."

He is silent.

"What madness grips you?"

"Madness, Mrs Mac?"

"They put men in stocks for such crimes. They also hand out sentences of five years in prison or transport to one of His Majesty's plantations in America. Is this the fate you seek for yourself?"

Though he tries to hide it, her prognosis distresses him. "I shall depart Alderford at once," he says, reaching for his hat. "That way, you will all be relieved of the responsibility."

Her quick reply betrays a plan. "We've a better idea," she says. "I have a stack of the master's recent music—or rather, music from when he was still actively composing. I would yet trust you to bring the manuscripts up to Dublin for delivery to the Neale brothers."

"The Neales have expressed an interest in issuing another collection of his tunes?" he asks. Their silence of late suggested otherwise.

Mary Mac ignores the question. "With proper grooming and attire, you could circulate within Dublin society for a spell," she says with the naiveté of someone who has never been to the capital, let alone experienced its society. "You may even borrow the name of one of my own sons, if it will help. Should Patrick Delany be willing to assist in the scheme and make introductions on your behalf, you could easily hide for six months or a year until we can resolve this dispute with Maguire. I've already sent the colonel a note, offering to pay for the missing volumes."

"You believe he brings the charge out of an interest in recovering the cost of two books?"

"Why else?"

Owen has to catch himself. Colonel Maguire still has more in common with Mary Macdermott Roe than he does. To insult him might be to insult her equally. "Then Dr Delany has agreed to harbour a fugitive in his home?" he says .

"Not as yet," she admits. "But he will be happy to comply. So Terence believes, at any rate."

Rising slowly, Mary Macdermott Roe crosses to the window. All energy has now faded from her manner, like light from a recessed corner of a sky. Her shuffle over the floor reveals what her unabated ambitions for Carolan and her unflagging censure of Owen can cause him to forget: her ladyship is a woman of seventy. A widow of many years, her hearth gone cold.

On a table is the locked box where she stores correspondence. Until two months ago the box, filled mostly with notes from children and bills from creditors, stayed open. These days it is kept secure, the key stored around her neck. The box is painted dove blue with floral patterns along the trim.

Privately, Owen doesn't give the Dublin scheme much of a chance, even if he does consent to be groomed like a legitimate Macdermott Roe. But her mention of such a ruse, with its implicit recognition of his resemblance to Sir Henry, is an opportunity he can't let pass. "Now that I have a trunk full of Sir Henry's clothing," he says, "I imagine I could dress up as one of his sons. With a shave and trim, naturally."

"I'm sure," she says, distracted.

"Henry Macdermott Roe was every bit a gentleman. And I, curiously, am every bit his double."

"Then we have a plan," she says, having moved to the doorway.

He goes to follow her.

"It's after five o'clock," he says in response to her expression. "I haven't seen Terence in nearly a week."

"Do you think it wise to be present when I show him this docu-ment?"

"Probably not."

"I shall say your head is yet sore."

"I do miss him, Mrs Mac."

"Tomorrow isn't so far off, is it? Perhaps by then we'll have a bet-ter idea of what's to be done with you."

He wishes she would do a better job of hiding her relief. Also, that he wasn't such her ladyship's dog at Alderford.

❊ ❊ ❊

During his thirty-six hours of confinement Owen amused himself by writing out Carolan's bed-bound schedule. The program rivals the itinerary of a slothful monarch holding court.

AM

9:00–10:00

Rise. Bath. Shave. Trim.
Prayer, one full rosary.

10:00–11:00

Breakfast: chocolate and tea, toast and butter, caudle.
Dr Lynch "examines" patient.

11:00–11:15

Owen Connor receives no instructions. Is ushered out.

11:15–noon

Discussion with Mary Mac of secret correspondence, incoming.

PM
Noon–2:00
Upstanding visitors. Bishop of Kenmare and Councillor Brady. Lord Mayo and Charles O'Conor. Various offspring, usually Maev and, until recently, Mary.
Refreshments: caudle and ale, bread and cheese-toasts, figs and nuts. Two or three pipes of tobacco, prepared by Flinn.

2:00–3:00
Light lunch.
First: turkey endive and boiled mutton.
Second: greens and soup, puddings and pastries.
Third: sweetbreads and collared pig, fricassee of eggs and pigeon. Salads, potatoes and cheese.
Dessert: creamed apple tart.
Claret and ale.

3:00–4:00
Nap.

4:00–5:00
Second bath. Fresh clothes. Nostril hairs trimmed and ears cleared. Nails clipped. Dictation to Mary Mac of secret correspondence, outgoing.

5:00–6:00
Owen's official "visit." No refreshments offered. No pipes filled. Peculiar topics: careers in East India Trading Company and on sugar plantations in West Indies. Soft summers in Nova Scotia and bears in Quebec. Annie MacManus, a fine lump of a girl. Annie, who'd make an excellent wife.

6:00–6:30
Dr Lynch again.

6:30–7:30
Mary Mac reads from *The Aeneid* and Old Testament. Ale and claret served. Carolan dozes.

7:30–8:00
Evening prayers with Father G—— from Keadew, or the bishop. Weekly confession on Saturday. Twelve Hail Marys and four Our Fathers, one each of Apostles' Creed and Act of Contrition. Rosary used to count penance.

8:00–9:00
Dinner.
First: beef and baked tongue, turkey and hare.
Second: soup and pâtés, partridge with vegetables.
Third: stuffed veal with parsley and cream, chickens with eggs and sauce. Rare mutton.
Dessert: almond cake and chocolates.
Claret and port.

9:00–???
Visitors of various standing. Charles MacCabe and Toby Peyton. Young Henry Mac from Greyfield. Brian Lynch, "off duty." Sundry musicians from surrounding parishes. Backgammon and bad jokes, songs and recitations.
Whiskey and ale.

Now, walking back across the pasture, a mist like blown snow creeping over the ground, Owen tries to discern a role for a guide in the itinerary. No matter how often he mentally scans the schedule, his presence in Carolan's room is required only twice daily. Fewer times than that of Mary Mac or Flinn. Fewer even than Annie, who is in and out of the chamber from morning until evening. Why, he has to believe his master derives more use from Grace the dog, who sprawls before his hearth most afternoons, once her arthritic joints permit her to climb the stairs, nails clicking over the wood.

All men crave purpose. They desire to act and for those actions to be of practical good. Francis Hutcheson believes the highest motivation for virtuous action lies in what he calls "benevolence." In *An Inquiry* the term seems interchangeable with "generosity" and "kindness." Owen tries not to be too hard on himself. He works to cultivate those qualities he lacks. He both carries and reads books. He also seeks out company that will ennoble his mind. If he appears deficient in virtue at present—after all, a document circulates accusing him of a crime—he hopes the condition is temporary. He isn't a bad person, or undeserving of love.

chapter three

December 24, 1737

He glances up from his oatmeal at the letter in her grasp. He finds her gaze. Panicking, Owen admires her mouth and neck and then, in spite of himself, the flour sprinkled in the seam between her breasts, like sugar over a plum pudding. His own gaze retreats to the safety of the servants' hall table, its unvarnished wood and dull grain. There is no cause for her to press upon him. Or if there is cause—she is kneeling on the bench and must keep her balance—there is also an effect. He leans back, as if in self-defence against a rearing horse.

"Well?" Annie says. "Are you going to read it?"

"In a minute."

He lays the envelope on the table and collects his spoon.

"You're not thrilled, Owen? I am."

"Yes?"

"Thrilled for you. It's brilliant news, I'm sure," she says, her breath a feather over his cheek. "One of those nobles who so admire your master. He's going to take you in until the trouble passes."

"And make a gentleman of me, to boot?"

"Why not?"

Owen, whose smile went missing when his front tooth was knocked out, can't suppress a grin. "What a sweet girl you are, Annie MacManus," he says.

The letter isn't from Dr Delany. The paper is rough cut and bears no seal. The penmanship belongs to a rustic Gael. Anyway, why would the present bishop of Down, bowing to the persuasions of his old harper friend, who must have posted a half-dozen letters to

Dublin in the last month entreating Delany's help, respond to the servant instead of the lord?

"How would you know if I am sweet?"

"Don't start. And don't stare at me," he says.

"I am trying to read your expression. How else am I to find out what's happening in your strange head?"

"You're certain you want to know?"

"I'm certain you think me too silly to bother with," she answers, climbing back down.

With Owen still on the bench, they are now eye to eye. He could take her by the waist and pull her to him, like any lad with his lass. He could plant a kiss on her mouth, forcing her lids closed, and then brush his lips over her outrageous lashes, a tickle akin, he imagines, to a cat's tail across a face. The servants' hall, incorporating the kitchen and dining area, is sweltering this morning. Half the table has been given over to loaves of bread left to rise beneath damp cloths. Counters and windowsills are crowded with cake pans and biscuit trays. In such a hothouse of scents—vanilla and cinnamon, ginger and cloves—her own fragrance mixes with the rest, sweetness on sweetness, until he summons images of such intensity he senses another rising, this one beneath his breeches.

Annie nestled on her back atop a loaf batch, blinking. Annie with a cake in her hand, nibbling the corners.

"I've no real wish to hide in Dublin, you know," he says, making a show of snatching up the envelope. "Even disguised as a Macdermott Roe and luxuriating in gentry hospitality."

The handwriting is unfamiliar. *Owen Connor, Esquire*, it reads. *Alderford, Co. Roscommon.* Esquire?

"Just for a spell," she replies, wiping her brow with her apron. "There is fear the sheriff will come any day."

"It's been a month."

"The thought of you under arrest in the Enniskillen gaol . . ."

"The conversation might be an improvement."

"But not the food."

As he breaks the seal, Owen feels her press upon him again. Odd, for she has not moved. Her brow is now flour-sprinkled as well.

"Should I read it aloud?" he says.

"Maybe it's not from Bishop Delany. Maybe it's from a secret lover."

"I've a woman in every manor in the land."

"And at Lakefield?" Annie says, referring to the cottage outside Mohill where the youngest Carolan daughters live.

He asks her meaning.

"There are two lovely girls as yet unwed, aren't there? I'm sure either Maev or Mary would be delighted to receive an offer."

"Silly maid."

Though it hardly seems possible, her pupils widen further.

"I've known those girls since they were babies," Owen says. "I attended Maev's birth, unlike her own father, who stayed here at Alderford, claiming to be ill. I played cup-and-ball and hopscotch and told them bedtime stories."

"I meant nothing by it, Owen."

"Even the suggestion is a disgrace."

She moves away.

"Don't you want to hear the letter?"

"I've work to do."

"I'll read it out without glancing at it first," he says in apology. "We'll share the surprise of the contents."

"The suggestion is a proper scandal, I'm sure," she says with her back to him. "As you believe all normal relations between men and women to be."

Annie stomps across the room to the sink. She is too short to work at the tub, a problem remedied years ago by the construction of a platform. Believing the pedestal renders her a statue, she usually refuses to mount it in Owen's presence. But today Annie MacManus climbs the three steps and shuffles around, her expression a cross between defiance and hurt. Hair falls over her brows.

He bows his head into the letter to escape her.

Owen Ballach,

It's what that pretty scullery maid calls you, is it not? Give the lass my regards, if you aren't already giving her a good deal more. The weather up here is foul and the politics are worse. Sheriffs raided the priory a fortnight ago, scattering us rebel friars to the winds. I fear for the regular people of Donegal. Their food may last the winter but their fuel is almost certain to run out. Agitations already in Omagh and Enniskillen, towns where I dare not show my face. You should be equally cautious, my bold lad. Rumours fly of your insurrection at Tempo and of the sheriff who has finally agreed to do Colonel Maguire's bidding—for a sum, it is presumed. This is no country for our kind, Owen. Not now, nor anytime soon, I fear. Haven't I been telling you so? There must be some land where men of high spirits but low breeding can leave a mark. Expect my knock on your door to make a strong case for flight. I pray you are still at liberty to hear it.

The Boatman

P.S.: I've news about your master's encounter in the penitent cave. Prepare to be contrite.

Friar Seamus. Owen is keen to raise a glass with him again, enjoy his mischievous glimmer and pirate's grin, the apostasies that slip from his lips as naturally as curses. He also has a proposal for the Franciscan. Instead of Isaac Newton and Francis Hutcheson he has been studying an unsigned pamphlet borrowed, with Mrs Mac's blessing, from the Alderford library. The document outlines a proposed navigation scheme for the Shannon River. If canals were dug and locks constructed, horse-drawn barges could travel from the mouth of the Shannon up through Clare and Roscommon and across into Longford. Half the width of the country by water, instead of the miserable roads, often little more than cowpaths, currently in use. Such a scheme, with its attention to the common good, is rarely considered outside Dublin. The Pale is the bright future, the countryside the grim past. The notion of being part of the project, if only as a simple labourer, gives Owen cheer. For all the talk of others about his supposed prospects, he has no desire to live abroad. He belongs right where he is.

He'll tell Seamus about the Shannon proposal, making a case for their involvement. He'll certainly put an end to any further chat about marching into an exile almost certain to be permanent. That course of action is for the defeated or the cursed.

Owen will dutifully inquire about the P.S. to the letter and try not to sound begrudging. But even Carolan has stopped claiming he conversed with his adolescent sweetheart on Station Island. He has also apparently quit bothering every maid who enters his chamber for the loan of her hand, to study her bone stems. No one has spoken the name Bridget Cruise aloud in ages, a pleasing conclusion to that history.

A serious discussion with anyone will serve as encouragement. Owen has scarcely managed a moment in private with his master these recent weeks. His appointed visiting hour still stands, but the pretence that the time is for him alone has been dropped. Even when the room isn't bustling with servants or other guests, the conversation flounders. He always cherished their horseback journeys together both for the exchanges they encouraged and the abstinences they imposed. Sober, Carolan is good company, curious and wise. Merry, he *is* the company, the entertainment, the bard at his unbuttoned best. He seems merry all the time now.

Slipping the letter in his pocket, Owen stands, intending to apologize into Annie's ear. At that moment Flinn bursts through the door from the manor with all the haste his ancient bones can muster. He stumbles down a step.

"Is he here?" the butler asks. "Is he?"

"Who?" Owen says.

"Owen Connor."

"Flinn?" Betty O'Neill says, abandoning the pot she is stirring.

"A stranger," Flinn gasps. "In the front hallway. He means business, he does."

"Should I go see if I can be of help?" Owen says. He stands just a few feet from the old man.

"Dear God," Betty O'Neill says.

"Do you mean the sheriff?" Owen thinks to ask.

"From Enniskillen," Flinn replies.

"Then I'd best be heading in the opposite direction."

"Owen!" Annie MacManus says.

The butler's chest heaves under his apron. "Mrs Mac advises . . ." he says. "She took me aside to advise . . ."

"Calm yourself, Flinn," Betty O'Neill says. The cook's stout physique and town-crier voice turn most of her comments into commands. At age fifty Betty O'Neill has supplanted Flinn and John Stamford as de facto chief of the household staff. Mother to five children and wife to a farmer in the village, she wields her authority with the same faint menace as she does the knife often clutched in her hand. Owen, frankly, is afraid of Betty and is careful never to cross her. One more woman passing judgement on his life, he sometimes thinks.

"Owen Connor should absent himself to the cottage and there hide, until he is sent for," the butler eventually says, speaking once more as though Owen isn't present. "The sheriff means to search the estate. Owen is to make no noise and light no fire, as the smoke would betray him."

"I'll go along," Annie says, descending the platform.

"You'll do no such thing."

"These birds can wait, Betty."

"And how will it look if the sheriff comes in here and finds a sink of half-plucked chickens and no scullery maid?"

"She's right, Annie," Owen says. He seeks her gaze again, intending to relay his gratitude. But she turns away. Her spine shows through the back of her dress, shaded in by sweat.

He crosses the kitchen.

"I may leave tracks," he says. "Could someone sweep them clean?"

Then he is through the back door and into the garden. The snow has stopped and the ground is hard, rejecting most prints. As he can't trace his own steps in the thin cover, he doubts the sheriff will fare any better. Much of the pasture, including its eastern rim where the path runs into the copse, is obscured by drifting mist, peculiar given the temperature. Though Owen can't see the horses through the brume, he assumes they are out there. Gull and Gem may be cold and bored, he decides as he hurries across the field, but at least they are at no risk of being torn apart by starving villagers. Another sight he once witnessed and now can't expel from his head.

✳   ✳   ✳

Annie's brow, flour sprinkled. Annie's breasts, beneath a cloth. In Dublin once Owen buried three pennies in his pocket and went seeking one of the women who lingered around Hoey's Court. It was an early evening in November and the light was wan, darkness gathering across the cobblestones. More bold than in daylight, the ladies—harlots, he perfectly understood—were soliciting men with bosoms bared and lewd remarks on their lips. "You're as long as you are tall, aren't you, pet?" a woman leaning against a wall said to Owen. Though his legs carried him to her, his mouth failed to form any words. Even so modest an interest induced the prostitute to cackle and lower the collar of her dress, revealing slopes of grimy cold-prickled skin. But the sight of the breasts activated Owen's empathy, not lust. Gathered in the hollow at the base of the woman's neck was a pool of sweat. In her eyes were the signs of a raging fever. He might have pressed the back of a hand to her forehead in concern had she not read his face and grown defiant. "Tell us how much you have," she said, seizing his coat sleeve. "And what you're hoping for it." Now mortified, Owen barely managed an answer. For two of those pennies, the woman said, she'd take him in her mouth. For the third coin, he could take her in any manner he wished. In either case, the taking would occur in the recess of the alley, a quiet spot, she assured him, out of sight of perverts. "What do you say?" she insisted, her expression now daring him to pity her to the extent, he surmised, that she pitied him. "You all want it the same, you know."

He fled then, naturally, and ever after believed himself still more disfigured from the shame. Because Owen did indeed want it like any other man. Because he would have paid those pennies, and so won release from the stockade of his sensual innocence, were it not for the sweat he couldn't help noticing between her collarbones and the illness in her eyes. His mistake—if that is the word—had been to conduct the exchange before night enveloped the city. Wretched darkness would have freed him to satisfy himself, and devil take the problems of some whore.

✳︎　✳︎　✳︎

As instructed, he leaves the fire cold. Light, squeezing through the door slats, expires a few lengths along the cottage floor. Owen considers hiding the books. If the sheriff comes, though, he won't surrender. John Stamford loaned him a hatchet and spade for house repairs, and either could cave in a skull. Ideally, a thwack across a backside will suffice.

Should he be ashamed? He certainly regrets the discomfort he is causing those around him. Indeed, he lies awake at night worrying about how his rebellion will play out. Badly, Owen senses—for him, anyway. But the consequences do not negate the bright justice, so to speak, of what he has done. He has a defence ready for any who will grant him the dignity of a listen.

The poor sheriff. The man has strayed far from his Ulster hearth. The Leitrim–Roscommon border must be a foreign territory, especially south and west of Lough Allen. The region, a sodden idyll of lakes and streams, glens and woodlands looks only to itself for judgements. Villages nestle along ridges and astride rivers. Manors sink into lots, windows askew and chimneys thrust upwards at queer cants. The landscape can strangely affect travellers descending from the highlands of Donegal or Mayo. While never blind, the outsider moves through Leitrim wearing blinkers, able to chart only what lies directly ahead. Landmarks elude recall and compasses stop working. One lake much resembles the next. Few crossroads are posted, and those that are shouldn't always be trusted.

Owen's master has called this remote corner of the country home since the age of fourteen. Fears of the open sea leave Carolan agitated during visits to estates and towns along the coasts. For all his wanderings the bard has never crossed the Shannon down into Munster. As for his native Meath, arguably the prettiest of the inland counties, the fields fertile and the estates affluent, it is certainly a familiar travel destination. But Owen required only a single tour of that countryside and a few nights among those lords to appreciate why Carolan was a contented inner-exile. Working the fields are numerous relations. Housed in the manors are one or two childhood friends. Then there are the ruins of chapels and priories sprinkled throughout the demesnes. They boast gravestones over their floors and swallows in their towers.

Leitrim–Roscommon holds fewer such associations. Ruins are

equal in number but closer to rubble than architecture. Estates tend to be small and sequestered, their squires known more for character and humour than achievement or notoriety. Alderford operates on a slightly larger scale—like the St Georges, the Macdermott Roes owned a forge at Arigna, the Iron Mountain—but still fits alongside its neighbours. Mary Macdermott Roe is neither a socialite nor a spirited host, despite accommodating any guests who journey up from Carrick to meet Carolan, a semi-permanent visitor to her house since the death of his wife four years before. Mrs Mac, of course, was herself widowed in 1727, when Sir Henry tumbled from a horse.

Each of those passages altered the estate. With Henry Macdermott Roe gone and his sons off married or carousing, life at Alderford turned inward. More exactly, it sank into the soil, like a cross at the head of a forgotten grave. From the moment Carolan suffered his loss, Mrs Mac began to devote her every breath to his recovery and their mutual bereavement. She paid a Mohill woman to move into the cottage and finish rearing Moira's children. She ordered new linens and kitchenware for their home, a gift she never made to either Moira, while alive, or her own child Henry, when he moved to nearby Greyfield. Her generosity recognized few limits, despite the eventual failure of the forge and the mounting costs of hosting the bard.

Even the manor has come to serve, if not actually resemble, its resident legend. A first-time visitor might well assume the peeling paint and scuffed floors, shabby furnishings and drab decorations to be the natural dwelling of a blind man. Windows are flung open in all weather for his beloved birdsong. Vases are kept brimming for the perfumes that intoxicate him.

Owen sometimes entertains the fancy that Alderford literally ceases to function when Terence Carolan isn't there. Betty O'Neill, motionless at the hearth. Annie MacManus, frozen on her platform. Flinn kneeling before a creel, as if in prayer, and John Stamford posed with a brush drawn over a horse's coat. And Mary Macdermott Roe? In her chair in the sitting room, gaze nun-sharp and lips pursed, the letter box in her lap.

The poor sheriff. He won't be capturing any fugitive on this hunt. He'll be lucky not to find himself wandering the streets of Carrick or Boyle at sunset, all direction lost, his mercenary outing ended in humiliation.

✳   ✳   ✳

She finds him shrouded in blankets, a book useless in his lap.

"It's freezing in here," she says, a shawl over her own head.

"I hadn't noticed," Owen replies. He wonders if he can swing his legs over the side of the bed. The cold has numbed them.

Annie is back in the cottage for the first time since November. She examines the room. "What are those tools for?" she asks in a voice about as warm as his hands.

"Braining nosy sheriffs."

Her features betray no amusement.

"I've a mind to build that chimney," he says, noting her mood, "as you suggested. The smoke is choking some days."

"When might this occur—once you've got the door to close properly and the shelf to hang at a regular angle?"

He has tried twice to correct the shelf, removing the brackets and repacking the wall with mud. The board still runs at a slant, obliging Owen to stack the final five books as a dyke. The pile diminishes the collection in stature, reducing it to a heap of volumes, organized without care or respect.

"I'm sorry about this morning," he says.

"Owen?"

"The Carolan girls. I realize you were only making sport."

"Who was the letter from?"

He has an answer ready. Noting her tone, he opts for greater disclosure than he first intended. Does Annie remember him speaking of a friar named Seamus he met in Donegal this past summer? Seamus operates the ferry out to Station Island during pilgrimage season and does odd jobs for the Franciscans the rest of the year. A brawny fellow, outrageous in manner and opinion. Closer in temperament to a rapparee, if not an actual highwayman.

"And he is a friend of yours, this Seamus?"

"We are conspiring together," he says to impress her.

"Conspiring?"

"Formulating plans."

"Does he have a last name?"

"Who doesn't?"

"And it would be?"

The truth is, Owen doesn't know. Seamus steadfastly refuses to divulge any personal information. He claims it is irrelevant to their destiny, which is to make their mark using wits and determination alone. Owen is especially lucky, says the friar, being a foundling. He has no clan to disown.

"He is from Galway, I think," he replies.

"And what did Seamus-from-Galway want with you?"

"Forget the letter, Annie," he says, running out of explanation. "Is the sheriff gone back to Enniskillen?"

"He's taking tea with Mrs Mac in the sitting room."

His smile drops away.

"The pasture is swallowed in a brume," she says. "I wandered it for several minutes seeking the path. Look what it did to my dress," she adds, holding up a muddy hem.

Owen looks, admiring an ankle clothed only in a stocking.

"Then I suppose a stranger won't find his way to us, will he?" he says.

"Not unless someone escorts him."

He is up on his feet.

Annie MacManus squats before the chest containing the wardrobe of Henry Macdermott Roe. The motion swells the thickness across her shoulders, as though she hides a sack of grain there, the fabric stretched tight as a corset. The contrast between her bloated torso and shapely ankles and wrists never fails to both move and vaguely disturb him. Even in summertime Annie won't wear a blouse with short sleeves. She sews her own clothes.

"Mrs Mac sent me with instructions," she says. "The sheriff is here to arrest a servant. You are to disguise yourself as a gentleman."

"Annie?"

"Her orders."

Opening the trunk, the maid transfers the top layer of garments onto the bed. She examines each article, sniffing for freshness and smoothing out creases. Next, she orders him to strip.

"You heard me," she says to his disbelief.

Owen peels off his jacket, vest and chemise, baring skin the colour of boiled fish.

"The breeches as well."

"Annie MacManus!"

"Shall I inform Mrs Mac you have disobeyed her again?"

He must sit back on the bed to remove his boots. His arms, thin as a crane's limbs, mortify him, as do his thighs. She is viewing the real Owen Connor now and shortly will be covering her mouth. In shock or amusement? Both, he suspects.

"Uncut velvet," Annie says, inspecting a coat. "Isn't it lovely?" She runs the fabric across her cheek.

Once again, even her simplest gestures stir him below. "I'd hardly know," he answers with a swallow.

"You mean you haven't even had a feel of Sir Henry's garments, in all the months they've lain in that trunk?"

"Please. I'm shivering."

"God, you're a pole," she offers, regarding him from top to bottom.

Her smile is too impish. But can he be certain she is codding him? He has to play along.

"First the breeches," she says. "Or do we start with these stockings and garters here?"

"Give them over."

"We want to get the order right."

"Give them."

He snatches the clothes from her. A struggle ensues, man versus stocking, and Owen find himself hopping across the floor. His drawers, which hang off his hip bones like a coat on twin pegs, threaten to fall down. His freckled member, if not his spotted sack, will send her bolting from the chamber, he is quite sure.

"Am I about to glimpse what no woman has seen before, Owen Connor?" she says. Her laugh is light and easy.

He blushes so hard, his eyes tear up. "Shame on you," he says. "Teasing a man so."

"Poor thing."

The garters prove no easier to manoeuvre.

"Do I position them above or below the knee?"

"Below. No, above."

Sir Henry's trousers could have been tailored for Owen Connor. The narrow-toed shoes with silver buckles are more of a squeeze, but he can still walk in them. Annie rummages for the fanciest shirt in the collection. The chemise has laced ruffles and crinkly sleeves. A "pagoda" design, she calls it—whatever a pagoda might be.

"The vest next, cut at hip length," she says, displaying a gold vest with gilded embroidery. "Then the coat. We'll save the scarf for last."

When he complains that the coat pinches across the back, she claims it is the fashion. She repeats the contention about the silk buttons running down to his groin. The trouser design baffles him. The crotch is too tightly stitched, driving fabric into his crack and pressing his genitals upwards, as if for better display.

A gentleman never ties more than two vest buttons, Annie notes. Nor does he expose himself to winds and risk having the coat-tails flap.

"How would you know such things?"

"Flinn told me."

"You talk to that awful creature?"

"Flinn isn't so bad. You just need to be patient with him. And gentle," Annie says. "As you do with most people, including your own self."

"He's never had any time for me."

She presses her lips together. "He doesn't know what to make of you, Owen. He isn't convinced you're one of us."

"Us?"

"A member of the household. A servant," she adds without a trace of self-consciousness.

"What else would I be?"

"Betwixt and between, it seems to me and to most everyone else. Flinn is confounded by this. It's his age showing."

Owen would sit back down in amazement at this observation were Annie MacManus not now positioning him with his back to the bed. She climbs onto the mattress, her bosom pressed into his shoulder blades and strands of her hair on his neck.

"You smell," she says.

"It's these clothes."

"It's you. I don't mind."

He blushes further. When she reaches around to tie the scarf, he inhales. She still wears the fragrances of Christmas baking, especially cloves. She still smells edible.

"You're choking me."

"Hold still or else!" she says, laughing again.

He steps away.

"I must look ridiculous."

"Glance in the mirror and find out."

Mercifully, the glass is too filthy.

"My appearance is ridiculous under the best of circumstances, Annie. I hardly need to make it worse with a costume."

"Red doesn't flatter you, it's true," she says, her arms crossed. "Not with those freckles and that hair. The wig," she says, bending back over the chest. "I forgot all about it."

"There's no chance I'll wear that thing."

"I've heard they used the hairs of plague victims back in the old days," she says, mounting the headpiece on her fist.

"It's hideous."

"Colonel Maguire will have provided the sheriff with a description of the carrot-haired thief . . ."

He grabs the wig. The net feels clammy, like the pelt of a recently slaughtered fox. He has gone so far as to lower the cadaver onto his skull when she bursts out laughing.

"Don't tell me," he says.

"The sheriff left Alderford more than an hour ago."

"Mischief maker."

"You deserved it."

"Mischief."

"And you look a real gentleman, Owen. With a shave and cut and a silver tooth in that gap, you'd be fit for any fancy occasion. You could even accompany Mrs Mac to the holiday ball at the St Georges' in Carrick next week, should she reconsider the invitation."

"She hasn't attended the ball since Sir Henry died."

"Maybe she would now, with you dressed like him."

"Do you remember Henry Mac?" he asks.

"Only from seeing him in the village. I wasn't yet employed here when he died."

He waits.

"You're his image, you know," she says.

"I am?"

"Betty remarks on it frequently, as does John."

Should he? He has vowed to share his theory with no one, until he has more evidence. But she has raised the likeness.

"Sit for a minute, Annie," Owen says. "Let me tell you about my trip last month to Sligo."

* * *

After she leaves, promising to return with "real" orders from Mrs Mac, he refolds the clothes as best he can. He has told her only what he believes to be the truth. Namely, in the summer of 1698 Henry Macdermott Roe made with child a young woman from the Ox Mountains in Mayo, who died giving birth. Sir Henry later rescued his bastard son from the Sligo charity school where he had consigned him, never revealing their relationship. The boy grew into a man, a taciturn fellow with a rare lankiness and an even rarer betwixt-between temperament. The freckles, he reckons, must belong to his mother's side. He bets if he inquires down near Arcale he'll discover more than a few spotted Connors or O'Connors, and one with a story of a daughter who vanished long ago and came, it was presumed, to a bad end.

He wishes Annie MacManus expressed astonishment, rather than incredulity, and delight, instead of trepidation, at his theory. He wishes she hadn't focused on the impropriety of his suggesting a blood connection with his superiors. For that matter Owen wishes his own response had been more assertive. The same dread that left him trembling after his confrontation with Colonel Maguire seized him again. An enormous act, taken without forethought. A colossal mistake, its consequences yet to be measured. But that is silly. How can a few remarks spoken in private with a servant be the match of a public exchange of insults with an officer notorious for his temper and likely possessed with a small arsenal of weaponry—half-pikes and daggers, firelocks and bayonets?

John Stamford finds him in a foul mood. The stable master has braved the terrain to deliver a message from Mary Macdermott Roe. When Owen asks about Annie, John admits that Betty O'Neill gave the maid a tongue-lashing for her absence earlier in the day. The message is succinct. Owen Connor is to present himself in the servants' hall at six o'clock. No visit with Master Carolan beforehand. Neither is he to linger in the library to pass the hours.

To Owen's halting inquiry about the sheriff's inspection, John Stamford confirms that the stables were searched. Did the sheriff ask him questions? And did John supply answers? he wonders.

But then his resolve to ask further questions falters, and the stable master leaves.

✳   ✳   ✳

"He lied for you, Owen. We all did."

His eyes stay lowered.

"Should Terence Carolan be forced to dissemble before the law for your benefit? Should I be? Or Flinn or John or Betty?"

"Not if you don't wish to, Mrs Mac."

"Wish to?" Mary Macdermott Roe says. She stands at the top of the staircase leading from the main floor of the manor down into the servants' quarters. The elevation projects her voice, which is steady today—the organ note, plangently sounded. "What choice did you leave us? We could hardly betray you." A cough, aimed into a raised handkerchief, interrupts her scold.

Owen has his back to the chamber. Behind him, Betty O'Neill and Annie MacManus pretend to be cooking. Flinn sits at the table, not pretending to do anything else but listen, with John Stamford puffing on his pipe.

Try as he might, he can't keep from swaying. He hasn't eaten since breakfast, and the air is almost coloured with Christmas scents. Owen thinks of boiled beef, the meat salty and tender, and of warm bread.

Hunger flutters his response. "Could we talk in the library," he says, "or even out in the front hall?"

"Why not here?"

"It isn't very private."

"And have you kept your troubles private from the rest of us at Alderford? Is your 'dispute' with Colonel Maguire, as you call it, still none of our affair, now that we have all broken the law by misinforming the sheriff of your whereabouts?"

She looks at him with a sharpness designed to peel away his clothes. She also delivers a line that has obviously been prepared for an audience of greater than one. "You do not deserve admission into my house," she announces.

"Mrs Mac . . ."

She repeats the assertion.

He nods, cap in hand. Good lad.

"The Ulsterman knows your face, Owen."

"He does?"

"He claims he met you on the road from Pettigoe to Enniskillen. A blind elder and his companion, a tall fellow with a temper on him. One look at Terence in his bed and the sheriff was on about the odd couple he stopped along a dangerous country lane in the dead of a miserable night."

Owen's memory of the encounter features more of the sheriff's bark than his muzzle. The air was black and their lantern would not stay lit. "He certainly interrogated us as if we were criminals," he says. "Which we were, I suppose, given that Terence had just completed the pilgrimage."

"He knew you were coming from Station Island," Mrs Mac says, "but had no interest in making anything of it. He has an interest, however—financial, I am inclined to believe—in arresting the thief who plundered the library at Tempo."

Plundered? His hands ball into fists.

"Terence has little recollection of the meeting. His forgetfulness contributed to the sheriff's ire this afternoon. Not," she says with mirthless pleasure, "that his sort requires much to turn bumptious."

Owen advances a step towards Mary Macdermott Roe. "I sometimes think his general infirmity can be traced back to that evening," he offers in as low a tone as he thinks will carry.

Her puzzlement shows in the usual cocking of the head.

"He has kept to his bed for four months now, Mrs Mac. His illness must run deeper than fatigue from the pilgrimage or even the after-effects of trying to toss that child. It must," he says.

"His illness?"

"Infirmity, if you prefer."

"What nonsense are you talking, Owen Connor?"

"Mrs Mac?"

"Your words offend both your master and your mistress."

He is dumbfounded.

"Terence is no more ill than—" She stops, her fire once again abruptly losing its flame. "This isn't the place to be inquiring after his health," she says in her own version of a hush. "Not that you have any right to pose such questions, at any place or time."

Her falseness and feeble efforts at intimidation irk Owen. "Then may I even inquire about his work?"

She swats the query away with her hand.

"Is he composing a new tune?"

"Possibly."

"With his nails being clipped daily by Flinn?"

"Eh?" Flinn says from behind him.

"Flinn does as he is instructed," Mary Mac says, once again

addressing the wider audience, "and has done so without fail or complaint for better than a half-century. Unlike other members of my household."

He drops his head in defeat. "I'd like to apologize to Terence in person," he says. "As I will apologize to every other occupant of this house."

She says nothing.

"I haven't spoken to him in ages. His room is forever full of friends and well-wishers and men who are unfamiliar to me."

"Not tonight."

"Then can I simply relay holiday wishes?"

"I will relay them on your behalf."

"Am I or am I not still his guide?" Owen asks. "Am I or am I not still in your employ?"

"Don't dare use that tone."

"Then am I permitted to remain in the servants' hall long enough to eat a bowl of beef? It is a courtesy you extend to any stranger who knocks on that back door, being kind of heart and a Christian."

"Now you would flatter me?"

"I make no such attempt."

"Impossible man!"

Though Owen rarely bows, he does so now. From the waist, curls flopping over his forehead.

"Stay the entire evening in the hall," Mary Mac says. "It is the eve of our Lord's birth, after all. Not even Owen Connor prefers the company of his books on Christmas night."

What would she have him say? Or do? He bows again, despite knowing the gesture will be interpreted as insolence.

"And I've brought you another something to read," she says. "A work I hope you will find edifying."

She holds out the tome she has been clutching to her chest. *Life of James, Duke of Ormond* by Thomas Carte. It is a quality volume, bound in custom leather and printed on gilt-edged paper. Published in the autumn of 1736, Owen recalls, at three and sixpence per issue. He could never afford such a purchase and isn't sure she can any longer, either.

"The duke," he says neutrally. "Terence would be delighted to have this read to him."

"We recommend it to you for a reason."

"Yes?"

"James Butler was a fine man," she says. "There is much a person can learn from how he conducted his life."

"James Butler was a rich man," Owen says.

"Excuse me?"

"Then Terence also believes I would benefit from Carte's biography?"

"We both believe it."

"I am grateful, Mrs Mac."

"Don't," she says.

"Beg pardon?"

"Bow to me. You look ridiculous."

"I'm sure I do," Owen says.

She turns and, cracking the door no more than is necessary, slips back inside her rightful domain.

chapter four

January 20, 1738

"My quip about Lady Tyreconnell's verbal joust with James had little sting, I grant," he says. "But Maguire's retort . . . Honestly, Seamus. It was the King William anecdote."

"Which one?"

"Concerning the boatman who asks the monarch which side emerged victorious at the Boyne."

"And?"

"You don't know it?"

"Remind me," the friar says.

Owen repeats the king's contention that, regardless of whether he retained or lost the throne because of the battle, the boatman's lot would not soon change. To his surprise, Seamus slams his fist into his palm at the slight upon his kind.

"Later, I even delivered myself of the Pope epigram," Owen adds. Noting his friend's expression, he recites the lines.

"Calling Hugh Maguire a dog was provocation indeed, Owen. It's no surprise he is having you hunted."

He wonders if he should challenge this interpretation of the poem. "Pope isn't name-calling, as such," he says with what he hopes is proper humility. "He is more asserting that every man serves some master, regardless whether he acknowledges the fact or is quite unaware of it."

"But we serve no one, do we?" his guest replies. "No ties to clan or land or obligations to any meddlesome wife or mewling infants.

None of that for the likes of Seamus-the-boatman and Owen Ballach."

Untying his cloak, Seamus reveals a flask slung around his shoulder. He inverts the spout over his mouth, squeezing the bladder until wine dribbles down his chin. The friar stumbled out of a storm an hour ago and might have perished in a snowdrift had a villager not escorted him to the estate gates. He first presented himself in the servants' hall. Presuming him a beggar, Betty O'Neill offered a chair by the hearth and a bowl of soup. Her emphatic denials that Owen Connor lived at Alderford obliged the Franciscan to unbutton his vest, showing the cross dangling from his neck.

"The servants protect you still," he commented. "All very admirable and good. But for how much longer?"

Now, soothed by liquor and the blaze, Seamus is in better spirits. Owen remembers him without a beard or such scraggly hair. He also recalls a taller, more robust figure, his eyes piercing rather than clouded and his manner commanding of respect instead of worry. Still, his own spirits lifted at the knock on the door, and he does not wish them brought back down so quickly. Not in January, with the season raging and his future as obscure as a sky of falling snow.

"A chimney wouldn't be a bad idea," Seamus says, waving at the smoke billowing from the hearth.

The tools remain in a corner, untouched.

"You certainly acted bold at Tempo," he continues. "There is talk of your exploits up and down the shores of Lough Erne."

"Carolan was the true bold one that night. He delivered a speech on his vocation that silenced Maguire with its eloquence and passion. He denounced the Tudors and Cromwell and all the others who have laid waste to this land. He also declared himself little more than a faint echo of the music gone by. It made me proud," Owen says.

"A speech?"

"A learned discourse, almost."

"So Terence Carolan admonishing a table of country lords is the match of his guide sounding off to a military officer who could have gutted him with his rapier, probably without consequences?"

"I am not comparing our actions."

"Why wouldn't you?"

"Seamus?"

"Let me guess," the friar says. "Because he is one of nature's chosen, his every fart a melody and his every belch a pleasing poem. Whereas you are a foundling, ill-bred and poorly educated, capable only of smelly, tuneless expulsions."

The remark tongue-ties Owen. Does he ever sound so bitter himself? He shades his brow with his fingers.

"Not suffering those aches you told me about, are you?" Seamus asks. He inverts the flask again, the bladder emitting a squeal, like an animal in a trap.

"They started back up in the early fall."

"Across the forehead?"

"The very centre of it," he admits, massaging the spot. "The aches are brought on by inactivity, I am convinced. The open air, the motion of riding a horse, perhaps even sleeping in different beds, keep them at bay."

"Then I've arrived not a moment too soon."

Owen asks.

"I am here to announce the end of this sore-brained interlude and the start of a period of head-clearing adventure."

"When?"

"Summer, at the latest."

"You've heard something? A rumour, perhaps?"

"A rumour about what?"

"That Carolan will be resuming his travels."

"Carolan?" the friar says. He cuts him with a look.

"I've not been dismissed from my position, Seamus," Owen says in his own defence. "I can't just abandon him."

"Owen Connor, Esquire?"

"I never claimed I was an esquire."

"And here I was thinking you were a fugitive. A criminal whose prospects, if he were fool enough to linger much longer in this hovel, could include years incarcerated in some prison or a one-way passage to the colonies as convict labour."

Owen works the sore spot with a fury.

"I think I preferred it when you just scratched your skull," Seamus says.

"I think I did as well."

The friar laughs and rests a conciliatory hand on his shoulder. Sensing frigid air from where the thatching has deteriorated along one wall, Owen adds another piece of turf to the fire. It hisses and crackles and then is engorged.

"How is the master, anyway?"

He outlines the situation.

"Five months in bed? That doesn't sound like a recovery to me."

"No?"

"More like a retirement."

For the first time Owen expresses aloud his belief that both Carolan and Mrs Mac have been attempting to find him employment, or even mere sanctuary, away from Alderford.

"I'm sorry," Seamus says.

"Sorry for what?"

"You can be of service to them no longer, Owen. They want you gone."

"You don't understand."

"Explain it, then."

"I live at Alderford," he says, "and have since I was twelve."

"Is this because of the girl?" Seamus asks, fixing him a more kindly gaze.

"Seamus?"

"The fetching scullery maid. I was hoping to catch a glimpse of her in the servants' hall before."

Owen has already questioned him about the hall. Only Betty was present when the friar appeared. Annie MacManus, ill for the past two days, must have been too weak to rise from her bed in the room beside it. She would have been tempted, especially once the stranger asked about Owen Connor.

Is he ashamed of her stunted body? He has no reason to be, exactly. A virtuous man would never entertain such a thought.

"It's not because of Annie," he answers now.

"There are loads of girls."

"It's not her."

"Then you truly feel responsible for Terence Carolan?"

"Why wouldn't I?"

"Who's the one being administered to by a bevy of adoring women and obliging servants? The one admired and revered and certain to live on in memory for ages to come? Not you, son. Nor me, for that matter."

The friar passes Owen the flask. He declines.

"You still haven't inquired about Station Island," Seamus says.

He does so, reluctantly.

"After our evening together in Devlin's," the friar begins, "and your master's tale of his reunion with his muse, I asked my fellow friars about the pilgrims on the island that week. There was no Bridget Cruise among the faithful."

"I'm sure not."

"But there was a woman who gave her name as Barnewall."

Owen stares into the flames, his cheeks hot.

"One friar, who has relations in Meath, was quite certain the bard's Bridget Cruise married into the Barnewall clan. He believed she wed Arthur Barnewall, second son of the famous Mathias."

"She did marry him," Owen says.

"Then?"

"It does not mean she was the same woman who made pilgrimage with Carolan. It does not mean he identified Bridget Cruise by her bone stems and then conversed with her in the cave."

"Bone stems," Seamus says. "A bird in the hand. It's a tender image, right enough."

"There is still no hard evidence, Seamus."

"Easy, lad."

"She was always in his head and never in his life."

"And what are you?"

"What am I?"

"Are you in either—his head or his life?"

Owen is seized by an attack of shivers, as though at the news of a death. Even his teeth chatter. "Could you fetch a cover from the bed?" he asks.

As the friar wraps him in a blanket, pushed air causes the fire to spark and smoke. Seamus then crosses to the bookshelf.

"Where all the trouble starts, eh?" he says.

"Careful."

"What, I'll damage one of your precious tomes?"

"The shelf," Owen says. "It isn't secure in the wall. You need to remove individual titles slowly, bracing the row with your hand."

Joining his friend, he demonstrates with his copy of Ovid.

The Franciscan surveys the spines. "Ovid and Tacitus, John Locke and George Berkeley. Anne Finch, is it? I am not familiar with her. *Persian Letters,* naturally, along with Mr Bunyan, featuring plenty of fearsome woodcuts, to be sure. Fine editions of Milton and Dryden," he says, extracting the latter book, "which it ought to be, belonging as it does to Lord Mayo. And what about Pope's Homer in soft black leather? 'Property of Edward Crofton.' Indeed," he adds with a chuckle. "Mr Crofton hasn't noticed it missing, I'll wager."

"He has, I'm afraid."

"Daniel Defoe, now, he can't be stolen property," the friar says, examining a book with frayed borders and no label. "*Journal of the Plague Year*. Even I've read this one."

"I found the volume in a stall in Smock Alley some years ago. Negotiated a fair price with the vendor."

Seamus must squint to decipher the titles. With a candle now lit, the cottage isn't particularly dim. Is he near Owen's own age? He imagined the friar his junior by as much as a decade.

"The travels of Lemuel Gulliver, of course—dedicated to your master, I recall your saying—and what's this? Faulkner's recent two-volume edition of the *Works*? That must have commanded a hefty sum when first issued. Ah," he says, glancing at the plate affixed to the endpaper, "has Manus O'Donnell of Newport also remarked on its absence?"

"He hasn't."

"More a gentleman of leisure than learning?"

"We found O'Donnell gravely ill our last visit to his house. He passed away not long after."

"And you lifted Faulkner's edition of Swift, figuring the end was near and no reader would seek the chilly consolations of the Dean in his final days?"

He is silent.

"Rogue," Seamus says.

Owen doesn't care for the friar's grin or the mirth in his eyes. His friend notes how it is only the damaged books, including a *Robinson Crusoe* which has clearly survived a fire, that he can claim to possess legitimately. All the quality tomes had to be filched in order to find an owner who requires them to serve as something more than props in a portrait. Seamus's indirect reference to the painting of Sir Henry Macdermott Roe in the sitting room at Alderford is, Owen realizes, both accidental and accurate. Still, he feels half compelled to mount a defence of country squires who like to purchase books for their libraries and be portrayed clutching them in paintings, without much bothering with their contents. He wonders at the impulse in himself. To his ongoing astonishment, not a single person—not Carolan nor Mrs Mac, Annie nor Betty O'Neill—has yet asked him *why* he is risking so much for the sake of a few volumes on a rickety shelf. No one has asked, even though the question is obvious and he would very much like to address it. Seamus hasn't inquired, either, and Owen suspects that the friar assumes the reason to be self-evident. Owen is taunting his so-called betters, country gentry of indifferent education and cretinous habits who consider fortunate birth or convenient marriage fair evidence of their right to enjoy the fruits of dumb luck.

He couldn't, and wouldn't, refute his friend's assumption outright. What he would do instead is give a reason for his actions, one unrelated to his circumstances. All Owen seeks is the chance to plead that case—these many months later.

Seamus, though, is no more likely to oblige him. Scanning the shelf, the friar falls upon what he designates as the "offending titles."

"Don't tell me you took the *Optics*?" he says.

"Newton is beyond me, I confess. But this anonymous work by Francis Hutcheson," Owen replies, pulling down *An Inquiry into the Original of Our Ideas of Beauty and Virtue*, "it contains remarkable notions."

His guest does not inspect the book. "I know the name," he says without enthusiasm.

"Hutcheson believes slavery to be an unnatural state. He argues that every man, whether captive or servant, has the right to resist tyranny."

"Does he?"

"Aren't those astonishing ideas?"

"No more than Cromwell's notions of nearly a century ago to abolish the monarchy and permit every landholding male a vote," Seamus says. "Why, Ironguts himself believed in freedom of conscience—so long as your conscience was in accord with his."

"But Cromwell was an invader, wasn't he?"

"And this fellow?"

"He is from Down, Seamus. Son of a minister."

"That's right. Not one of us," the friar answers.

Owen winces at this characterization of Francis Hutcheson. "I'm fairly certain I met him. In the Dublin home of Patrick Delany, where Carolan and I often lodged. A short fellow, stocky and badly shaven. Very friendly," he says, warming once again to the memory. "We must have talked for an hour. Discussed the Penals, if you can believe it, which he declared an abominable set of laws."

"As I said before . . ."

"He was certainly different from the Dean. Swift looks right through a man he does not think merits his attention. The one time I was in his company he failed to acknowledge my presence. To be honest, he treated Terence like some rare variety of bird brought in from the wilds. I don't believe he is much interested in the music, or the people, out here."

Aside, he means to add, from an almost untenable compassion for the plight of those people. No other motive could have stirred an author to produce a work as devastating as "A Modest Proposal." Using the flesh of starving children in ragouts and flaying their carcasses to fashion gloves for ladies? Even Owen, aware that Swift wrote the pamphlet in the wake of the same 1726 famine that he witnessed—probably at closer proximity than the Dean of St Patrick's Cathedral—finds the satire extreme. But then, it has never occurred to him to tell Carolan, let alone the reading public, about his own worst nightmares.

"And yet you admire his writings enough to steal a collection of his works from a dying man?"

No easy defence comes to mind. Owen has long maintained that Francis Hutcheson is one of only two individuals he has met to possess the eyes Terence Carolan lost. The other claimant is Jonathan Swift. Swift's eyes are globular and distended and rendered near black by dense, slightly alarmed brows. They never slice a fellow. Instead, they examine his features with the dispassion of a flame thrust into a face. Swift emits a force of probity—or he did in his heyday, before the madness began to overtake him.

"It's the same with the duke," Seamus says. He indicates the duke of Ormond biography, which Owen was reading when he arrived. "Another great Irishman lacking other than a passing acquaintance with his subjects."

The book lies open on his bed, its binding supple and its typeface refined. Were he alone, Owen might raise the volume to his nose and inhale its scent, a mix of ink and calfskin. He might press the page to his lips.

Annie MacManus assured him the other day that, come springtime, they'd go wandering through the fields below the manor. "We'll dip our tongues in blossom cups," she said.

And yes, he coloured.

He explains that he is reading the Carte biography to assuage Mary Macdermott Roe. "I also borrowed a document from her library outlining a scheme for the Shannon," he says, recalling his many imagined conversations with Seamus about the proposal. He holds the pamphlet out to him.

"You can't bring them along, you realize," the friar says, ignoring it as well.

"Beg pardon?"

"These books. Once we settle on a destination, we'll need to travel light. On foot. On the run, quite possibly."

Owen says nothing.

"I'm heading down to Clare to wait the winter out. Daniel MacNamara says he'll find me work free-trading with his sons in Kinvarra Bay."

"Smuggling?"

"Wood, hides and butter for the French. Brandy, wine and silk for our own gentry. Land the cargoes after dark, unload and move them before sunrise. An honest night's labour," Seamus says.

"What about the customs office?"

"What about the Enniskillen sheriff?"

The friar, a smuggler? The trade attracts the shiftless the way horse dung attracts flies. Hardly the pursuit of men of destiny. For the first time Owen notices the broken veins along his friend's nose and the sacks pillowing his eyes. He knows Seamus only in passing, he is forced to acknowledge, and is largely unfamiliar with the contents of his heart.

"I'll swing around for you in April," the Franciscan says.

"Then it's settled?"

"France in the summertime, son. Us in embroidered coats and shoes with stone buckles. Chapeau bas atop our heads and French fillies in our arms. What do you think?"

Owen has no firm thoughts about France, aside from a comment and a name. The name, mentioned in a whisper by those who hold progressive views, is of a Frenchman called Voltaire. A radical, by all accounts, and yet another of Swift's outrageous acquaintances. As for the comment, it stands in his mind as no less a mystery and far more of a disturbance. "There are bullets in Europe with our names already engraved on them," he says.

"What's that?"

On repeating the remark, Owen decides he has made a mistake giving it voice.

The friar's hand, which had been back on his shoulder in fraternity, is withdrawn. "Nonsense," he says.

"Why not involve ourselves in something worthwhile instead? Like rendering the Shannon a network for barges and such."

Scowling, Seamus snatches the pamphlet, flipping through its pages. "The scheme will come to nothing," he says. "Waylaid by connivance or venality or the statutes. These things always fail."

"A career in the Irish Brigade doesn't tempt me much, Seamus. I hardly see myself as a soldier for hire in some foreign war."

"How you see yourself isn't at issue. Rather, it's how others judge you that generally wins the day."

Still another thought that Owen hadn't intended to voice escapes him. "I've always aspired more to scholarship than any other profession," he says. At least, he has since receiving the endorsement of Francis Hutcheson.

The Franciscan refuses to stay the night. As he bundles back up, he chides Owen with traces of his former authority. "We've been through this, lad," he says. "There's nothing for us here. The people abide by a set of laws they ought to take up arms against. Rebels recall Limerick and the Boyne or even the Cavaliers and Roundheads for inspiration. The age cannot produce a single respectable passion. Nor can it give us one good reason to squander our lives in obscurity."

At the side gate, where a departure on a January afternoon may pass unnoticed—the village is marked by coils of blue smoke rising above the skeletal trees—Owen promises to consider the Irish Brigade.

"Retain Swift as an idol, if you must," Seamus says. "He is a book-fed fantasy, after all. But this other master, Owen, lovely harper and natural gentleman though he may be, cannot remain. Break free of him with haste. Fail to do so, and you'll never be free yourself."

A bark shatters the hush. The sky is sunless and almost flat, like the blade of a sword. Some quality to the light, as though it contains no depth, with objects clearly resolved five or fifty paces away, reminds Owen of his dream. A storm should soon follow, the ceiling collapsed. Blowing snow and brutal cold.

He says as much, the words unbidden.

"This is no dream," the friar corrects. "Not for the likes of you and me. It's waking life, and it's plenty murderous."

"Your own last name?" Owen remembers to ask.

Seamus shrugs.

"Suppose I need to find you down in Clare? There may be more than one Seamus free-trading around Kinvarra Bay."

But his friend—or is he Owen's partner in desperation?—is obstinate. They are destined to travel far and wide and without the burden of names. "It's what I see for us," Seamus says.

✻ ✻ ✻

What does Owen Connor see for himself? If he is being honest, he can't get much beyond a tableau. Two riders on a high country path at sunset. Slopes of bracken and thistle and, further up, white scree. Shadowy massifs jutting out like foreheads, with birds—hawks and cormorants, perhaps—arcing over the expanse. A valley floor below, half of it in shadow, stony moorlands bereft of habitations or grazing sheep, the desolation stretching west to a serrated rim of sea. A sky of deep violet, streaked with red in the middle tiers and grey in the upper margins. The wind a colour no one can quite identify.

Travellers on horseback, alone in the vastness. Skirting the valley down into a glen, fording a stream and following the shore of a lake. Back up the slope through heather and dog roses onto the side of a slumping bare-backed mountain. Forever between destinations and away from hamlets and farms. Chatting about this and that, without agreeing. Going quiet for a spell, the silence companionable. *Swish-swish*, the horses swishing their tails. *Cheep-cheep*, the cry of a bird.

❋   ❋   ❋

"Betty O'Neill said I should stop by," he says from the doorway.

"Then do so."

"Here I am, Annie."

"And here I am, in this bed," she answers. She sits up, pulling a blanket to her chest.

He asks after her health.

"Better, thanks."

"Dr Lynch paid a visit?"

"This morning."

"And?"

"He couldn't cure a dog of its fleas, could he?"

Owen smiles at her smile. He wishes the room had a chair. There is space for two beds and a table. A narrow window, set high in the wall, directs a rectangle of light onto the floor on bright days and a dull patch, like milk spilt over stone, on overcast ones. The walls are bare. He remembers asking Seamus about the cells where the anchoresses volunteered their own incarcerations. They had only a tiny opening to receive food.

She shifts to allow him to sit next to her. "I won't say a word to cause you a blush," she says. "Promise."

He perches on Bridget O'Donnell's bed instead. "I'm sorry for you."

"Don't be."

"You have difficulty breathing sometimes? Pains in the lower back and across the ribs?"

Also in the legs, he has been informed, discomfort so intense Annie has to grip a table or wall to keep from toppling. As a child she was confined to bed for more than a year after falling ill. Once back on her feet she learned to weather the daytime spasms and night-time aches, the strange sense, she once confided to Owen, that her body was growing slowly apart from her head. Mrs Mac hired her at age seventeen out of pity, most believed, and to enliven the house with her spirit and beauty. Few expected the girl to see twenty. A thirtieth birthday still strikes all concerned, including Dr Lynch, as improbable.

"You've been talking to Betty?" Annie replies.

"Everyone within five miles of Alderford knows about your condition."

"They do?" she says, rehooking hair behind her ears. But then she smiles again. "Are you having me on?"

"Maybe."

"Owen Connor, making light of things?"

"I'm not that grim, am I?"

"Just so serious."

He frowns at the description, however apt.

"You had a visitor this morning?" she asks.

"My friend Seamus."

"The one who won't reveal his last name?"

"That's him."

"He wants you to go away, doesn't he?"

Owen's resolve to honour Annie MacManus with the truth is put to abrupt test.

"I've known it all along," she says, reading his face. "And I knew he'd come for you one day."

"Seamus has plans," he says. "Wild ones, really. But hardly more wild than Mrs Mac's determination that I book passage on the next ship leaving Cork, regardless of the destination. Everyone now seems anxious to send me away not merely from Alderford but from this entire island—as though they were one and the same."

An absurd notion, he decides at once.

"People hold you in high regard," she says.

"I doubt that very much."

Annie picks at the blanket. Owen is about to ask a question he isn't even sure he wants answered—"Is exile what you wish for me as well?"—when the maid reaches behind her pillow. To twist her torso she must bend forward and then pivot her upper body with the caution of someone suffering a pinched neck. The action seems to block her throat, gagging her. Her hand emerges with a stack of envelopes bound in ribbon.

"If the missus ever finds out . . ." she says.

"Annie?"

"You need to be aware of all that's been done on your behalf these last months. The efforts of Mrs Mac and the master, the devotion they have shown."

Owen's mouth is suddenly full of ash. He crosses to her bed. When Annie is unwell, her skin turns translucent and her eyes hollow, as though her spirit has withdrawn to safer ground. Her hair, too, seems to lose its lustre—probably from going unwashed for days.

"You've read them yourself?" he asks, still standing over her.

"You know I can't."

"But you're sure their contents will be a consolation?"

She shows no inkling.

"May I?" he says, indicating the mattress.

"Don't be silly."

He sits and unties the ribbon, wishing it was the ribbon of her nightgown.

"Aloud?" he says.

"They're private."

"Right."

He spreads open the first letter, running his finger over the broken wax seal. The text is long and the handwriting is tidy. He scans the lines for relevance.

My dear Terence,

Apologies for the tardiness of this reply. I do recall your most recent guide, Owen Connor, if dimly. Your wish to see him resettled beyond his current situation is commendable. My own ability to be of assistance is limited, I am afraid, especially given his background and education . . . Dublin is, after all, a city of accomplishment . . . As well, I must confess, Terence—and forgive my bluntness—to not retaining an especially positive impression of the fellow. He seemed ill at ease with his station, often adopting a manner unwarranted by rank. I might hesitate to recommend him solely for his behaviour in my home one evening some years ago, when he tested the patience of a guest, a promising young professor of philosophy, discoursing with the man as though they were old school chums . . .

In addition, I have been apprised of a rumour, one which I would be remiss in not now relating, given how it affects your own standing. Are you convinced this Owen Connor is of sound moral character? The rumour concerns the thieving of properties from the very houses you have graced with your presence. I fear he has taken advantage of both your infirmity and kind-heartedness in order to rob others of their possessions and you of your reputation . . .

"Owen?"

He reads the first paragraph again. Dr Patrick Delany, bishop of Down, has to be referring to his encounter with Francis Hutcheson. There have been no other conversations at other soirees even remotely like it. For accomplished men such a meeting was probably routine and forgettable—a tedious chat with a nervous little Northerner. For Owen it meant the world.

"The way you stare at those words . . . Is the news so terrible?"

"Patrick Delany regrets he can't be of assistance in procuring me a position in Dublin," he answers. "Much as he would wish to." His smile probably resembles a rictus.

"There's a pity," she says too brightly.

Mary Macdermott Roe has isolated all correspondence related to him. Owen flips through envelopes containing replies from lords and ladies residing on estates located in, by his quick count, nine counties spread across three provinces. None of the letters require even a hasty scan. Their hidden existences confirm a rejection, along with a judgement.

A letter from Belanagare causes him especial dismay. Among Carolan's friends, Denis O'Conor was always the most gracious. By the time Denis died in 1732, his son Charles had already established himself as a scholar and gentleman. The opinion of Charles O'Conor, with whom Owen has spoken freely over the years, matters a great deal. A favourable opinion could grant him the resolve to act decisively. A poor opinion may prove unbearable.

His hands tremble unfolding the pages. Glancing over at Annie, he confirms a face fast draining of its remaining colour, the way motherhood drains a woman of her youth.

The letter runs to six pages, terse by its author's standards. Owen has been reading O'Conor's missives to Carolan for ages and knows how to edit, and occasionally paraphrase, the texts. Suspecting that Charles would begin kindly, he searches the opening paragraphs for his own name. It does not appear until page three.

. . . Owen Connor is indeed more virtuous than his recent actions would suggest, and I agree that he possesses, as you put it, a "humane and elevated mind." Perhaps the deprivations of his childhood have left their mark. Perhaps, too, he is simply out of sorts with the times. His nature, if not his present dilemma, will render his every attempt at self-improvement fraught. Society, in which we all must make our cautious ways, will not easily forgive Owen. The obduracy is not vengeful. It is, rather, a mechanism for stability and continuity—"Things as they are, and forever must be," as my dear father used to say . . .

Therefore, Master, you are justified in seeking for your guide a situation abroad, where his efforts might find consideration for their merits alone, and he will not be hastily judged as a certain class of man. I urge you to overcome your doubts about this course of action and pursue it both vigorously and, given what I have heard of the agitations of Colonel Maguire, urgently. I only wish I could be of more aid in what must be the cruellest of tasks: banishing one whose companionship is held dear . . .

From there, Charles turns his attention to a book of fables he is composing, as well as his latest efforts at compiling genealogies for the Roscommon O'Conor clan.

"You weep, Owen?"

"No."

"Your eyes?"

"It's the script. Charles O'Conor has dreadful penmanship."

A *humane and elevated mind*? In truth, his mind is neither. How kind of Terence to venture the claim, though, especially now, in the wake of Owen's latest crimes.

"You'd best return these to the box, Annie," he says, retying the ribbon. Noticing hair fallen across her eyes again, and feeling strange, he rehooks the strands. They are fine as gossamer, and as fragile.

The action is still rude. Of course, Owen Connor lacks moral character. He is also a clod, incapable of erecting a shelf or finishing a book, most likely a volume he has pinched. A shiftless man, deserving the company of his own sort.

When Annie's eyes manage to further widen, without any apparent strain, she becomes a sky containing both sun and moon. But is it his sky?

"Mrs Mac," she says, her cheeks glistening, "she's gone to Carrick for a visit. I've her key . . . Oh, Owen!"

"I need to see him."

Removing a handkerchief tucked up her sleeve, Annie wipes away the tears that he should be stemming with his lips. But are they his tears?

"She said you aren't permitted a visit this afternoon. On account of a cold he has caught. He is asleep more often than awake these days."

Owen stands with such haste, the bedposts knock against the wall. "I offered to take on new duties, you know, tasks unrelated to my former status as guide. Haul trays of food up the stairs. Ensure that decanters are kept brimming. Fill his pipe correctly—Flinn, I happen to know, packs the bowl too tight—and empty his chamber pot. Twice I asked Mary Mac if I could please be of some direct service to my master and to Alderford."

"How did she answer?"

"Initially, she claimed Flinn would not countenance my working alongside him. Then she said I hadn't been trained for those tasks."

"They are particular."

"What sort of duties do you think I managed on the road? Carrying the harp and setting him up to perform were only a small part. Even in houses where the host assigned a manservant, I was still forever fetching a glass of ale and helping clean and dress him. I've darned the man's stockings, Annie. I've cleaned sickness off his shirt and wiped his . . . when his hands were shaking too violently."

"All right, Owen."

But it isn't all right, and the bottle containing his feelings has been shattered. "She knew very well what I was asking," he continues. "To be with him, or even just close by. To be useful! She knew this, and still she prevented me." The sentiment sounds peevish to his own ears.

Annie sniffles.

"I miss him so," he says.

"I know."

"Can I be expected to respond otherwise? Twenty-one years as his companion, with tasks most every day, and now this—nothing, aside from the rare visit, with him three sheets to the wind and in his cups with MacCabe or Peyton or some Italian. Is it ridiculous? Am I without dignity?"

"Feelings can't be helped," she says softly.

"That's right. They can't."

"Is he like a father to you as well?"

"He is. No," he amends, "more a friend and confidant."

"As a wife could be?"

"Beg pardon?"

"He *is* ill," she hastens to add.

"That isn't really the case, Annie. All these months he has stayed in bed on account of . . . those letters."

"Mrs Mac still sends them out. Fewer than before Christmas, mind," she says. Then, after a hesitation: "And she hides the letters Bridget Cruise mails to Master Carolan. It's wrong, I think."

His face cannot mask the shock of this information. Annie might as well have told him that his own real father—not Sir Henry, in the end—had been secretly corresponding with Mary Macdermott Roe all these years.

"Four letters since the summer, at least," Annie says. "From a Mrs Arthur Barnewall, on an estate in Meath. My mistress says she'll show them to him once he has his strength back. But I don't believe she will."

"Bridget Cruise," Owen repeats. A name that won't sink into obscurity, either in music or, it would seem, in life.

Annie MacManus draws a fluttery breath before speaking further. "You'll notice changes in Mr Carolan. He rarely rises from his bed now, even to chatter with birds. In the autumn it did seem as if he was recovering or waiting for some event to occur. Now, though, I worry he is truly feeble."

He can't hear this diagnosis.

"Will I fetch you a cup of tea?" he asks.

"Dr Lynch says if I rest today, I'll be fine by tomorrow."

"Then rest you shall have," Owen says from back at the door.

She replaces hair behind her ears again. But is it his hair?

"Your head," she says with a sadness so unhidden it could erase the smile from the portrait of a child. "You haven't knocked on it with your fingers even once."

He shrugs.

"Maybe it's because you know you won't be confined here much longer."

"Rest, Annie."

"You'll be off having adventures."

"Close your eyes."

"I'm not very tired."

"Close them."

Finally, she does.

chapter five

February 26, 1738

"Who's that?"

"Owen."

"Owen Connor? At long last."

"Terence?"

"I'd nearly given up on you, my boy. Thought you might have left me for greener pastures. Come close now."

Owen enters the chamber. Weeks of waiting for the appointment, his first since before Christmas, have left him anxious. Of late the pain has been migrating over his skull and down into his neck, a winter cap of discomfort, obliging longer periods of rest to quell the nausea. He worries he may betray the tumult, both physical and emotional, yet within him. He is already near tears at the decline—irreversible, he sees at once—in his master's health.

Grace the hound flops before the hearth. Two birds lift off the sill.

"I'm thinking of her," Carolan says, "and the children. All the time now, thanks to you."

"Me?" he says, drawing a chair next to the bed. From there he can whisper directly into Carolan's ear.

"Of course. Just as you promised."

Owen waits.

"'Let me guide you, Terence,' you said. 'Let me do my job.' Or words to that effect."

"And here you are."

"And here *we* are, Owen. All of us, in the four-poster bed. Martha and Siobhan and Tadhg and Anne, Eileen and Maev and Mary. Every one bright and alert. I wrote a tune for each, you know."

"A tune?"

"Seven babies, seven tunes."

What is he witnessing? To all appearances, the room has been laid out for a wake. The window is open, in case of smells. The walls are lined with extra chairs. On the table are a bottle of whiskey and stacks of glasses. In a vase are flowers from last summer, dried and pressed by Mrs Mac. The corpse, too, has been prepared. It lies tucked beneath tidy sheets and blankets, the arms exposed and the hands folded. Skin looks waxed and cheeks shaven. Ears have also been trimmed, strands of hair pasted to the skull.

Except that this corpse is talking, his lips blue and spittle-flecked. He is spouting fiction—there are no tunes bearing the names of his children—but in a tone of such conviviality that Owen hasn't the heart to correct him. Unless he is mistaken, he is up inside Carolan's head, a place he has always wished to visit. He assumed he'd never get there.

A bird calls.

"A bluetit," Carolan says, "flicking and picking along the branches outside. A pleasant surprise, in this weather."

"The snow is melting."

"Remark how the call begins with three or four deliberate notes. *Dee-dee-dee-dee.* Then a run of lower ones, uttered faster and faster until they are a near trill. *Dee-di-de-ree.* Or better," he adds, the fingers on his left hand drumming over the back of his right, *"pwee-pwee-tee, tee-tee-tee-tee."*

"I hear it."

"Lucky the husband, eh?"

"Master?"

"Don't call me that. She never did."

"No, she didn't," Owen says, guessing the identity.

"She laughed at the pomposity of the title. 'An honorific, wife,' I would say. 'Sheer silliness, husband,' she would reply. Why, the woman wouldn't even call me by the title in bed. And there I surely *was* one."

Owen stifles a smile.

"I heard it. How you take air through your nose. Got you to smile, didn't I? A master between the sheets!"

"Aren't we perky this afternoon," he says.

"Why wouldn't I be? I sleep all night and much of the day now. And I've not a care, have I?"

"I suppose not."

"I'm done for. I'm way past my natural time. But stop," he says. "Come closer. Come right up into me, if you can. You'll see me better."

Assuming Carolan means "hear" him, Owen hunches over so that his lips brush the bard's earlobe. Until a week ago he had plans to use the meeting to convince his master to send out word to his children, now scattered from Dublin to Sligo, requesting that they assemble at Alderford for a final reunion. Until a few moments ago he had also intended to beg for the return of his old life or, failing that, counsel on what he should do. *Guide me, Terence,* he was even prepared to say. The reunion of the Carolan offspring with their father, Owen now understands, is impossible—there is no bed large enough to accommodate such a gathering. But is the parent as abstract to the grown children as they are to him? He suspects not, and he commiserates with Tadhg Carolan and his six sisters: a mother lost to disease and a father who was kindly but, at the close of day, unable to be with them. As for raising the matter of his own fate, the concern abruptly strikes him as ungracious. Who has been the luckiest by far of the bard's progeny? Easy. Owen Connor, who has had Carolan's company, and his confidence, for better than half his thirty-nine years.

"I've a story ready for posterity," Carolan says. "Tell me what you think of it. I'm at death's door and about to knock. Calling to Flinn, I request a glass of the finest whiskey, which I polish off in a swallow. Then with a smack of my lips I declare the libation a 'parting glass from my most ardent lover,' and myself fortified for whatever lies beyond."

"You've written the script?"

"MacCabe thought it prudent, as did Toby Peyton. When the time comes, I'll likely be drooling and delirious. What chance any words from my mouth will be worth repeating in public houses and at hearth sides? The same applies for the tune expected of a harper. Composing it in your actual dying moments makes for a far better story than melody."

"Then you've considered composing as well?" Owen says, damping the excitement in his voice. He opens his eyes momentarily. The sight is strange: a corpse murmuring, a mourner attending his every breath.

"A farewell composition, you mean?"

"I'd thought it was too late."

"It is," Carolan says. "Too late or too early!"

Owen is quiet.

"Just as you said. About bonding with real people rather than imaginary ones. I tried it with Grainne Connelly and Brian Maguire and even poor Thady Bourke. Couldn't be of any good. Couldn't mitigate a thing. It's only in the bed here that I'm at all useful as a father and a husband."

"The bed," he repeats.

"They were forever crawling in with Moira and me, especially on cold nights. Always room for one more, I told her. The raft is never too crowded . . . But stop a minute. Listen."

"Another bird?"

"Listen."

Owen listens to a lengthy whistle, sustained for twenty seconds and then restarted after the briefest interlude.

"A song thrush, high on a branch," Carolan says. "Notice the length of the repetitions and the music of it. As well, observe how the intonation can be both dropping and rising. *Peter-peter-peter* and then *bopeep-bopeep-bopeep*."

For each *peter* he flicks his first and second fingers in pattern. For every *bopeep* he taps out a sequence of one-two-three-two-one.

A tune.

In the harper's head.

With Owen Connor in there as well. Or nearly.

"Lovely," Owen says.

"It is all so lovely, isn't it?"

He agrees.

"How are Gem and Gull?" Carolan suddenly asks.

"Gull's rheumatism worsens when he is confined indoors. He is reluctant to lie on the ground for any length. Gem is restless and misses her master."

"My wife loved those animals."

"That she did."

"She had the most wondrous hands, dear Moira. Her bone stems, in particular. Delicate as a swallow's wings."

"Moira?"

"I used to entreat her to let me hold them. When did she pass away, Owen? Was it long ago?"

"Not so long."

"I can't breathe sometimes for missing her."

"And yet while she lived . . ." he says, the anger threatening to surface.

"I can't breathe!"

Surprising himself, Owen finds it easy to abandon the complaint he has been nurturing for two decades. He is inside a great artist's melody. Truth is different in here. "The loss remains a fresh hurt?" he asks.

"I've not been the same man since, have I?"

"I'd never say such a thing."

"I've been no man, really. Himself, and no one else. Who else could I be?"

He chuckles again.

"Whiskey, Terence?"

"What's this—Owen Connor tempting a reprobate with the very cause of his dissoluteness?"

"Maybe I am abandoning my old self as well," Owen answers. Here is another startling notion sprung into his head, which now seems full of the oddest ideas.

"I won't drink a parting glass with you, my boy."

"No?"

"Because we shan't be parted. Not truly. Neither in this life nor the next. I won't allow it."

Owen sobs without reserve. He makes no move to cover the emotion with a hiccup or any other disguise.

"There, there," Carolan says without stirring.

"I'm sorry."

"But if the glass is offered in simple companionship, I couldn't very well say no, could I?"

Pouring the whiskey allows him to recover his composure. Annie MacManus outlined the procedure. The patient can no longer sit up or even raise his head. Owen must slip his right hand behind Carolan's skull and elevate it. Then he has to press the rim of the glass to his lips. Don't be too cautious, Annie warned. Your master still likes a proper draught.

In fact Carolan drains the measure off in a swallow, running his tongue over his lower lip to catch stray drops. Owen then sips from his own glass, the whiskey scalding his throat.

Should he ask? He feels he must.

"Have you heard lately from Mrs Arthur Barnewall?" he says, his voice a tone below audible.

"Who?"

"Her. Bridget."

"The chambermaid?"

"Bridget Cruise."

Carolan's forehead does not crease and his mouth remains in its usual vacant smile.

"Not in a while," he replies.

"I have to apologize for not believing you."

"Not in more than a half-century, come to think of it," he continues. "Myself, a lad of fourteen, and her a year younger. She was a charming girl."

Owen closes his eyes again.

"Another lifetime, really," Carolan says.

"Of course."

"It's down to poor Mary Mac now."

"In what regard?"

"Everyone else is safely in the bed. The bairns, of course, all seven of them, and Moira, tasting of butterscotch. Plus you, Owen."

"I'm there with you?"

"Naturally."

"And Mrs Mac?"

"She tried so hard. Wanted it so badly. But it can't be that way, can it? A husband and wife, along with their children. It's a sacred and solitary pact. A raft adrift in a claret-dark sea."

Should he also inquire about Henry Macdermott Roe? The mystery is as vexing as that of Bridget Cruise and no less important—to Owen, anyway. Carolan will remember if Sir Henry had cause to visit the Ox Mountains late in 1698. And if Henry Mac confided his secret to anyone, it would have been the bard.

"In my own mind," Carolan says before Owen can decide, "I've always assigned you to the largest clan by far—the nation itself. She must be your father and mother. She must provide you care. Fanciful, I grant," he acknowledges.

Overcome again, Owen dares not speak.

"As for your friend," the harper says.

"Friend, Terence?"

"The fellow you met in Ulster. What's his name again?"

"You must be thinking of—"

"Shane, is it not?" he interrupts. "He emigrated to Quebec, as I recall, rather than enlist in Donegal's Regiment. Isn't that so?"

This decision, too, is easy. "Quebec, aye," Owen says. "A ship out of Cork back in the autumn."

"Excellent. For the best, you know. I am familiar with his kind. Not up to your quality at all. Speaking of quality . . ." Carolan says with unmistakable intent.

Owen repeats the procedure with a fresh glass of whiskey.

"Courage, son."

"That is your counsel?"

"Courage!"

The thrush calls once more. The bird calls and the composer's fingers duplicate it: one-two-one-two for the *peter-peter-peter* and one-two-three-two-one for the *bopeep-bopeep*.

"There it is," Owen says, keen to be free from his grinding thoughts.

"Indeed."

"The tune doesn't feel racing."

"Not a bit," Carolan says.

"Nor jaunty."

"There is elegy in this part. And sorrow, I think."

"Tap it out."

"One, two, three."

Slowly, Owen begins to feel it—the emptiness, the freedom.

"Your typical Oriental is convinced his existence is akin to that of a man awakening from a sleep in which he dreams he is a butterfly," his master says.

"And what does the fellow wonder?"

"Am I a man dreaming I am a butterfly?"

"Or a butterfly . . .?"

"Dreaming I am a man?"

"A parable," Owen says.

"A melody, pure and everlasting."

"Aye."

"But you're not yet ready for such music, are you?"

"I may be."

"You're a young lad still, with a future. A brilliant one, I am convinced."

"Thanks."

"Tell me about Annie MacManus."

"I'd rather talk about the melody a bit more. I like it here, Terence. I like being where you are."

"Aren't her eyes mesmerizing?"

Owen pauses.

"You're not tapping your forehead?" Carolan asks.

"No."

"Because you are on the road already?"

"Maybe."

"Her eyes, then?"

Owen tells him about the eyes of Annie MacManus. How they are impossibly huge and occupied, not at all like the eyes of a person in the choke-hold of death. How he cannot imagine eyes containing more spirit or hope, a certain indication that she will defeat the doctor's predictions. Long, happy life to Annie MacManus. No one deserves it more.

"Well now," Carolan says, apparently surprised by the summary. "But the poor girl isn't very tall?"

"She is a grown woman, Terence."

"And she is sickly?"

"A man would be lucky to call her his wife," Owen insists.

"The good doctor claims that attempts on her part to birth a child could end in disaster, for one or possibly both parties."

"Lynch is a . . ."

"Quack, quack," Carolan says. "Quite so."

"It's complicated," Owen finally says.

"Is it?"

"You know."

"Tell me still."

Owen has a notion to talk about anchoresses and their cells. Wisely, he suppresses it. "She can't see who I am," he says instead. "She can't see that I am no farmer or labourer, let alone a tradesman or squire. Why should she be able to? She lives right here and now, and has been nowhere else. She can't imagine the varieties of men, and their preoccupations, out in the world. We would be a mismatch, I fear. She would end up disappointed."

"Not like a pleasing tune about some girl, eh?"

"Terence?"

"All those songs about love make it sound as easy as plucking a flower in a meadow. Living the love is more demanding."

Owen draws air into his nose again, to show that he wears another smile.

"There is one further matter," Carolan says.

"I've been waiting."

"Could you grant me the great favour?"

"I've already agreed to it with Mrs Mac."

"She outlined the terms?"

"Not in so many words. But I have surmised what is expected of me and am willing to comply."

Carolan details the task. Because the instructions differ so fundamentally from what Owen has been led to think—the dates and destinations, even the purposes—he asks to hear them a second time.

"You are perturbed by my request?"

"I am honoured to perform these duties for you."

"As my guide?"

"As your manservant."

Two travellers, Owen thinks to himself, in a colossal landscape. What king can survive without his fool? What knight without his squire? Only alongside Terence Carolan, in his service and his shadow, does he feel purpose. Only there is he not lost.

A warble of exceptional pitch and volume floods the room like water through a collapsed dyke.

"To the window," Carolan says.

Owen hesitates. If he stands, the audience will be ended. But then it has been on the wane for several minutes, and Owen already feels blessed. He should leave the harper to his task.

He is at the sill.

"Is it . . .?"

For once, the bird's name comes to him. "A skylark," he says, "out over the wheat fields."

"They prefer cultivated land."

"It hangs high up. Two hundred feet, easily."

"Must be at the top of its arc," Carolan says. "Soon it will drift sideways down."

"There it goes."

"Listen."

Owen listens.

"Quite the warble, isn't it? Shrill and continuous and far-carrying. As breathless in pace as the song of any chaffinch."

"Astonishing," he says.

"God is blind, Owen," Carolan says in a voice now drained by exhaustion. "I understand that finally. He does not see our sufferings, as I once believed. He can't make the night as bright as day, despite the psalm's claim. He is as afflicted as I am. He dwells in the same darkness."

He waits.

"So much makes sense once you realize this truth. So much that you thought beyond acceptance becomes a cross to bear gladly. All the Lord can do is suffer alongside us, manage to be present, like any father or friend. We are not alone in our sorrow. Nor are we alone in feeling forsaken. How can we be? God is as pitiable, and worthy of compassion, as the next creature."

"Is this music as well?" Owen has to ask.

"No, it is silence."

"Silence?"

"Hush, my boy. Hush."

chapter six

March 7, 1738
The journey. Owen kept to the itinerary as best he could. He actually jotted down Carolan's orders after their conversation, both to avoid error and retain a record. His master was exacting in his wishes. He also demanded secrecy. Owen was to discuss the trip with Flinn and no one else. Even Mrs Mac needed to know only that Carolan's guide was carrying out his instructions.

They were as follows:

1. Depart Alderford on March 1. Travel to Pettigoe via Manorhamilton and Belleek. Keep to west shore of Lough Derg.

2. Find Cinnamon the cat. Confine animal inside airy sack. Settle debt with James Devlin.

3. Carry on to Kesh under cover of darkness. Visit Connelly family. Leave provisions and gifts. If Deirdre is yet ill, send back to Pettigoe for a physician. Pay any fees in advance.

4. Return to Alderford using same route, no sooner than March 6. Do NOT take the road through Enniskillen.

Most of which he managed.

It snowed for the first time in a week the morning he left. The ride to Drumkeeran passed without incident, smoke rising from the farmhouses scattered along the lower slope of Arigna. The mountain loomed to the lee side of the path, marking the divide between the border region and the hills and glens of north Leitrim. At Manorhamilton, a village along the River Bonet, the sky faded to ash and the wind expired, the cold catching in his nose like pinches of crude snuff. Gull, whose joints could foretell a turn in the weather, started to fret towards the late afternoon. They pressed on for Garrison, Slieve Bembo prominent to the west, man and horse equally uneasy within those barren valleys, before taking shelter in a gutted priory whose transept retained only a part of its roof. Owen lit a fire using kindling from the saddlebag, smoking out birds in the spire. The temperature dropped overnight, and by morning the air crackled. The path ahead was now treacherous, rivulets forming in the ruts. When he stamped his boots, the clack resembled the report of a distant firearm.

He saw few humans the second morning and no birds, aside from a crow perched motionless on a well. The people he did spy stood at a remove from the track, their forms bowed. The clang of shovels left him content to disavow the usual greetings. He spotted one farmer dismantling a fence to protect a corpse from dogs.

At Garrison, a mean settlement of hovels lacking chimneys or windows, Owen met a young girl wearing boots fashioned from strips of sack. Her dress ended at her knees and her shawl allowed light through it, like the wings of a decomposing moth. Though he knew the direction, he asked her for the bridge over the River Drowse, offering a farthing for the information. Snot hung from a nostril and clumps of hair scraped against her cheeks. If her eyes still showed greater curiosity than terror, it was only from naiveté. The child examined the coin as though it had no use, being inedible.

Was there a new famine in the land? He had no stomach for gloomy predictions. But he remembered this kind of cold, and these sorts of encounters, and shuddered.

The moon came out that evening, a glow of starlight guiding them onwards. The frigid air drew the sky into relief, the stars distinct in one quadrant and smudged, like drifting pipe smoke, in another. A band of black ran through the middle, as though a portal to a second, deeper heaven. Near Belleek, Owen forced Gull into an abandoned cottage. The horse's flanks brushed the door frame, causing the walls to shudder and the roof to heave, raining dust and hay. Once he convinced the animal to lie down, he buried him in straw that yet retained the scent of the humans who once used it for bedding. He did not light a fire, fearing a conflagration, and awoke with a pulse flaring in his neck and a fever searing his brow the same gold-red, he imagined deliriously, as an unsmoored fire. Gull hardly touched his morning feed, even though Owen rubbed his joints and then his poll, in case the horse was suffering from the rheumatism.

He did not debate giving up. Nor did he consider staying in the cottage until the weather improved or his fever abated. He had tasks and a schedule and was a capable servant, a trustworthy guide.

That morning he began offering coins to every woman—there seemed to be no men left in Donegal—who emerged from her house to greet or simply observe the traveller. "What am I to do with this?" one asked, examining the half-penny. Another, eyeing the sack strung across Gull's flanks, wondered if he could spare a few cups of flour instead. A third woman stared blankly at the coin. She stood wrapped in just a blanket, revealing as much womanliness as he had ever seen—breast and belly, dark hair in a patch between her legs. He clicked his tongue twice at the spectre, ordering Gull to trot.

Rider and horse were coming down into Pettigoe when a cat darted across the path. Owen had undertaken the journey with two silent assumptions. The first was that Deirdre Connelly hadn't lasted more than a week beyond their visit the previous August. The other was that Cinnamon had also long since died. On dismounting, however, he received a series of urgent head-butts against his calves. The creature wrapping itself around him matched his vague memory of the cat, including the filthy coat and blunted tail. Without further ado he hoisted it by its scruff and dropped it into a burlap sack.

"By the blood of my forefathers," he envisioned Carolan announcing at Alderford, "this is the paw of Cinnamon the cat."

Then he carried on to the crossroads, over the bridge and back up out of the village, without stopping at Devlin's to settle their debt. Owen couldn't decide why he disobeyed this command, except that the innkeeper had overcharged them the previous summer—a penny too much, at minimum, for such appalling fare and pissy ale—and he had already lightened his purse by half. He might require the remaining coins for a doctor, possibly for himself.

Owen retraced their steps from Pettigoe to Kesh in still another snowfall, arriving in the hamlet at sunset. After trying the Connellys' house, he advanced to the brother's, rapping until his knuckles turned blue. At the only cottage showing signs of habitation he received a cheerful welcome from Maude Sheedy, an elderly spinster who squinted at him from behind veils of cataracts. She recalled the visit of Terence Carolan the previous summer, including his performance for the Connellys and public display of affection with their daughter. While she did not remember any guide accompanying the bard—due, no doubt, to her dimming sight—Maude was happy to take Owen at his word. The bedded embers of her fire gave off a scorching heat, and her farls and cheese tasted as good as one of Betty O'Neill's four-course meals.

As feared, Deirdre Connelly succumbed to diphtheria three days after Carolan left. More shocking by far was the fate of her mother. Never particularly strong, Grainne Connelly surrendered to grief within a fortnight of the child's death, stringing a rope around a branch while her husband was harvesting down at the lake. "May God have mercy on her soul," Maude Sheedy said, blessing herself. A stricken Patrick Connelly forsook the house he had built and went off to Belfast, intending to enlist. Next, his brother lost a son to the same disease. Believing the hamlet cursed, the remaining Connellys also left for the city, hoping for better luck selling their spinning and weaving outwork. Since early January Maude had been the sole resident of Kesh. "Except for the ghosts," she said.

She listed them:

Glow seeping through the window glass of a deserted cottage.

Footsteps fading up the lane at night.

A child singing *ladly-fol-da-dee*.

Owen trembled at the tale. He insisted Maude Sheedy accept the flour, sugar and oats he had brought for the family. He had no use for the goods now, and his horse should not have to carry the load back to Leitrim. But once he relieved Gull of the sacks, he announced his intention to leave. Her face went vague at the decision, as though suddenly lost in the past. She had a spare bed and the fixings for breakfast. Could the gentleman not stay until sunrise, if only to keep an old woman company?

Sadly, he could not.

Back at the Connellys', Owen forced Gull through another narrow doorway. Groping in the dark—light from the recently revealed moon was wavering—he lit a candle, building a small fire using an armful of turf borrowed from Maude Sheedy. The fire showed all of Gulliver's fifteen years, especially about the face: the hollows above the eyes and wrinkled lids, the loosely hanging lips. Poor creature. Owen wept for the horse's decline hard enough to recognize that he was lamenting his own death, imminent and inevitable. Would he be remembered? Not for long, he had to assume.

Recovering from his second bout of tears in both two weeks and, he estimated, twenty-seven years, he dispensed Carolan's generosity. A cob-pipe and packet of Virginia tobacco were left on the table, a handkerchief of gingerbread cookies on a stool. The third gift, provided by Mrs Mac herself, Owen carefully unwrapped. All three plates had survived the trip. He examined their images before lining them along the shelf where Grainne Connelly had stored jars. One plate depicted a country manor nestled in a valley, the second a garden party with children and hounds. On the third plate a family sat at a dinner table laden with a feast.

Next Owen slumped on his side atop a bed of bulrushes, ready to receive her. An arthritic horse and a skittish cat could hardly be substitutes. But he guessed that, were he simply to pass out on the floor and submit to his own chronic nightmare, Deirdre would soon come to him, and he could fulfil his final promise to his master.

Starving children, *ladly-fol-da-dee*.

An abandoned cottage, light seeping through glass.

Absent parents, footfalls in the lane.

He found the graves behind the house the next morning. Crude wooden crosses canted at their heads, like mourners bent over canes. Briar wreaths had been laid upon the mounds during the recent thaw. The stones protecting Grainne Connelly were intact, but those intended to shield Deirdre had been scattered. Someone or something had dug the smaller mound up, flinging black earth across the snow. Now in the clutches of a roaring fever, Owen did not remain long enough at the site to learn whether the girl's body still occupied its grave.

A thought gripped him then with the same clarity that Carolan must have been gripped by melodies. Owen Connor might wish to be a father someday. He might enjoy that settled existence.

The notion, and little else, stayed with him the ride home to Alderford. He retained no memory of where he spent the nights and could not account for a single meal or conversation along the way. But he did come to understand as he passed through Drumshanbo on the morning of March sixth that he had strayed once more from the itinerary. Drumshanbo, only five miles east of the Macdermott Roe estate, was situated along the bottom shore of Lough Allen. It marked the near conclusion of the traditional route down from the North, the path he had been forbidden to travel. Sensing his rider's incapacity, Gulliver had obviously made the decision for them both and headed south along the east shore of Lough Erne, through the scruffy island town of Enniskillen—whose modern stone gaol, Owen seemed to recall, was situated on the main road—across the west bridge back over the River Erne and then further south through Derrynacreeve and Ballinamore. He mapped it out on the horse's neck:

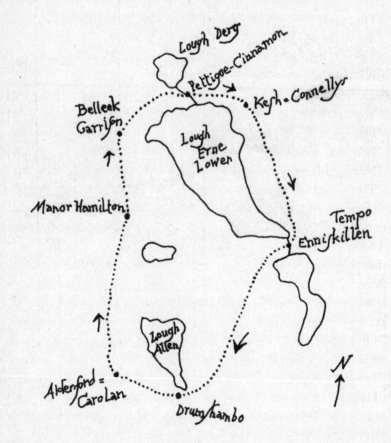

Even in his delirium he recognized the symmetry. Saw it plainly, in fact. The journey as a circle. Half of it his choosing, the other half chosen for him.

✳   ✳   ✳

"Proceed no further, Owen Connor," Mary Mac says in the staff hall the evening of his return. "You are not welcome here."

"But I have business with my master."

"You lied to us. Again."

"I did not."

"To me, especially."

"I serve Terence Carolan," Owen says. His will being stronger than his body, he flattens a palm on the table for balance. "All other allegiances come second."

"You are not fit."

"I am quite ill, since you mention it."

"Now you mock me?"

"Not for an instant, Mrs Mac."

"Then leave the manor at once."

"I promised him a summary of my findings. I promised him a cat in a sack," he says, raising the sack.

Cinnamon meows. Behind Owen, Annie MacManus giggles, her defiance already strained.

Mary Macdermott Roe struggles to hold a grim smile. "Then tell me what you wish relayed to Terence," she says. "I shall convey it directly. As for some flea-ridden Ulster stray . . ."

"I'm afraid I can't," Owen answers. "The matter is private."

Believing it prudent, he bows at the waist.

"Private? From me?"

"Like certain letters," he begins to say. But he, too, would be content if the letters from Bridget Cruise were destroyed.

"In my own house?"

He bows a second time.

"You have brought shame upon Alderford."

"I apologize."

"And been the direct cause of your master's latest downturn."

Owen must sit. The floor will do fine, he resolves, especially since neither Flinn nor John Stamford, both sucking on pipes at the table, have any intention of propping him up. Some obscure estate law appears to decree that his every humiliation should occur before the entire household.

A cloud of mundungus drifts in his direction. He draws in a lungful, hoping the scent will steady him.

"You insist you were not aware that the sheriff had made it known he would visit here the first week of March?" she asks.

"I was not."

"And Terence, by your account, just happened to select that period for you to carry out his secret missions to Pettigoe and . . . what is the name of that village in Fermanagh?"

"Kesh."

Owen wondered about the timing, naturally, and guessed that his master had received a warning letter from Brian Maguire, which Flinn somehow hid from Mary Macdermott Roe. But he couldn't quite see the butler defying his mistress to spare Owen an arrest or even a flogging.

"But how could he have known the dates of the sheriff's return? Unless there was a communication . . . Flinn?" Mary Mac says, looking past him.

The butler suspends his smoke in mid-puff.

"Have any letters arrived from Tempo in recent weeks that were not brought to my attention?"

"Mrs Mac?" the butler asks. With his chin lowered, Flinn's eyes are thickets of brow.

"It hardly matters," Owen intervenes. "I accept responsibility for the debacle. And the sheriff, I take it, was none too pleased to find me gone?"

He is reminding Mary Macdermott Roe of her options. She can interrogate a trusted servant in front of his peers and learn that he deceived her, in conspiracy with her beloved house guest. Or she can boast of how her Leitrim estate dealt with the intrusions of an ill-mannered Northerner.

The strategy of a diplomat, he thinks to himself. Carolan would be proud.

She chooses wisely. "He was displeased, in point of fact," she replies, "and soon became displeasing to me. Such a person deserved neither a bowl of Betty's soup nor a sup of my whiskey, regardless of whether he had frostbite in his toes. Such a person deserved what he got," she adds. "An escort back to the gates and instructions to return him home via counties Cavan or Longford. Isn't that so, John?"

"The man may still be wandering as we speak," John Stamford says.

"Quite right."

"He'll not darken this door again, Missus."

With household solidarity re-established, everyone can breathe again. In a few moments, Owen is aware, attention will shift back to the real enemy—him. He has a notion to use the remaining seconds to explain to Mary Mac and the others that, far from dragging the estate's name "through the bog," as she earlier complained, the incident with the sheriff will add to the legend surrounding the manor where the bard hung his cloak his final days. One has only to be out in the countryside—as he has been, and they have not—to remark on the gathering roar of tales concerning the twilight adventures of Terence Carolan. This newest story is a corker, rife with mischief, along with just the right note of harmless insurrection. Before long it will be travelling across Connacht and Leinster, a tale worth both amplifying and exaggerating, with the names of the house and the guide still prominent in the telling. Only later will the title "Alderford" go missing, or be confused with Mohill or Nobber, other sites associated with the harper. As for the name "Owen Connor," the fellow who stole the books and picked the fights, it will suffer first from errors—"Owen Cleary was his name" or "They called him Conn the Freckled"—and then from indifference. Before long he will simply be the "lad" who played a part in the legend of Carolan's confrontation with the Ulster regiment that marched southwards to arrest the bard for some witty slight upon King George—calling the monarch a dog, perhaps, or a boatman.

"You don't have an actual cat in that sack, do you?" Mrs Mac says, ignoring the noisy evidence to the contrary.

"Named Cinnamon," Owen answers.

"And you stole it from the streets of Pettigoe?"

"As per his request."

"You think a cat will help him now?"

Owen says nothing.

"He suffered a fit while you were traipsing about Donegal," she says. "A massive attack. On your account it was, too."

"Not fair," Annie MacManus says.

He turns to her. She stands on her platform, chin raised gloriously high, poised for a fight she can't possibly win.

Mary Macdermott Roe, clearly puzzled by the epidemic of insubordination infecting her servants, cocks her head at the maid.

"Quiet, Annie," Owen says.

"One arm and leg paralysed," Mrs Mac resumes, "and his powers of speech lost. Even his mental faculties . . ." She stops to gather her composure, as though it is a shawl that keeps slipping from her shoulders. "All this happened the very morning after the sheriff's raid. Is there anyone else to blame for such an unexpected reversal?"

"Unexpected?" Annie says. "But Dr Lynch—"

"No one," Owen interrupts.

"Then you accept full responsibility?"

"I have already said as much."

"And you accept that I must take the necessary action to protect Carolan against . . . Have you a comment for your mistress, Annie MacManus?"

"I do."

"She does not," Owen corrects. Having seen and heard enough, he stands. "I accept blame for his condition and the lies I forced you all to tell. I shall remove myself to the cottage shortly and after that from Alderford itself. I give you my word. Just as now," Owen says, brushing past Mary Mac to the stairs, "I must keep my word with Terence."

"Flinn!"

But Owen is already in the hallway and climbing the main staircase. Carolan's chamber is open and he walks in, halting at the foot of the bed. His master lies in much the same pose as ten days ago. The difference this evening is the rictus that has collapsed the left side of his face, like a watercolour blurred by rain, and the drool pooling at one corner of his mouth, which he is either unaware of or else can't clear away with his tongue. Curled in his undamaged hand is the rosary, the crucifix dangling over his thumb.

"Terence," he says in a tone of such shrill cheerfulness that Grace the dog, malingering by the fire, whimpers. "I'm afraid I can't stay long. Cinnamon requires a wash and a trim of the nails, for your own protection. But here he is, pretty much as you left him last summer."

He lowers the sack to the floor, untying the string. With a dog nearby the cat won't venture out.

"Hear the meows?" he asks.

Carolan attempts a reply. His lips quiver, as though he is praying the Hail Marys, but only on one side. The effort releases a trickle down his chin.

Unable to watch any longer, Owen studies the floor. He hears footsteps on the stairs.

"As for the Connellys of Kesh," he says. "I can report good news. Patrick thanks you for the provisions and tobacco. Grainne was delighted with the plates. And Deirdre the dancer . . ."

He staggers. From fatigue and illness, or the size of this latest lie? He can't be sure. Hands grip both his arms in support. One grip belongs to an old woman, the other to an even older man.

"She is yet sickly and, to my mind, too slight for her age. But she is grand and squealed at the gift of the biscuits. 'You'll not catch me,' she said, dancing about the cottage like a sprite. 'I'm the gin-her-bread man!'"

"Look," Flinn says.

Even Owen glances back up. Carolan's mouth has curved into a deformed smile, slack on the damaged end. It is a rare physical expression, as confident in its worth as a father's smile to his son. Mary Macdermott Roe crosses to the bed to end his indignity with a handkerchief.

"My duties are fulfilled," Owen says.

He withdraws.

* * *

Annie catches up to him in the pasture. She has neglected to bring a shawl and must keep raising her skirts out of the muddy snow. Owen removes his cloak and wraps it around her, a third of the fabric dragging on the ground.

"You seem tired," she says. Lifting onto her toes, she touches his scratched cheek. "The cat did this?"

"Getting him out of the sack was one matter," he admits. "Getting him back in, quite another."

"Was the travelling difficult?"

"A little, thanks for asking."

"It isn't fair, Owen."

"Don't say or do anything to further anger the others, Annie. Don't do that to yourself."

"To myself?"

"It's for the best."

She presses her lips. "Why do they treat you so?"

"Revenge, I suppose. Intimate and bloody-minded. Like Cinnamon," he says, running his own fingertips over the scratches.

Annie vows to bring him his meals and keep him informed about Carolan, even if her actions land her in trouble or cause her to be dismissed. Owen thanks her with his eyes.

"He's dying, isn't he?"

"I'm sorry for you," she says.

Then she brings a dark flush to his scratched cheek.

"And I could come to you, Owen Connor," she offers, her gaze unblinking. "I could, anytime."

CHAPTER SEVEN

March 24, 1738

Three more weeks go by, and still no resolution. Carolan yet lies dying. Owen, banned from the manor, yet awaits arrest. The death watch, as reported by a breathless Annie MacManus, has been festive. He can't blame the girl for being awestruck by the lords and ladies descending on Alderford to pay their respects, or for assuming these guests to be a higher category of citizenry. For Owen, Lord Mayo is a hapless philanderer living in a leaky castle and Fanny Power, now Mrs Robert Conmee, a wily charmer not to be trusted at whist. But for Annie and the other servants, such individuals are not only transplants from a ball at Dublin Castle—the silver brooches and white kid gloves, the coach driven by a groom in splattered uniform—but the fruits of musical alchemy. Nearly every new arrival has corresponded with an existing composition by the master. How could the servants fail to be astounded? "They hardly ever look like their tunes," Annie tells him once. "Except for Grace Nugent. She's lovely."

Bets are on among the servants, Annie says, as to when Flinn will finally announce "Mrs Arthur Barnewall, of Trimlestown." What a reunion that will be! Bridget Cruise and Terence Carolan, together again at last. They will be humming the famous melody in the hall throughout the afternoon. They'll also be squabbling over who gets to bring Bridget her cup of tea or glass of port, and thus glimpse the lady's regal manners and flaxen hair.

Owen does not mind too much that, according to Annie's reluctant count, only one guest has inquired after Carolan's guide. Edward

Crofton, of all people, whose thieved edition of Homer, translated by Alexander Pope, adorns the bookshelf in the cottage. Flinn apparently informed Mr Crofton that the employee in question no longer resided on the estate, having immigrated, it was thought, to New France. Nor does Owen miss having to suffer the inattention or, worse, the abuse of these gentry folk. Thanks to the letters he read in Annie's chamber, he now knows how little they think of him. Shifty and untrustworthy and disposed to taking on airs. Damaged beyond repair by an upbringing devoid of shoes or warm fires or parents' affection.

But then, hasn't he been levelling similar incriminations at himself in a letter to Friar Seamus? The floor beneath his bed is littered with versions of the text. The current draft is still a muddle of thoughts, revealing, in his view, a weak intellect matched by an incomplete character. He would certainly not be quick to see the letter published, even under a pseudonym.

Boatman, the letter begins. *Greetings from her ladyship's dog at Alderford. Here is a pen name worthy of the Drapier: "Her Ladyship's Dog." Or perhaps the "Betwixt-Between Man" or the "Peasant-Philosopher"? All three would serve as cloaking and as summary . . . My sojourn at this estate is near ended, I suspect, and no, my master, though beyond recovery, yet graces the living. The proper discharge of a service to him last month is what finished me off. No good deed goes unpunished, does it? . . . Sir Isaac Newton claims there are two types of matter and men. A few are strong and undivided and never lose a night's sleep in worry over their opinions or rank. Most, though, are fated to twist in their straw beds, bedevilled by such concerns. We knock about our entire lives, inclined first in one direction and then the other, lacking surety in our judgements or, more severely, our worth. Fragments, the scientist calls us, forever seeking to form and reform through a clinging friendship or a dutiful wife. It's a deficiency of love that makes us so, I am convinced . . . But France and the Irish Brigade still hold no allure. It's right here where we should make our stand. Establish our names and connections, as patriots and husbands, even as fathers. Swift says a man cannot be reasoned out of something he hasn't first reasoned himself into. That is my position also, I think . . . But hammer on my door again, so I might convey it better. Or perhaps I will soon come looking for you, S the Smuggler, in Kinvarra Bay, County Clare, chased by death and disgrace and a mercenary sheriff or two . . .*

And so on. Lucky for Seamus, and probably for Owen as well, the mailing address is incomplete. Already he envisions the letter "posted" into the hearth, the paper smoking along the edges before being consumed.

Poor Annie arrives with his supper one evening just as the directionless missive, and another raging head, have made a wreck of his sanity.

"You're sure he has not performed a new composition for these visitors?" Owen says to her, fingers busy on his skull. "The harp must be woefully out of tune."

"Owen!"

"You'd tell me if he played for them, wouldn't you?"

"He cannot raise his head or lift his right hand," the scullery maid answers. "I doubt he realizes who is present in the room much of the time."

"The majority of those lords and ladies couldn't distinguish a planxty by a great composer from a fiddle tune dredged up in a public house. Affluence does not breed musical taste, I have observed."

"He has not played, I swear."

"His nails would preclude it," he agrees, contradicting himself.

"But I'll tell you something he is aware of," Annie says. "Every day I whisper your name in his ear, when tidying the bed or spooning him broth. 'Owen is fine,' I say, 'though he misses you terribly.' He smiles, Owen. At least, his lips quiver, which is all he can manage. I see the affection and concern. I see it plainly."

"What, in his gaze?"

She looks at him. At once he shifts his focus to the wall. When Annie grabs at the hand covering his face, pulling it away from his brow, he allows her. She does not let go.

"I'm pleased to hear it," he says in apology. "I am."

"You think he has forgotten you?"

"I think *I* have forgotten me."

"I visit you every day."

"I am grateful."

"And I see you," she says. "I see the sadness in your eyes. Also the gentleness, and the pain."

Releasing his hand, she turns away. The shelf is before her, and in a gesture he finds touching she feigns studying the spines of the books.

"Do you enjoy reading these?"

"Enjoy?"

Annie is silent.

"I enjoy some of them, yes," Owen replies. "Others are more tasks, like the lessons I received during my schooling."

She keeps her back to him. He can admire her then, her nut-brown hair and pretty ears, the high slope of her cheek. When his attention fastens, as it does, on the bulge across her shoulders, the not-quite-hump that thrusts her head forward, Owen is ashamed once more. He is also seized by a melancholy that is hopelessly philosophical. How people look to each other, and to themselves. The pitiless light of day upon all our faces. The tyranny of conventional vision.

"They taught you about books at the charity school?"

"Hardly. Sir Henry put me in class with his own boys. We used the small sitting room," he says. "Our tutor lived in this very cottage."

"And he was a queer lonely man as well?"

"James Egan? I don't recall him being so."

"On account of the reading, I mean. You're on your own for hours, your face buried in words."

"It's the only way to get the job done."

"Someone could read to you aloud, couldn't they?"

"I read to Carolan most nights we travelled," Owen says.

"The Bible?"

"Or Virgil."

Her expression, discerned in profile, invites him to expound.

"The story of the Roman warrior Aeneas who washes ashore in a town called Carthage. He takes a fancy to the queen there, named Dido."

"But she takes more than a fancy to him, does she not?" Annie says. "My father told me the story as a tale rather than a book. Doesn't she end up falling on her own sword?"

"With him back out at sea in his ship, noticing a huge funeral pyre and wondering who might have died." *Aeneas caused her death and lent the blade,* Owen recites to himself. *Dido by her own hand in dust was laid.*

"Her heart and soul, sacrificed for that fellow. He probably wasn't worthy of her, you know."

"Almost certainly not," he says.

It feels curious talking to Annie MacManus about books. Actually, it feels curious talking to anyone about them now. Owen's last decent conversation was with the friar in January.

"Girls get all in a lather about love," she says.

"That they do."

"It's generally a mistake."

"No doubt."

She is back to staring at his face. For clues, he suspects.

"And the books that you . . . that people claim you . . ."

"Stole?"

"I don't believe it myself," Annie says without conviction.

"These two," Owen says, pulling down the Newton and Hutcheson. Handing them to her, he sits on the bed.

"Are they brilliant stories?"

"Not exactly," he answers with a grin he hopes she won't misinterpret.

"Then why bother?"

"Different reasons."

"And they mean so much to you?"

He nods.

"I'd like to understand, Owen," she says with sudden shyness, "if you aren't opposed to explaining."

"I'd be honoured," he says. His explanation takes only a minute. Books, he begins, can't be owned. Neither their ideas nor their appeal to truth. He learned this from Carolan. For years he was witness to the birth of wondrous melodies, courtesy of his master's gift. No question who composed the tunes or whose name belonged on them. Still, once played in a hall or drawing room or even at a crossroads dance, the melodies ceased being the property of the harper Terence Carolan. They belonged to any and all who listened, were delighted and stirred, and later hummed them to their children. Such things—art, he supposes, though the word is a bit grand—created in a spirit of freedom must, in turn, be freely given away. "And *that*," Owen concludes, his voice rising with passion, "is the true liberty loose in this land."

Her silence is as least as long as his reply. He watches for signs of impatience or scorn. The good opinion of this scullery maid, he acknowledges, is essential to him.

"Then you should read them to me," she finally says.

"I might, some time."

"Share that liberty with others."

He blinks.

"There's no real difference between having those books locked away here or in someone's library with an actual lock on the door, is there?"

"I suppose not," Owen admits. In truth, he is shaken by her accusation and her insight.

But then, just when her anger is having an effect, the fight goes out of her. "It would be better if you had never looked at me at all," she says woefully.

"Annie?"

"Better that you'd never looked at my face, along with the body the Lord has seen fit to provide. Then you'd have been like your master with his missus, obliged to focus on a person's nature, not her appearance. You'd have taken a fancy to me regardless and not have jumped back on that ship, like Aeneas."

These words astound him even more.

"Blow out the candle, please," she says.

He complies. Guessing her intention, he slides over. Annie joins him in the bed, both of them fully dressed.

"I've some claim to you," she says. "To come to you or, better, for you to come to me. Lying in the rhododendron glade up beyond the stream. Dipping our tongues in blossom cups. In May, when everything is in bloom. It's what men and women do together. It's who we are."

He takes her hand.

"I've some claim," she says again.

"I'm flattered," he answers, meaning it.

"But?"

"You are so young," he says.

"Twenty-one now. Late to be marrying."

"It's a dream of sorts," Owen says. "Feeling bright and hopeful and certain your fate will be different. But then you awaken and find out it isn't true."

Neither of them speaks.

"Can I still stay?" she eventually says.

"If you like."

"Even just to feel your bony hip and long spine. Even just to smell you."

"I blush."

"I can see it."

She laughs. Then she starts to cry, a steady, resigned whimper, strangely similar to a keen.

"Hush, Annie," he says, enfolding her in his arms. He can manage this small gesture. Console her. Nurse her sore body.

"This must be enough," she says. "It must be."

"Hush."

The rain starts up, a patter of wet snow and droplets. The winter, a wrathful deity, is expiring at last.

He is tired. Sleep, even with a woman in his bed, won't be denied.

"How is the head now?" she says from a distance.

"Improved."

"You're surprised?"

"I am, to be honest."

"It's because you're anticipating another journey."

"Maybe."

"It's all that keeps you from exploding."

"If you say so."

She continues to weep. Or is it the rain? He shifts onto his side, away from her. She presses against him.

She says something else.

"Aye," he replies, not really hearing her.

"How can I . . .?" she repeats.

How can I not be enough? Annie might be saying. He could ask her to repeat the remark a third time, but doesn't.

"Hush," he says.

Her hair smells of ginger and her body of oatmeal. An anchoress in her cell, Owen thinks dreamily. Alone with her stone womb and her god.

* * *

When he opens his eyes, it is light. And she is gone.

* * *

It is mid-morning before Owen finally gives up waiting for breakfast to be brought to the cottage. As promised, he has kept clear of the servants' hall. Now he removes his cap and kicks his boots at the door. Two girls he does not recognize stand at the counter, one plucking a bird and the other stirring a pot. Three strange men sit by the fire supping noggins of ale. In profile, a man with a shaved skull and square jaw seems familiar. When the stranger winks at him, Owen recoils.

"Has anyone seen Annie MacManus?" he asks.

"Who are you?" the maid holding the chicken says.

The same man speaks without turning to Owen. "He's the lad, he is," he says in the orotund accent of east Ulster. "Aren't you, Owen Connor?"

The girl gasps at the name.

"Have you Mrs Mac's permission to be in the house?" Betty O'Neill says, emerging from the pantry.

"I'm looking for Annie," he says.

"Are you now."

"Please."

"You could try her mother's in the village, where she has likely fled, having burst in here at dawn wild-eyed and bawling. She gave her notice and then left without so much as a goodbye. As if," the cook says, "the reason for her distress wasn't written over her face. What else have you stolen from this estate, Owen? What else?"

"Once a thief, always a thief," the man at the fire says.

Owen glances at the profile again. Gordon Smith, the butler at Tempo? What is he doing at Alderford?

"Have you no decency?"

"You've known me since I was a boy, Betty."

"I don't know you, sir. Not at all."

"I'll go speak with Mrs Mac," he says, crossing the hall.

"I wouldn't recommend it," the cook says.

Mary Macdermott Roe stands in the front hallway between two gentlemen. On sighting Owen, her scowl dissolves into an expression of concern that is tender and vulnerable and, as such, a strain upon her hardened features. He recognizes the bulk of Brian Maguire and the ruination settled over the man's face. The second guest slaps his gloves in his palm. Colonel Hugh Maguire, in a cloak and riding boots. Owen recalls the colonel as taller and broader across the shoulders. He recalls him as more dashing.

"Owen," Brian Maguire says helplessly.

"Speak of the devil," the colonel says.

In an instant Owen is back down in the servants' hall and striding for the door. Though he is chased by the laughter of just a single fellow servant, he still feels the birch switches across his backside. The pasture squelches underfoot. Ground fog once again provides a natural defence, and he wades through the brume.

❊　❊　❊

Hours pass. Owen can tell by the cold embers and the light through the slats. His thoughts, too, at once alert and tranquil, confirm that he has slept. He has a plan. Peeling off his clothes, he opens the trunk, selecting the same outfit Annie tricked him into sporting on Christmas Eve. He dons the stockings and garters, breeches and chemise. He ties two vest buttons. He even forces himself into the narrow-toed shoes with the silver buckles, to complete the imitation. Next, he consults the same looking glass he once resisted.

Time does not allow for a shave. Tugging a comb through his hair, he splashes his scalp with water, to suppress the curls. Annie loaned him a pair of grooming scissors a while back. Taking them up, he clips his sideburns and bangs, clears his ears and snips at the hairs in his nostrils. His eyebrows flare dramatically, the wrong look for a gentleman. He nearly pokes an eye out trimming them.

A sound stops Owen between the fireplace and bookshelf. He hears a horse neigh and recognizes Geminiani by the grunt at the end of her call. Has Gulliver sunk a hoof in mud and stumbled?

At the shelf he pulls out *An Inquiry into the Original of Our Ideas of Beauty and Virtue,* steadying the plank with his hand. Scanning the titles for Newton, he slides a volume from between its neighbours. As he does, he notes the name Isaac Newton further along the row. Realizing he has the wrong book, he attempts to file one title while removing another. A bracket comes unstuck and the shelf collapses. Owen cradles a dozen books in his arms, the rest plummeting to the ground. A volume lands spread open, the text face down. It is the *Optics,* a page ripped and another folded over and smeared.

He curses.

In the pasture he halts his frantic pressing of the bent page against his chest to take in a sight. Gull and Gem stand by the fence at the north end of the field. Neither horse appears to be ailing. Rather, they are trading plaintive neighs, heads raised and ears alert. From where he stands it is obvious the animals are directing their calls at a manor window.

The hall is now empty, except for Flinn. The butler, a gnome in an oversized apron, sits at the table examining the surface and either does not notice, or chooses not to comment on, Owen's flight across the floor. Back in the front hallway he takes in the absence of cloaks on the stand and the chapel hush of the air. He calls out to Mary Macdermott Roe, twice.

"In the sitting room," she answers.

He finds her in a chair by the window, the letter box in her lap. Aside from the brief viewing earlier on, Owen has not seen Mrs Mac—or Flinn, in fact—in twenty-one days. She strikes him as a small, sorrowful widow, her disappointments stored in a box. He wonders if he has shrunk as well.

"Mrs Mac?"

"Sit."

"Am I permitted?"

"I won't have you towering over me," she says. She looks him up and down. "My late husband," she offers. "Tall as a tree and skinny as a reed. There you are."

His attention drifts to the portrait above the mantel. Does he truly resemble Henry Macdermott Roe? He has hesitated to compare details until now. Sir Henry's brow was heavier and his nose more aquiline. His chin also ended in a bony tip, in contrast to Owen's horseshoe jaw. As for the eyes, the artist's rendering is cursory. But Owen can remember his patron's cool eyes, and if he cares to admit it—which he does today, for some reason—he must acknowledge that in the thousands of times Sir Henry's eyes met his own, at table or in the barn, among company or in private, not once did the exchange suggest a connection between father and son. He suspects he should have seen this truth some time ago.

He has a speech prepared. "I've come here this morning to do what is right by Colonel Maguire," he says.

"It's past four o'clock, Owen."

"It is? At any rate I've brought the books along. The Newton is a bit worse for wear, but if we press it under another volume for a period, the paper will flatten out."

"He is gone."

"The colonel?"

Her sob is closer to a choke.

"No," Owen says.

"Gone, and I don't know how I will carry on without him."

He repeats the denial.

"These last weeks . . ." she says. "Such splendour and finery. I never really appreciated his importance to them. Out there among our nation's nobility, behaving in a manner that won him only admiration and love. For his music, of course, but also, I now realize, for his person."

"His gentleness and civility," Owen says.

"He disappointed not a single patron. He said and did nothing to cause discomfort or social upset."

Owen pauses before these attributes.

"The stories those nobles told," she says. "Mostly old tales, some too ribald for my ears, along with a few new ones as well. Both Flinn and I overheard guests leaving the house with the story of his parting kiss and farewell composition, performed on his deathbed." Mary Mac frowns, as though just recognizing a striking collision between fact and fiction. "It was an honour to host such esteemed persons," she adds to herself.

He sits down.

"My best wasn't good enough," he says. "Not for the likes of Terence Carolan. I know it for certain now. For all my love and attention to my duties."

His remarks lift her gaze back up. "Circumstances will change at Alderford. It is inevitable."

He nods.

"And what are you doing in Sir Henry's clothes?"

"Mrs Mac?"

"He took you in all those years back. We both welcomed you into our home. Why have you required further affirmation? Annie MacManus told me of your theory this morning, in response to my own question concerning your shocking behaviour of late. Your insolence about being a Macdermott Roe, the product of an illicit relation between my husband and some country girl—can you explain it?"

He can, now that he has forsaken the insolence. According to Francis Hutcheson, a high birth makes it more probable a man can redeem a low character and learn to practise virtue. By extension, a foundling with bad habits must stand almost no chance. That leaves Owen Connor forever mired in himself, a hopeless case.

Instead, he simply apologizes.

"And is this truly the cause of your cruelty towards Annie? A belief that you are gentry by blood, if not by upbringing?"

"I am not worthy of the girl," he replies. "And I am very sorry she mentioned my silly conjectures to you."

"She was in distress, Owen. You've gone and broken her young heart." Mary Macdermott Roe sighs and clutches her box. "I've the composition right here, at least," she says. "For posterity."

"The composition?"

"Charles MacCabe transcribed it. He went over the notes with Terence, humming the melody and counting out the beat, to ensure he had taken it down correctly. The piece was composed entirely in his head."

"When was this?" he says above the pounding inside his own skull.

"While you were evading the sheriff."

"Has it been played?"

"I am to hire an itinerant, preferably an Italian, to perform the music at the graveyard in Kilronan. Terence worked on this bit of theatre with MacCabe and Peyton the day before the final attack. I am glad they did, for I find such preparations ghoulish."

"Then no one knows how it sounds?"

"Charles O'Conor, who made a study of the score this Friday last, claims it is irregular in structure, which is no surprise, and in the traditional range. A beautiful melody, Charles believes. But he also remarked . . ."

"Yes?"

"I am not versed in music, Owen."

"What did Mr O'Conor say? His exact words. No need for you to try interpreting them."

She rebukes him with a mild frown. "He spoke of the piece being unusually grave. He detected an ambition, and a yearning, new to Terence's music. I find these qualities worrisome. His compositions are usually so easy with themselves, a reason why they are so pleasing to the ear, I suppose."

"He wrote it for her, you know."

"He did not."

"He told me as much. A musical record of a man remembering, or even rediscovering, his affection for a companion he has lost. His gratitude for love, expressed in melody."

"His final composition is in honour of that woman?"

"Moira was hardly any woman."

"Moira? I took you to be referring to Bridget Cruise."

"It has to be her," he says under his breath. "There can be no one else."

"Here it is, regardless," Mrs Mac says, unrolling a scroll of parchment paper.

"May I?"

She holds the sheet out, and he crosses the room to collect it. Recalling his master's final remark about music and silence, he half-expects the score to be blank. As it is, he can no more read the text than Annie MacManus can declaim *The Aeneid*. Owen doubts he will ever hear the composition performed. But it is enough to know it exists and must be the music he witnessed being created, in a room filled with birds and inside a mind filled with melodies. It is enough to hold the paper in his hands.

"I had not intended to mention this to you," Mary Macdermott Roe begins. She has adjusted her chair in order to stare out the window, a palm flat against the glass, as if to cool the fire within her. "Terence expressed a wish that the tune be named 'Owen Ballach,' in reward, I expect, for your faithful service during the better times. Several friends, including myself, convinced him it must bear the formal title 'A Farewell to Music,' both to keep with tradition and to match the tale he was constructing about his final hours. He accepted our reasoning only after argument."

Owen is unable to speak.

"Betty O'Neill has laid the body out," she says. "Go to him."

"I don't think I can."

"It's those ridiculous shoes you wear. I could never understand Sir Henry's fondness for narrow toes."

The statement urges him to his feet.

"Changes are inevitable, here and everywhere," she says, her fingers squeaking over the glass. Light from the window catches her profile, showing her without pity.

He leaves the score on the table, next to the books.

❊   ❊   ❊

At the top of the landing he pauses to smooth his hair and check the buttons on the vest. The door is open once again, and the chamber emits a rare light for that hour—due, no doubt, to its western exposure. Bird call fills the corridor as well, a clamour of peeping and chattering, as if from a busy cage. Grace occupies her spot by the hearth. On noticing Owen the dog rises with a groan and a yawn.

In the Name of the Father, he says silently, sliding his hand down his chest, And of the Son, and of the Holy Spirit, Amen. Afraid to look, Owen crosses to the window, expecting to find a choir loft of birds on the sill. A single winged creature, the same bluetit, perhaps, as in February, takes two hops before fluttering away. He peers southwards out the window, beyond the field where he once tracked the skylark. Gem and Gull maintain their now silent vigil in the pasture.

Cinnamon catches his eye first. According to Annie, the cat has rarely left its post on the bed since its arrival at Alderford. She swore the animal was informed in advance of its duties. The cat sang throat songs to a fading musician. It licked a dying sensualist's cheeks and chin and pawed his lips. Cinnamon even figured out to sprawl next to Carolan's functioning hand, allowing him to knead the now soft, glistening coat, and so double the volume of purrs.

Noticing the intruder, and possibly remembering the evil man who once stuffed it in a sack, the cat growls. Owen resolves to let Cinnamon claw him in exchange for a spot on the mattress. He can't bring himself to examine Carolan's face. He can't even touch the hand with the rosary beads woven like briar between the fingers, the polished crucifix flat on the chest. Slipping out of his shoes, he lies next to the body, a boy seeking warmth from a sleeping father. The bed frame is a foot too short. His ankles extend beyond it and he crooks his neck, his right arm pillowing his own head. He inhales talcum. His sight, lifting up over the scene, blurs and finally goes blind before a light that can only be described as harmonic.

Within that light, Owen thinks, I am not a servant masquerading as a nobleman and he is not a childlike corpse laid out to rest. Within that radiance, we are seen for who we are and loved the more because of it. There is a country no one would flee, a place of lasting peace. A ruined priory by a stream, why not? Sunlight through a gap in the wall. Swallows reeling in the tower.

He improvises a prayer. Earth, receive this great, good and foolish man. Lord, include him in your harmony.

Will we ride out, Master? he then asks. Footloose and wind-tossed and up the lane? The horses are keen for the exercise and the nation longs for your return. No endless seas or vaulting skies, I promise. No valley where the birds don't sing. We can keep right here in south Leitrim, among the brimming lakes and sodden bogs, the moss-floored woodlands. The glens are snug and the paths well-trod. A soothing countryside, one that protects those wise enough to stay within it.

What will we hear and smell on our journey? What will we observe? In the woodlands there will be foxes and fallow deer, hares and woodmice. By lake's edge otters and badgers may stir. Birds will serenade us wherever we wander: wrens and song thrushes, wood-cocks and kingfishers. Expect moorhens and mallards along the shorelines, cormorants and snipes out on the water. Yes, a grey heron slowly lifts off. Yes, a mute swan rides among the reeds.

And in the glens? Carpets of primrose and yellow iris, bluebells and blackthorn further up the slopes. White willow and orange hawthorn berries; honeysuckle and wild dog roses. Dog roses are red, like certain trees in the rhododendron glade at Alderford. Honeysuckle is as it sounds—the gold of fresh honey, poured into a mug.

Gold, like the hair of young girls in sunlight?

Then you can summon colours?

A little.

And images—they aren't entirely vanished?

Not entirely. The swan in the current, for instance. Can you see it?

I can.

Head bowed and beautiful?

Aye.

Its path leaving no wake?

Hardly at all.

That must be lovely.

It is.

Delicate.

It is.

Mutable.

Aye, Master. It is lovely. It surely is.

Part III

A FAREWELL TO MUSIC

Night. Lucky the husband who puts his hand beneath her head. Amused, the father cuffed on the nose by a child's shin. Who sleeps upside down? Which one sprawls crossways and mutters about sugar cubes? Happiest three, five or nine in the four-poster bed. Running nails along spines and over scalps. Whispering *hush* and *dearie, move aside*. Scent of dough and flavour of butterscotch. Raft in a claret-dark sea.

Day. In his chair with pipe and noggin, his breakfast griddle-sizzling. The bairns are all fed? he asks. Fed and washed and scampering about, she answers. Let me give you a scrub as well. Sit and make tea instead, my glowing girl. Glowing? Lamp loses light next to you, Moira Keane. Stop it, she says. You are a good wife. Easy to woo and easier still to wed. I am a simple country woman, she replies.

Night. Music must listen to her least whisper, as he will soon attend her every moan. Her, kissing his scars. Him, scratching her everywhere, until she is a tumble of brown hair. Raise the gown, woman, I can contain myself no longer. But I've a baby in my arms, she says. What say we shift Maev over to the other side? Mary, she answers. This one is called Mary.

Day. Another pipe? she asks. Another roll in the hay? he replies with some sort of grin. Daddy, can you see my new dress? Show Daddy, her mother corrects her. Here you are, he says, lifting the girl into his lap. All cylinder flesh and lilac scent, squirms and giggles and coos. Owen Connor may be coming by this afternoon, he tells the child's mother. Wouldn't that be a surprise? she says. They share a laugh.

Dirige, Domine, Deus meus, in conspectu tuo viam meam.

Night. Only on her side will they not start the raft shaking, the water seeping in. His arm her pillow, lucky husband, his other steadying her hip. She reaches behind and shifts his nightshirt above the waist. We'll kiss without scandal, he whispers, and be as quiet as church mice. You just think you will be, she says. Neck and shoulders, waist and thigh—all that we desire. Plus breasts.

Direct, O Lord, my God, my way to Thy sight.

Day. Up in the garden behind the cottage. His straw chair, his pot of ale. Children *tra-la-la* about him. Look, Daddy, look what Eileen did. Collect some flowers for me, girls. You and you and you over there. Bring your sister Mary along. But Mary can't even walk? Maev, I mean to say. That's me, a tiny voice says. I see you, Daddy! Will he give this bairn a toss? Into the air, the sky, with never a fear or fall?

Night. He is in her and she in him. Kissing without scandal in four-poster bed. Most excellent wife and mother! Most pleasing tumble from scentless, soundless grace. He should stay by her more. He should not be away so often, even just away in his head. Happiest here. Happiest three, five or more upon this raft. Wisha, wisha. My dearest dear.

Day. Alone in the garden, the pot long drained. Children picking flowers below in the meadow. Owen Connor up in the kitchen sipping tea with the wife. Who is this Terence Carolan, master and man? He is no one, dreaming the music that soon will play him. He is himself, dreaming the lucky fellow and his blessed life.

epiLogue

In 1765 a grave in the cemetery at Kilronan was disturbed. A skull was separated from its skeleton and a hole drilled into the forehead. Ribbons of green silk were then used to moor the skull to a niche in the wall of the Macdermott Roe chapel. Locals began to venerate the object. Some believed that by boiling milk in the cranium, or by mixing powdered fragments of bone with water, they could cure children of illness. Others thought merely touching the forehead would bring them good fortune. The skull of harper Terence Carolan remained on display at Kilronan until the end of the eighteenth century, after which it vanished.

A group of Belfast music lovers put out a call in 1792 for harpers to join a competition. Only eleven musicians answered the summons, ranging in age from a boy of fifteen to ninety-seven-year-old Denis Hempson. A contemporary of Carolan, Hempson alone performed in the "old style," associated with the vanished bardic tradition, using brass strings and long fingernails. An amateur musicologist named Edward Bunting acted as copyist, and his efforts preserved dozens of melodies that would have been lost otherwise. Stories of Carolan's skull circulated at the gathering, and several participants expressed a desire to hold it, hoping the contact would bring inspiration.

❋   ❋   ❋

The Irish played a role in many eighteenth-century European wars. Tens of thousands of Irishmen, having left their homeland in the decades following the Battle of the Boyne and the introduction of the Penal Statutes, served with various armies, usually in their own brigades. The disbanding of such units in the French and Spanish services in the 1730s caused intrepid Gaels to drift eastward in search of commissions, mostly to Austria and Russia. In April 1741 the War of the Austrian Secession began with the Battle of Mollwitz in Silesia, now part of Poland. Among the Irish serving on the defeated Austrian side were two raw recruits. One was listed as "Seamus Boatman," an unlikely and presumably false family name. The other was "Owen Connor," also spelt "Conner" and even "Eoghan O'Conhuir." Though Owen Connor passed into the record as a casualty of battle, eyewitnesses claimed he collapsed before any contact with an enemy bullet. He is said to have dropped to his knees, head clutched in his hands. A letter addressed to a woman on an estate in County Leitrim was found among his possessions. It is not known whether the letter was delivered.

* * *

The previous winter, one in three residents of Ireland died of starvation or disease. Grain and potato crops failed due to a wet autumn and then a long, hard frost, and in February 1740 epidemics of typhus and the bloody flux broke out in the countryside. In Dublin, where food riots were common, seventy-three-year-old Jonathan Swift, still two years away from being found of unsound mind by a Commission of Lunacy, stayed in his bedroom, avoiding the icy streets and desperate beggars. His colleague, George Berkeley, whose *Essay towards a New Theory of Vision* had adorned Owen's bookshelf, began handing out twenty pounds in gold or banknotes per week to help feed the destitute of Cloyne. Berkeley also ceased powdering his wig with flour, as had been the custom among gentlemen.

Historians talk of the period as the longest known spell of

extreme cold in European history. *Bliadhaïn an áir,* it was called in Ireland—"the year of the slaughter."

At Alderford, weakness of spirit took away Mary Macdermott Roe in June, while Betty O'Neill died from a bout of the flux, likely brought into the manor by an itinerant to whom she served a charitable bowl of soup. John Stamford had already lost his life in a riding accident, which led to the brown bay Gulliver being put down as well. Flinn the butler survived famine and disease equally. He died a decade later at the age of ninety-eight or thereabouts. On his grave marker was the name Joseph Michael Flinn.

Though she returned to assist in the funeral preparations for Terence Carolan, Annie MacManus declined to resume her duties as scullery maid. She married William Duigenen of Keadew shortly thereafter and was soon pregnant with the first of six children. A historian found her alive and well in 1785, a "very small, very aged beauty spinning wool." Annie offered up vivid reminiscences of Carolan and Mary Macdermott Roe, including the story of how a garrison of soldiers tried to arrest the bard in the wake of some indiscretion committed by a manservant. The historian, describing her cottage at Mount Allen, remarked on the surprising presence of two books on a shelf. The volumes were dust-covered and tattered and showed no signs of having been read. One volume was by Sir Isaac Newton. The spine of the other was too badly deteriorated to offer up a title or an author.

autior's note

A few borrowed biographical details aside, *Carolan's Farewell* is a hopeless work of the imagination. By its very nature, for instance, the novel
spreads one major historical inaccuracy. Outside The Pale, eighteenth-
century Ireland was predominantly Irish- or Gaelic-speaking.Gaelic was
both Carolan's native tongue and the language of his largely forgettable
lyrics. His English was said to have been fluent but indifferent. Minor
details have also suffered in the fictionalizing. Take the concert hall in
Fishamble Street where Handel's Messiah received its debut. It wasn't
completed until 1740. But as I needed the hall finished three years earlier, I advanced the work schedule. Recent scholarship, in contrast—
specifically, the study of faded watermarks on manuscripts—has cast
doubt over whether the Neale brothers did issue their collection of
Carolan's music during his lifetime, a development I have elected to
ignore.

There is also debate about which versions of the Bible were avail-
able to Irish Catholics during the first half of the century. While
Bedell's Gaelic translation of the Old Testament was the choice in
certain quarters, other citizens definitely read the King James.
Some probably had access to both. Since this novel isn't written in
period English, however, I have opted simply to cite the most pleasing versions of passages from that book. As well, readers familiar
with Irish literature may recognize aspects of the tale of the for-
tune-hunter Hugh Maguire and his stubborn English wife from
Maria Edgeworth's novel *Castle Rackrent*, written in 1800. As
Edgeworth admitted to borrowing from a real-life tale for her

fiction, so I confess to the same. Two centuries later, it still makes a good story, if ever more murky history.

A word, too, about the music. Though the "real" Terence Carolan continued to compose after his wife's death, the tunes from his last years aren't his finest. But the piece usually called "Carolan's Farewell to Music" was indeed designed as his deathbed composition. It is a wondrous creation, sombre and dignified, and its quirky structure, in particular a middle passage that sounds of spring rains and autumn sorrows alike, lends it the quality of inspired improvisation. Still, it is entirely my fancy that the piece marked a late deepening of his vision, or had anything to do with his wife or their four-poster bed.

acknowLedgments

Thanks to Barra O Seaghdha, Becky Vogan, Mark Abley, Denis Sampson, David Manicom, David Wilson, Jackie Kaiser, Iris Tupholme and Maggie Bakker for help with the manuscript at various stages. Stephen Scharper, Peter Kennedy, Tanah Haney and Ann Dooley provided sundry forms of expertise, while artists Liz Bierk and James Lahey were generous with their time and talents. All the illustrations in this novel are by Liz Bierk. Michael Cullen assisted with technical matters, and John Fraser of Massey College, University of Toronto, was a great support, as always.

P.S.

About the author

About the book

Ideas, interviews & features

Read on

Author Biography

CHARLES FORAN, who was raised in Toronto, attended the University of Toronto and later the University College in Dublin, where he received an M.A. in Irish literature. He has lived in many countries, including Ireland, and has written several books with that backdrop, most notably *The Last House of Ulster* and *Carolan's Farewell.*

Foran is an award-winning author and journalist, and his work appears regularly in publications in Canada and abroad. Among his books are the novels *Kitchen Music, Butterfly Lovers* and *House on Fire,* and the nonfiction titles *Sketches in Winter* and *The Story of My Life (so far).*

Says Foran: "I didn't start reading seriously until I was sixteen, and I didn't try writing until I was almost twenty. Still, within a few hours of buying the paperback of Gabriel García Márquez's *One Hundred Years of Solitude* in my local mall, I sensed that I was a terminal case. It took years to find the words to diagnose the condition. But some part of me understood then and there that my adulthood was going to be about books or nothing else. The design and creativity, yearning and faith, implicit in a novel like *One Hundred Years of Solitude,* were qualities that literally took my breath away a quarter century ago. My breathing still turns choppy every time I read something possessed by that ambition and humility."

The author now makes his home in Peterborough, Ontario, with his wife and two daughters.

JAMES LAHEY

Charles Foran

An Interview with Charles Foran

The melodies of the real-life Terence Carolan were the inspiration for your novel. For you, what links exist, inspirational or otherwise, between music and literature?

Prose, sadly, can't ever attain the clarity of music. It is too noisy and argumentative, not to mention too muddy. That said, good writing has cadence, and it has pitch. A wrong word in a sentence is a wrong note in a melody; one sentence too few, or too many, in a paragraph can have the same effect as a tune that suddenly goes out of key. If the music of a sentence is right, Northrop Frye once said, the sense will take care of itself. The elusive "voice" of a writer may be, in effect, the musical tone of his or her talent, transcribed into language.

What is known of the real Carolan, and how much did the facts figure into your story?

Although Turlough O'Carolan, as he is more commonly known, was revered in his own time, the first surviving written account of his life appeared more than a decade after his death. It is fanciful and riddled with errors. As such, the "facts" about the "real" Carolan were, from the start, doubtful, and somewhat beyond being checked for accuracy. Historically speaking, he is mostly legend, though a sense of him as a man—mischievous and good-humoured, fond of people and of drink—does come through. This is often the case with figures from history. Dates and details may go missing, but character survives. It must speak to what humans need in order to understand stories. ▶

> **This is often the case with figures from history. Dates and details may go missing, but character survives.**

3

An Interview with Charles Foran (*continued*)

Things known for certain about Carolan were happily used as character pegs in the novel. The dates of his life, for instance, are true to the record, as are many biographical details. Turlough O'Carolan did lose his sight to smallpox at eighteen and did begin training on the harp only once he went blind. He never achieved more than ordinary skills as a player, and apparently wasn't especially troubled by this limitation. He is said to have married late and fathered seven children, six of them girls. His wife, whose real name is thought to have been Mary Maguire, probably died around 1733. None of his children's names has survived, curiously, including that of his only son, who is believed to have tried a career as a harping instructor in Dublin, trading on the fame of his father.

> " I wrote a novel about friendship and art, love and death. "

Carolan's Farewell **is a work of fiction, yet you decided to use the musician's real name and life story as a rough framework. In retrospect, do you feel that was the best decision?**

I wonder now if it was wise. To my surprise and disappointment, a lot of the initial critical attention paid to the novel fixated on mundane matters concerning its presumed accuracy to the historical figure and my presumed interpretation of Irish political history. And yet, settings in novels are always portals to an author's genuine concerns. I wrote a novel about friendship and art, love and death. I did not write a biography of a harpist or a history of eighteenth-century Ireland.

How did you go about researching the period and inhabiting, for a time, the mind of an eighteenth-century character?

The novel took three years to complete. Year one consisted of being intimidated by how little I knew about the age in which the story was set. Interestingly, the more I "researched," via reading books from the period and travelling around Ireland, the less confident I felt that I would find a literary path back into that time and place. Year two involved a moratorium on books and travel, and an immersion in Carolan and Owen Connor. I had to get to know them as evolving characters. They had to get to know me as their aspiring scribe. Once we'd established a friendship, I did what all novelists do: I begged my creations to guide me into the story, to relay what they saw and heard, thought and felt. Year three of the process, then, involved following them on their journey, notepad in hand.

In the scenes from Carolan's perspective, did you find using more dialogue and less visual description restricting or freeing?

The quantity and quality of the dialogue was appropriate for the story. For twenty years Carolan and Owen have been travelling together. They've spent countless hours on horseback, proceeding at walking pace through the bird-loud countryside, most often on their own. What else are they going to do except chat and argue, trade quips and jibes? These conversations can't help but be familiar, the same ground trod upon over and over, the same jokes retold to death. They can't help ▶

> “ I had to get to know them as characters. They had to get to know me as their aspiring scribe. ”

5

being the same largely affectionate, occasionally exasperating old song and dance.

More generally, eighteenth- and nineteenth-century novels tend to be crowded with the garrulous and, occasionally, the gasbag. People had the leisure to talk. They made entertainment of their conversations and storytelling; eloquence and wit were prized, a pleasure for all concerned. Verbal skills were also part of a man's social armour, necessary to his advancement or even mere survival in society. In *Carolan's Farewell*, for example, the long chapter at Tempo estate involves a number of duels, most of them using words rather than rapiers.

> The long chapter at Tempo estate involves a number of duels, most of them using words rather than rapiers.

Owen speaks of "the tyranny of conventional vision." What does Terence, in his blindness, see that others do not?

Maybe, just maybe, in many of us the visual overpowers and occasionally overrides other faculties, leaving us prone to believing more what we see than what we think and feel. Maybe, just maybe, the eye is an unreliable judge of character or even of attraction and we are all at the mercy of the tyrant that is our impulse to go on appearances, and probe no deeper.

"I dwell too little in the real world. Most men, in contrast, dwell too much in it." This is Carolan's take on the world, but is it also yours—as an individual or as a writer?

Carolan has a notion: "A pilgrim whispered something to me the other day," he says to

Owen. "He said your typical Oriental believes his life to be akin to a fellow who falls asleep and dreams he is a butterfly. Upon awakening, he wonders, 'Am I a man dreaming of being a butterfly or a butterfly dreaming of being a man?'" The parable, attributed to the Taoist philosopher Lao Tzu, captures how I feel at the end of a good day at my computer. Between sleep and wakefulness, the line between the story I am writing and the story I am living is so fine that it is hard to tell what is real from what was merely a dream.

In the end, did you find it hard to say goodbye to this appealing duo, Carolan and Owen, or did writing the final lines bring creative closure?

I found the company of all the characters pleasing. And once I'd done with the book, I was content when Annie MacManus and Mary Macdermott Roe, Colonel Maguire and Friar Seamus took their leave. But Carolan and Owen refused to depart from my head. They carried on their journey, still chattering and arguing, for several months afterwards, and I continued taking dictation from them. I had to will myself to stop this and to pluck up the courage to ask them to please be gone. Now, while I miss them still, and still grieve the injustice of Owen's fate, if I want to find Carolan and Owen I have to go read from the novel, like anyone else. The business is done, and I am once more a man dreaming he is a butterfly. Or is that a butterfly dreaming he is a man?

"Carolan and Owen refused to depart from my head. They carried on their journey, still chattering and arguing."

How the Journey Began

The novel did not start out as story and history. It started as music and landscape. Music I first heard in 1981, thanks to a Derek Bell recording called "Carolan's Receipt." I was twenty, a Canadian tending bar in County Limerick for a summer. My big discovery was a new Dublin band called U2. But in the village where I lived, the wistful, light-infused melodies of a harper dead for more than two centuries cleared all contemporary furniture from the room of my imagination. The room stood empty, save for the sound of plucked brass-strings, while my eyes flooded with a landscape.

Ruins. They were everywhere. Across from the bar was a thousand-acre estate still occupied by the last earl of a clan that had retained this title since before the reign of Elizabeth. By the river near his manor stood a friary and a castle, now the fringes of a golf course. The castle dated from the thirteenth century, the friary from 1464. Its spire was crumbled and its transept floor was covered in graves. Birds sang from lofts. Sunlight angled through gaps in the wall.

I even courted a girl in the friary, a French waitress. The courtship—what a word for a twenty-year-old U2 fan to employ—was no less sweet or tinged with melancholy. It played out like one of those Irish melodies, grace notes expressive and sad. It played out like Carolan's music, echoing in ruins in a rain-muffled landscape. Time, layered and indifferent. Human dramas, furtive and predictable, and soon forgotten.

Next came the history. The eighteenth century, I was taught at graduate school

❝ The room stood empty, save for the sound of plucked brass-strings, while my eyes flooded with a landscape. ❞

in Dublin, functioned as a kind of interim. We studied the collapse of old Ireland, culminating in the Battle of the Boyne in 1690. We charted—did we ever in 1983–84, with the latest Troubles raging in the North—the rise of the modern state, born, it was argued, from the rebellion of 1798. But in between those dates was little or nothing. Nothing major, at least. Nothing to merit the rank of history with a capital H. There were the Penal Laws, petty legislation aimed at extinguishing Catholic ownership of land. There were famines, foreign wars and some unusually bad weather.

And there was Jonathan Swift, dean of St. Patrick's Cathedral in Dublin, author of *Gulliver's Travels* and the thinly disguised *Drapier's Letters*, among other great works. He went mad on account of Ireland, it was said. He alone provided a worthy monument from a minor age. W. B. Yeats famously summarized it: "Swift has sailed into his rest; / Savage indignation there / Cannot lacerate his breast."

I wondered about this. In the basement of Fred Hanna's shop on Dawson Street was a copy of *Carolan: The Life Times and Music of an Irish Harper* by Donal O'Sullivan. The book, first published in 1958, had lately been reissued in two volumes, the bulk of the text being transcriptions of music, along with notes on the sources. The volumes cost twenty-two pounds. That was a week's rent. That was the price of multiple restaurant meals superior to anything I could cook. I debated the purchase for a winter and a spring.

The dates of Carolan's birth and death jumped out: 1670–1738. He had been born ▶

> **❝** Jonathan Swift went mad on account of Ireland, it was said. **❞**

How the Journey Began (*continued*)

into the Restoration and come of age around the tumult of the Boyne. As an adult, he'd had a passing acquaintanceship with the lacerated Swift. Carolan, moreover, not only had been renowned in his lifetime but had contributed dozens of tunes to the permanent Irish repertoire. *Gulliver's Travels* was indeed an eighteenth-century classic. But so were "Mr. O'Connor" and "Fanny Poer" and the finest of the Bridget Cruise compositions.

Except that few who heard those melodies now realized they belonged to an actual man, rather than to the proverbial artist known as "Traditional." Except that Carolan's life, which I gleaned by skimming chapters, included one or two facts and many more embellishments and legends. He was, in effect, as obscure as the epitaphs on those friary graves. Indecipherable or rubbed clean by weather. Erased, like so much else, by time.

In the end, I bought the biography without quite knowing why. I did not glance at the volumes again for nearly twenty years.

The music, though, took up residency in my head. I listened to Carolan's tunes while working on all kinds of projects. I had them on while travelling to countries profoundly unlike that Ireland of landscape and history. Eventually, I began to know the melodies the way one knows a friend. I liked the person who had composed them. He had to have been a fine fellow, genial and refined, in a rough-hewn sort of way. He was probably inclined to melancholy, if never to piety or undue self-regard. He surely composed with the same ease that birds sing. The notes

❝ Carolan contributed dozens of tunes to the permanent Irish repertoire. **❞**

10

flowed too perfectly, and were too perfectly right, for it to be otherwise.

Slowly, an image emerged for this Carolan, the first inklings of a story. The image was almost a cliché: two travellers on horseback along a country path. Knight and squire. Lord and manservant. It was Quixote and Panza, and Diderot's Master and Jacques. It was a thousand tales of itinerant musicians and actors found soaked and starving in miserable circumstance. Landscapes were grander back then, and men were, in one sense, more humbled. A hundred-mile journey was epic, full of incident and, often enough, peril. Regular folk rarely ventured a day's walk from where they were born. The far slopes of that valley, the lands beyond those hills, were distant indeed.

The image sent me back to O'Sullivan's book. In the biographical sketch were compelling details about the musician. He went blind from smallpox at eighteen. He was admired for his music but loved for his conviviality. He held sobriety in disregard. It was said he was reunited with his childhood love, Bridget Cruise, by the shores of Lough Derg, in the wake of having made the pilgrimage. It was said he often composed on horseback, fingers clacking on cloak buttons. *Duh-dah-dah-dah*, clacked Carolan. *Dah-la-lah-la*. Another lovely tune, just like that.

Here, I decided, was one rider on the path. Here was the blind harper.

And the other? In the figure of the foundling, the young man or woman of no means and uncertain destiny, the eighteenth century had its favourite literary subject. Tom Jones and Moll Flanders are the best-known ▶

> " A hundred-mile journey was epic, full of incident and, often enough, peril. "

of the cast. The world was widening. Beyond the sea lay adventure and opportunity, be it as a soldier-for-hire or an immigrant to the colonies. Beyond the sea lay places where a man or woman might be allowed to transcend his or her station. Philosophers were thinking more and more about individual rights and liberty. The air was bright with ideas free from the ancient shadows of religion and duty and humility before kings. It was enough to get a foundling believing his talents might win out.

For some reason, I knew the foundling character as well. It could be because my ancestors fled to Canada during another famine in another century. More likely, I recognized Owen Connor, and instinctively liked him no less, because hopeless ambition and shy longing, the worry of belonging nowhere, of being of no real use, is something writers just know about, in their bones.

Here was the other rider on the path. Here was the guide.

Carolan and Owen Connor. Harper and guide, master and servant. Father and son, friend and friend. Finally, the story I could tell in that landscape and against the backdrop of that history. Finally, the story I could set to that wistful, light-infused music. All I needed now was to command their horses to walk, *cluck-cluck* with my writerly tongue, and it—the journey of *Carolan's Farewell*—could begin.

> **The air was bright with ideas free from the ancient shadows of religion and duty and humility before kings.**

Carolan and Owen:
Ireland, Past and Future

At first glance, the 1730s might seem an awkward fit for Terence Carolan. He is, after all, practising a craft that belonged to a vanished Ireland of chieftains and their courts. Two centuries earlier, the blind harper would have formed part of an aristocratic inner circle; even a hundred years earlier, he would have held high rank in society. Friends and strangers alike yet hail Carolan as "the bard," and courtesy keeps him from correcting them. But he knows better: the tradition, and his role within it, have vanished, leaving him a mere itinerant musician, commissioned to entertain; to sing, like every other poor player, for his supper. Likewise, his music lacks the purity of the great harpers before him. He loves those Italians too much, going so far as to name his horse after the composer Geminiani; his creativity is too instinctive, and too quirky, to replicate the old marches and laments. *As a composer of music,* he thinks while performing for the villagers in Kesh, *Terence Carolan belongs to a clan of exactly one.*

And yet he does not feel dispossessed. Secure in his talent—secure, perhaps, in his infirmity as well— he carries himself with authority and ease. The son of a tenant farmer, he accepts both his own exceptional fortune and the fact that, for most men, there is a "way that things must be." His faith grounds him, as does a medieval, or maybe pre-modern, sense of destiny. Some of the old Ireland, in other words, its values and mores, lives on within Carolan, informing his views. At Tempo manor, during ▶

> **❝** Some of the old Ireland, in other words, its values and mores, lives on within Carolan, informing his views. **❞**

a besotted dinner where several local lords, their own loyalties and values divided, behave without dignity, Carolan silently acknowledges the enduring stability of his nature. *Whole and undivided,* he thinks. *If still a codger.*

Owen Connor is less sanguine. A low birth denies him standing, and his foundling status precludes any of the securities granted by family and clan. Nor does his taciturn nature allow for the necessary skills to compensate with charm. By his own admission, Owen is the "Betwixt-Between Man," neither peasant nor lord, farmer nor scholar. He clings to his role as Carolan's guide for the simple reason that without it he is, in effect, superfluous. The Ireland where an individual of his sharp intelligence and self-possession might thrive is a half-century away or longer. Owen will not live to see the emergence of a modern notion of state and citizenry. He will not hear the echo of his hopes in the proclamations of Wolf Tone.

His own age, meanwhile, has no use for him. "This is no country for our kind, Owen," his friend Friar Seamus complains in a letter. Better to seek exile across the ocean, or find work as mercenaries in some European war. Owen disagrees. "It's right here where we should make our stand," he writes back. "Establish our names and connections as patriots and husbands, even as fathers." But that is wishful thinking, especially once he steals those books. The times are not right for Owen, nor he for the times. Not all men are lucky enough to be easy in their skins and their age alike. Some are fated to struggle and defy, almost always paying a high price for such integrity.

> " Not all men are lucky enough to be easy in their skins and their age alike. "

Recommended Reading

To my knowledge, only one non-fiction book exists devoted to Carolan. Happily, Donal O'Sullivan's *Carolan: The Life Times and Music of an Irish Harper*, first published in 1958, is magnificent, and I am indebted to it. Likewise, I wish to acknowledge *Grace's Card: Irish Catholic Landlords 1690–1800* by Charles Chenevix Trench, *Irish Life in the 17th Century* by Edward MacLysaght, *Irish Folk Ways* by E. Estyn Evans, *Dublin 1600–1860* by Maurice Craig, and *Letters from Georgian Ireland*, edited by Angelique Day. John M. Hull's memoir of blindness, *Touching the Rock*, was a revelation, and I relied on *Jonathan Swift: A Portrait* by Victoria Glendinning for details about the dean. For Virgil, I used Rolfe Humphries' translation of *The Aeneid*.

Austin Clarke's "versions" of the lyrics of "Mabel Kelly" and "Peggy Browne," while probably belonging more to Clarke than Carolan, were too delightful not to employ, especially given their eighteenth-century spiritedness. I first discovered them in *The Faber Book of Irish Verse*, edited by John Montague.

Readers may also enjoy the following:

Castle Rackrent by Maria Edgeworth
Gulliver's Travels by Jonathan Swift
Irish Classics by Declan Kiberd
Jacques the Fatalist and His Master by Denis Diderot
The Shape of Irish History by A.T.Q. Stewart
Tom Jones by Henry Fielding
Waiting for Godot by Samuel Beckett

Web Detective

www.contemplator.com/carolan/index.html
Dedicated to Turlough Carolan and his music, this website provides background and offers links to many related sources.

www.harpspectrum.org/index.shtml
On this site, read "The Rediscovery of Carolan," by Gráinne Yeats. (Click "Folk Harp" on the home page.)

www.shamrockirishmusic.org/id31.htm
You can learn about Irish folk music through the Shamrock Traditional Irish Music Society, Inc.

www.harp.net/CnaC/CnaC.htm
Check out Cairde na Cruite, an organization dedicated to reviving the long-dormant interest in the Irish harp.

To receive updates on author events and new books by Charles Foran, sign up at *www.authortracker.ca.*

www.askaboutIreland.ie/feature 3.html
The story of the Irish landed estates, or "big houses," from the early eighteenth century onward, is told here through text, prints, photos and maps.

www.historyworld.net
Search the index with the keyword "Ireland" and take a tour of Irish history.

www.charlesforan.com
Visit Charles Foran's site, which offers background on all his books, as well as author news.